A TIME OF DREAD

JOHN GWYNNE studied and lectured at
Brighton University. He's been in a rock 'n' roll band,
playing the double bass, travelled the USA and lived in
Canada for a time. He is married with four children and
lives in Eastbourne, running a small family business
rejuvenating vintage furniture. His debut novel,
Malice, won the David Gemmell Morningstar
Award for Best Debut Fantasy.

By John Gwynne

The Faithfull and the Fallen

MALICE

VALOUR

RUIN

WRATH

Of Blood and Bone

A TIME OF DREAD

JOHN GWYNNE

A TIME OF
DREAD

Of Blood and Bone

BOOK ONE

MACMILLAN

First published 2018 by Macmillan
an imprint of Pan Macmillan
20 New Wharf Road, London N1 9RR
Associated companies throughout the world
www.panmacmillan.com

ISBN 978-1-5098-1295-0

1 3 5 7 9 8 6 4 2

A CIP catalogue record for this book is available from the British Library.

Map artwork by Fred van Deelen
Typeset by Ellipsis, Glasgow
Printed and bound by CPI Group (UK) Ltd, Croydon, CR0 4YY

Visit **www.panmacmillan.com** to read more about all our books
and to buy them. You will also find features, author interviews and
news of any author events, and you can sign up for e-newsletters
so that you're always first to hear about our new releases.

For Harriett,
whose smile is a window into her heart,
which lights up the darkest of rooms,
and sends the storm-clouds fleeing.

And for the Intensive Therapy Unit's team
at Eastbourne District General Hospital:
you are all angels without wings.

ACKNOWLEDGEMENTS

It's a wonderful feeling to be back in the Banished Lands for this new tale. As ever, this book did not happen without help. There are many people to thank.

Always first, I must thank my family. My darling Caroline for her unflinching love and support. She is the engine room that drives the Gwynnes and without her I would never get anything done, and nor would I have the will to do so. My sons, James, Ed and Will. Their passion for the Banished Lands is a constant inspiration, and their desire to dress up like a Viking and stand beside their old dad in the sheildwall is a wonder and a joy to me.

And of course, my wonderful daughter Harriett, whose courage and radiant smile is a blessing all of its own.

John Jarrold, my agent, for his wisdom and guidance, which more often than not takes place over a delicious meal in the Mermaid Inn, Rye.

The always-wonderful Bella Pagan with her constant support and advice, and of course her team at Pan Macmillan who work ceaselessly to spread some love for the Banished Lands far and wide – Phoebe Taylor and Don Shanahan, I'm thinking of you.

Julie Crisp, my fierce and bloodthirsty editor, for her commitment to the Banished Lands, her ability to see straight to the heart of a story, and of course her red pen.

Will Hinton, my editor at Orbit US, and his team, your efforts on my behalf are much appreciated.

My copy-editor, Jessica Cuthbert-Smith, who has worked with me since Malice and saved me from errors far too numerous to contemplate.

My small band of fearless readers, who have all given their time in a world that seems full of far too many things to do, and whose enthusiasm for this story has been such an encouragement:

Acknowledgements

Caroline, who loves the Banished Lands as much as I do, and whose insights and feedback are always spot on.

Ed and Will, whose knowledge of the Banished Lands seems to far exceed mine, fortunately. Their enjoyment and passion for this new tale with its new characters has been a great source of motivation to me.

Sadak Miah, my oldest friend and sometime duelling partner. I promise to let you win next time. And I promise there will be dragons, just be patient.

Mike Evans, reader, friend and advisor on all things military – mostly the details that people should just not know.

Kareem Mahfouz, a friend who would make the perfect shieldman, and whom I suspect has the blood of Balur One-Eye flowing in his veins.

Mark Roberson, whose enjoyment of all things Banished Lands has ever been an encouragement.

Usually most of my research is textual, drawn from the wonderful written page. For this book I tracked down an expert on recurve bows – Steve the Bowman – who provided me with a wealth of information on the construction and use of the Hunnic recurve bow. Of course, I'm writing fantasy, so all errors are my own.

And of course, I must thank all of you readers who have invested both time and money to join me in this journey through the Banished Lands. It is a constant source of surprise and joy to me that you have enjoyed the tale so far, and I'd like to say a big thank you for your messages and support.

Whether you are returning to the Banished Lands or this is your first foray into the wilds of Forn Forest, I hope that you enjoy your time in this world.

Truth and Courage,
JOHN

Cast of Characters

The Desolation

Aed – resident of Kergard. Son of Calder the smith.

Asger – a trader who lives in Kergard.

Bodil – a trapper of the Desolation and part-time resident of Kergard.

Burg – leader of a group of workers from the Kergard mines.

Calder – a smith of Kergard, a friend of Olin.

Drem – a trapper of the Desolation. Son of Olin.

Fritha – a newcomer to Kergard. Granddaughter to Hask.

Hask – a newcomer to Kergard. Grandfather to Fritha.

Hildith – a resident of Kergard who owns a mead hall. Member of the Assembly.

Olin – a trapper of the Desolation. Father to Drem.

Surl – Fritha and Hask's hound.

Ulf – a resident of Kergard and a member of the Assembly. A tanner by trade.

Wispy Beard – a newcomer to Kergard.

Land of the Faithful

Alcyon – a giant who resides in Drassil.

Aphra – sister of Riv. Daughter of Dalmae. Captain of a hundred. A White-Wing of Drassil.

Balur One-Eye – father to Ethlinn, Queen of the Giants. He resides in Drassil.

Dalmae – a former White-Wing. Mother to Aphra and Riv.

Estel – a White-Wing of Drassil.

Ethlinn – Queen of the Giants. Daughter of Balur One-Eye.

Fia – a White-Wing of Drassil.

Garidas – a White-Wing of Drassil and captain of a hundred.

Jost – a training White-Wing of Drassil.

Lorina – a White-Wing of Drassil and captain of a hundred.

Vald – a training White-Wing of Drassil.

Riv – daughter of Dalmae and sister to Aphra. A training
   White-Wing.

Order of the Bright Star, Dun Seren

Byrne – the High Captain of Dun Seren. A descendant
   of Cywen and Veradis.
Cullen – a young warrior of Dun Seren. A descendant of
   Corban and Coralen.
Fen – one of Keld's wolven-hounds.
Hammer – Sig's giant bear.
Keld – a warrior and huntsman of Dun Seren.
Rab – a white talking crow of Dun Seren.
Sig – a giant. Weapons-master of Dun Seren who travels
   widely to hunt the Kadoshim.
Tain – the crow master of Dun Seren. Son of Alcyon.
Varan – a giant of Dun Seren.

Ben-Elim

Adonai – a Ben-Elim of Drassil.
Israfil – the Lord Protector of the Land of the Faithful. High
   Captain of the Ben-Elim.
Kol – one of the Ben-Elim of Drassil. One of Israfil's captains.
Kushiel – one of the Ben-Elim of Drassil. One of Israfil's
   captains.
Meical – once High Captain of the Ben-Elim. Now frozen in
   starstone metal, sealed with Asroth in Drassil.

Kadoshim

Asroth – Lord of the Kadoshim. Frozen within starstone
   metal in the Great Hall of Drassil.
Gulla – High Captain of the Kadoshim.
Rimmon – a Kadoshim.

THE
BANISHED
LANDS

Kavala mountains

Grinding Sea

ARCONA

old

Drassil

Oriens

Isle of Kletva

ORN FOREST

Haldis

ME FAITHFUL

ihan

Halstat

Bairg mountains

erolin

Agullas Mountains

Balara

Tethys Sea

Ripa

TARBESH

PELSET

Telassar

NERIN

'Like one, that on a lonesome road
Doth walk in fear and dread,
And having once turned round walks on,
And turns no more his head;
Because he knows, a frightful fiend
Doth close behind him tread.'

Samuel Taylor Coleridge,
The Rime of the Ancient Mariner

A TIME OF DREAD

The Book of the Fallen

*A tattered extract discovered upon the corpse of a Kadoshim demon,
the Year 131 of the Age of Lore:*

They think we are broken.
We are not.
They think we are defeated.
We are not.
*For over two thousand years, my brothers, we have fought our noble
war, against Elyon the Great Tyrant and his servants, the Ben-Elim.
Two thousand years our battleground was the Otherworld, that place of
spirit, where all things are eternal. And then, little over a century ago,
we saw the fulfilment of our long-crafted plan, to break into this world
of flesh, to become flesh, so that we might wage war upon Elyon's creation, mankind; to conquer and rule, or destroy, as we see fit.*

*But we were betrayed, my brothers, and lured into a trap of the
Ben-Elim's making. On that day we fought like warriors-born,
shaming the heroes about whom the people of this world tell tales. On
that dread day of tribulation we fought with sharp iron, tooth and
claw. Blood was spilt in rivers, but alas, we were outnumbered by the
Ben-Elim and their allies, who were led by a maggot that men called
a hero, Corban the Bright Star.*

*Pah, I say to that, for Corban is long dead, and yet we are still
here. One day I will spit on his grave, dig up his corpse and feast on
his bones, for it was Corban who dared raise a blade to our master,
our great Lord, Asroth, and it was Corban's kin, Cywen, who cast the
spell that entombed Asroth within a prison of iron.*

We fought on, long after that day, a hundred years of war, but always they were too many, and our numbers dwindled.

And now the Ben-Elim hunt us, as do the followers of long-dead and thrice-cursed Corban.

So, my brothers, I say to you that we must change the way we wage this war. Retreat to the shadows, dwell in the dark places and gather your strength. Bide your time, for our triumph is coming. The day when we unite again, when we set our Lord Asroth free, when we take back what is rightfully ours.

Only do this: answer the call when it is given.

They think this is the final chapter of our long defeat.

But they are wrong.

So written by Gulla, High Captain of the Kadoshim until the restoration of our king, Asroth the Great.

CHAPTER ONE

BLEDA

The Year 132 of the Age of Lore, Reaper's Moon

'I should be down there,' Bleda said, knuckles whitening on the grip of his bow. He was crouched upon the steep slope of a hill, looking down upon a scene of wonder.

A war.

Horses and their riders swirled upon the plain in constant motion, from this height seeming like two great flocks of birds looping ever closer, the distant rumble of hooves setting the ground trembling beneath Bleda's feet. As he stared in envy and fascination, the faint echo of hurled challenges and insults, the harbingers of violence, drifted up to him.

'No, you should *not* be down there,' a voice said behind him, Old Ellac absently rubbing the stump where his right hand used to be. The skin around his eyes creased and cracked like old leather as he squinted at the battle about to begin on the plain below.

'Of course I should,' Bleda muttered. 'My mother is down there, leading our Clan. My brother rides one side of her, my sister the other.'

But not my father.

'Aye, but they are all more than ten summers old,' Ellac pointed out.

'So?' Bleda snapped. 'I can fight, am more skilled with a bow than most. Than you.'

3

'That's not hard these days.' Ellac snorted and cuffed Bleda across the head with his one hand.

Bleda immediately felt shame at his remark, more painful than the slap. He knew that neither of them wanted to be sitting on this hill while their kin fought and bled on the field below.

Your tongue is sharper than your sword, his father used to say to him.

'Look,' Ellac said, pointing with his stump. 'Altan.'

On the plain below a lone rider separated from their Clan, instantly recognizable to Bleda as his older brother, Altan.

Seventeen summers is not so much older than me. Yet he is old enough to fight, and I am not. Bleda scowled at the injustice of it, though none of his ire was directed at Altan. He loved his brother fiercely.

Altan was galloping hard, curling close to the enemy warband. As he did so a rider emerged to meet him, galloping just as fast. Both warriors dipped in their saddles, arms extended as they drew their bows.

Bleda felt a jolt of fierce pride, as well as a cold fist of fear clench around his heart.

Aim true, Altan. I cannot lose you as well.

The world seemed to slow, sound dimming as Bleda stared at the two champions.

And then Altan was wheeling away, the other rider swaying in his saddle, toppling sideways, falling to the ground, dragged along as one foot snagged in a stirrup. Ellac let out a grunt of admiration and Bleda punched the air with his fist, whooping and yelling his pride. He felt Ellac's disapproval at his burst of emotion, the warriors of his Clan were supposed to wear the cold-face like a shield, but that was Altan down there, and he had just felled a champion of their ancient rivals.

A swell of cheering rose up to them, changing into battle-cries as the two warbands came together with a concussive crash. Bleda gulped, a squirm of anxiety uncoiling in his belly. He had seen death before, held his da's cold, wax-smooth hand, heard the tales of warriors back from their raids, even helped stitch their wounds – but this . . .

The death screams of men and horses echoed up to them, within moments the plain becoming a choking, seething mass of bodies, the splash of blood, the harsh clang of steel.

'What's that?' Ellac said behind him, pointing to the skies. 'Your eyes are better than mine.'

'Vultures and crows,' Bleda said as he squinted into the searing blue and glimpsed the silhouettes of wings.

'Too big,' Ellac muttered.

Bleda tore his eyes away from the battle and stared. More and more winged shapes were appearing in the sky, speeding towards the battlefield, growing in size with their approach. Great white wings beating through the air, then Bleda saw the glint of sunlight on steel.

'The Ben-Elim,' he whispered.

Winged warriors wrapped in gleaming mail swooped down to the battle-plain, skimming above men's heads, stabbing indiscriminately with spear and sword, lifting men into the air, rising up steeply and dropping them, screaming, limbs flailing.

'No!' Bleda hissed, hand reaching for arrows in his belted quiver as he stood, about to launch into a scrambling run down the hillside. Ellac grabbed his wrist.

'We must help,' Bleda shouted. 'This is not the Ben-Elim's fight; thcy should stay out of it.'

'They said they would come, would not allow the Clans to go to war,' Ellac said. 'And whether it's their fight or not, they are here now. Look.'

To the west of the battle the realm of Arcona stretched into the horizon, a never-ending sea of grass, the vast plains punctuated here and there by clusters of low-lying hills. From around the closest range Bleda saw a wall of dust rising up, knew such a cloud could only be stirred by the tramp of many feet. A great host was coming.

The Ben-Elim's Holy Army. Giants upon their great bears, and their wall of shields.

Then Ellac was dragging him back up the hill, towards their tethered horses.

'What are you doing? We must help my mother,' Bleda yelled, but Ellac ignored him, hoisted him into his saddle, and then, mounting agilely for a man with one hand, grabbed Bleda's reins. With a click of his tongue and touch of his heels against his horse's side they were cantering up the hill.

'Please,' Bleda cried. As a prince of the Sirak it was a word that rarely touched his lips.

Ellac looked between Bleda and the battle.

'I cannot let you go down there,' the old warrior said. 'Your mother would have my other hand, and my eyes as well.' He spurred his horse on, up the hill and away from the battle. Bleda looked back as they reached the crest and his heart lurched in his chest. On the field below all was chaos and blood, winged warriors diving and swooping, slaying any who came within reach. Then the battlefield was gone and they were riding hard for their camp.

Bleda stared at the horizon as he paced a track in the grass before their camp, still clutching his double-curved bow in his hand. His brother Altan had made it for him, taking moons for it to be finished, Bleda watching and learning with fascination.

It is too big for you, Altan had said to him, tousling his black hair. *It is a man's bow, the draw too great for you, but how else will you become strong, eh?*

That had been over a year ago, and now Bleda could loose his third arrow before the first had struck its target.

Tension was thick in the air as everyone waited, behind him a crowd amassed of the young, the old and the infirm; all else who could sit on a horse and draw a bow had gone to fight. Gers and wagons stood empty and unattended, dogs barking, goats bleating.

'There,' a voice said behind Bleda, and all looked to the skies. Winged shapes were appearing. And on the ground beneath them a dark smudge, riders approaching.

'Mother,' Bleda whispered, recognizing her before all others.

Erdene, Queen of the Sirak, rode into their war-camp. Her helm was gone, head bowed, a long cut upon her shaved scalp. The thick warrior braid that had been neatly bound and coiled about her shoulder like a sleeping serpent was now torn and frayed, matted with blood. That morning her shirt of scale-armour had glistened in the sunlight, but now it was dulled and dented. What was left of her honour guard rode about her, silent and battered, and curled behind and around them was a sight that took Bleda's breath away.

Huge bears, great shambling beasts of tooth and claw, and sitting upon them were giants: men and women wrapped in leather, steel and fur, axes and war-hammers slung across their backs. Swirling tattoos of vine and thorn coiled up their arms.

Erdene reined her horse in and her warriors stuttered to a halt.

Where is Altan? Where is Hexa? Bleda thought, his eyes searching the riders for his brother and sister, and then his feet were moving as he ran to his mother, Ellac stumbling behind him, trying and failing to catch him.

Erdene saw him and shook her head, but it was too late, and in heartbeats Bleda was at her side, staring up at his mother, bears and giants towering about him.

'Altan and Hexa?' Bleda called up to his mother as he grabbed her boot.

Erdene looked down at him with an expression Bleda had never seen before.

Shame.

She blinked, as if not recognizing Bleda for a moment, then Erdene's eyes snapped into focus.

'Run,' his mother said to him.

Bleda didn't know what to do; his mind and heart were filled with the Sirak iron code, which told him to wear his courage like a cloak, to live free and fight to the last breath for his Clan. To show no sign of weakness or fear, and to never, ever, surrender. But his mother had spoken. She was also his queen, and she had told him to *run*.

He turned, looked around wildly, saw the camp in chaos, giants and bears everywhere. Others were arriving, columns of normal-sized warriors on foot, clad in black leather, with huge, rectangular shields upon their arms, silver wings embossed upon them. They spread in tight-packed lines about the camp, surrounding everyone within it, and their shields came together with a resonating snap. Bleda glimpsed shadowed faces in silver helms, smaller figures appearing amongst them: children, he realized, offering water skins after a hard march. As he stared, he saw a figure staring back at him, pale and fair-haired, a girl, holding a water skin up to a warrior, even as she stared straight at him.

Shadows flitted across the ground and the sound of wings filled Bleda's ears as the Ben-Elim swooped low. One flew lower than the rest, great wings beating as he hovered above Erdene and Bleda a long moment, grass and dust swirling, then he alighted gently upon the ground. He was tall, taller than any man Bleda had seen, his hair raven-black, wearing a coat of bright mail and gripping a spear in his fist. Blood crusted the spear's blade.

'Is this him?' the Ben-Elim asked, eyes lingering on Bleda a moment, then rising to Erdene.

Erdene was silent for so long that Bleda thought she would not answer.

'You must be strong,' Erdene said to Bleda.

Fear trickled through Bleda, then, at something in his mother's voice, and in the way the winged warrior had looked at him.

He tried to master his fear, to control the prickling in his eyes that threatened tears.

No. I am Sirak. I am son to Erdene, Lord-of-all-she-sees.

'Good.' The Ben-Elim stooped down and grabbed Bleda by the collar of his tunic, hoisting him into the air. Bleda instinctively snatched for an arrow from his quiver, nocking it to his bow, but with a flick of his wrist the Ben-Elim slapped it from Bleda's grip, sending his bow falling to the ground. Bleda glared at the Ben-Elim, expecting his mother to intervene, to protect him, as she always had done, but she just sat upon her horse, looking at him with her grey eyes.

'I am Israfil, Lord Protector of the Land of the Faithful, and you are coming with me,' the Ben-Elim said. 'A surety that your mother will keep the peace once we are gone.'

'What? Where?' Bleda said, the Ben-Elim's words seeping through to him slowly, as if through water.

'You are my ward, Bleda, and Drassil will be your new home,' the Ben-Elim said.

Ward. Drassil.

The words set Bleda reeling as if they were blows. Drassil was the Ben-Elim's fortress, far to the west.

I am to be their ward. A prisoner, he means.

'No,' Bleda whispered. 'Mother?'

A long silence, a look between Erdene and Israfil that spoke of pride and shame, of the victor and the defeated. The fear returned then, a chill in Bleda's heart, seeping into his veins, carrying a tremor to his lips.

The cold-face. Do not shame Mother. Do not shame my people.

'It is agreed,' Erdene said, her face a mask, only her eyes speaking her message.

You must be strong.

'It is the price that must be paid,' the Ben-Elim intoned.

'There will be peace in the Land of the Faithful. There is only one enemy, only one foe who shall be fought: the Kadoshim and their followers.'

'No,' Bleda said, both denial and refusal. He felt hot tears bloom in his eyes, snatched at them, knowing the shame they brought.

'Altan and Hexa will not allow you to do this,' Bleda said, anger and fear twisting his voice, then there was a rushing of air and a beating of wings as more Ben-Elim sped from the sky, alighting around Israfil. The first was fair-haired, a long scar running from forehead to chin. He threw something at Israfil's feet. They dropped with a thud, rolled in the grass and fell still.

Two heads, eyes bulging, blood still dripping.

Altan and Hexa.

The world went silent. Bleda's vision was reduced to the severed heads of his brother and sister. He heard something, distantly, realized that it was him, that he was screaming, twisting and bucking in Israfil's grip, hands reaching to gouge the Ben-Elim's eyes, but Israfil held him at arm's length until slowly Bleda's strength drained away, like wine from a pierced skin. Israfil regarded Bleda with dark, emotionless eyes, then finally shifted his gaze to the fair-haired Ben-Elim who had cast the heads at Israfil's feet. Although Israfil asked no questions, did not even utter a word, the blond Ben-Elim spoke as if answering a reprimand, his eyes dropping.

'They would not surrender,' he said, his feet shuffling in the dirt. 'They slew Remiel.' His eyes came up, fierce and defiant, and met Israfil's. 'They slew a Ben-Elim, gave me no choice.' Israfil held his gaze a long moment, then gave a curt nod. With a flick of his wrist he threw Bleda into the air, a giant catching him and placing him on the saddle in front of him. Bleda found new strength, fighting and squirming, tears blurring his vision, but the giant held him tight.

Israfil waved his hand and then the giant was tugging on his reins shouting a command, and the huge mountain of fur and muscle beneath Bleda was turning, lumbering away from the Ben-Elim and Bleda's mother, from his kin and people, away from everything he knew, away from Bleda's whole world.

Towards his new home.

Towards Drassil.

CHAPTER TWO

DREM

The Year 137 of the Age of Lore, Hunter's Moon

Drem grunted as he lifted another shovelful of earth and hurled it out of the pit he was digging. He rested a moment, drank from a water skin, looked up and saw a cold blue sky through dappled branches that were swaying in a breeze. Birdsong drifted down to him; the angle of the sun told him it was close to sunset. The pit was deep, now level with his head, but he kept digging, swapping his water skin for a pickaxe that he swung with practised rhythm. Ten swings with the pickaxe, loosen the ground, fill his shovel and throw it out of the pit. Back to the pickaxe. His shoulders and back ached, sweat stinging his eyes, but he ignored the discomfort, blinked the sweat away and continued to hack remorselessly at the iron-hard ground.

A sound seeped through the rhythm of his labour and the noise of the river beyond the pit. Footsteps. He dropped his pickaxe, grabbing his spear and pointing it upwards.

A shadow fell across him.

'That'll do,' Olin, his da, said, looking down to him through a mess of iron-grey hair.

'Not deep enough,' Drem grunted, putting his spear down and picking up the axe again.

'It's deep enough to hold any elk I've ever seen,' Olin said.

Drem had been digging pits since he was ten summers old. *How deep?* he'd asked his da all those years ago. *Twice your height*, his da had said to him. Back then his da had been digging the pit with him, breaking up the soil and Drem doing the shovelling. Now, though, eleven years later and Drem did most of the digging himself, his da setting other traps along their hunting runs with noose and rope. He had to remind himself that he didn't need to dig hunting pits twice his height any more, not now he'd grown into a man, and a tall one at that. It still made him uncomfortable to stop, though. He liked to do things the way he was told the first time, didn't like change. With an act of will, he slammed the pickaxe into the ground one last time, felt it connect with something solid that sent a shiver up his arm.

'Sounds like you've found the mountain's root,' Olin said. 'Come on, let's eat.'

Drem yanked the pickaxe free, threw it up to his da, then his shovel; last of all held his spear shaft out. Olin grabbed it and held tight as Drem pulled himself out of the pit. His da grunted with the strain, even though he seemed to be made of muscle lean and knotted as old roots.

Drem turned and looked at his handiwork.

'You chose a good spot,' Olin said, looking at a well-worn path that the pit cut across. It led down out of the foothills they were standing in towards a fertile plain, the ground around the river there soft and marshy.

Drem smiled at his father's praise.

Together they cast a lattice of willow rods over the pit, then a thin covering of branches and leaves, finally some bark and lilies.

'To an elk that tastes nicer than hot porridge and honey on a winter's day,' they said together, the end of their ritual, and then they turned and made their way up a steep slope towards their camp, the river foaming white alongside them.

The sun was a line of fire on the edge of the world by the time Drem was turning a spit over a small fire-pit, fat from a quartered hare spitting and sizzling as it dripped into the flames.

'Smells good,' Olin grunted as he finished tending to their packhorses and furs, then came and sat down, wrapping a deer-skin about Drem's shoulders and pulling one tight about his own. Drem felt cold now that he had stopped digging, the night's chill seeping into his bones. Rolls of skins surrounded them, tied and piled high. It had been a bountiful hunting season, and now they were almost home.

Drem carved the meat with his favourite knife, the wide blade was wicked-sharp and longer than was usual for a hunting knife.

They call a blade like that a seax in this part of the Banished Lands, his da had told him when they'd forged it together.

Drem didn't care what it was called; he just knew that he loved it, that it felt a part of him, his permanent companion. The bone-antler hilt was worn to a perfect fit for Drem's fist. He shared the meal between them and they sat eating in com-panionable silence. They were partway into foothills that led up to a range of snow-capped mountains at their back, but Drem was staring in the opposite direction, out over the land-scape that unrolled below them. A great lake dominated the view, its waters dark and shimmering in the setting sun, about it a patchwork of tree and meadow that was tinged with red and gold as autumn slipped into winter. Between Drem and the lake the lights of a large town flickered into life, tiny as fireflies from this distance. A sturdy stockade wall ringed the town, dotted with torchlight. It was Kergard, the most northerly town of the Desolation, built by hard people to survive in a hard environ-ment. Drem liked the look of it all, the colours merging, lights glowing soft and warm like candles. Other lights sputtered into existence beyond the stockade walls, homesteads scattered across the land. Drem's eyes searched out their own home, a little to the north and nestled amongst the fringes of woodland, though he knew there would be no fires lit, no torches or candles burn-ing at a window.

Home, if I can call anywhere that, when I've spent most of my life travelling from one place to the next. This will be our fifth winter in the same place, though, and that's the longest I can remember staying anywhere since Mam . . .

He was looking forward to returning home after half a year of hunting and trapping in the Bonefells. He liked his life in the Wild with his da – loved it even – but his da was right: winter was almost upon them, and that was not the time to be sleeping on root and rock.

As he stared at the speckled landscape he saw a new cluster of lights appear, further north and east from his home, close to the northern bank of the lake.

'That wasn't there when we left,' he said to his da, pointing.

'No.' Olin frowned. 'Looks like Kergard's grown. Hope they know what a winter this far north is like. The land won't be green like this for much longer.' His da looked from the panorama before them and then up and over his shoulder at the snow-capped mountains and darkening sky, watching his breath mist before him. 'Winter's following close behind us.'

'Aye,' Drem grunted, pulling his deer-skin tighter. 'Strange that this land is called the Desolation,' he murmured, struggling with imagining the landscape before him as an uninhabited wasteland of rock and ash.

His da grunted, licking fat from his fingers.

'And that lake was once a crater?'

'Aye, it was,' Olin said. 'The Starstone Crater, where a rock fell from the sky. Started a lot of trouble, did that rock.'

Drem knew all about that, had listened to the tale-tellers speak of how the Starstone had crashed to earth, though he struggled to imagine such a thing happening. The tales told of Seven Treasures that had been forged from the Starstone, and that the first war had been fought over those Treasures, men and giants shedding a river of blood. It had taken a god to stop it; Elyon the Maker had unleashed his legions of Ben-Elim, raining a judgement of death and destruction upon the world and its inhabitants. Elyon had only stopped when he realized that he had been tricked, lured into the plan of his great enemy, Asroth, Demon-Lord of the Fallen. Elyon had walked away then, abandoning the world of flesh and banishing both his own Ben-Elim as well as Asroth and his Kadoshim hordes to the world of spirit, the Otherworld, where they remained trapped for two thousand years as men and giants slowly rebuilt their shattered world.

Until just over a hundred years ago, when the Kadoshim found a sorcerous way to break their bonds in the Otherworld. They returned to the Banished Lands in an explosion of hatred and slaughter, but the Ben-Elim followed them, their eternal war spilling into the world of flesh.

'Much has changed since the coming of the Ben-Elim,' Drem said.

'Aye,' Olin grunted. 'And not much of it good.'

Drem's da was not a supporter of the Ben-Elim. It was rare that he would even mention them, despite Drem's attempts to lure him into that conversation.

'Turning the Desolation into this is good, though,' Drem said, waving a hand at the vista before them.

'This *is* good,' his da agreed, 'but the Ben-Elim didn't do this. *They've* done it,' he said, pointing to the settlement beside the lake, 'and others like them. People like us.'

'We're trappers, hunters.'

'Aye, well, I mean people that have travelled north and settled here, irrigating, farming, planting, growing. The Desolation has become this because generations of people like us made it a better place. Though I suppose the Ben-Elim are the reason behind that as well, their *protection* in the south was what drove many here.'

Drem thought about that a while. Stars prickled into life in the crow-black of night as darkness seeped into the world around them.

'They'll come here, too, though, won't they?' Drem said

into the night. 'The Ben-Elim. Sooner or later, as they have elsewhere, to hunt the Kadoshim.'

He'd said that last word quickly, knowing his da did not like to hear it uttered.

Kadoshim. Dread demons of Asroth who had escaped their bonds in the Otherworld and entered Drem's world to become creatures of flesh and blood, monsters come to destroy all that lived in these Banished Lands. His da hated them, hated the very sound of their name.

Because they killed my mam.

He didn't like to upset his da, could hear his breathing was sharper, his frame tense, just from those few words, but if he could get him to talk of the Kadoshim, maybe he would then be able to talk of Drem's mam, too . . .

'Aye,' Olin growled, spitting on the floor beside him. 'The Ben-Elim will be here one day. But later rather than sooner, I hope. May they linger in Drassil another hundred years. And every day until then shall be better for their absence. I've searched many a year for a place where we can live free.' He drew in a breath, seemed about to say something more, but only silence followed.

Drem breathed deep, the scent of pine trees and winter heavy in the air.

'Have you seen Drassil?' he asked, a new tactic.

Olin gave him a sidelong look.

'I have, as you well know.'

Drem opened his mouth to ask another question.

'Enough,' his da snapped as he stood quickly. 'A long day on the morrow, I'm for my bed.' He stamped his feet, stood there hesitantly for a moment, looking down at Drem. Then he walked away and lay close to the fire. Drem heard the rustle of furs and popping of a cork as a skin of mead was unstoppered.

Drem sat and stared into the darkness, listening to the sounds of the night.

*

Drem woke to a great crashing. Staggering to his feet, furs falling away, wet with dawn's dew, he looked to his da, who was on his feet, a short-handled axe in one hand, knife in the other. The stillness of dawn was shattered by a roaring that echoed through the foothills, startling birds from branches.

'The pit,' Olin said, and then he was off and running. Drem stooped and swept up his spear, his long legs carrying him after his da, who was already disappearing amongst the pine trees that cloaked the hillslope.

The path curved close to the river, which frothed and foamed with icy water fresh from the mountains. Drem closed in on his da as the ground began to level, and then saw him skid to a halt, twenty paces ahead.

Drem caught up, breathing heavily, staring in disbelief at the sight that had caused Olin to stop.

The elk pit was a mass of limbs and fur, a great-antlered bull-elk with head and shoulders scrabbling on the ground as it tried to heave itself out. It was lowing frantically, clouds of cold breath misting and billowing, a terror and agony in its cries.

Because something else was in the pit with it. Or part of it was, its bulk too great for the pit to contain.

Behind the thrashing elk Drem caught a glimpse of white fur, of long claws and a wide, gaping maw full of teeth as they clamped down upon the bull-elk's muscled neck.

A bear. A giant bear. What's it doing here, so far south of the Bonefells?

Scythe-like claws opened up bloody tracks across the elk's chest, the bear gave a vicious shake of its head and Drem heard the crack of bones breaking, the elk slumping, slipping slowly back into the pit.

Even through the fog of shock, Drem realized he'd never seen a *white* bear before. Beside him his father stood as frozen as he was, awestruck by the savage power before them.

'What do we do?' Drem whispered.

The bear's head reared up from the pit, jaws red with gore, white fur stained pink, and it looked straight at them.

'Run like hell,' his da said, pushing Drem back up the path. In a handful of heartbeats they were both sprinting, legs pumping, behind them the sound of the bear extricating itself from the elk and pit, the thunder of its gait as it lumbered after them, Drem feeling the ground shaking beneath his feet.

They ran amongst pine trees, where the ground was spongy with forest litter and pine needles. Drem's heart felt it was bursting though his chest, a great crashing behind them as the bear barrelled into a tree, the sound of wood splintering. Then sudden pain, Drem's foot plunging into a hole, his body flying through the air, crunching to the ground. He tried to rise, but a sharp pain shot up his ankle into his leg and he dropped to the ground.

He rolled onto his back, saw the bear powering towards him, a mountain of fur and muscle blotting all else out, small eyes gleaming in its huge head. Fear coursed through Drem. Bone-chilling, limb-numbing fear. He knew he should do something, move, run, hobble, anything, as death hurtled closer and closer, but he could do nothing, only stare wide-eyed as it came to claim him.

And then his da was standing over him, axe and knife in his fists.

'Run, Da,' Drem wheezed.

Olin drew his arm back and hurled his axe with all his might; the axe spun through the air, slamming into the bear's shoulder with a meaty *thunk*. It gave a rumbling growl but surged on. Drem remembered his own hand-axe at his belt, fumbled to draw it from its loop as his da grabbed Drem's spear and sent that too hurtling towards the creature. Before knowing if the weapon had struck true, Olin threw himself upon Drem, covering him with his body.

The world turned dark, the sound of the bear like a thunderclap overhead, a roar of pain, the smell of his da's sweat, the ground shaking as the bear closed on them. Then his da was dragging, pulling and rolling to the side, the bear so close Drem could smell it and feel the air of its passing. He lashed out with his small axe at a paw bigger than his head as it thumped into the ground less than a handspan away, tasted the copper tang of blood on his lips. Scythe-like claws raked the ground, spraying soil as the bear's momentum carried it on.

'*Up*,' Olin grunted, hauling Drem to his feet. Pain lanced up from his ankle and he almost fell, his da grabbing an arm and hauling it over his shoulder. A score of paces away the bear was skidding to a halt, turning, Drem's spear protruding from its chest. With a swipe of its paw, the spear was ripped free; blood welled, the shaft splintered. The beast lumbered back towards them.

Abruptly Drem was hoisted like a sack of grain onto his da's back and carried away from the path. Drem saw the bear lurch after them, pounding through the trees, closer and closer.

Fear enveloped Drem like a fog, snatching his breath away, but through it one thought pierced the haze. His da was going to die trying to save him. A wave of love for his da drove back the consuming fear of imminent death, but a new fear rose up, that his da was going to die.

'Leave me, Da, save yourself,' Drem breathed. A grunt from Olin was the only response. Then Drem glimpsed where his da was running.

Towards the river.

And then Olin was leaping, the bear swiping at them with its claws, his da crying out, an arc of blood in the air and they slammed into ice-cold water. Drem gasped in the white foam, then was pulled under, not knowing which way was up, hands flailing, feet kicking, lungs burning. His head broke water and he sucked in a great lungful of air, spluttered as the current grabbed and spun him, slammed him into a rock. He pushed away, glimpsed his da bobbing on the water ahead of him, speeding through icy spume, then disappearing as the river fell away. He swam after, the current catching him again and sending him speeding in the same direction. Behind him he glimpsed the white bear leaning over the river's edge, roaring its rage.

CHAPTER THREE

RIV

Riv's spear slammed into the target with a satisfying thud, piercing the straw man's heart. She gave a fierce snarl as it swayed and fell backwards, her eyes flickering to the crowd that stood about the weapons-field, watching her and a score of others at their warrior trials. Her eyes found her mother and Aphra, her sister, looking like a warrior-born in her best war-gear, white wings embossed upon a black leather cuirass that gleamed beneath a cold winter sun. Their eyes met and Aphra's shone with pride, making Riv's chest swell.

'Shield wall,' a voice boomed, echoing off the stone walls of Drassil, and Riv focused again, speeding towards her companions, slipping her shield from her back as she ran, hand reaching for the wooden short-sword at her hip. She was one of the first in line, her comrades settling around her, raising shields, setting feet. Vald pushed into her left side, dark where she was fair, all muscle and sweat, half a head taller than Riv, and almost as wide as he was tall.

'Nearly there,' Vald grunted. 'Won't be long and we'll be off on the Long Night.'

'If old One-Eye doesn't break our bones to kindling first,' Riv replied, and grinned at the speed with which Vald's smile twisted into a frown.

A horn blast rang out, and all along the line wood and iron thudded together, great rectangular shields overlapping, Riv and her companions pressing tight together as they had been drilled countless times. Riv peered over her iron rim to see Balur One-Eye step out from the crowd, captain of the Ben-Elim's legion of giants, his battle fame almost larger than his own huge form. He stood a man and a half tall, his white hair bound in a thick warrior braid, moustache knotted with leather, and tattoos of thorn and vine swirling up his thick arms. Wrapped in leather and fur, he strode towards them, gripping a long-hafted war-hammer in his massive fists. More grim-faced giants followed him, striding towards Riv's shield wall. A worm of fear threaded through her belly at the sight of old One-Eye and she fought the urge to laugh, a wild joy leaping up inside her.

I have dreamed of this for so long, since I was born, it feels. Sixteen summers of wishing I was a warrior of the White-Wings, and now it is so close I can taste it.

'Ready,' she called out, her voice trembling with the emotion of this moment, and she tucked her head down and pressed her shoulder firmly into her shield.

Vald grunted unintelligibly as shields from the second row rose up to cover the heads of those in the front row, and then Balur was there, the air whistling as he spun his war-hammer and slammed it against them, wood cracking like a burst of thunder. Riv felt the power of it shudder through the shield wall, a tremor that rippled through wood and iron, flesh and bone, but as far as she could tell no one had fallen and the wall held. A thud from further away, one of Balur's companions joining the fray, and another, much closer, an explosion that numbed her shield arm and rocked her backwards, feet digging grooves in the turf as she fought to stay upright. Riv blinked sweat from her eyes. Still feeling the vibration of that last blow in her bones, she saw there was a crack running partway down the centre of her shield.

Come on, give the order, Riv thought, her right hand clamped around the hilt of her short-sword, but she knew to draw it early would be to fail this warrior trial.

She snarled a curse and gritted her teeth.

More blows rained upon them, grunts and gasps all about as her companions tried to hold and weather the storm, digging deep. Even having practised this so many times before and knowing that it was not real combat, there was still an edge of fear snaking through them, something different about the way Balur and his giants were pounding at the shield wall, a savagery that Riv had never encountered before. A shield burst into so much kindling somewhere above and to the right, followed by a sharp scream.

A horn rang out, two short blasts, and within a heartbeat Riv's wooden blade was drawn and she was stabbing out through the small gaps above and below her shield. She felt resistance, heard a grunt and smiled. She tried to peer out past her shield to see if it was Balur she had struck, but saw nothing but fur and the byrnie rings of a mail shirt.

Another combination of horn blasts rang out from the rear, a signal for the wall to prepare to march, then one more long note and Riv took a staggering step forwards, pushing against the pressure upon her shield, Vald keeping pace beside her, the rest of the wall rippling forwards, gaps appearing between the shields as the pace varied, but closing up quick enough.

The horn blew again, the sound initiating a movement Riv liked to think of as the death march, when the enemy was close to breaking and the advance of the wall aimed to crush any spirit remaining amongst those that fought on. Riv continued to stab over and under her shield, sweat stinging her eyes, dripping from her chin, Vald holding his own beside her.

A shouted command from the other side of Riv's shield, muffled, and then the pounding against the shield wall stopped, followed by one more horn blast, long and lingering, and the wall rippled to a halt. Riv lowered her shaking shield; those about her were doing the same, all of them sweat-soaked and aching, bruised and battered by Balur's assault. One-Eye and his companions were grinning at them, his empty eye socket puckered with mirth.

'Well, they weathered the storm of iron,' Balur called out loudly to ringing cheers that spread amongst the onlookers around the field. Balur dipped his head to Riv and the others about her.

Apart from Jost, Riv thought, looking at one of her training companions as he was carried stumbling from the field, one arm hanging limp and broken.

There was just time for Riv to wipe the sweat from her brow, run her fingers through her short-cropped hair and enjoy the sense of relief at finding herself still standing, and then there was the beating of wings. Several Ben-Elim rose from behind the crowd and swooped down onto the field, landing gracefully between Balur and Riv. Israfil, the Lord Protector, was first amongst them, clothed in gleaming mail, hair raven-black, eyes like coals. He strode straight towards her, a wooden practice sword in his hand. His companions spread about him to engage Riv's companions in the final trial.

Israfil raised his sword, dipped his head and then he was attacking her, his weapon arcing down from above. Riv lifted her shield, knocking Israfil's wooden blade to one side, then countered instinctively with a chop to his neck. He pivoted away, as a man, not using the advantage of his wings, and set about striking at her with combinations of the forms she had been taught, which she knew more intimately than any friend.

In no time at all she was sweating, wrists, elbows and shoulders aching deep as her bones, the power in Israfil's blows shocking her, even as he maintained perfect balance and poise.

He hits harder than Vald, and faster than anyone I've ever come across.

Then Israfil was stepping back, giving her space and a moment's respite. His white wings, held furled behind his back, were twitching as he marched back and forth before her, his bright eyes appraising her, head cocked to one side like a predatory bird. With a flick of his wrist he indicated for her to drop her shield. Even before it hit the ground he was coming at her again, his blade slicing from all directions as she retreated before him. Even her speed, which she was well known for amongst those that used the weapons-field, only just saved her from a dented skull and cracked ribs. And then, without word or warning, his wings gave a great beat and he was lifting into the air, above her, behind her, Riv twisting desperately to fend off his blows, grunting as his sword grazed her shoulder.

What better way to test if we are ready to hunt Kadoshim? The Ben-Elim are the closest thing to our enemy.

Riv ducked a blow that would have taken her head and rolled away, jumping back to her feet and leaping at Israfil as he followed, which, judging by the brief twist of his lips, caught him by surprise – Riv's sword snaking through his defence and stabbing into his thigh.

If it was cold steel you'd be bleeding like a speared boar now, she thought, then grinned.

'You try too hard,' Israfil said as he swept in closer, his sword chopping at her head, deflected, sweeping into a slice for her throat, knocked away, coming back to stab at her face, Riv swaying, stepping back, thrown off balance by his words, not his blade.

I have tried hard all my life to be the best I can be, to be worthy to wear the white wings, to fight for the Ben-Elim. How is that wrong?

'You fight to prove yourself to others,' Israfil continued, voice low and fierce, meant only for her ears. 'Pride drives you, and you think it makes you strong.' His words pounded her as hard as the flurry of his blows that followed. Riv staggered backwards, her parries and blocks wilder, her counters slashing only empty air. 'But you are wrong,' Israfil ground on, 'your pride is your *weakness.*'

She felt a squeeze of pain in her chest at his words, the

world dimming around her, her vision focused solely upon Israfil.

'It makes you brittle,' he said, lips sneering in disgust and disappointment.

Riv reeled, spinning into open space to give herself a moment to recover; she was gasping as if she had just been gut-punched.

Brittle? No. I am strong, have trained every day, all my life for this.

Israfil's blade slipped through her guard but her quick feet pivoted her away, its edge grazing the leather of her jerkin.

'Is it because you have no father?' Israfil said as he swirled around her. 'That you feel you must try so hard to prove yourself?'

'What?' Riv spoke for the first time, feeling her shock and hurt shift into something else, edged in red. 'No,' she said in a snarl, 'my sister is a White-Wing, as was my mam before her. I have enough to admire . . .' More blows, driving air and words from her lungs, Israfil's wooden blade connecting with her shoulder, one blow flowing into another, cracking into her ribs. A great pulse of his wings and she was stumbling back, slipping to one knee, the pain in her side fuelling the anger that was swelling in her gut, outrage at being so wronged by someone she had respected completely and utterly until only a handful of heartbeats ago.

My father? He is long dead.

She looked up at Israfil, who hovered above her, mouth twisted in some unreadable emotion.

'You are *weak*,' he said to her.

Riv leaped at Israfil, a red rage flooding through her. She grabbed his belt and hauled herself higher, saw his mouth was moving but could only dimly hear his shouted words because there was a roaring in her head like a storm shaking the trees of Drassil, and then her fist was slamming into Israfil's face, once, twice, blood gushing from his nose, and his wings were beating, lifting them higher. Part of her was appalled at what she was doing, but that part of her was small and powerless, an observer to events, nothing more, watching as she rained blows upon the Ben-Elim. Even then all she could hear were his words, *you are weak, you are brittle*, and then the red mist filled her head and her vision until she saw and heard nothing except her own wordless howl.

Riv blinked awake and sat up with a start. She felt a pressure upon her chest and saw her mam's face staring down at her, eyes creased with worry.

'Easy, Riv,' her mam said. 'Rest a while.'

As if I ever took that advice. Riv snorted, pushing her mam's hand away. She sat up, saw that she was still in the weapons-field, her mam kneeling beside her, a crowd gathered in a half-circle around Vald and the others who had completed their warrior trial. They were standing in a line, faces glowing with exertion and pride as Israfil stood before them, commending them on their prowess.

You are weak.

Riv put a hand to her head, squeezing her eyes shut, remembered frozen moments: leaping at Israfil, blood from his nose, rising into the sky.

'What . . . happened?' she muttered, an ache in her back between her shoulder blades pulsing up into her head. She twisted, rolled her shoulders.

'You attacked Israfil,' her mam said, a horrified whisper.

The voices of her companions and friends rose up, reciting the first lines of the Oath.

'I am defender to the Faithful,' they all began, voices ringing out.

I should be there, beside them, she thought. *They should be my sword-kin, now, except that they have passed their warrior trial, and I have failed.*

'I am the sharp blade that will slay the Fallen,' echoed across the field.

She looked back to her mam, who was regarding her with sad, disappointed eyes.

With a choked sound in her throat, Riv pushed past her mam and ran. She saw heads from amongst the gathered crowd turn and stare at her; her sister, Aphra, her pride-filled gaze of earlier a thing of history now.

And then she crashed into someone, both of them tumbling to the ground. With a grunt, she climbed to one knee, saw the other person spring agilely to his feet. The youth was staring at her, lean and sharp-featured, with deep, almond-shaped eyes and dark, weathered skin, almost the same colour as the alder-wood hilt of her sister's short-sword. She knew him, or at least, knew his name. Bleda, the Sirak prince who was a ward to the Ben-Elim. Riv remembered the day he had been taken, all those years ago when she had been her sister's attendant, her shield-carrier, weapon-cleaner, water-giver and all other manner of tasks. She had loved it. But not that one, long ago, moment. The scene flashed through her mind, seeing the boy's proud face, his curved bow falling from his hand, face stricken as his kin's heads had been tossed into the dirt before him, tears streaking down his face as the giant Alcyon had carried him away.

Bleda looked at her now, standing over her, his face as emotionless as the Ben-Elim, eyes dark pools.

'I heard what he said to you,' Bleda whispered. He reached a hand out, not to help, but to wipe a tear from her face. He looked at it, glistening upon his fingertip. Something about him changed, but it was only in his eyes, his face still as carved stone.

'*This* is his victory, your defeat,' he said, showing her her own tear.

She stared back defiantly, letting him see her anger and

shame, allowed another tear to roll down her cheek. Her own form of defiance.

'You will come back, stronger.' He shrugged, then put a hand on her arm to help her rise but she shook it off, leaped to her feet, and then she was speeding around a corner, where buildings hid Bleda and the weapons-field from view.

Riv ran through the streets of Drassil. The huge giant-built towers of stone loomed all around her, and high up, above even their rooftops, the leafless branches of Drassil's great tree soughed in a cold wind. Faces passed Riv in a blur, some uttered or nodded greetings, but Riv ignored them all, shame a cold fist clenching in her guts, her need to be away from the weapons-field driving her on. She slowed to a walk, looked around her and saw that her feet had taken her to the courtyard before Drassil's Great Hall.

It reared before her, a huge dome of stone built around the trunk of Drassil's great tree, which in itself was wider than any man-built tower that Riv had ever set her eyes upon. Broad steps led up from the courtyard to massive iron-banded gates of oak, flung open so that the entrance looked like a gaping, shadow-filled mouth in a giant's skull. Riv crossed the court-yard and padded up the steps, earning a stare from the guards who stood around the doorway, a dozen White-Wings in their black cuirasses of boiled leather and bright silver helms. They knew her, though, and so Riv passed through the doorway without opposition. Once inside she hesitated a moment upon the threshold and looked into the chamber.

It was one huge circular room, the dome's arc rising high and cavernous above her, sounds echoing and magnified; even the breath in her throat sounded loud and harsh to her own ears. The floor dropped away from her in a curve of tiered stone steps that cascaded down to the ground a good fifty paces below her. Riv went down the steps, firelight from great iron braziers washing over her. She glimpsed a Ben-Elim standing in an alcove high above, others gliding gracefully through slanting beams of winter daylight that filtered down from shuttered windows set into the dome's walls.

She reached the last dozen steps and stopped, looking into the chamber. Below her the ground levelled, crossing a wide expanse towards the room's centre, where the trunk of Drassil's ancient tree rose. Before it stood a row of muscle, flesh and steel: a score of Queen Ethlinn's giants set about a dais. Shield-breakers, they were called, some of them the very giants that had stood and fought against the Black Sun's shield wall more than a hundred years ago, out on the plains beyond Drassil's walls. Asroth and his host of dread Kadoshim had filled the skies that day, while his champion the Black Sun had led a warband thousands strong upon the ground.

And yet we won. The Ben-Elim saved us, Riv thought, sinking down onto one of the cold steps and staring over the heads of the giants below her. Her gaze fixed onto the dais behind them, at what they guarded.

Two statues forged from black iron, they seemed at first glance. One Ben-Elim, one Kadoshim, joined in battle. Their wings were spread, one feathered, one with wings more akin to a bat, things of leather and skin.

But they are not statues.

She stared at the Ben-Elim, his features strained with exertion. Meical, once captain of the Ben-Elim. She could even see a bead of sweat running down his forehead. And in his grip, the Lord of the Kadoshim.

Asroth, Lord of the Fallen.

His hair was long, bound with braids and wire, his face regal and handsome, exuding a fierce pride.

And a deeper malice.

I'm supposed to stand against that malice, supposed to protect the Faithful and slay the Fallen. What is wrong with me? Why did I do that on the weapons-field? And to the Lord Protector, of all people.

And why did he say those things to me?

She felt her belly churn at the echo of his words, a pain

deep inside sharp as any skinning knife. Hot tears came to her eyes and she sniffed, wiping them angrily away.

Footsteps echoed behind her, a familiar stride that Riv would know anywhere. Confident, full of purpose.

Her sister, Aphra, dark-haired where she was fair, calm and controlled where Riv was not.

The footsteps stopped.

'You might as well sit,' Riv muttered, slapping the flag-stoned stairs.

Aphra sat quietly, waiting.

'I hate myself,' Riv whispered into the silence.

Aphra took a deep breath. 'It's a setback,' she said. 'Not the end of your chances to join the White-Wings.'

'I punched the Lord Protector in the face,' Riv pointed out.

'Aye.' Aphra nodded, running a hand through her dark hair, close-cropped like all of the White-Wings. Practical and uniform. 'Granted, a big setback, then.' She looked at Riv, her hand twitching to reach out and wipe away the stray tear that rolled down Riv's cheek. Riv saw her fist clench in the effort it took to resist that urge.

'Why?' Aphra said, instead. Not accusing, or judging.

'Because . . .' Riv's voice caught in her throat at the memory of Israfil's words. She took a deep breath, controlling the emotion that was stealing her voice. 'He told me I was weak because I have no father,' Riv said, and then the rest spilt out in a torrent of whispers, Aphra listening in her calm way.

When Riv finished, Aphra sat there nodding, eyes staring into nowhere. Looking at her sister, Riv saw a few strands of grey in her hair, was surprised at that. Her sister always seemed so strong and capable. Fierce and wise, never-changing.

She's getting old.

'He was testing you,' Aphra said.

'What?'

'Many of us are fatherless, and motherless. We are born of warriors, Riv, and warriors die – that is the way of it. Our da was a White-Wing, he fought and died in service of the holy war. It is just a part of our life.' She was silent a moment, her eyes distant.

'What was our father like?' Riv asked. She had never known him, a White-Wing like her mam, but slain on a campaign, soon after Riv was born.

Aphra looked down at her, stroked Riv's hair. 'A warrior.' She shrugged. 'A White-Wing, he gave his all for the cause, died for it.'

'I know that,' Riv said, 'have heard it a thousand times. But what was he *like*?'

'Ah, Riven ap Lorin,' Aphra said, using Riv's full name for once. 'He was like you: wild, like the north wind.'

Riv liked that, though she thought that quality might not have helped her warrior trial today.

'So it's our father's fault I punched the Lord Protector, then.'

'I don't think that will be an acceptable excuse to Israfil.' Aphra smiled. 'Though I wouldn't worry,' she added with a shake of her head. 'Israfil did not mean what he said.'

'Then why did he say it?' Riv growled.

'Think,' Aphra said, poking Riv in the temple. 'The warrior trial is not just about skill of arms, Riv. Think about it. It is all a test to deem if we are fit to face the Kadoshim in battle. For that you need blade-prowess, of course, because the Kadoshim are strong, yes, fierce and deadly, that too. But they also have dread-cunning, and will exploit any weakness. Imagine you were in a shield wall and the right insults wormed their way into your head and heart – what if the rage took you then, and you leaped from the wall in a red-murder haze? The wall would be shattered, and your sword-kin would die.'

Riv thought about that awhile, and whatever way she looked at it there was no getting away from the sense of it.

'That smacks of truth,' she conceded, 'but it doesn't mean it *is* the truth.'

'This time it is,' Aphra said. 'A similar thing happened to me, on my warrior trial.'

'Really?' Riv asked, wanting it to be true. It was a far better option in her head than the Lord Protector secretly being a wicked, malice-filled bastard. 'The Lord Protector?'

'No, it was Kol that sword-schooled me.' Her eyes took on a faraway look. 'But he said some hard things to me. Things that were close enough to truth; if you looked at what he said in a shift of light you could almost think, maybe . . .'

'Aye,' Riv agreed, a hiss of breath.

'But they were *not* the truth,' Aphra said, shaking her head. 'Kol spoke to me afterwards, and told me it was only a test.'

'Will the Lord Protector tell me the same, then?'

'Well, I'm thinking, no,' Aphra said. 'I controlled my anger, unlike you, and still passed my trials, remember, where you have failed. You will have to take them again, so the Lord Protector will not want you knowing. I shouldn't have told you.' She looked sternly at Riv. 'Don't tell a soul, not even Mam.'

'I won't,' Riv grunted, almost insulted, as if she would ever betray her sister's trust.

'And then there's the matter of punching the Lord Protector in the face,' Aphra continued.

Riv hung her head and put her face in her hands.

'An apology may be the wisest step,' Aphra said.

Riv's gut instinct was to snarl *NEVER*. Israfil's words were still a sharp knife in her soul, but, if it had all been a test . . .

It does make sense, and is something the Ben-Elim would do: testing every aspect of a warrior, mental as well as physical.

'It was a great honour, the Lord Protector choosing you to fight, to test. He must see greatness in you,' Aphra said. 'As do I.'

'Huh,' grunted Riv. *Shame I didn't live up to it.* 'I'll apologize, then,' Riv said grudgingly.

'Good,' Aphra said, taking Riv's arm and tugging her to her

feet. 'Now let's go and find Mam. She's searching for you all over Drassil.'

Riv stood, feeling some of her hurt and anger drain away.

'When do you think the next warrior trials will be held?' she asked her sister.

'A few moons, most likely. As soon as there are enough recruits reaching their name-days to make a shield wall.'

Maybe still this year, then, Riv thought, *before Midwinter's Day*.

'Before then you're going to have to do something about that temper of yours, though. It seems to be getting worse, not better, and that's not the kind of quality the Ben-Elim want in their White-Wings. Discipline, control,' Aphra said, putting an arm around Riv's shoulder and steering her up the stairs towards the open entrance.

'Aye,' Riv agreed, knowing that was a truth harder in the doing than the saying.

I've never been the calmest, never as calm as Aphra, but she's right, it is getting worse.

'Otherwise one day it is likely to get you into a whole lot of trouble.'

I think it already has.

'Why did you come here?' Aphra asked her.

'Don't know.' Riv shrugged, though she did know, pausing and looking back into the chamber, her eyes drawn to the figures of Meical and Asroth upon the dais.

They had been frozen like that since the great battle, over a hundred years ago. The Seven Treasures had all been present, forged from the Starstone, and it was by the Treasures' power that a portal had been opened between the Banished Lands and the Otherworld. Through that gateway the Kadoshim had poured like a dark plague, death and destruction their sole purpose, but fortunately the Ben-Elim had followed close behind them, saviours of humanity.

Somehow the Treasures had been destroyed, reduced to

molten metal, and Asroth and Meical had been caught up in their destruction, coated in the cooling ore, frozen for all time. Whether they were dead or alive, no one knew, but the Ben-Elim in a humbling act of self-sacrifice had elected to stay and guard mankind against even the possibility of Asroth's return, and to hunt down and destroy the Kadoshim that had survived the Battle of Drassil.

That was why she had come to this hall. To remind herself why she had trained so hard, each and every day of her remembered life; to remind herself of what was at the heart of all the blood and sweat, the dark mornings, the muscle straining, the exhaustion, sacrifice and discipline. Something that was bigger than her insignificant life. Something that gave her meaning and purpose.

The great fight. The holy war. And I must be a part of it.

CHAPTER FOUR

DREM

'Grab the branch!' Drem heard his da shout. He splashed about wildly, saw the branch as it loomed close and reached out, the fingers of one hand wrapping around it. He felt the river current still tugging at him, his arm and shoulder muscles stretching and straining – for a moment he was sure the river was going to win – then Olin was pulling him into the shore, a hand under his arm helping him rise. Drem hobbled onto the riverbank, his ankle a throbbing pain.

Olin didn't look much better, grey hair hanging lank, his face pale and gaunt, dark hollows under his eyes. The sleeve of one arm was torn, a long red wound beneath it pulsing blood.

'Need to l-l-look at that,' Drem said, trying to stop his teeth from chattering.

'Let's get warm first,' Olin muttered, eyeing the darkening sky.

The river had carried them out of the foothills and into the plain that surround the Starstone Lake. Drem looked back up at the hills and mountains, his mind filled with the memory of the white bear that had come so close to killing them both. He shivered.

Fire.

Both their kindling pouches were soaked through, but they found dead rushes close to the river and gathered great bundles of them, then used their striking irons to set sparks leaping.

Drem groaned in pleasure as the first warmth of the flames lapped against him. They stripped their wet clothes and hung them close for drying. Both of them were covered in cuts and bruises where the river had introduced them to rocks and branches on the turbulent journey from the foothills to the plain. Drem's bone-handled seax had managed to stay within its sheath; he kept it close, the white bear never far from his mind.

Olin splinted his ankle, which was swollen and bruised purple, but didn't feel broken, and then Drem set about stitching his da's arm. A claw from the bear's parting swipe had gouged a long furrow almost from shoulder to elbow. Drem boiled some water, let it cool awhile and then cleaned the wound out. He took a fish hook and thread from a pouch on his da's belt and began methodically stitching the wound up.

'Last time you did this I'd drunk half a skin of mead first,' his da hissed, grunting each time Drem pierced flesh and popped through skin.

'Quiet,' Drem whispered, wiping fresh blood away and concentrating on his stitching. It was a task he enjoyed, found it fascinating, seeing the flesh pull together. There was something appealing about the regimentation of the stitches, and something wonderful in the fact that this act helped the body to heal itself, that it would allow flesh and skin to grow and knit back together.

When he was done Drem sat back, smiling at his handiwork. His da twisted to inspect it and nodded approvingly.

'Ever decide you're done with hunting, you'll make a fine healer,' he said. 'Or maybe a seamstress.' His lips twisted in a smile.

'So, what now?' Drem asked.

'We could limp home to our cabin,' Olin said, 'but what would be the point of that, when we've got half a year of trapping sitting back in those foothills?'

'The point?' Drem said, raising an eyebrow. 'I'd imagine it would be avoiding death by giant bear.'

'Aye.' His da laughed. 'And that's a good point. But that bear should be long gone by now. He's meal enough in that elk he felled to last him a ten-night. He only chased us because he thought we might be after a bite of his supper.'

There was logic in that, and Drem liked logic. More than that, logic was the cadence by which he walked through life. But the memory of that bear, its claws and teeth, was still vivid in his mind.

'And we need those pelts to sell, if we don't want to starve through winter,' Olin added. 'We're not farmers, have no crops to see us through.'

Drem looked up at the foothills and mountains beyond, solid slabs of darkness now as night settled like a shroud about them.

'Back to the camp it is, then.' He nodded.

'With first light,' Olin said.

They settled about the fire, dressed in their dried-out clothes, but all the time Drem was going over the bear attack in his mind. He'd travelled and lived in the Wild for many years with his da, and he was no stranger to the savagery of the Banished Lands and their bloodthirsty predators. Packs of wolven, blood-sucking bats – once he'd even seen a draig. But never had he come across something that had affected him like that white bear. He'd been frozen with fear. There was respect, too; for the staggering majesty of its power, and for its indomitable will. Any creature that made the wild of the Desolation its home was a force to be reckoned with.

He thought of his da, standing over him as the bear charged.

And my da is not so different from that bear. He is indomitable, too.

'Thank you,' Drem whispered.

'Huh?' Olin grunted, his back to him. Drem had thought he was asleep.

'I said, thank you. You saved my life.'

'Well, I'm your da. It's my job.'

'Life and death is no jest,' Drem muttered.

His da shifted to look at his son, his face deep-lined, all dark grooves and shadow in the flickering firelight.

'No, you're right.' He sat up, pulled his knees up to his chest. 'The truth of it is, there are not many things I've done right in this life. Getting handbound to your mam was one of them. You're another, Drem; the one good thing I have left. And I'll be damned if I'll let anything take you from me. Not without a fight, anyway.'

Drem felt a surge of emotion at his da's words. They were both practical men, both viewed life logically, rarely given to emotional displays. Neither of them were much for long words or long conversations, and Drem had never heard his da say such things as this to him.

Maybe it's coming so close to death. We both stared it in the face this morning.

His voice did not cooperate as he tried to speak. He coughed, cleared his throat.

'I wish I could remember more of Mam,' he said. 'If I think hard enough I can see something of her face, her eyes. Her smile. But no matter how hard I try, I can't remember her voice.'

The fire crackled between them, the only sound as Olin stared into the flames.

'Her voice was beautiful,' he eventually said. 'Like a river to a parched man. At least, it was to me.' He smiled to himself. 'She laughed a lot, cried little. She liked a good jest, did your mam. Ach, she would fall off her chair she laughed so hard.' He shrugged, finally looking at Drem. 'She loved you fiercely.'

As I love her.

His memories of his mam were vague and half-formed, like figures in the mist.

Long, dark hair, laughing eyes.

Fractured memories flickered through his mind. A song, hummed in his ear, a tight hug. Another face, a woman, tall, blonde, a stick in her hand, bending down to lift him up. A tower on a hill.

Drem had only been a bairn when his mam died, three or four summers old, but he remembered how she made him feel: a warm glow in his chest, edged with the melancholy of loss.

Safe, and loved, that's how I feel when I think of her.

'I hate the Kadoshim,' Drem growled.

Olin just stared into the flames, his eyes glistening with reflected firelight.

'Why did she have to die? Why did the Kadoshim kill her?' Drem said, more to himself than to his da, but Olin looked at him.

'Because this world is a hard and cruel place,' Olin breathed. 'That white bear, nothing else you have ever faced matches the malice that the Kadoshim bear towards us, towards mankind. They are wickedness made flesh.'

Drem thought about that awhile; the silence grew between them.

Kadoshim and Ben-Elim, ancient enemies waging their eternal war against each other.

An ember crackled and popped on the fire.

'If it was the Kadoshim that murdered my mam,' he eventually said, 'why is it that you hate the Ben-Elim so much, when they hunt the Kadoshim?'

'Aye, I suppose it would not make sense to you.' He scowled into the darkness. 'I do not like to talk of these things, have tried for years now to leave them behind, to carve a life for us free of their stain and influence. Talking about it only digs up the hurt that I've spent a long time burying.' Olin sighed. 'But, always the questions.' He drew in a deep breath. 'So. An answer for you, and then maybe you'll give me some peace. The Ben-Elim *do* hunt the Kadoshim, are their ancient enemies. But it was the Ben-Elim who plotted and schemed for the Kadoshim to enter these Banished Lands in the first place. The Ben-Elim used the Kadoshim to open a portal between the Otherworld and the world of flesh, and then the Ben-Elim followed them through, their spirit-bodies becoming flesh in the process, just like the Kadoshim.'

Drem frowned at that. 'Why? Why did the Ben-Elim do that?'

'They had their reasons,' his da said, 'the telling of which I do not have the time or the inclination for. Just trust me on this. The Ben-Elim are not our friends or allies because they hunt the Kadoshim. The Kadoshim would not be here in the first place if not for the Ben-Elim.'

'But—'

'Ach.' His da spat. 'Answer this, then. The bear and the wolven, they both hunt the elk, do they not?'

'Aye, they do.'

'Are bear and wolven friends, then? Would they share a meal one with the other?'

'They'd most likely fight,' Drem answered. 'Or maybe one would walk away, depending on how hungry they were, how big the bear was, and how many wolven in the pack.'

'Aye, you have the right of it, lad. Things are rarely clean cut, black and white, right or wrong. Life's more complicated than that. And so it is between the Ben-Elim and human-kind. Or so it should be . . .' Olin's hand dropped to the knife at his belt, fingertips brushing the worn leather hilt. 'Besides, the Ben-Elim are not the only ones who hunt the Kadoshim.'

'Who else does, then?' Drem asked, leaning forwards.

'Is there no end to your questions?' his da muttered. 'You'll get no more out of me tonight. We've an early start and a long walk on the morrow. I'd recommend getting some sleep.' And with that he rolled over.

What's wrong with questions? Drem thought, feeling frustrated. *They are all I have.* Absently he lifted two fingers to his throat, searching for his pulse. Something about its steady rhythm soothed and calmed him when he felt anxious or troubled. He counted the beats, a whisper of breath.

'Drem,' his da said. 'Stop taking your pulse, or at least, count in your head.'

'Aye, Da.'

'There it is,' Drem said, pointing as the elk pit became visible on the path ahead of them. It was closer to sunset than highsun, both of them slowed by their injuries from the day before. They separated, slipping into the cool shadows of pine trees either side of the track, moving forwards slowly and searching for any signs of the white bear. There was none and they met beside the elk pit.

The elk was gone, snagged fur and dried blood staining the bottom of the pit, the earth churned and scattered, great gouges from the bear's claws and ruts in the soil from the elk's death-throes.

'Taken it back to its den – some cave or safe place,' Olin said. 'Where it can eat in peace.'

Must be a cave the size of a mead-hall, Drem thought, looking at an imprint of one of the bear's paws.

'Well, as long as it's far from us, I'm not caring,' his da said. He sniffed and looked around; the hillside was quiet and still.

'Let's go see what's left of our camp.'

Their path wound into the pine trees close to the river, and Drem saw the spot where he'd fallen, where his da had stood over him. For a moment he felt his blood run chill at the memory of it . . .

I wish I had Da's courage.

A patch of blood and Drem's axe lay amongst the forest litter close to where he'd fallen, beside it a claw, long and curled, a tuft of fur and flesh still attached to it where the axe had severed it from the bear's paw.

'There's a keepsake for you,' Olin said as he crouched and

passed the claw to Drem, who whistled while turning it in his hand, the claw measuring from the tip of his finger to his wrist.

'Not that you'll need reminding of that beast,' his da said.

'Not likely,' Drem muttered, the claw bringing back a kaleidoscope of memories of him lying on his back staring at the onrushing bear.

They found his da's axe close by, its blade blood-crusted black.

'Good axe, that,' his da said with a smile, 'Glad not to have seen the last of it.'

Their camp was mostly untouched, the piles of furs where they'd left them. One of their packhorses had slipped its rope but they found it only a few hundred paces away, contentedly eating grass. Something had been through the leftovers of their supper and ripped open a bag of cheese but, judging by the teeth marks, it was more the size of a weasel or stoat than a giant bear. It did not take long for them to break camp and soon they were winding their way back down the hillslope, leading three ponies, all piled high with bundled furs and kit. It was close to sunset but they'd agreed to get as far away from this spot as possible before darkness forced them to stop. Drem felt much better for a thick cloak about his shoulders, the spear he held in his hand and the axe hanging at his belt, not that weapons had done him or his da much good yesterday.

When they reached the elk pit Drem marvelled again at the carnage caused by one beast. Looking into it, something else caught his eye. Not a gleam, more the opposite: a matt darkness. Something black and solid.

Drem scrambled into the pit, careful not to take any weight on his injured ankle as he dropped the last few handspans, then crouched in the soil.

'What is it?' his da called from at the pit's rim.

'I don't know,' Drem answered as he scraped and dug at his feet. Then he sat back, frowning.

It looked like a slab of rock, black and pitted. It was roughly the length of his forearm, loosely shaped like a teardrop, cold to the touch. As Drem tried to pull it free of the soil around it, he realized it was heavy, much heavier than he would have expected of a slab of granite, or iron ore of a similar size.

Feet thumped to the ground beside him as Olin joined him.

'What is it?' his da asked again.

'You remember I hit something hard when I was digging the pit – you called it the mountain's roots,' Drem said.

'Aye. It was a joke,' Olin muttered.

'I think this is what I hit. The bear's claws have raked around it, dug it free.' Drem shuffled aside to show his da, who crouched down and reached out to touch the rock. He pulled his hand away, hissing as if he'd been burned or bitten.

'What's wrong?' Drem asked.

Olin looked pale. 'Get me my shovel,' he said.

CHAPTER FIVE

SIG

Sig sat in her saddle, hunched over from the rain, and stared into the darkness. Beneath her, Hammer shifted her huge paws and gave a low, grumbling growl, more a vibration in the great bear's belly that shivered up through Sig's bones than an audible sound. Horses whinnied and stamped, no doubt unsettled by the great mass of muscle and teeth that they were standing with, too close for their liking.

It is not so easy for a giant such as I to stay hidden, but silence is at the heart of it, and I am making a better job of it than they are!

Sig frowned admonishingly down at the men gathered about her, even if the closest rider to her was Elgin, Battlechief of Ardain. He looked old to her in the darkness, deep lines in his face, though his straight back and the strength of his grip when she had arrived had told her all she needed to know.

It is not the first time we have hunted and fought together. Not many that I'd trust at my side beyond my sword-kin, but he is one of them.

Once this would have been unthinkable to her: a giant of the Jotun Clan, standing amongst the race of men in companionable silence. But now the giant Clans were reunited, and peace had been made with mankind.

Although the Banished Lands are not yet at peace.

'How much longer,' Sig heard someone whisper, a bodiless voice in the gloom.

'Whisht,' Elgin silenced the voice.

Sig sniffed the air and looked up at the sky, though there was naught to see except darkness and the sensation of rain-patter upon her face.

It is always darkest before the dawn.

She shrugged, loosening stiff muscles, a ripple of her broad shoulders that set water cascading as if shaken from a tree, shifting the weight of her shield and the sheathed longsword across her back. The moon slid out from behind rag-torn clouds, silvering the woodland they were standing within, soft-ening the solid dark of the hill before them, a glimpsed snarl of twisted hawthorn and wind-beaten rock. Sig looked to her right, saw Cullen sitting straight-backed in his saddle, ring-mail glistening black with rain, a spear in his white-knuckled fist. His red hair was bound tight at the nape, a round shield like hers slung across his back with a white, four-pointed star painted upon it.

The bright star, sigil of our Order.

'Now?' Cullen mouthed up to Sig. She gave him a scowl in return.

Anticipation and energy exuded from the young warrior and, not for the first time, Sig wondered at the wisdom of bringing him fresh from his Long Night into such a trial as this.

That decision's long-made, now. No going back on it. Besides, he was the best of his year, which was no surprise with the blood that runs in his veins.

Sig twisted the other way in her saddle, a creak of leather and ringmail, and glimpsed faces about her, men cold, wet and tired from their night-long journey and vigil, but their faces were stern and set in hard lines. She liked what she saw.

I asked for hard men. They'll need to be.

Grey trickled into the world, dawn making shadows shift and form where there had been only the crow-black of night. A whisper of wings overhead, the hint of something much bigger than owl or hawk as a darker shadow flitted above the trees, speeding towards the hill. Sig strained eyes and ears, but there was nothing more.

A hundred heartbeats later, a new sound. The pad of foot-falls, then a flicker of movement. Shapes appeared: one man, two hounds slipping through the grey. Great beasts, chests broad and solid with muscle, muzzles flat and wide, bristling with the threat of sharp teeth. One was brindle-dark, the other grey as mountain slate. Sig felt men tense at the sight of them, quickly followed by whispers and pats to calm horses, but Sig grinned to see the wolven-hounds, so named because of the mixed blood that flowed through their veins. For a moment Sig was a hundred leagues away, and over a hundred years, seeing in her mind the original parents of this line: the great wolven, Storm, and her mate the brindle hound, Buddai, fighting and rending Kadoshim on that Day of Days. She felt a flush of pride, muted by sadness at glories and friends long past and faded.

The man with them was clothed in leather, fur and soft skins, his eyes dark shadows above a tangle of beard. He too wore a round shield slung across his back, as all in the Order did. A single-bladed axe hung from a loop at his belt, kept company by a brace of knives. He held an unstrung bow in one hand. Keld, her huntsman. Sig only needed one look from him to know it was time. A jolt of excitement rippled through her, which surprised her.

But then, it is not every day that you track a Kadoshim to its lair.

'Guards?' Sig said, her voice grating like an old iron hinge.

'Aye, there were, but the bairns saw to that,' Keld said, patting the big head of one of the hounds.

'All right then,' Sig grunted, feeling the imminence of violence begin to course through her, a tremor in her bones, a wildness fluttering in her blood, and she looked at Elgin.

He pulled himself straighter in his saddle and nodded to her.

'*Aghaidh*,' Sig whispered and Hammer lumbered into motion, out of the trees and across a windswept open space towards the hill in front of them. The rising sun washed the land in pale light, making deep valleys of shadow amongst the boulders. Elgin and his three score swords followed, all proven men, handpicked from Queen Nara's honour guard. They spread into a wide line behind Sig, Cullen and Keld.

Elgin raised his arm and signalled his warriors; a number of them peeled away to circle the hill, spread to watch for any hidden boltholes.

The ground began to slope upwards, Sig's eyes fixed on the darker shadow ahead of her, not much more than a crease in an exposed section of the rock of the hillside.

A cave. A lair.

Keld hooked his unstrung bow onto Sig's saddle and gave the rain-ragged clouds above a dark look – *too wet to bother stringing his bow.* The huntsman gave a low whistle and his hounds padded left and right, merging with the shadows.

Sig rode past a knot of hawthorn, saw boots poking from it, the stain of blood dark and slick on the grass where the guard had been dragged by Keld into cover. Hammer gave the corpse a cursory glance and sniff as she padded past it.

Only fifty paces from the crease in the rock face, then figures detached from the cave's entrance: two, three, four of them emerging as if from the very rock itself. Their bowed heads were hooded, cloaked for the rain, one holding a spear, the others with sword hilts poking from their cloaks.

'Cullen,' Sig said as she drove Hammer on, the bear jerking into a lumbering run. Behind her the red-haired warrior stood in his stirrups and hurled his spear as the first figure looked up and saw them. His mouth opened wide as he sucked in a gasp of air but the spear punched into his chest before any warning cry could be uttered. The force of the blow threw him back into his comrades in a dark splatter of blood, taking one man to the ground with him in a tangle of limbs. The other two reached for blades as Keld's hounds leaped in from either side, a blur of motion, a crunch of flesh and bone, a succession of snarling and wet tearing sounds, a gurgled rattle of a cry.

Hammer reached them as the last survivor climbed from the ground, gasping out a warning cry, a glint of steel as he dragged his blade free of its scabbard. Hammer swiped a paw at him, claws as long and sharp as daggers raking across his face and chest and he dropped faster than he'd risen in a spume of blood-mist and gore.

And then there was silence, just the wind and rain, the creak and jangle of harness, one of the wolven-hounds lapping at pooling blood. Keld tutted and the hound stopped. Sig sat high in her saddle, one hand on the hilt of her longsword still sheathed across her back, the other resting upon the weighted net that hung at her belt. These were the precarious moments, when the entrance was still open and unguarded. When escape was still possible for their enemy.

They waited, frozen, all seeming to hold their breath, even the wind dying down for a few heartbeats.

No new enemy emerged from the shadows, and Sig slid from her saddle and approached the entrance. There was a long rasp as her longsword slipped from its scabbard. Cullen tugged his spear from the dead man and joined her in the approach to the Kadoshim's lair. Keld was at his shoulder, his short-handled axe in one fist, knife in the other. Behind them Elgin and his warriors dismounted and followed.

A dozen paces into the tunnel a torch-sconce was hammered into the stone wall. It flared and sputtered, below it the remains of a burned-out fire. A spit rested above the fire and a pot sat beside it, a few cups of wood and leather about it. No one was there. Keld crouched to touch the ash and embers and his hounds padded past him. Together they stopped, sniffing the air and their hackles rose. As one they growled, a low, savage snarling. Keld looked back at Sig.

'It's here,' he breathed.

A thrill of excitement threaded through Sig, everything around her becoming a little sharper.

Six years gone since the kin last hunted a Kadoshim to bay and killed it.

Cullen swept past her – an unblooded hound eager for the kill.

Sig grabbed his shoulder with her iron grip and scowled a warning at him.

She strode past him and Keld, following the tunnel as it twisted deeper into the hillside, sloping gently upwards. Torches flickered periodically, light then darkness. As she climbed higher the air seemed to thicken, a smell of things long dead, a corruption in the air.

The tunnel opened ahead and Sig came into a small chamber. A single shadowed exit on its far side. A fire-pit sat in the middle of this chamber, embers still glowing, and around the edges furs and blankets were splayed, a rack of weapons, spears and rusted swords leaned against one wall, though there was no sign of the living. Cracks in the wall oozed damp earth, worms as thick as rope were wriggling within it.

'Fifty-two,' Cullen said, counting the furs spread about the chamber's edges. He shared a look with Sig and Keld.

Never this many. So, the rumours are true.

'A better fight, if they're all here,' Cullen declared, not able to keep the grin from his face.

Sig gave him a flat stare.

The hounds growled, paws splayed as they half-crouched, hackles a ridge upon their backs, lips curled to reveal sharp teeth. Keld hissed a command. Then a tendril of sound drifted down to them, emerging from the darkness of the exit on the far wall: voices, joined together, chanting, a cadence to it rising and falling. They set a chill trickling down Sig's spine, and behind her she heard muttering amongst Elgin's men.

Sig strode into the darkness, the chanting growing louder as she climbed higher, past another flickering torch. She felt her flesh goosebump, a creeping dread seeping into her, thick in the air, making her limbs grow heavy. The urge to stop and go back wormed into her mind.

Something is at work here.

'Truth and Courage,' she hissed at the darkness and saw either side of her Cullen and Keld straighten at those words, the Order's battle-cry and mantra. And then, in front of them was an arched doorway, a form silhouetted against the fire's red glow. The chanting was loud, echoing down the tunnel, filling Sig's head and heart with dismay.

Go back, go back, fear's voice whispered in her head.

'Truth and Courage,' she snarled back at it and surged forwards. The silhouette turned, a man, head shaven to scabbed stubble. His mouth opened at the sight of Sig storming out of the darkness, hounds and warriors about her. A spear in his hands levelled at Sig but her great sword was already cutting upwards, shearing through the shaft, lopping half of his hand off with it. The man stumbled backwards, amputated digits spinning through the air, his eyes fixed on the stumps where his fingers had been. A roll of Sig's shoulders and her sword came back down to chop into the meat of him between neck and shoulder, a wet sound like an axe cleaving damp wood, bones cracking, and the man was falling back in a spray of bloody froth. Sig ripped her blade free and stood over his twitching corpse.

A circular chamber spread before her, high and wide, the roof hidden in shadow and smoke. Braziers of fire belched red light, casting misshapen shadows. A crowd of men and women at least forty-strong gathered around a dais at the chamber's centre, chanting in a tongue Sig had never heard before. They were all shaven-headed, and Sig glimpsed the gleam of chain-mail and weapons.

These are not disgruntled farmers, or deluded dissenters, Sig thought. *More like warrior-acolytes.*

Upon the dais was a wooden cross-frame; a figure was bound wrist and ankle upon it, a man stripped naked.

And close as a lover to this man stood a figure, tall, head shaved, its skin pale as alabaster, mapped by dark veins. It wore a shirt of rusty mail, a sword sheathed at its hip, and from its back great wings of leather and skin were furled. Power and malice pulsed from it like a heat haze.

Kadoshim.

Something inside Sig leaped at the sight of it, a jolt of hatred racing through her, burning away any remnants of fear that lingered in her veins. Once she had seen these Kadoshim in their thousands filling the skies above Drassil, and since then she and those like her had hunted these dread creatures, over a hundred years of blood and war. At first the fighting had been constant, but in the last score of years the Kadoshim were rarely found – so much so that her Order was questioning whether the creatures had been brought close to extinction in the Banished Lands.

Not extinct yet.

As Sig stared, the Kadoshim thrust a knife into the belly of the prisoner, a gush of blood and coiled entrails splashing from the gaping wound. There was the sudden rush of blood-stink and hot metal in the air as the man screamed his agony over the fevered chanting from the crowd.

Then the Kadoshim saw Sig and the shadowed figures of her companions behind her. Their eyes met and the chanting about the chamber stuttered and died.

The Kadoshim pointed its blood-slick knife at Sig, faces turning.

'Kill them,' it rasped.

CHAPTER SIX

BLEDA

Bleda stood upon the walls of Drassil, looking down at the weapons-field below. All manner of warriors were training, learning the craft of spear, bow and sword, as well as other things.

'Strategy, they call it,' his friend Jin said as she pointed to a shield wall that had formed near the centre of the field. She was a ward of the Ben-Elim, too, taken the same day as him. That had been grounds enough for a friendship.

'Cowardice is what I call it,' she continued, head cocked to one side as she considered the warriors far below. Her jet hair was short-cropped to her head, the sharp features of her cheeks and the slight hook of her nose reminding Bleda of the stooping hawk that was the sigil of her Clan. 'A warrior should stand one against another, whether with bow, spear or blade. That is skill, that is honour. Not *that!* Hiding behind your weapons-kin, hiding behind wood and iron!'

'Huh,' Bleda grunted, his eyes drifting from the shield wall to the figure of a mounted warrior galloping, spear raised, charging a straw man. The drum of hooves drifted up to Bleda, simply the sound of it stirring his blood, even if the horse was a huge, muscle-bound beast as far from the swift and hardy ponies he had grown up riding as he was different from a giant.

Ah, to ride through the plains of grass with nothing but wind and sky before me. A recollection of doing just such a thing filled his mind. It was a dim, faded memory, more precious to Bleda than gold, silver or jewels. He closed his eyes a moment and concentrated, almost feeling the wind whipping across his face, could almost hear the distant echo of his laughter mixing with his brother's, who had been riding at his side on that long-ago day.

Altan.

Before he had a chance to control it, another image flashed through his mind. His brother's severed head in the dirt, eyes bulging, tongue lolling. With an act of will he pushed the memory away, forced it into a shadowed hole in his mind and let out a long breath, as if he had completed some physical exertion.

'They are cowards, no?' Jin said, clearly enjoying her rant against the warriors of Drassil, and wanting Bleda's support on this point. It was not often that they were alone enough to be able to speak like this, always someone was around teaching or watching over them. Even now they were supposed to be with a loremaster and hard at work learning their letters. Instead they had sneaked off and made their way onto Drassil's walls, finding a rare spot between guards on watch duty.

'Their ways are strange and without honour,' Bleda said, and in truth many of the Ben-Elim's ways still seemed so to him, even after five years of living amongst these people as their ward. But there was much more to the Ben-Elim and their allies than that. Much of what had once seemed strange now made a lot more sense.

And they are not cowards, as much as I would like to agree with Jin on that point. But Bleda kept his opinion to himself, as he often did. *I'll not argue with my only friend, the closest thing I have to my kin in this strange land.*

In truth, Jin should have been his enemy. Until Bleda had been snatched away by the Ben-Elim on that dark and distant day, Jin *had* been his enemy: daughter and heir of the Cheren's lord, the Clan that Bleda's people had been fighting the day the Ben-Elim came. Technically there was blood feud between

Bleda and Jin, as Bleda's da had been slain by members of Jin's Clan, and in return Jin's older brother and heir to the Cheren Clan had been slain by the Sirak. But now, for five long years, all they had had was each other, each of them acting for the other as some tenuous bridge to home.

The thrum of arrows leaving bows dragged his eyes from the galloping horse, in time to see a score of straw targets shudder as loosed arrows hit their mark. Even Bleda could not stop his lip from curling in a sneer at that.

Great longbows of ash or elm. How could you string or shoot one of those from the back of a horse?

He saw one archer give a congratulatory slap on the shoulder to another.

No doubt thinking they have great skill. I was hitting such targets as that when I was eight summers old. And when is a fight ever like that? Your enemy standing helpfully still while you take careful aim?

He shook his head, disgusted, and Jin grinned to see it.

'They would be no match for the Cheren,' she said, following his gaze, 'or even the Sirak,' she added with a twitch of a smile.

'They defeated both our Clans, though,' Bleda muttered.

Jin scowled at that. 'They took them by surprise,' she spat.

'Aye, they did. But there was more to their victory than surprise. I was there. I saw it.' It was a fact he never failed to remind her of, giving him a slight advantage in their discussions of home.

'Still, if our Clans had been ready, and stood together,' Jin said, jutting her chin out.

'Aye, maybe,' Bleda agreed, though he was not so sure.

'As they will when we return home and rule our Clans.' She flashed him a grin.

'Just so,' he replied, hiding the doubt in his heart.

Bleda turned away from the weapons-field and stared out over the walls of Drassil. High above him the branches of the great tree arched, spreading wide over the plains that surrounded the ancient fortress, dappling the meadow-grass in sunlight and shadow. The plain to the west was covered in cairns, thousands of them, burial mounds of moss-covered stone raised over those who had fallen on the day the Ben-Elim came, the day the Kadoshim were defeated. A road ran through the centre of them to the gates of Drassil.

A road watched over by the dead, Bleda thought.

In the distance a forest ringed Drassil: ancient Forn, though its trees had been cut and thinned for over a hundred years now as the Ben-Elim had rooted Kadoshim from the dark places. Slicing through the forest were roads that radiated out from the fortress, north, south, east and west, like spokes from a wheel hub. They were wide and straight, connecting Drassil, the Ben-Elim's seat of power, with the rest of the Land of the Faithful, and it was along these roads that their armies marched, whether it was to fight Kadoshim or to enforce *peace* upon lands within their ever-expanding boundaries.

Bleda found himself looking east, as he often did, imagining that he could see the rolling plains of his homeland beyond the green-leaved bulwark of Forn Forest. This time, though, he saw a column upon the east road, marching steadily towards Drassil, the distant ripple of banners snapping in the breeze.

He slapped Jin's shoulder. She was still pouring scorn upon those in the weapons-field, but her eyes narrowed as she saw what he was pointing at.

'Giants and bears at the front,' she whispered.

'And Ben-Elim above,' Bleda said, spying shapes circling in the air above the column.

'But banners?' Jin said. 'Not Ben-Elim troops, then.'

They stood in silence, wondering who these approaching visitors were, important enough to warrant such an escort. A shadow crossed over them and there was a gust of wind, light footsteps and a Ben-Elim landed close by. He was tall, graceful and beautiful as a fine statue, as were all the Ben-Elim, though he was fair-haired where most were dark. Bleda felt a stirring of anger in his blood at the sight of him, for this was Kol, the Ben-Elim who had thrown the heads of his brother and sister at his feet.

'Many are looking for you two,' the Ben-Elim said. 'You are wanted in the keep.'

'What for?' Jin answered, haughty as if she were already Queen of the Cheren.

'You have visitors,' the Ben-Elim said, looking out onto the plain before Drassil.

The approaching column was still a way off, but close enough now for Bleda to see the swirl and snap of the banners. Jin gasped, her eyes always a little keener than his, but he recognized the images soon enough, and his heart lurched within his chest.

Two banners, one with a stooping hawk upon a blue sky, the other with a rearing stallion in a field of green.

The Cheren and the Sirak Clans.

Our kin have come.

Bleda sat at a table in a chair too big for him, fidgeting and picking at a scab on his thumb. In response to their barrage of breathless questions, Kol, the Ben-Elim, had given them nothing, except for a dark scowl. The only thing Bleda really wanted to know was who rode beneath the Sirak banner.

Has my mam come to claim me? Finally to take me home?

Jin was seated beside him and he could see her trying to look calm and indifferent despite him being sure she felt the same mixture of fear and excitement as he. The Lord Protector swept through the open doors, a dozen White-Wings marching behind him. Israfil's expression was as emotionless as usual.

His mastery of the cold-face would earn even my mother's respect.

There was something in his stride that spoke of something else, though.

Agitation?

Israfil stood before Bleda and Jin, somehow managing to hold both of their gazes at once. Bleda noticed a twitch in his wings sending a ripple through the white feathers.

'You were not at your letters,' Israfil said, a statement. 'You could not be found when you were needed and, as a result, you have not been briefed on the arrival of your Clansmen, or been able to prepare for it.'

Bleda returned Israfil's gaze as long as he could, felt Jin doing the same beside him, felt her shift as her head bowed. He was not long behind her.

'You are given every advantage here. Learning – language, your letters, the histories, all manner of knowledge. You are taught your weapons, no less than our greatest warriors. Food, clothing, everything that you could want for, you are given; a preparation for the great task ahead of you, to rule your people, to spread the peace of Elyon.'

To be trained as your puppet king and puppet queen of the Arcona Clans, you mean.

'You are given the utmost respect; are you not?'

Bleda and Jin were silent a few moments.

'We are, Lord Commander,' Bleda said. He could not deny that they were treated well.

For prisoners.

He felt Jin's eyes burn into him, a look that did not go unnoticed by Israfil.

'All that is expected of you is a measure of that respect returned,' Israfil said, frowning at Jin.

Jin remained darkly silent.

Bleda clamped his lips shut. Part of him agreed with Israfil, knew that his behaviour was insolent and rude, and felt a stirring of shame for that. But another part of him remembered, would never forget. His brother. His sister.

I represent my Clan, here. Am the face and voice of the Sirak.

'I apologize for our rudeness,' Bleda said, seeing Jin's head snapping around and ignoring the look of disgust she sent him.

'Good.' Israfil nodded and heaved a long sigh. Bleda felt his neck flush red.

And then horns were ringing and the open doorway of the keep was full of figures, a handful of giants entering first, axes and war-hammers slung across their backs, ringmail shirts gleaming. Jin hissed as the giants moved to one side, revealing a stern-faced man, head shaved apart from a long dark warrior braid curling across his shoulder, an iron-grey beard upon his chin. He wore a fine sky-blue deel, edged in gold thread, belted with soft-tooled leather, his breeches bound tight from ankle to knee, and baggy above. His eyes locked with Jin's and his stern face softened, eyes creasing in the hint of a smile.

'Father,' Jin whispered, half rising.

'Stay, child,' Kol murmured from behind them and Jin sat back down.

And then everything else in the room faded for Bleda.

His mother, Erdene, Queen of the Sirak, strode through the doorway.

She was older, with lines in her brown, weathered face that had not been there the last time he'd seen her, streaks of grey in her thick-bound warrior braid. A white scar stood out across her shaven head.

She looked as fine a Sirak lord as he had ever seen, dressed in a richly woven white deel tunic, fox fur trimming its collar and hems, a thick leather belt dressed with chains of silver and gold about her waist, and his heart thumped with pride to see her march towards him. He felt his face shifting, mouth stretching into a smile.

Her eyes looked into his, saw his smile, but he received nothing in return, only her cold-face, flat and impassionate. He gritted his teeth together and with an act of will wiped all emotion from his face.

Behind Uldin and Erdene walked a small retinue from their courts. Bleda saw an old face staring at him.

Old Ellac!

Bleda's heart leaped a little with joy at another familiar face. The old warrior stared straight at Bleda, though he too showed no spark of emotion.

'Welcome to Drassil,' Israfil said as they were all shown to seats around the table. Food was brought and drinks were poured as Israfil continued his greeting, speaking of the journey from Arcona and the new peace in the Land of the Faithful. His voice became a blur of sound that Bleda did not hear, all his attention focused on his mother, and on maintaining the required facade of indifference.

Is she ashamed of me? Five years since I saw her last, and not even a nod of her head. He was suddenly painfully aware of his appearance, how little he now looked like a Sirak prince. Especially his hair, which should have been grown long enough for a warrior braid, the rest of his head shaved and the long braid bound upon completing his warrior trial and Long Night. Instead his hair was cut short, the same way as the other training warriors at Drassil wore their hair.

To her it must look as if I have become one of them. Does she think I have betrayed my Clan?

Bleda felt all this raging within him, rearing and lashing at him, like a wild stallion's hooves. A bead of sweat rolled down his forehead with the effort of keeping it all hidden.

I will not shame her more than I already have.

And then Israfil's voice faded and Bleda realized a silence had fallen over the table.

'My thanks for your courteous welcome,' Uldin of the Cheren said, his voice warm and strong. 'It is a pleasure to be in fabled Drassil. Truly, it is a place of magnificent wonders, greater even than we had ever imagined, and I am only left with the question of why have I not journeyed here before. Why have I left it so—'

'What Uldin is trying to say,' Erdene interrupted, her voice calm and flat as a windless sea, 'is: why are we here? Why have you summoned us?'

Israfil inclined his head to Erdene.

'Five years have passed since your two Clans went to war,' Israfil said, 'breaking the peace of the Faithful. Breaking Elyon's Lore. And in those five years your two Clans have known unbroken peace, is this not so?'

'This is a truth,' Uldin said, glancing at Erdene, who just gave a curt nod.

'We Ben-Elim are here for one reason: to protect the creation of Elyon. *All* the peoples of these Banished Lands. Asroth led his legions of the Fallen, the Kadoshim, into this world, and so we followed them, to protect you as best we could. The war with the Kadoshim was fierce and bloody, and many of my kin fell in battle on that fateful day. Even so, we won that battle, saved mankind from a dread fate, but the war is not over. Asroth remains, imprisoned within a skin of starstone iron, and many of his Kadoshim survived, secreting themselves away to fight on with stealth and cunning. So we stay to guard the body of Asroth, and we fight on against the Kadoshim.'

'This is a tale we all have heard,' Erdene said. 'You did not summon us over a hundred leagues to tell us this.'

'No, I did not,' Israfil said, betraying no sign of annoyance at Erdene's interruption. 'I have received word of the Kadoshim moving in your lands, of deaths at their hands.'

'Aye, this is true,' Uldin said. 'Some foul sacrifice was performed.'

'We will find these *monsters* and root them out,' Israfil said, a hint of snarl and iron in his voice, the closest thing to emotion that Bleda had ever seen in the Lord Protector. 'But we are stretched, the Banished Lands vast, which is why we are blessed with the allies we have. Giants, as well as warriors from throughout the Land of the Faithful; they are a tithe of thanksgiving to aid us in the practicalities of this war that we wage.'

Israfil stopped then, allowing his words to sink in.

'What are you saying?' Uldin grated, his voice less warm than before.

'He is saying that he wants us to fight the Kadoshim,' Erdene said flatly.

'Yes, and more,' Israfil said. 'It is time for you to show your gratitude to the Faithful, time to prove your commitment both to peace with each other and to the great war. It is time that you committed a tithe of warriors to the cause, just as the other peoples that dwell within the boundaries of the Land of the Faithful do.'

'Well, now we have it out on the table and plain for the seeing,' Uldin said.

'If that is the whole of it,' Erdene said.

'That is the meat of it,' Israfil said, 'though there is a little more. We want a tithe of warriors soon, and after that, a yearly tithe of your young, to be trained here, at Drassil.'

Bleda felt his face twitch at that, a momentary slip of his cold-face.

They would steal the heart from our people, and deny our culture to each new generation. He controlled the sneer that threatened to twist his face. *They would make puppets of us all, turn us into them, pious, wingless pawns.*

Uldin and Erdene just stared at Israfil, giving no clue as to their inner reactions.

'And to cement your peace with one another and your commitment to the cause,' Israfil said, 'a symbolic act to bind your Clans further in peace, your two heirs shall also commit to one another.'

For the first time a twitch upon Erdene's face.

'What does he mean?' Jin whispered to Bleda.

'I . . .' Bleda said, his voice not working right, his head spinning, for he was sure he knew exactly what Israfil was saying.

'Bleda and Jin shall be wed,' the Lord Protector declared.

CHAPTER SEVEN

SIG

Men and women in hooded cloaks charged at Sig, iron glinting red in the flickering firelight as weapons were drawn, and, from behind her, Keld's wolven-hounds bounded forwards, crashing into the onrushing crowd, an eruption of blood and screams and snapping, slavering growls. Sig strode forwards, Keld and Cullen close behind, Elgin shouting a battle-cry and leading his men charging from the tunnel entrance.

Sig punched her sword through the belly of the first man to rush her and kicked him in the chest as she ripped her blade free, sending him hurtling into those behind, a snarl of limbs as they went down. Cullen leaped into the space and stabbed down with his spear, ducking a sword-slash from a man who knew his blade-craft a little better, not that it helped him much as Keld's axe crunched into his skull, wrenched free in a spray of bone and brains.

Sig marched on, longsword swinging in great loops, sent a head spinning through the air, a jet of blood erupting from the stump of a severed neck. Her sword-kin stabbed and hacked to the left and right of her, the wolven-hounds wreaking bloody havoc in the shadows, and Elgin's warriors spread wide as the Kadoshim's followers hurled themselves in a frenzied attack.

Sig wiped sweat from her eyes, searching for the Kadoshim. It was still upon the dais, passing something to one of its shaven-headed followers, leaning to hiss in the man's ear.

Sig shouted, pointing with her sword at the Kadoshim, and Keld and Cullen answered, moving towards the dais like ships through a storm-racked sea.

A woman came at Sig, wielding sword and knife, a swirling attack that stopped Sig's advance, the clang of steel as Sig parried the sword, a grunt as the knife slashed at her belly, stopped by her ringmail shirt. She slammed an elbow into the woman's jaw, then hacked though the woman's forearm, which dropped to the floor still clutching its sword. The woman staggered and fell to her knees, face draining white as her life's blood pumped into the ground. She toppled sideways, cursing Sig as she died.

Sig forged on, the din and stench of battle in this subterranean chamber immense: death screams, battle-cries, the wounded mewling and shrieking in their pain. She saw the Kadoshim push its companion on the dais away, sending him running for a shadowed alcove. A sword hissed into the Kadoshim's fist, its wings unfurled and flexed, a beat of air that carried the stench of corruption as it lifted from the ground, Keld's axe whistling through empty air where it had just been standing.

Sig burst onto the dais through a knot of the attackers, her bulk scattering them. A jolt of power shuddered up through her boots, sudden nausea making her stagger; a glance at the dais showed runes scratched and scribed into the ground. She shook her head and strode towards Keld and Cullen. A glance at the prisoner bound to the wooden frame showed there was no helping him, slumped in his bonds, his entrails heaped about his feet. His chest was still, a string of spittle hanging from his slack jaw.

'Keld,' Sig said, pointing at the hurrying messenger who was disappearing into what Sig had thought was a shadowed alcove, but as she looked now she saw it was an exit from the chamber.

'The Kadoshim gave him something,' Sig said. 'Whatever it was, I need to see it.'

'It's done,' Keld grunted, running and leaping from the

dais, two fingers in his lips and whistling, an answering snap and snarl came from within the chamber.

'Where is the Kadoshim?' Sig growled, standing back to back with Cullen as they turned slowly, searching for the Kadoshim in the guttering red-flicker of light and shadow.

'There!' Cullen yelled, as the Kadoshim swooped down from the murk of the chamber's roof, chopping at one of Elgin's men, lifting another one bodily into the air and burying its sword in his belly, hurling the dying warrior back down into the chaos.

Without a word the two of them left the dais, forging a way towards the Kadoshim.

A man leaped at them, axe raised over his head, Cullen's spear darting out and punching through his open mouth, dragged free in a burst of blood and teeth. Cullen shrugged his shield from his back, caught a sword-blow aimed for Sig, slammed the iron rim into the sword-wielder's throat and sent him gasping and choking to the ground. Sig stamped on the fallen man as they pushed on, bones cracking beneath her iron-shod boots.

Then the Kadoshim was only a handful of paces before them, hovering above the conflict as its wings beat up a storm of dust.

'FALLEN ONE,' Sig bellowed, her cry ringing through the chamber, a momentary lull as both sides paused. The Kadoshim stared at Sig, saw Cullen beside her raise his shield, the bright star of their order upon it, and hissed at them, spraying spittle. Then it was flying at them, a dark blur. Sig hefted her blade and swung two-handed, the Kadoshim's wings tucking tight together and somehow it was spinning, Sig's sword slicing wide by a handspan. A crack as Sig turned, Cullen grunting as the Kadoshim swooped over him, raining down a flurry of blows, Cullen bending beneath them in a burst of incandescent sparks as the Kadoshim's blade crashed into the iron rim of his shield, shearing through it.

Cullen yelled in fury and stabbed up with his spear, the blade grating along the Kadoshim's mail shirt, links twisting and snapping. The Kadoshim just laughed and grabbed the shaft of Cullen's spear, ripping it from his hands.

Sig charged in, her sword slicing an overhead arc at the Kadoshim, who somehow saw the giant coming and with a beat of its wings swept higher, Sig's sword-tip cutting through the leather of its boot. Blood dripped a spatter of red rain from the wound as it hovered above them.

'You're a long way from Dun Seren,' the Kadoshim snarled down at them, its guttural voice cutting through the din of battle.

'We'd travel twice as far to carve some pain into your stinking hide,' Cullen yelled back.

The Kadoshim hissed at them.

'Who are you?' Sig shouted. 'Gulla?'

The Kadoshim laughed, the sound of nails scrapping across chalk. 'Over a hundred years, and yet you know nothing of us.'

'Gulla is chief of your kind, I have heard,' Sig said, eyes fixed on the Kadoshim, circling to her right. 'If not Gulla, who are you, then?'

'I am Rimmon,' the Kadoshim snarled. 'I am your death.'

'Like to see you try,' Cullen snapped back, grinning.

Rimmon screeched and swooped down at them, hacking, chopping, stabbing.

Sig leaped away and the Kadoshim turned in mid-air, blade slashing at Cullen as he rushed in, sending the young warrior staggering away with a gash across his forehead. He disappeared amongst the press and heave of battle.

Sig bellowed a battle-cry and stabbed, but Rimmon twisted and Sig's lunge sliced only air. Battle raged about them as she held her ground against the creature.

Enough of this.

Sig leaped close and the Kadoshim's blade met hers in a shower of sparks before he fell back before her.

Rimmon's wings beat hard; the Kadoshim grabbed a fallen spear as he swept back into the air. Sig reached a hand to her belt, felt the mesh of her weighted net, unhooked it and with a flick of her wrist snapped it open.

She raised the net, whirled it about her head as the Kadoshim drew a hand back and hurled the spear down at her. Sig twisted, a figure leaping in front of her and fouling her net throw. It was Cullen, his battered shield taking the force of the Kadoshim's spear. Sig stumbled as Cullen's weight slammed into her. He fell to the ground, Rimmon crowing in victory, before speeding away across the room. Sig took a step after him and then heard a groan.

Cullen.

The young warrior was pale as milk, red hair sweat-soaked and plastered to his head. The spear had burst through his half-splintered shield and pinned his arm to his body. He tried to say something but his breath was a wheezing hiss. Sig had no way of telling what the wound behind the shield was like, but from the look of him she feared the worst.

Waiting won't make it better.

She put one big boot onto the remains of the shield, gripped the spear shaft and pulled it free.

Cullen grunted, face twisting with pain, and Sig knelt beside him. She breathed a sigh of relief as she lifted the shattered shield away. The spear had pierced his bicep, punching clean through and out the other side, but Cullen's chainmail shirt had slowed it there, done enough to save the lad. A few rings were shattered, the spear-point cutting through the wool and linen beneath, a bloom of blood, but it was only a shallow wound.

Not that the fool boy will be doing much more leaping around for a ten-night or two.

'I can fight on,' Cullen mumbled, trying to stand. His eyes rolled white and he slipped back to the ground with a groan.

'No, you can't,' Sig said.

'Will I die, then?' Cullen whispered, struggling for breath.

'Of old age, most like, but not this day, laddie,' Sig said and stood, raising the spear in her hand. She saw the shadowed streak of Rimmon as he sped towards an exit from the chamber, hefted the spear a moment, finding its balance and judging its weight, and then she threw. It flew straight as an arrow, punching through one of the Kadoshim's wings, low, where it thickened and joined the shoulder. There was a scream, Rimmon plummeting to the ground.

'Got to leave you awhile,' Sig grunted down at Cullen.

'Bring me its head,' Cullen mumbled.

Sig ploughed through the chamber, smashing any before her out of her way. In heartbeats she was at the spot where the Kadoshim had fallen, saw the spear she'd cast at the Kadoshim lying on the ground, its blade dark with blood. Darkness thick as smoke filled the tunnel, so Sig grabbed the weapon, tore a dead man's cloak from his back, wrapped it around the spear shaft and stabbed it into a fire-filled brazier. Soon flames were crackling and she lifted the torch and glanced back.

There were knots of combat still raging about the chamber, but to Sig's eye Elgin and his men had the measure of it, far more of them still standing than their frenzied enemy.

They can finish here. I've got a Kadoshim to kill.

Sig gritted her teeth and ran into the tunnel, no time for care or caution.

Darkness retreated before her; the tunnel sloped upwards, closing tight about Sig, constricting and claustrophobic after the high-roofed chamber. Soon the noise of battle faded. Side tunnels breached the main path, but fat spots of blood showed Sig the way, leading her ever higher in the main tunnel. Then she saw Rimmon running ahead, a shadow at the edge of her torch's reach, the tunnel too close for him to unfurl his great wingspan.

Or perhaps my spear throw has injured his wing.

Rimmon stumbled, one shoulder scraping against the

tunnel wall, righted himself and ran on. Sig increased her pace, no need for stealth. Rimmon knew she was there; knew she was gaining.

A light ahead, bright in the darkness. Daylight, not torch or fire.

A spurt of speed from Sig, twenty paces behind the Kadoshim now. Ten. Cobwebs draped Sig's face. Daylight loomed, bright and blinding, the Kadoshim a black silhouette.

Squinting into the white glare, Sig threw the spear. It arced forwards, trailing fire and smoke, and Sig saw the dark shadow of the Kadoshim tumble and fall. Moments later she burst out into a winter's sun, a pale, cloud-choked morning almost blinding her.

They were on the hilltop with the squawking of disturbed crows, around them open air and the wind snatching at clothes, setting Sig's blonde warrior braid fluttering. In the far distance she saw the stain of the Darkwood and the towers of Uthandun before it.

Rimmon rolled upon a flat patch of grass, the spear tangled between his legs, guttering black smoke. Sig swung her sword overhead, aiming to carve the beast in two. With a snarl the Kadoshim swept to the side, part-roll, part-beat of wings, a heartbeat later and he was upright, sword in his fist, though Sig saw one of the wings was twisted, like an injured arm. Malice radiated from the Kadoshim's dark eyes.

With a snap, leathery wings were unfolding and Rimmon rose unsteadily into the air, a blast of wind rocking him, one wing leaking blood at the shoulder-joint. For a moment the Kadoshim hovered in the sky, the sun behind framing him in a luminous halo.

'Finish this another time,' Rimmon hissed. Another pulse of wings and the Kadoshim veered away, swerving through the air like a man after too much mead. He tested his wings, darted forwards again, well out of reach of Sig's sword as the giant ran to the hill's flat edge and swayed a moment, risking a long, bone-breaking tumble to the ground far below. The Kadoshim sank a little in the air, another beat of his wings taking him further away, though hugging the hillside.

'I'd rather finish you now, Rimmon of the Kadoshim,' Sig muttered.

She unclipped her net and swung it over her head, a whistling sound as the cord and weights in its four corners cut air, then she released it, high, arcing up and then down, dropping gracefully, corners spread.

The net folded around the Kadoshim, snaring his wings, wrapping around limbs, and Rimmon screeched, twisting in the air as he thrashed, spitting and biting, trying to tear his way free, but with every movement the cords snared tighter and the Kadoshim folded and plummeted to the ground.

Sig sheathed her sword across her back and launched herself over the edge, skidding and sliding down a grassy slope. She toppled and rolled a hundred paces, righted herself, saw the Kadoshim still falling, close to the hill's base now.

'HAMMER,' Sig bellowed through cupped hands and heard a faint rumbling roar drift up to her as the Kadoshim hit the hillside and bounced away, spun through the air a good fifty paces and crunched and rolled as the ground levelled out.

Sig continued her sliding fall down the hill, saw Hammer appear lumbering out from between boulders. Rimmon had stopped rolling now, was still for a few moments and then slowly extricated himself from the net and began to drag and crawl away through the grass, wings trailing behind.

Hammer stopped at the foot of the hill, looking up at Sig, who yelled snatched commands as she made her way down the slope. The bear turned, head swaying on its thick-muscled neck, and then thundered after the Kadoshim.

The ground levelled beneath Sig and she half ran, half stumbled towards Hammer. The huge bear stood over the Kadoshim, one paw upon his chest, pinning him to the ground.

Rimmon writhed and squirmed beneath the bear's weight, limbs and wings batting feebly at it, but Hammer did not move.

Sig drew her sword as she reached them and stood over the Kadoshim. He was bloody and broken, limbs and wings twisted, one leg showing bone, his pale, dark-veined face splattered with blood, but his eyes still radiated a malefic fury.

Sig levelled her sword at the creature's throat.

'I would like nothing more than to kill you now,' she grated, 'but I have questions for you: so many followers here? The man you sacrificed – why? And the message you sent?'

The Kadoshim stilled a moment.

'I will tell you nothing,' Rimmon spat, voice as broken as his body. A trickle of black blood leaked from the corner of his mouth.

'We shall see,' Sig said, retrieving her net from the ground a dozen paces away. 'Perhaps not now, and I am not the most patient of questioners. But I shall take you back to Dun Seren . . .'

Something swept across the Kadoshim's face at the mention of Sig's home, the fortress where the Order of the Bright Star were based.

Have the Kadoshim learned to fear us? A hundred years of bloodshed has given them good cause.

Suddenly the Kadoshim had a knife in his fist and he was stabbing frenziedly at Hammer's paw, sinking deep, blood spurting. The bear roared and jerked away, the Kadoshim – abruptly free – was up and stumbling at Sig, knife lunging for her belly.

Then Hammer's jaws clamped around Rimmon's torso, lifting him bodily from the ground, jaws snapping tighter as it shook the Kadoshim furiously, blood spraying, bones snapping. The bear hurled the Kadoshim to the ground, slammed one paw upon the winged demon's torso and grabbed its head, ripping it from its shoulders with a wet, tearing sound.

Sig stood and stared. It was all over in a handful of heart-beats.

'I think you are more bad-tempered than I am,' she muttered, patting the bear's neck.

CHAPTER EIGHT

RIV

Riv cursed under her breath, a continuous muttering as she scrubbed the floor of one of the many communal latrines in Drassil. It was early and she was on latrine duty, not her favourite of tasks at the best of times, but even less so today. Her sleep had been troubled with bad dreams. In the light of day they were ephemeral, only a vague memory of weightless, endless falling.

'What's that?' Carsten said. Just like Riv, he was the child of a White-Wing, born in Drassil and raised to become a warrior of the White-Wings. He was a year younger than Riv, as were all on the latrine team with her; because she had failed her warrior trial, all of her friends were training on the weapons-field as White-Wings, but not her.

'For my shame,' she muttered, then looked up at him. 'What's what?'

Carsten was supposed to be pouring buckets of water over the long stone seating block that Riv had just scrubbed, but he had stopped. The walls behind him were filled with pastel depictions of Ben-Elim casting Kadoshim from the skies, a reminder of the great sacrifice they had made to protect man-kind from the evil of the demon horde. Riv was just about to give Carsten a piece of her mind for shirking his duties when he said it again.

'What's that?' he said, and then she heard it, filtering in

through the unshuttered window and open doorway. The blowing of horns.

'That's the call to the Lore Chamber,' Riv said, leaping to her feet. Usually the Lore Chamber convened once a ten-night: Israfil and his captains gathering in Drassil's Great Hall and sitting in judgement upon all manner of issues brought before them, whether they be disputes between residents of Drassil, petty charges of drunkenness or minor disobediences to more serious matters, even murder.

But the next meeting's not due for another four nights.

The horns blew again.

'Come on,' Riv said, making for the open doorway.

'But, the latrines,' Carsten said.

'It's excrement, it'll still be here when we're done.' Riv strode out into the streets of Drassil, hearing Carsten following her.

The streets were full, all those not on essential duties making their way to the great chamber of Drassil.

'What's going on?' Riv asked a White-Wing in the street.

'Ethlinn and Garidas are back,' she said.

The horns blew again and Riv began to run, feeling aches in her joints that hadn't been there a few days ago.

Can't sleep, and I'm aching like I have a fever. I'll visit the healers when I have some time.

Crowds grew thicker as Riv reached the courtyard of the Great Hall, people pouring through the open gates, Riv elbowing through them. Inside everyone was filing along the tiered stone steps, using them as benches, hundreds already sitting there. Riv saw her mam, Dalme, a few rows down and squeezed and shoved her way through the crowd to reach her.

'Hello, my darling,' her mam said.

'I hear it's Ethlinn and Garidas returned,' Riv whispered as she sat beside her mam.

'Aye, it's true,' Dalmae said, gesturing to the hall's floor below them.

75

The iron-covered statues of Asroth and Meical were where they always were, tall and brooding before the trunk of Drassil's ancient tree, and ringed about them were Ethlinn's giants, as always. On the wide space between them and Riv a dozen chairs had been set, for Israfil and his captains sitting either side of him. Blond-haired Kol sat at the far end. Riv found her gaze lingering on the scarred Ben-Elim. He seemed different, somehow, from the Ben-Elim he sat beside, his perfect features altered by the scar that ran down his face, changing the straight line of his mouth. Perhaps he felt her eyes on him, because he looked up, straight at her, as if she were the only person in the room. She held his gaze a few heartbeats, then looked away.

Before the Ben-Elim was a wain, something bulky upon it, covered with a sheet of stitched hides. A score of White-Wings and giants were standing about it. Riv saw Garidas, who was captain of a White-Wing hundred, just as Aphra was. He was standing straight-backed and stern, as always, short-cropped dark hair framing a serious face. Riv liked him: he was a devout man, utterly committed to the Ben-Elim, and a fine warrior. He'd given Riv a fair few bruises on the weapons-field, although recently she usually gave as good as she got. If anything, Riv thought, it wouldn't harm him to smile more.

Beside Garidas towered Ethlinn, Queen of the Giants. She was pale as milk, long-limbed, even for a giant, slimmer and less muscled than most, though there was an obvious strength in her musculature. Black hair knotted in a thick braid coiled about her shoulder and a thin torc of silver rested about her neck.

'Where have they been?' Riv asked her mam. There had been rumours, but no one really seemed to know, even Aphra, which was rare, because Aphra always seemed to know everything that was going on.

'I think we're about to find out.' Dalmae shrugged.

The murmuring of the crowd stilled as Ethlinn strode to stand before Israfil.

When Israfil sat in his chair on the Lore-Giving days, he would start the proceedings with a prayer to Elyon and a reading from the Book of the Faithful, but today was different. He stood, the hall settling into immediate silence.

'Faith, Strength and Purity,' Israfil intoned.

'For that is the Way of Elyon,' Riv responded automatically, along with all the others.

Israfil sat and gave a nod to Ethlinn.

'The rumours were true,' Ethlinn said. 'We found a Kadoshim lair, though recently deserted. There was evidence of large numbers dwelling there, thirty, forty at least.'

Gasps and murmurs rippled around the crowd. Kadoshim sightings were rare; the last one had been in the Agullas Mountains far to the south, over a year gone. It had been hunted and slain, a half-starved, pathetic thing, by all accounts, only a handful of deluded servants with it, more farmers than warriors.

'Where?' Israfil asked.

'In Forn. Thirty leagues south, between here and Brikan,' Ethlinn said.

So close. How dare they? Riv thought, her anger flaring.

'How do you know it was a Kadoshim lair,' Kol said, 'if it was deserted?'

'We found a body, nailed to crossed timber. He'd been sacrificed, runes upon the floor, written in his blood.' She paused. 'Terrible things had been done to him.'

Israfil said nothing, but the other Ben-Elim about him whispered to one another.

'And we found this,' Garidas called out, at the same time ripping off the hide covering from the wain.

A cage of iron bars lay underneath, within it a figure. Riv stared, straining to see properly. One man, heavily muscled and shaven-haired, clothes ragged and torn. He sat upon his knees, a chain hanging between his wrists. There was something . . .

wrong, about him. Then he moved and something shifted on his back. At first Riv thought it was a cloak, but it was *moving*.

'It cannot be,' her mam hissed beside her.

Because the man in the cage had wings.

'Is that a Kadoshim?' Riv asked. It was not what she expected, looked nothing like the paintings on the latrine walls she'd just been looking at. It appeared far more human than she had been led to believe, and although he was sitting, he seemed short, definitely shorter than the tall, elegant Ben-Elim.

'No,' her mam said.

'Bring him closer,' Israfil ordered, a tremor in his voice that spoke of fury.

White-Wings unlocked the cage and dragged the winged man out. He did not put up a fight, just walked towards Israfil, with Garidas and half a dozen White-Wings about him. Riv saw the winged man pause, staring at the dais and the entwined figures of Asroth and Meical. Garidas yanked on his chains and he stumbled forwards.

'You are a half-breed. Spawn of improper relations between a Kadoshim and a woman, are you not?' Israfil said, barely able to keep the rage from his voice.

'I am,' the man said, standing tall before Israfil, his voice deep and guttural.

'Kneel before the Lord Protector,' Garidas said; one of the White-Wing guards slammed a spear shaft across the half-breed's shoulders. He swayed but remained on his feet, another blow and he dropped to one knee.

Shouts and angry yells echoed from the benches around Riv. She looked about, saw White-Wings and many others shouting curses and shaking their fists. Amongst the crowd a few stood still and emotionless: Bleda the ward, alongside those from his Clan who had arrived recently. He was staring at Israfil and the half-breed, his darker skin and almond-shaped eyes drawing Riv's eyes to him. His companion, Jin, saw Riv's gaze and nudged Bleda. Riv looked away.

Israfil stood, a ripple passing through his wings, and he strode closer to the half-breed.

'Whose seed are you spawned from?' Israfil asked. 'Who is your sire?'

The half-breed looked up at Israfil, eyes cold with hatred.

'You are a filthy abomination, a tainted stain upon the land,' Israfil said. 'Your very existence is justification for the war we wage against the Kadoshim. They have broken the greatest law, mixing the blood of eternal with mortal, and you are the result.' Israfil's face twisted in disgust.

A movement drew Riv's eyes away from Israfil to the Ben-Elim seated behind him, to Kol. A flash of anger flickered across his face, making his scar twitch, then it was gone.

'Who is your sire?' Israfil repeated.

'Why would I tell you?' the half-breed said. He spat at Israfil's feet.

A cascade of blows fell upon the half-breed, head, shoulders, back. He fell forwards, onto his hands.

'Hold,' Israfil snapped.

'Who is your sire?'

'We know of you, Israfil, petty pawn of the Tyrant,' the half-breed said. He smiled through bloodied lips. 'Your days are numbered.'

'No, half-breed scum,' Israfil said. 'It is you who will soon be taking your last breath. But not before you are put to the question. It will not be quick – there are Ben-Elim who have mastered the art of keeping a body alive indefinitely, on the knife-edge of death. By the end we will know everything that you know. It is surprising how long even a piece of corrupted filth like you can live.' A look of contempt and loathing. 'It is not a task I take pleasure in, but my holy charge is to protect Elyon's creation, and you and your ilk are a corruption that must be eradicated.' Israfil raised a hand, signalling for the beating to continue.

'Drekar is my father,' the half-breed blurted. 'And I am Salk.'

'You have no name, should not exist. You are a pestilence,' Israfil said. 'Where is Drekar, now?'

'You will see him, when he chooses,' Salk said. 'But for now he sends you a message.' With a burst of unbelievable speed and strength, Salk surged to his feet, leathery wings beating as he threw himself to the side, crashing into one of his White-Wing guards, wrapping the chain that hung from his manacled wrists about the warrior's neck. Other White-Wings stabbed with their blades, but the half-breed was faster, leaping from the ground in a burst of powerful legs and wings, other warriors rushing forwards.

There was a collective gasp throughout the chamber, Riv jumping to her feet and vaulting through the tiered crowd, though she knew she was too far, too late.

The half-breed lurched into the air, hovered above his captors, the White-Wing in his grasp fighting and twisting, but Salk gave a last savage wrench of the chains and there was an audible *crack*, the White-Wing's limbs suddenly dangling, head hanging slack. Salk hurled the body at the warriors below him, snatching a short-sword from the dead man's scabbard, tucking his wings and hurtling towards Israfil. He bellowed a wordless cry.

Israfil drew his own sword, other Ben-Elim behind him taking to the air.

Salk's lips drew back in a primal snarl as he levelled his sword at Israfil.

Ethlinn stabbed her spear into the half-breed's shoulder, bursting out of his back in a spray of blood. She kept hold of it, swinging and slamming Salk to the stone floor, where he twisted and writhed on her spear like a stuck salmon.

Israfil and a score of others rushed to him, but before they could reach him Salk had the short-sword at his own throat.

'Father says he will send you back to the Otherworld,' the

half-breed said, and then he was dragging the sword across his neck, a jet of arterial blood.

'No,' Israfil yelled, Ethlinn kicking the sword from the half-breed's hand, but it was too late: a pool of blood was widening about him. In moments he was gone.

Israfil stood over the corpse, shaking his head. 'We could have learned much from him.'

'When he was captured we searched him, found this,' Garidas said, reaching into his cloak and pulling out a tattered scrap of parchment.

'What does it say?' Kol asked, standing at Israfil's shoulder.

Garidas looked to Israfil, waiting for his permission. 'Perhaps you should see this in private,' the White-Wing captain said. The Lord Protector nodded.

Ethlinn spoke out anyway, her voice echoing through the chamber.

'It says *Go luath*. Soon.'

CHAPTER NINE

DREM

Drem limped along beside his da and their string of packhorses, not for the first time wishing he was sitting upon the back of one of those horses, rather than struggling along beside it with his ankle throbbing. The fact was, though, that they had too many furs and skins to carry, and when faced with the prospect of leaving those skins behind or walking . . .

Olin had been happy to leave a bundle or two behind, but Drem knew how long and hard they'd worked for those skins, risking life and limb, and they needed them to sell if they wanted to eat through the winter.

The palisaded walls of Kergard loomed higher the closer they came to the new town sitting upon the rim of the Starstone Lake. Noise and activity rolled off it like heat from a dung heap.

'It looks bigger,' Drem said, and that was because it was. Bigger than when he had last seen it, six moons ago. Fresh-built holds and houses of timber and stone, roofed with thatch and sod, spilt down the slope and into the meadow and woodland about Kergard's walls.

Olin didn't respond, just stared with a frown upon his face. Without a word, he led their lead-pony off the main road to Kergard and onto a rolling meadow, skirting the town and heading north-east, towards their home. He had been like this since their discovery in the foothills three days ago. Drem saw his da reach out and put a hand upon the lump of black iron they'd hauled from the elk pit, wrapped and hidden now within half a dozen skins.

He is convinced it is starstone metal. And it is strange: twice as heavy as it should be, and a black that seems to suck light into it. I've never seen anything like it. But starstone . . . ?

The more Drem thought about it, though, he had to admit that there was a slim possibility that his da was correct, regardless of how farfetched the likelihood seemed. Besides, his da was a practical man, not given to wild theories or flights of fancy. Local legends told how the lake beyond Kergard was supposedly a crater formed by the original Starstone as it crashed to earth. He looked back over his shoulder at the foothills they had only recently left, one hand coming up absently to stroke the bear claw that he had tied to a strip of leather about his neck.

Behind those hills reared the jagged teeth of the Bonefells, looking as if they were holding up the sky. He squinted his eyes and tried to imagine the Starstone coursing over those mountain peaks, spitting great gobs of fire and smoke and blazing a trail of flames.

He blinked and nodded to himself.

Who is to say that part of the Starstone did not crack and fall away as it plummeted to earth.

He frowned, unsure of what it meant if what they carried hidden in their pack was *indeed* a piece of the fabled stone.

'No time to stop, we're almost home,' his da called back to him.

I hope it's not a piece of the Starstone. Look what happened last time – blood, war and death throughout the Banished Lands.

With a sense of unease seeping through him, Drem hobbled on.

Drem smiled to see their homestead appear, the rooftop of their barn visible beyond a copse of oak and alder. It was not as isolated as it had been when he and Olin had left. A handful of fresh-built homes were running along the line of a stream that curled out of thickening woodland to the north and fed into the lake. They passed a fence line belonging to the last of these new homes and turned onto the grass-choked path that led to their homestead. A dog barked and a voice called out. Drem saw a big hound standing in their path, lips curled back in a snarling growl. He was old, scars criss-crossing his dun coat, one ear half-chewed. A voice called out, an old man was hurrying from the porch of a timber house, a hobbling run using a long staff for help. A younger woman appeared a dozen steps behind him. The old man reached his fence, gasping for breath and leaned upon the timber rail for a moment, though he still managed to wave the tip of the spear he was carrying in Drem's direction. Drem had thought it a walking staff, but the old man seemed to have other ideas as he pointed it at Drem and his da.

'That your hound?' Olin asked, keeping one eye on the snapping, snarling creature.

'It is,' the woman said as she reached them. She was of an age with Drem, as far as he could tell, hair as yellow as the sun, tied and pinned tight to her head, blue eyes creased with worry as she reached a hand out to the old man.

He snatched his arm away and tutted at her.

'I'd be grateful if you'd call him off.' Olin nodded at the hound.

'Maybe I will, and maybe I won't,' the old man said. 'Who are you? And what business do you have to come creeping about my home?'

'We're not creeping!' Drem said, annoyed at the unjust and inaccurate accusation.

The spear-point levelled at Drem's chest.

'That's our hold,' Olin said, stepping between Drem and the old man and pointing to their home.

'No one lives there,' the old man snapped. 'Been empty since we came here.'

'It's been empty for a little over six moons,' Olin said, 'and like as not it is cold and damp inside and needs a hearth-fire lit. It's our home, though, built by our own hands. Didn't have neighbours when we left, but looks like we've more than a few now.'

The woman looked at their packhorses, the skins and furs tied in big bundles.

'Calder the smith said that trappers built that place, Grandfather,' she said to the old man. 'He said they'd be back for winter, as well.'

'He did?'

'He did,' she said.

'Huh, then why didn't you say so?' he snapped at Drem and his da.

'We just did,' said Drem.

The old man lowered his spear-point, a little begrudgingly, Drem thought.

'Your name is Olin, is it not?' the woman said.

Olin frowned at that, but eventually nodded into the growing silence. 'Aye, it is.'

'Well met and welcome home,' the girl said. 'I'm Fritha, and my grandfather is Hask.'

'Well met,' Olin said. 'And this is my son, Drem.'

'It'll be good to have some neighbours out here,' Fritha said, 'so close to the forest and mountains.'

Drem looked where she was pointing, at woodland just behind his own hold, and hills beyond.

'They're not mountains,' Drem corrected, not liking it when things were said wrong. His da gave him a flat stare.

'Well, whatever they are, we're happy to meet you,' Fritha said. 'Isn't that right, Grandad?'

'What? Yes, I suppose we are,' Hask muttered. 'Can never be too careful,' he added with a shake of his spear.

'True enough,' Olin said.

The hound was still growling and barring the way. Olin looked pointedly at it.

'We've been sleeping on root and rock for six moons; it would be nice to light a fire and see our beds.'

'Of course,' Fritha said.

'Surl, enough,' Hask snapped and the hound slunk over to his heel with one last snapping growl and then it was silent.

Olin bade them farewell and led Drem and the line of ponies on.

'You can be very diplomatic when you put your mind to it,' Drem said to his da as they drew near the gates to their hold.

'Don't have to use a sharp edge to deal with every situation,' Olin replied. 'More often than not a kind or polite word will fix a disagreement.' He looked a long moment at Drem. 'And you don't have to correct every inaccuracy you hear in a conversation.'

'I just don't like it when people get things wrong.' It was more than that – a compulsion far beyond habit or annoyance. Drem felt that he had to do it, a pressure would grow within him until he voiced his corrections. He knew his da didn't like him doing it, had often spoken to him about it.

'I know that, son, but other people, they can take it wrong, think you're criticizing, being rude. Some people don't react well if they think you're disrespecting them.'

'But—'

'I know, you don't mean any harm, but just think before you speak, eh? And hold your tongue if that's at all possible. Even if you don't understand why it's important. Do it for your old da.'

Drem winced, knowing that it would pain him, but he nodded. 'I'll try,' he conceded.

Olin smiled and patted Drem's shoulder.

It was good to be home. Olin unloaded the packhorses in the yard, all except the rock they'd dug out of the elk pit. He led the horse with the rock still upon its back around the rear of the barn, telling Drem to carry on until he returned. So Drem did: fires were lit, cobwebs and rats were swept and evicted from rooms, the horses rubbed down and put out to paddock, and a stew was set to simmering in a pot over the hearth. As he was seeing to these routine tasks Drem thought on his da and the lump of black rock they'd dug up.

I wish we'd never found it, and bringing it home with us! If it is what Da thinks it is, then a war that consumed the world began over something very similar.

That was not a comforting thought, and Drem resolved to talk to his da about it. He was carrying their pelts into the barn when his da joined him, hands and boots sticky with mud. Drem gave his da an enquiring look but received no response, so he carried on moving the pelts, his da washing down in a rain barrel and then silently helping. Once all the skins were under cover Drem began sorting through their tools in preparation for tanning.

I hate tanning skins, he thought, wrinkling his nose as he got a whiff of lime milk. It felt as if it singed off all the hairs up his nose.

'We'll start the tanning on the morrow,' Olin said. 'Just prepare for it now, then we'll go and put some hot food in our bellies.'

Watching his da rest a hand upon the pile of skins, bow his head and pinch the top of his nose, Drem thought he looked more troubled than he had ever seen him.

Because of that stone we've found? I'm troubled, too.

'Da, should we have brought that stone here? It's—'

'It's better with me than anywhere else,' Olin said, cutting him off.

'But we could have left it there, buried it again.'

'I could not live with the knowledge of it out there,' Olin said, 'just waiting to be found. At least with me, I know it cannot be put to any great evil.'

Evil!

'But—'

'Enough,' Olin snapped. 'Let it lie, Drem, I'll not be changing my mind.'

Drem sucked in a deep breath, weighing up the worth of continuing.

Once he makes up his mind, there's rarely any changing it. For now.

Drem loved his da, but more and more of late, he was feeling frustrated at how his da treated him, avoiding questions, treating him like a bairn.

Twenty-one summers old. I'm a man.

His da rolled his injured arm, the one Drem had stitched.

'How is it?' Drem asked him.

'Itching,' Olin said, then shrugged. 'A good sign. Your ankle?'

'Throbbing. I'll live.'

'Aye, well, let's get this finished, stable the ponies and we can look forward to some hot food, a cup of mead and a bowl of hot water to soak our feet in, and we can compare injuries.'

Drem liked the sound of that and the thought of it put some fire in his limbs. It made the job of finding and dusting off the buckets and barrels of quicklime, salt and oak bark less of a chore.

Drem's belly was rumbling by the time they finished bringing the ponies in from the paddock and settling them in the stables. As tempting as it was, they'd learned the hard way last year that you didn't leave animals outside through the night. The north had predators that liked the taste of horse.

The clouds were low and bloated, the sun just a faint glow on the horizon when they left the stables and made their way across the small yard to their cabin.

The sound of approaching hooves broke their companionable silence, growing steadily louder. They paused on the cabin steps, Drem noticing his da loosening his knife in its sheath and taking a step closer to the wood axe that was leaning against a timber post.

It was Ulf, the tanner. He trotted into the yard on a bay pony that looked too small for him, raised a hand in greeting and dismounted stiffly, approaching them with his halting gait.

'Thought you were back,' Ulf said with a grin, pointing at the smoke rising from the chimney.

Ulf was a few summers younger than Drem's da, but looked older. Mostly grey with a few streaks of black still in his hair, fat-bellied and fingers stained with the chemicals of his trade. He was one of the few people for whom Olin had more than a passing time, and last winter they had spent many an evening round a fire in each other's company.

Maybe it is because he was like us, once. Before his injury.

Ulf had been a trapper, like them, liked to boast that he had helped sink the first posts in Kergard's walls over a score of years ago and used to trap along the Bonefells every spring and summer. After his injury – a tale involving a wolven that became larger and more fearsome with every telling – Ulf had retired from trapping and become the town tanner, buying skins and pelts from those who still hunted this far north and turning them into tooled leather. He was a skilful man; Drem's da said he'd never had a pair of finer-fitting boots than the ones Ulf had made. When Drem and Olin had come to Kergard five year ago Olin had struck up a friendship with the tanner, who had helped them build their cabin and surrounding homestead.

Now, though, Drem could see a tension in his da at the appearance of the tanner, his eyes flickering beyond the barn, just for a moment.

He's worrying about that lump of rock.

'A good season's hunting?' Ulf asked.

'Aye, good enough,' Olin said.

'I was hoping to buy or trade your skins,' Ulf said.

Please, thought Drem. He hated the tanning process far

more than the cold nights and hard rock and root of the hunting.

'We were just talking about starting the tanning on the morrow,' Olin said, tugging on his short beard.

'I'll give you a good price and save you the hard work, and the smell . . .'

'We're not afraid of some hard work, are we, lad?' Olin said.

'No, Da.'

But the smell. Please . . .

Olin saw Drem's look.

'Well, it's something we'd not be against discussing, I suppose, is it, Drem?'

'No, no, it's not,' Drem said, trying not to let his hope spill all over his face.

'We'll come into town on the morrow, talk on it some more,' Olin said.

'Well, I'd like to talk on it now, if it's all the same to you. Don't like to go to bed with unfinished business, gives me gut-ache and then I can't sleep. But it's hard with the smell of that food cooking,' Ulf said, smacking his lips and raising his head to take a big sniff. 'Distracting, it is.'

Olin frowned, his eyes flicking beyond the barn again, but then his face cracked in a smile. 'Best we do something about that hole in your belly, then,' and with that they all entered the cabin.

'Kergard's bigger than when we left,' Olin said, dipping some black bread into his bowl.

Ulf had produced a loaf from a saddlebag strapped to his horse. 'Never go anywhere without a loaf of bread – makes every meal better,' Ulf had pronounced, and Drem had to admit it had certainly made his bowl of stew much better as he ripped off a large chunk and soaked up the last of the thick gravy glistening with fat and onion juice at the bottom of his bowl.

'Aye, it is, sure enough,' Ulf said as he sat back and quaffed his mead, emptying the cup without taking a breath, then belched as long and loud as Drem had ever heard. His da filled Ulf's cup and sipped some of his own. Night had fallen long since, a strong wind outside making timbers creak and sending the flames of the fire flickering and coiling as darkness pressed in upon them, making shadows dance and writhe on the walls.

'Close to four hundred new souls living around the crater, I'd wager,' Ulf said. 'All of them arriving since you wandered off in the spring towards the Bonefells. Not that I'm complaining: they'll all be after fur-lined boots and cloaks once they have a taste of winter up here.'

'Any trappers like us?' Drem asked.

'Aye, a few. Not like you two, though,' Ulf said. 'Six moons living wild in the Bonefells, now that's what I call commitment to the job. Most of the others have been back at least a moon, those that are coming back.'

'Not everyone's returned, then?'

'No, Vidar and Sten are still out there, though they're almost as insane as you two, so there's still hope they've survived the Wild another season. Old Bodil isn't back, either, which isn't so good. Don't expect to see him, now. He's wintered eight years in Kergard, and he's always back before the end of Reaper's Moon.' Ulf squinted at Olin through one eye, a sure sign that the mead was having some effect. 'Didn't see him on your travels?'

'No. Not him nor any other soul,' Olin replied.

Hope he's all right, Drem thought. He liked Old Bodil, though most called him cantankerous and ill-tempered. Drem thought most of that was just straight talking, without any dressing.

'Ah, well. He'll not be the first trapper to end his days up in those mountains, or the last. Maybe he ran into the kin of the

wolven that ended my trapping days. Course, I doubt they'd
ever be as fierce a beast as I had the bad fortune to come across,
roaming up in the high places.'

They probably are, wolven don't become less fierce, thought
Drem, gritting his teeth so that he didn't blurt the words out.
He was trying to take his da's advice and not unwittingly insult
Ulf; not that he saw any insult in correcting a mistake, but he'd
learned to take his da's advice on such subjects, no matter how
much it bothered him. And it did bother him. Listening to
someone make a mistake and not correct it was like listening
to nails scraping across slate and not asking them to stop.

'Big as draigs, they were, those wolven.' Ulf rubbed a hand
along his thigh, leg out straight before him, eyes distant.

'There's more than wolven to watch out for up in those
hills,' Olin said. 'We came across a giant bear. White as snow,
it was.'

Ulf grunted and sat up with interest. 'A white bear pelt;
now that would fetch a rare price. Why didn't you bring it
home?'

'We were too busy trying not to let it eat us.' Olin smiled
ruefully.

Drem nodded his head vigorously.

Ulf raised an eyebrow.

'It was big,' Olin said, 'bigger than any I've seen before,
even those with a giant on their backs.'

'Pffft.' Ulf spat with a smile. 'Animals grow in the telling,
I've learned.' Nevertheless, Drem saw him give Olin an
appraising look.

Ha, you're a fine one to say that! Drem thought, almost grinding his jaws together to stop himself from saying anything.
Instead his hand reached up into his woollen shirt and he
pulled out the bear claw tied around his neck, dangling it for
Ulf to see.

Ulf whistled and held his hands up. 'Fair enough,' he said,

eyes wide. 'The beast on the end of that must've been a rare sight.'

'We didn't stand still to admire it,' Olin said.

'No, spent more time running, and swimming,' Drem added.

'And near soiling our breeches,' Olin put in.

Ulf spat a mouthful of his mead onto the fire, which hissed, flames leaping.

'Ah, I miss those days.' He laughed wistfully.

'And even then we didn't get away free of harm,' Drem added, pointing to his ankle and his da's arm.

'Good job Drem can stitch a wound,' Olin said.

'Like that, eh?' Ulf nodded knowingly. 'Man-eater, then. I've come across them before. I wonder . . .' Ulf gazed at the fire, falling silent.

'Wonder what?' Drem prompted.

'Not just trappers lost to the Wild. Townsfolk have been going missing, too. Lads out hunting, mostly. Some near the lake.' He shrugged. 'And a bairn or two. First I thought it was southerners not having enough respect for a northern winter. Too many, though. Then I thought a wolven pack may have come south early. Thought I heard howling, the other night, off to the north-east. Might have been the wind. But maybe it's your white bear. Once they get a taste of man-flesh . . .' He looked to the flat dark of a shuttered window, and suddenly Drem was imagining the white bear padding through their yard.

'That was just a wild animal protecting its kill,' Olin said with a wave of his hand, though he looked troubled by what Ulf had said. He looked hard at Ulf. 'Tell me, these new arrivals at Kergard. Has this ever happened before? So many coming north in just one season?'

'Not since I've been here,' Ulf said, 'and that's over a score of years. Most I remember is a dozen in one year. Usually it's people like yourselves, coming up in twos, threes, fours. Sometimes a family.'

Olin nodded thoughtfully. 'Why so many, do you think?'

'Two reasons, far as I can tell,' Ulf said. 'They've found iron ore, lots of it, close to the northern rim of the lake. A mine's sprung up, all sorts coming north to work it.'

That would explain the lights we saw the other night, Drem thought, sharing a look with his da.

'And then there's the other reason,' Ulf continued, looking about the room, hunching closer to Olin as if there were spies in the shadows. Drem did the same. 'There's trouble in the south,' the old tanner said. 'Hard to get the truth of it, a rumour here, another there. A lot of unrest, I'm hearing, people not happy.'

'Not happy with what?' Drem asked.

'The Ben-Elim,' Ulf said. 'There's another side to their so-called peace, and to living in their Land of the Faithful.' He took a large sip from his cup. 'I saw it all those years ago, but apparently it's getting worse.'

'What is?' Olin asked, his voice impatient.

'You know the Ben-Elim demand a tithe for their peace and protection. Coin or goods, and flesh?' Ulf said.

Olin nodded.

How is it that Da knows this, and I don't.

'What do you mean, flesh?' Drem asked, looking pointedly at his da, who just frowned, avoiding Drem's eyes.

'I mean people, Drem,' Ulf said. 'The Land of the Faithful keeps growing, and there aren't enough Ben-Elim to patrol it, so they want a tithe of warriors. Course, they've got the giants, or most of them, apart from those at Dun Seren, but that's still not enough. They demand youngsters they can train in their ways of making war, to go out and fight for them.'

'Oh,' Drem said. 'That just seems wrong. I don't like it.' He felt the urge to take his pulse, fingers twitching, but controlled himself.

'No? Well, you'll not like this, then. Up till now, the Ben-Elim have asked for a flesh tithe. But now they're just taking it. Seems not everyone's happy to send their young away to Drassil for warrior training, and so the Ben-Elim are just taking their tithe, whether people are willing or no.'

'That's close to slavery,' Drem gasped.

Olin glared at the flames.

'You're not the only one to think so,' Ulf said, 'and a lot of those that think the same are ending up here, where the Ben-Elim don't rule.'

'Good enough reason,' Olin said.

Ulf looked at them both a long moment, the room silent except for some wood cracking in the hearth.

'And then, there are the other stories I'm hearing,' he said.

'And what are they?' Olin asked. Drem could feel a change in Ulf, even before he said it. A change in his voice, in the set of his shoulders.

As if he's scared.

'Well, no one talks about it at first, but my job, well, I see a lot of people and, believe me, I hear a lot of folk's tales. After a while they tell me things, serious things. And it seems like there's one thing everyone agrees on.' He paused, took another drink from his cup. Drem saw a tremor in his hand.

'Go on,' Olin prompted.

'The Kadoshim are at the heart of it.'

Drem's da stiffened at that, a tension in his jaw.

'What do you mean?' Olin asked.

'I've heard talk of a Kadoshim cult arising. And talk of strange rituals. Of sacrifice.' His voice dropped to almost a whisper, and Drem felt that even the flames and darkness were leaning closer, straining to hear.

'*Human* sacrifice.'

CHAPTER TEN

RIV

Riv drew the arrow, the yew bow creaking as muscles flexed in her arms and back, until the feathers tickled her cheek. She sighted along the length of the shaft, raised the head a little and loosed.

The string thrummed as the arrow flew, arcing up across the archery range of the weapons-field, wind snatching at it before it dipped down and thudded into a straw target. It struck lower than she'd intended. She swore.

If that was my enemy, at worst they'd be walking with a limp now.

Sword and spear, she was a match for most of those she trained with, but she still had a lot to learn with a bow.

A chuckle sounded behind her. Riv turned to see the two wards from Arcona, Jin and Bleda, standing at the head of a small crowd.

'You see, Father, they use a bow as long as a spear, and most of them are about as skilled as any five-year-old from the Cheren.'

Jin's head was twisted over her shoulder, talking to a man behind her. His head was shaved, apart from his warrior braid, like all the warriors Riv had seen from the east. He was standing with a handful of others, men and women all of a similar appearance.

The leaders of the Cheren and the Sirak, and their attendants.

Riv saw Israfil and Kol amidst their ranks. A memory of the half-breed in Drassil's Great Hall flashed through her mind, Israfil standing over him, face twisted in revulsion.

Usually he is so calm, so controlled. How deep must be his hatred for the Kadoshim, and for the breaking of Elyon's Lore.

The Lord Protector was talking to a woman close to Bleda, and behind them all were two giants.

Riv had heard of the arrival of this party from Arcona, and news that they were here to discuss a tithe of their warriors had spread through the White-Wings faster than sickness through a camp. Riv had mixed feelings about that, as she liked the way things were at Drassil, and having newcomers with new ways felt like a threat to her way of life.

Israfil will not allow that. They will have to become like us, followers of the Lore, not the other way around.

The distinct feeling that she was now being mocked did not ease her concerns. She felt her cheeks flush red, a burning sensation.

'Why don't you show me how it's done, then?' Riv said, the words escaping her mouth before she'd realized they were even there, and at the same time she was throwing the bow at Jin. Riv was a little disappointed at the ease with which Jin caught it, a moment's surprise flashing across the girl's face even as she stepped forwards and deftly plucked the bow from the air.

Jin held it her hand, studying it with her flat, emotionless face as she twisted it from left to right.

'This is not fit for firewood,' she pronounced with a curl of her lip and passed it to a man behind her, an older man, with a beard the colour of iron. Another Cheren warrior handed Jin a curved bow, already strung, and a bag of arrows. Riv's eyes flickered to Israfil, saw him staring at her and she quickly looked away, back to Jin, who strode forwards a few steps, pulling a handful of arrows from the bag. She nocked one, the others held loosely in the hand that gripped the bow, drew and released in one fluid motion. Even as the arrow was rising high into the air she was drawing the next one, loosing, and then a third. She let the bow drop to her side and stared at Riv, not even watching to see if her arrows would find their target.

Riv did, though, and saw the first slam into the chest of the same target Riv had selected, with her arrow still protruding from its leg. The second arrow took it through the throat, the third piercing what would have been a shoulder, the straw man rocking on its base with the impact of the arrows.

'You should close your mouth, it is not a becoming look,' Jin said to her.

Riv just stood there, torn between admiration and respect for the feat of skill she'd just witnessed, and a bubbling anger that didn't take too kindly to being humiliated. An image of her fist connecting with Jin's disdain-set jaw flashed through Riv's mind. It was very tempting. But even through the first tendrils of red mist seeping through her she knew that it was a humiliation she deserved.

Israfil is watching. Show him you have learned a lesson. Show him you have control of your anger.

'That was . . .' She hesitated, her jaw tight and clamping on what she knew she should say. 'Good,' she ground out, not quite what she intended, but better than a host of other responses that were filling her mind.

'Pah,' Jin said. 'It is no more than any child of the Cheren could do. Our warriors do the same from the back of a galloping horse. To my shame I am a little out of practice.'

Riv searched for words to answer that, but couldn't find any, so she just nodded stiffly and walked away.

As she stepped onto the flagstoned road that led from the weapons-field she stopped and looked back. The field was alive with activity, as it always was: different cohorts of troops training in shifts throughout the day. There were giants upon the field, now, sparring with wooden hammer and axe, making the ground tremble, and Ben-Elim swooping and diving in mock aerial combat.

And there was Vald, her friend and, until recently, training partner. He was with the others who had passed their weapons-trial and Long Night. He stood proudly amidst a unit of White-Wings, being drilled on shield wall formations and flanking manoeuvres.

No, not amongst the White-Wings. He is a White-Wing now.

The sight of it twisted a knife in Riv's gut and she wrenched her eyes away, back to Jin and the others. It looked as if Israfil was showing the two lords from Arcona something of warrior training and life at Drassil.

The Lord Protector was talking to the man Jin had given Riv's longbow to. Jin's father, Uldin, Riv presumed. The others were lined up watching riders galloping at targets with sword and spear. As Riv watched, she saw Bleda amongst the crowd, but he wasn't watching the riders. He was staring right back at Riv. A woman, Bleda's mother, leaned close to him and whispered in his ear. Riv remembered her well: Erdene, sitting upon her horse, bloody and bowed. She was still clearly a warrior-born, solid and wiry as a twisted rope, head shaved clean except for a coiled warrior braid.

Riv saw a jolt go through Bleda at Erdene's whispered words and he leaned away from her, looking into her eyes, his face twitching with more emotion than Riv had ever seen from him since the day he had been torn from his Clan and kin. Then the emotion was gone, face swept clean as if it had never been there. He gave his mother a curt nod and turned to look at the riders as they galloped by.

Riv turned and left the weapons-field. She felt agitated, troubled by her encounter with Jin and her resulting humiliation, and something about what she'd just witnessed between Bleda and his mother bothered her, making her frown.

The streets of Drassil were heaving with activity. Riv walked through a traders' market thick with the sounds and smells of food and drink, vendors cooking all manner of meat and fish, a blend of herbs and spices mixing into a heady aroma.

Close by, fat steaks of auroch and sliced onions sizzled on a charcoal griddle, making Riv's stomach growl, but she walked on, the streets thinning a little as she left the market behind, the roads changing as she moved through the potters' district, with all manner of jars, vases, cups and plates on display upon tables before workshops. And then she was through them, passing through the clangour of hammer on anvil, the hiss and steam and rolling heat of the blacksmiths' quarter, and then, finally, she was standing before the barracks of the White-Wings: a series of stone buildings on either side of a wide street, great arched doorways leading into entrance chambers as big as a keep.

The military might of the Faithful was split into different disciplines. There were the White-Wings, the infantry heart of the army, masters of the shield wall, of sword and spear. There were the archer units, smaller bands of men and women who scouted and foraged during campaigns and formed solid blocks of archers during any battle. There were light cavalry, skilled with horse, with spear and lance, used mostly in battle for swift flank attacks and the harrying of routed forces. Then the giants, fewer in numbers, who when on foot acted as the shock troops of the army and became the heavy cavalry when mounted upon their giant bears.

And of course the Ben-Elim, death-from-above.

There were rooms enough at Drassil for the full strength of the Faithful's army, in total over twenty thousand strong, the White-Wings alone numbering over ten thousand swords, but the bulk of the army was spread throughout the Land of the Faithful, stationed at outposts and garrisons along the far-flung borders, at the Tower of the Bay at Ripa in the south, at Gulgotha in the east, at Brikan and Jerolin and Tarba.

So many of the buildings before Riv were empty and dark. At Drassil now there were around a thousand White-Wings, and they were split into ten units, each hundred its own compact fighting force. Riv's sister, Aphra, was captain of a hundred.

Riv remembered the day Aphra had been promoted, her wings presented to her by Kol, one of Israfil's captains. Riv had thought she would burst with pride.

Now she walked through the open doors of the hundred that she had been assigned to for as far back as her memory reached. The same hundred that her sister commanded, and the one that her mother had served in before that. Two generations, lives dedicated to the White-Wings and the Ben-Elim. It was all Riv knew. The centre of her life, around which all else revolved.

The feast-hall was empty, the fire-pit cold, as Riv expected. The whole hundred should be out on guard duty and then training in the weapons-field, so Riv was surprised when she opened the door that led to her barrack chamber and heard voices. A woman, not shouting, but voice raised, in anger or alarm. And another voice, quieter, calmer, deeper. Riv cocked her head to one side, straining to listen. She climbed a few of the stone steps leading up to the chamber she shared with her mam and sister and the other members of their hundred, ten warriors and their attendants, all sharing the same sleeping quarters, bonds forged by a lifetime of eating, sleeping, training, fighting, living and dying together.

The woman's voice grew louder, tremored with emotion, the other lower, an edge of iron to it. Both were blurred, the words unclear.

The door behind Riv grated shut and the voices beyond the closed door at the top of the stairwell fell silent, quick as a snuffed candle.

Riv paused a moment, only the sound of her breathing, then decided to go on.

I live here, they're my quarters, too. And besides, she was intrigued to know who the voices belonged to.

The door at the top of the stairs opened, a figure was striding down towards her. It was Fia, tall and dark-haired, her sister's closest friend. She saw Riv and nodded a greeting,

though she did not stop, just carried on past her. She was looking away, but Riv noticed that Fia's eyes were red-rimmed.

Still looking over her shoulder, Riv entered the chamber, a
sizeable room that was home to almost thirty people. It was one
long, large room, neat rows of cots along two walls, chests at
the bottom of each cot, an aisle running down the middle.

There was no one else in the chamber.

Riv frowned.

Strange.

The shuttered window over her cot was open and she
looked out into the street, but there was no sign of anyone. Riv
shrugged and walked to the end of her cot, kneeling before her
chest, home of all her belongings, although in reality they were
not *hers*. The White-Wings renounced all worldly possessions,
emulating the Ben-Elim in their devout desire to serve Elyon.
All that they owned was given to them by the Ben-Elim, every
item useful for the furtherance of Elyon's kingdom on earth.
She unlatched the bolt, slid it across with hardly a sound – the
White-Wings taught discipline and cleanliness as if it were
the path to holiness – and raised the lid, pushing it back to
rest against the frame of her bed. Inside was an assortment
of items: clothes, boots, a pair of iron-shod sandals, belts, her
best cloak, her fire-making kit, knives of various blades and
lengths, a short-hafted axe, rags and oils for the maintenance
and care of her small armoury. She rummaged through them,
reaching deep, and then pulled out an object concealed in a
sealskin cloak. She laid it on the floor before her and carefully
unwrapped it, revealing a curved bow.

Bleda's bow.

A ripple of guilt at seeing it; it was not hers, had not been
allocated to her by the Ben-Elim, and so in a way could be considered as her own possession, something that was forbidden.

*But it is not mine, it is Bleda's. I have just been looking after it
for him.*

She had seen him drop it on the day the Sirak had been

cowed, all those years ago, the same day he had been taken by the Ben-Elim as a ward. It had just lain in the dirt long after Bleda had disappeared into the horizon and Erdene and Israfil had moved on to the privacy of a tent for Israfil to talk over the terms and details of the Clan's surrender. As the sun had sunk into the hills Riv saw the bow still lying there on the ground, and without thinking had picked it up, wrapping it in a cloak and storing it with her sister's kit. She'd brought it all the way back to Drassil with her, not really knowing why, except that something inside her had gone out to the boy as he'd been held in the air by Israfil, his brother and sister's decapitated heads strewn upon the ground at his feet. She had thought how she would feel if it was her, with Aphra's head rolling in the dirt. Not that the Ben-Elim's actions were wrong, she knew that. The Sirak and Cheren had disobeyed the Ben-Elim's Lore: to preserve life, to only slay Kadoshim and their servants. And the deaths that day had established a peace that had lasted five years, so Riv was satisfied that they were justified.

But the look in Bleda's eyes . . .

She felt a wave of sympathy for him, because Riv knew that Israfil had punished Kol for the terrible act. Kol should have chained Bleda's brother and sister and brought them before Israfil for judgement, but Kol had a reputation for taking things into his own hands, for being more spontaneous than most Ben-Elim.

All this time later and she had never returned the bow to Bleda, even though she had resolved to do so a hundred times. Something always stopped her.

She brushed the grip with her fingertips, worn leather smooth and sweat-stained from Elyon knew how many hours Bleda had practised with it.

Hundreds, if he is anything like Jin. To be able to do that, after five years of inaction.

The bow was about the same size as the one Jin had used with such skill, less than half the length of the longbow Riv had

been practising with, significantly shorter even than the hunting bows used by Drassil's scouts and trackers. There was an
elegance and beauty of design in the pronounced curves of its
limbs. Riv ran her fingers along them, the layers of wood, horn
and sinew smooth and cold to her touch.

I should return it to him. Perhaps he could teach me . . .

The slap of boots on stone drifted through an open shutter
to Riv, in the street outside, then echoing as they entered the
hundred's barrack. A few heartbeats and she heard the door
open and feet pounding on the stairwell. Hastily, Riv wrapped
the bow in its sealskin cloak and buried it back in her chest,
closing the lid and snapping the lock shut even as the dormitory room opened and her sister ran into the room.

'What are you doing here?' Aphra asked, though she
seemed distracted, not even looking at Riv, instead her eyes
scanning the dormitory.

'Nothing,' Riv said with a shrug as she sat on her cot, a cold
breeze from the open shutters ruffling her short hair. Aphra
marched up and down the central aisle, looking between beds.

'What are *you* doing here?' Riv asked her.

Aphra stopped her searching and looked at Riv.

'Have you seen Fia?'

'Aye. She was leaving as I arrived. She didn't look very
happy.'

'Where did she go? Did she speak to you?'

'No, she passed me on the stairwell. Didn't say a word to
me.'

Aphra studied her a moment. 'If you see her, tell her I was
looking for her, and that I need to speak to her.'

'What about?'

'None of your business.'

Riv's scowl followed Aphra through the door as her sister
turned on her heel and left.

CHAPTER ELEVEN

DREM

Drem sat in the seat of their wain, the reins held loosely in one hand, his da beside him. The sky was a pale winter's blue, making Drem think of ice, and a cold wind swept down from the Bonefells, Drem's nose and ears *feeling* like ice.

'Get on,' Drem said, a flick of his whip adding some motivation to the two ponies pulling the wain as they reached the slope that led up to Kergard's walls, their snorted breaths great clouds of vapour in the cold air. The wain was loaded full with the pelts they had hunted, six moons' worth of their life being sold to Ulf the tanner, for which Drem was thankful.

Da negotiated enough coin to see us through winter and longer, and I don't have to spend half a moon with my nose plugged, a cloth wrapped around my face and my hands stained orange.

New holds had been built beyond the timber walls of Kergard, sprawling on both sides of the track with no apparent plan or design, a snarl of timber, wattle and daub and thatch, fences, pigs, goats, chickens, dogs, a cacophony of noise as Drem and Olin rode by.

'Looks different,' Drem remarked.

'Aye, and smells different,' Olin said, frowning at the advancement of civilization all around him.

The smell didn't improve much once they'd rumbled through the open gates, Olin nodding to the man on guard duty. Kergard wasn't ruled by a lord or king, the Desolation was free of such rulers and authority, free even of the Ben-Elim for the time being, as it was newly settled land. A group of Kergard's founders had worked together in the building of the village and had decided on a democratic council with no one man to lead or rule them. They'd called themselves the Assembly, and over the years some had died or left Kergard, while some of the new settlers had been invited to join the Assembly, but the core of the Assembly was still the same as it had been some twenty years ago. Ulf the tanner was one of them. Between them they organized a tithe from those who lived within the village's walls, and that tithe paid for roads, building repairs, labour and, amongst other things, for a small unit of guards. It was the Wild, after all, and crops, herds and homes often needed defending from the predators that lurked and roamed within the dark and storm-racked north. Most of the guardsmen were older men, retired trappers and huntsmen, whose days of roaming the Bonefell's were behind them.

Drem guided the ponies through busy streets of hard-packed earth, more people about than he had ever seen in Kergard before. They made their way through the village and towards the eastern fringes, where Ulf's tanning yard was situated. Drem could smell the place before sighting it, the sharp tang of his lime-water vats and the sickly stench of fat-scraped hides lying thick as smoke in the air.

Ulf met them with a grin and a bag of silver, and set two of his sons to unloading the wain of its pelts while Olin and Ulf chatted, mostly about mead and sore heads.

A woman entered the yard as they were talking, tall and stern-faced, an otter pelt cloak about her shoulders. Two men walked a step behind her, both muscled and scarred, belts brimming with axe and knife.

'Hildith.' Drem nodded a greeting. She ran Kergard's mead-hall, had helped build it with her own hands and was one of the original members of the Assembly.

'Still alive, then,' Hildith said to Drem and Olin.

'Aye,' Drem said.

Just, as he thought of the white bear.

'Forgive me, but I cannot stand here in conversation,' Hildith said, pulling a sour face. 'The smell is too much. I've come for my new boots and cloak, Ulf.'

Ulf ran to fetch them and Olin led Drem back to their wain, now unloaded.

'Come see me at the mead-hall and tell me your trappers' tales,' Hildith called after them.

Olin raised a hand.

'A good deal,' Drem said to his da as he drove the wain out of the tanner's yard, wheels bouncing now the load was lighter. They turned into a wide street, where clouds of steam were hissing from the roof of Calder the smith.

'Huh,' Olin grunted, making Drem frown. His da had been like this since they had found that lump of black rock in the elk pit – distant, quiet, uneasy, no matter how hard he tried to hide it.

It is the starstone that worries him so, if that is what it is. I do not blame him; I am worried, too. Despite his da's reasons for taking and keeping the lump of black rock, Drem thought it would be better for all if they took it and buried it again, or dumped it in the Starstone Lake.

'Here,' Olin said, pointing, and Drem whistled and pulled on the reins. They were at the market square, all manner of tents and stalls selling a variety of goods. Drem followed his da round and listened as Olin bartered and haggled, Drem carrying each purchase back to the wain. It was not long before the cart was groaning with the weight of grain sacks, barrels of salted meat and fish, and a fair few skins of stoppered mead. Olin had also bought a crate of ten chickens and two goats, who were now tethered to the wain.

A group of men were standing close to the cart, seven or eight of them, some trappers by the look of them, clothed in furs and deer-skin, knives and axes hanging from their belts.

One of their number, a man with red wisps for a beard, was prodding the butt-end of a spear at the feet of Drem's new goats, making them dance. He was finding it much funnier than Drem considered it to be.

Drem loaded a huge round of cheese into the wain, looking at Wispy Beard.

'They don't like that,' Drem said.

'They must do, or they wouldn't be dancing,' Wispy said, laughing so hard at his joke he started coughing and choking. One of the men with him, hooded face in shadow, touched his arm and Wispy raised a hand.

'All right, I'll stop then,' he said, 'if you think they're all danced out.'

A ripple of chuckles through his companions.

'Thank you,' Drem said, remembering his da's advice to always be polite.

The hooded man looked at Drem. He appeared to be bald beneath the hood of his cloak; Drem did see a scar running across one cheek, through the edge of the man's mouth to his jaw, giving him a permanent scowl.

'We're new to town,' the hooded man said. 'Heard there was a mine nearby, needing men.'

'Aye, that'll be up to the north of the lake,' Drem said. 'Easy to find.'

'And somewhere to wet our dry throats while we're here?' Wispy asked.

'Hildith's mead-hall – that way.' Drem pointed, then he headed back to the market.

There were new faces everywhere, some amongst the traders, but mostly those who were walking the market streets looking to buy rather than sell. Olin was talking to a stall holder about it when Drem returned.

'Feels crowded for the north,' Olin was saying.

'Aye,' the trader said, Asger, a short, round man, his fore-arms so hairy Drem could hardly see the skin beneath. 'Lots of new faces in Kergard, holds springing up all over. And there's that mine on the north shore of the lake. A few faces have disappeared, though.' He leaned closer to Olin, glancing left and right. 'I don't mean packed up and moved on. I mean gone. Just vanished. If it was all newcomers I'd put it down to them not respecting a winter in the north. But it's some of the townsfolk, too, ones that have been here years, like Hakon and his brood. They're gone. Cattle still in the barn, all their belongings still there.'

He tugged on a bushy beard.

'I've heard wolven howling at night. Maybe a pack's come down from the Bonefells . . .'

'Could be,' Olin said, looking thoughtful.

'Not complaining about the newcomers,' Asger continued. 'It's good for business. Though sometimes it's not.' Asger looked both ways and leaned close again, dropping his voice. 'Thieving's becoming a problem. Was a time when I didn't need to lock my barn doors. Wouldn't dream of leaving them open, now. It's those new miners. Not the same as good, honest trappers, if you ask me.'

Drem snorted. He'd met many a trapper that would have happily put a knife in his back to take his furs, a few had tried, though his da had taught them the error of that decision.

'Though they've hired their own trappers to keep them fed and clothed. They're more like thieves, I reckon.'

Drem would have liked to stay and hear more, but his da loaded him up with a barrel of apples and so he trudged back to the wain. He thought about what Asger had said, about thieving, thought about those men near the wain and resolved to wait there until his da was finished in the market.

As he turned a corner and the wain came into view he saw a woman in the street, pale yellow hair revealed as the hood of a cloak blew back in the wind. It was Fritha, his new neighbour, a large basket of latticed willow hooked over one arm. She didn't see Drem, as she looked to someone calling out to her: Wispy Beard, part of the group of trappers and miners that Drem had seen.

'Need some help with that?' Wispy said, stepping close to Fritha.

Drem didn't hear what Fritha said, but Wispy didn't seem to like it, stepping in front of her, blocking her way. She tried to go around him but he mirrored her, stepped with her. Some of his companions laughed. Drem put his barrel of apples in the wain, looking over his shoulder at Fritha.

Words passed between Wispy and Fritha, unheard but clearly angry in nature. Then Wispy slapped the basket, emptying its contents onto the ground. Red berries.

Berries picked from the woods, to sell in the market? Drem thought.

Fritha crouched down to scoop them back into her basket and Wispy raised a boot to stamp on them.

Before he'd realized he'd done it, Drem was standing over Fritha, Wispy sprawling on the ground. The sneer on his face quickly transformed into a snarl. His companions stepped away from the wall they'd been huddled around, seven of them, all giving Drem dark looks. The cloaked man pushed his hood back, revealing a shaved head and intense blue eyes.

'Shouldn't have done that,' the bald man said.

Probably not, Drem thought. *But what choice was there?*

Drem didn't like fighting. He hated it, in fact, thought it was pointless. He'd had one fight in his twenty-one years, when he was thirteen summers old, had broken the lad's jaw. Sometimes at night he could still feel his knuckles slamming into flesh, the slap of meat, like a hammer hitting a steak, the crunch of jawbone and grind of teeth knocked loose. The memory of it made him feel sad.

'I'm sorry,' he said to Wispy on the ground, and offered a hand to help him rise.

'Walk away,' Fritha hissed to him, taking a step towards the market.

Wispy gripped his hand and pulled himself up, grinning.

Ah, see. Da was right. Polite and friendly fixes most problems.

Wispy was still grinning when he punched Drem in the gut, doubling him over.

A crunch in the side of Drem's head, white light exploding in front of his eyes, something cold slamming into his face.

Dirt. Realized he was face-down on the ground.

'Uh,' he grunted, pushing up onto one elbow, the world out of focus for a moment. He blinked, saw Wispy was standing over him, still grinning, holding Fritha's arm.

'You'll regret this,' she snarled and slapped Wispy furiously, raking her nails across his cheek. Wispy howled, spat a curse and put his fist in Fritha's face; her legs suddenly went wobbly, only the trapper holding her up.

Drem punched Wispy between the legs, hard, saw his eyes bulge with the pain of it, then Drem was somehow on his feet even as Wispy was dropping to his knees, another trapper coming at him, swinging a punch. Drem didn't like fighting, always avoided it, but he was big, taller than most, and stronger than most, too. He caught the man's fist in his own, stopped it dead. Felt an anger flare in his belly at these men. At the pointlessness of this conflict. He could understand the white bear chasing him, the drive to survive, to protect its kill.

But this! For what?

He wrapped his fingers around the man's fist, squeezing and twisting the wrist and arm, felt the crackle of finger bones snapping, the trapper yelling, and he put his knee into the man's ribs as he bent at the waist to get out of Drem's grip. More bones breaking, ribs this time, and the trapper collapsed to the ground.

'Let her go,' Drem said to the man holding Fritha.

There was a moment's silence.

Then men were lunging at him from all directions, blows raining down upon him. He blocked a punch to his head, swept it away, threw a punch of his own, felt his knuckles connect with flesh, grunted as a fist slammed into his side, a kick to the back of his knee sending him stumbling forwards. The bald man appeared in front of him, grabbing Drem's shirt and head-butting him in the face. An explosion of stars and the world spun, the salt taste of blood in his mouth and he was somehow on his knees. There was a lull, men pulling back for a moment, and Drem found he was close to Wispy, who was also strug-gling back to his feet. They both looked at one another for a long moment.

'Fancy yourself a bear-hunter, eh?' Wispy grunted, and Drem saw that his bear claw was hanging loose about his neck.

'I'm going to take that claw and give you a new red smile with it,' Wispy snarled.

Then those on their feet were moving in again, more blows, and all Drem's hard work to reach this position was for nothing as he toppled to the ground, trying to curl up, cover his head with his arms. Distantly he was aware of screaming – *Fritha?* – wanted to do something about it, but his body wouldn't cooperate, kicks and punches merging.

Slowly he became aware that the blows had stopped. He opened his eyes, saw boots in a half-circle around him, saw Wispy climbing back to his feet, and the man whose hand he'd crushed and ribs he'd broken dragging himself away. Fritha was leaning against the wain, a purpling bruise spreading across her jaw.

And beyond the boots around Drem there was another trapper on the ground, unconscious, a man standing over him.

Drem's da.

'Step away from my boy,' his da said, voice tight, cold as frost-bitten iron.

'Stay out of this, old man,' a voice answered, a new pair of boots stepping over Drem. The bald man.

Old man? Is he talking about my da? The thought shocked Drem, even through the fog of pain that was pulsing through him, but as he looked at his da he saw a man whose hair was mostly grey, deep creases around his eyes and mouth, weathered and worn by living in the wilderness, his body lean and wiry.

He didn't speak like an old man, though.

'This is *over*,' Olin said. His eyes flickered to Drem, then across the men before him, five of them still standing, by Drem's counting, and finally back to the bald man. 'I'll ask you again. Step away from my son.'

'I don't take orders from the likes of you,' the bald man said, taking a step towards Olin and spitting on the ground.

'Not ordering, just asking,' Olin said. 'I'll not ask again.'

Drem tried to get up, needed to get up, knew these men were not going to back down, and he didn't want to see his da beaten to a pulp like him, or worse. But only his fist opened and closed, and one foot scraped the dirt. He dribbled blood and spittle.

'We're not finished with him,' the bald man said, jutting his chin at Drem. 'So fight us or leave, old man.'

Olin stretched his neck left and right, bones clicking. 'I'll fight you if you wish. But know this: I am old for a reason.'

'Ha, listen to the o—' the bald man began, but then he was staggering backwards and choking. Olin had lunged forwards and punched him in the throat, strode after him and followed up with a fist to the chest, and the bald man tripped over Drem and went sprawling. Others rushed at Olin, a burst of violence as punches flew, too fast for Drem to follow. He heard grunts of pain, a loud crack followed by an even louder scream, the thud of a body hitting the dirt. The chaos cleared for a moment, Drem seeing his da duck a punch and step in close, land a blurred combination of blows to the gut and head of Wispy, who it seemed had climbed back to his feet. An uppercut from his da lifted him from the ground and then he was lying in the dirt again beside Drem.

Men backed away from Olin, three left on their feet, panting, spreading in a half-circle. Olin stood with his feet spread, balanced, blood on his knuckles, a thin trickle of blood from a cut below his eye.

How is he still standing?

'He's broken my arm!' someone screamed beyond Drem's vision.

The bald man appeared again, stepping into Drem's view, this time with a spear in his fists, the tip levelled at Olin's chest. Drem heard the sound of steel scraping free of sheaths, the other three pulling blades. Something changed in Olin's eyes and he shifted his feet, drew the short axe at his belt with his right hand, a knife with his left.

Maybe the bald man saw the same change in Olin's eyes that Drem saw, because he hesitated a moment; only the sound of the wind, the groaning of men with broken bones, the scraping of dirt as Drem managed to drag himself to one knee.

Then voices were shouting, footsteps drumming, and Drem saw Calder the smith appear, a huge man, bare-armed and bare-chested apart from a thick leather apron, a hammer in his hand. Hildith and her two burly guards were with him. Asger and other traders from the market appeared from the other direction, coming to stand behind Olin.

The bald man stood there a moment, then he was shrugging, stepped back and lowered his spear. He helped one of his comrades stand, the others still on their feet doing the same, moving away, carrying those who couldn't do it themselves.

'Do they need throwing into Kergard's gaol?' Calder asked Olin, a scowl on his face.

'No.' Olin shook his head, slipped his knife and axe back into their homes at his belt and hurried over to Drem.

'Slowly,' Olin said as he knelt beside him, face all twisted with worry. He helped him stand, checking limbs for broken bones, holding a finger before Drem's eyes, ordering him to track them. Asking him questions, like what moon it was.

'What about kind and polite words fixing a disagreement?'

Drem wheezed at Olin, his mouth thick with the copper tang of blood, his split nose throbbing, pulsing with his heartbeat.

'There's a time for that,' Olin said. 'But sometimes, son, the only answer is blood and steel.'

CHAPTER TWELVE

SIG

Sig unwound the bandage from Hammer's paw, the bear rumbling dolefully.

'That's what you get for standing on a Kadoshim,' Sig said.

The stab wounds were healing, no pus or scent of rot, for which Sig was relieved. Gently she washed them out, then reached for a fresh poultice of honey, yarrow and comfrey, packing it tight into the many red punctures and finally binding it back up with a fresh bandage of clean linen. She stood and patted the huge bear's neck. Hammer's muzzle sniffed Sig's face, a blast of air sending her blonde braid flapping.

'You're doing fine, my faithful friend,' Sig murmured. 'We're not leaving for a few days yet, not until you're ready for it, so just rest easy, and eat.'

Hammer licked Sig's cheek, leaving a trail of saliva.

'Lick this brot instead, it'll taste nicer than me,' Sig said, pouring a thick, viscous liquid into a bucket, more like porridge than anything else. It was the giants' staple travelling food, incredibly nourishing and possessing healing agents as well. Hammer sniffed it and began to lick it up with relish.

Sig slapped the bear's muscled shoulder and left the converted stable block. Hammer was now its sole resident, as the horses of Uthandun had made it clear they were not comfortable sharing their stables with a giant bear.

The courtyard of Uthandun was awash with activity, warriors in the grey and green cloaks of Ardain everywhere, the honour guard of Queen Nara newly arrived from Dun Vaner to the north-west. Word of the Kadoshim coven had spread quickly and there was a sense of menace and tension in the air.

Warriors parted for Sig as she strode across the courtyard, their faces a mixture of unease and admiration. Giants were rare in Ardain, even with the close relationship between Ardain's Queen Nara and Dun Seren's Order of the Bright Star, but word of Sig's Kadoshim-slaying had circulated quickly, and that was a feat respected by all.

Though I didn't actually kill the beast, Sig thought as she made her way up a stairwell to the walls above Uthandun's southern gate. A cold wind blew from the north, reminding her of winter's approach.

Hammer should get the credit for that deed.

Cullen was there, waiting for her, his wounded arm in a sling, but apart from that looking for all the world like the happiest man alive.

'How is it?' Sig grunted, jutting her chin at his wounded arm.

'That, oh, it's fine. Just a scratch, hardly know it's there.'

'The spear pierced your arm and came out the other side,' Sig said. 'Even by my judgement, that's no scratch.'

Cullen shrugged. 'A tickle, nothing more.'

'Make a fist,' Sig said.

Cullen's eyes pinched as the fingers on his left hand twitched and slowly formed a loose fist. A bead of sweat dripped from his nose.

'Huh,' grunted Sig. 'You'll not be holding much in that hand for a while. Next time, look before you leap.'

Cullen blinked at that. 'I took a spear meant for you,' he said, somewhere between angry and upset.

'What, you thought I needed saving?' Sig growled. 'I would have dealt with the spear, without losing the use of an arm. And you fouled my net throw, which would have ended the battle then and there.'

Cullen withstood Sig's gaze a moment, then looked away.

'I—'

'No,' Sig snapped. 'You acted recklessly. Truth and Courage does not mean hurling yourself in front of every thrown spear.'

Cullen was silent.

Sig stared at him, knew that she had hurt his pride and felt a glimmer of sympathy for him.

He is young and reckless. I can remember that feeling. But I would rather have him ride back to Dun Seren beside me with his pride injured, than be carrying his corpse tied to a horse.

'Give your arm time; rest it properly and it won't be long before you're back to risking your neck,' she said.

Cullen grinned. 'Can't wait,' he said.

Sig rolled her eyes.

'You didn't come away bloodless, either,' Cullen said, looking at the lattice of cuts upon Sig, on her face, forearms, legs. She felt them as she moved, scabs pulling, tight skin itching. A long gash cut across her new tattoo of vines and thorns, added to the one already curling up one arm and down the other, a tale of the lives she'd taken.

'Aye, but mine *are* just scratches.'

'Well, it was a good fight, so it was,' Cullen declared, 'and no denying.'

Tell that to Elgin's dead sword-brothers. Twelve men beneath a pile of stones, now nothing more than cold sacks of meat. He's like a young pup, feeling invincible and too eager to please.

She didn't say anything, though. Cullen had fought well, with courage and skill, and acted to save her life without a thought for his own.

'The Kadoshim is dead, its followers slain,' Sig said by way of agreement.

'We for home, now?' Cullen asked.

'Hammer needs another day or two.' Sig shrugged. 'Should give Keld the time he needs to get back to us.'

'Thought he'd be back by now. He ever been gone this long before?' Cullen asked.

Sig didn't answer, just looked out over the meadow that rolled away from Uthandun's walls towards a bridge that arched across the river Afren, which flowed slow and sluggish to the sea. On the far banks of the river a wall of trees grew, the fringe of the Darkwood, quickly becoming a sea of green and gold and russet that filled the southern horizon.

Where are you, Keld?

In truth Sig was worried about her huntsman. It had been four nights now since the assault on the Kadoshim coven, four nights since he'd gone in pursuit of the shaven-haired acolyte who had fled on the Kadoshim's orders.

Four nights since she'd asked Keld to pursue the Kadoshim's servant.

Keld can look after himself, she reassured herself, burying the worry that stirred within her. *And Elgin has sent his own hunts-men out in search of him.*

And I want to see what the Kadoshim gave to that messenger.

There was more to her worry than Keld's delay. The whole mission was unsettling. Never before had she seen a Kadoshim surrounded by so many fanatics, and they were clearly more than a collection of feeble-minded zealots. They were organized, knew their weapons and were *stealthy*. They'd built a defensible maze within a dozen leagues of Uthandun.

Why? What is behind it?

A dread had filled her, a chill in her blood and bones ever since she'd heard the chanting in the tunnels of that hill, set eyes upon the Kadoshim as it sacrificed its prisoner. And saw the runes inscribed in a circle around the human offering.

This is some new strategy, and I do not like not knowing what it is.

Movement drew Sig's eye: a pinprick in the sky above the

Darkwood. A bird, standing out as different from those others in the air about it because of its flight. Where the others wheeled and soared, riding currents, this one flew straight and unerring towards Uthandun.

Cullen saw it, too, stared with head cocked.

'Is that who I think it is?' he said as the bird drew closer.

'Aye,' Sig rumbled. 'It's Rab.'

A white bird flew to the walls of Uthandun, saw Sig and Cullen and circled above them, squawking raucously as it descended in a flapping of wings, alighting on the timber wall. It was a white crow, its pink beak long and thick, feathers ruffled and poking in odd directions.

'*Finally,*' the crow croaked. '*Rab been searching everywhere for you.*'

A warrior standing guard upon the battlements shuffled away, muttering under his breath.

'Well, you've found us now,' Cullen said to the crow.

'You bring a message from Byrne,' Sig said. It wasn't a question.

'*Rab does,*' the bird answered, hopping along the wall, flexing its wings wide. '*Rab sore,*' it muttered. Cullen reached out his good hand and stroked the bird's wings, Rab leaning into the caress.

'It's a long way to fly from Dun Seren,' Cullen said with a shrug.

'The message,' Sig prompted the white crow.

'*Yes,*' Rab squawked with a clack of his beak. '*First, check that Sig and her crew are safe, Byrne said.*' Rab paused and pointedly looked them over with a beady, red-tinged eye, lingering on Cullen's arm in a sling and the cuts and gashes all over Sig.

'*Hammer. Keld. Hounds?*' Rab squawked.

'Hammer has a knife-wound in her paw, but is healing fine,' Sig said. 'Keld and his hounds are missing; chasing after a man who escaped our raid.'

'*Raid?*' Rab cawed. '*No. First Rab finish message. Byrne wants you back, Dun Seren, Dun Seren. Things happening.*'

'Does she? What things?' Sig frowned.

'*Byrne not tell Rab,*' the crow squawked sadly, shaking his head. '*Rab just messenger.*'

'I know, I know,' Sig said, holding a hand up, having listened many times to the crow's opinions on keeping information from him.

'*Sig go back to Dun Seren, soon as Sig can,*' Rab finished.

'I'm just waiting for Keld,' Sig rumbled, not for the first time thinking of going in search of him herself. But Keld knew Uthandun was the rendezvous point, and Sig was no tracker. Then a thought struck her.

'You could look for Keld, Rab. The sooner we find him, the sooner we can all go back to Dun Seren. We last saw him there,' Sig said, pointing north-east towards a line of hills.

The white crow puffed his chest up, white feathers bristling.

'It would be very helpful,' Cullen said, scratching Rab's neck. 'We're worried for Keld. And we'd be grateful.'

'*Rab is helpful,*' the crow squawked, his head bobbing up and down. '*And Rab like Keld.*' The crow looked up at Sig. '*Rab look for Keld,*' he said, as if the idea were Rab's own.

'Thank you,' Cullen said, nudging Sig with his elbow.

'My thanks,' Sig said with a grunt.

'*Welcome,*' Rab said and hopped off the rampart, wings spreading, catching an updraught, and then the crow was climbing higher, circling over their heads.

'*Rab back soon,*' the crow squawked, and then it was winging away.

'Ah, he's a good bird,' Cullen said with a smile.

Sig raised an eyebrow.

'He is,' Cullen said. 'Always eager to help, that one. And I feel sorry for him. The other crows in the tower are not always kind to him.'

'Are they not?' Sig frowned.

'No. I think it's because of his feathers.' Cullen shrugged. 'To my mind it's wrong to fault a bird for the colour feathers it's born with, don't you think?'

'Huh,' Sig grunted. She did agree, but she was wondering more about why Cullen knew so much about the behaviour of crows in their tower at Dun Seren. Rab was not the only talking crow that resided at the fortress.

'Well, I'm glad Rab has you to look out for him,' Sig said. She sighed, long and thoughtful. 'Come on,' she said. 'I'm hungry, let's find us some hot food. And after that, I need to talk to Queen Nara, and you'd best come with me. She is your distant kin, after all.'

Nara, Queen of Ardain, was sitting in the high chair of Uthandun's great keep, tall, for a human, dark-haired with a pale face. She was wrapped in a thick bear pelt, silver wire wound through her hair, a long knife sheathed at her belt, which Sig approved of. The feast-hall was mostly empty, one man poking at the central fire-pit, stirring embers up and adding logs. As Sig and Cullen arrived, Queen Nara was deep in conversation with Elgin, her battlechief. He had a bandage wound around his head, souvenir of the battle with the Kadoshim's acolytes. Another man stood at Nara's shoulder: Madoc, the Queen's first-sword.

Sig stopped a respectful distance away, Cullen at her side, but Nara gestured them forwards with an impatient flick of her wrist.

'Well met, Queen Nara,' Sig said, giving her best try at a bow. It was more a stiff lean from her hips, for Sig was not used to bowing. Cullen made a better job of it, though his arm in a sling didn't help.

'Enough of that,' Nara said, looking up at Sig. 'There's no need for ceremony between us, Sig. I have long hoped to meet you, who knew my great-grandparents and founders of the realm of Ardain. To think that you spoke with Queen Edana and King Conall,' she said wistfully. 'And you, Cullen, my cousin.' Nara looked Cullen up and down a long moment, serious eyes fixing on his face, her lips pursed. 'There is a statue of King Conall in Dun Taras, and I can see his likeness in you.'

'I am told I am most like my great-grandmother, Coralen, who was Conall's sister,' Cullen said.

Perhaps that is why you throw yourself so willingly into every battle, Sig thought, remembering Coralen fondly. Sig had admired Coralen's ferocity and skill, remembered the first time she'd seen her, fighting traitorous giants from Sig's own Clan, the Jotun. She looked at Cullen, at his red hair and the set of his shoulders and jaw. *But there is something of your great-grandfather in you, too. A kindness about you.* Sig's mind was suddenly full of Corban, the man who had founded their Order. The Bright Star after whom it was named. The man she had grown to respect above all others. She felt a stab of pain at the thought of Corban, barely dulled by the passage of time.

You are greatly missed, Bright Star.

'Perhaps, if you are staying here long enough, you could tell me something of my ancestors,' Nara said to Sig. 'It would be a fine thing to talk to someone who actually knew Edana and Conall, who spoke with them, drank with them, fought with them.'

'I did all of those things,' Sig said. 'Edana and Conall were strong allies in those early days in the fight against the Kadoshim, and faithful friends to Corban, the founder of our Order.'

'Aye.' Nara nodded. 'And nothing has changed there; there will always be a bond between my realm and the swords of Dun Seren.'

'I do not doubt that,' Sig said.

'To prove that my words are not just air, I have something for you,' Nara said. 'A group of my young warriors-in-training have volunteered to accompany you back to Dun Seren. More than forty or so who wish to become warriors of your Order.'

'That is good news,' Sig said, 'for which I am most grateful. The fight goes on, and fresh recruits are ever needed.' Her eyebrows knitted together. 'Riding to Dun Seren does not mean they will remain, though. Our training is hard. It tests both strength of sinew and strength of heart.'

'As it should,' Queen Nara said. 'It is a noble cause.'

'Aye,' Sig agreed.

'All the volunteers know this.' Nara shrugged. 'There is no insult or dishonour in trying and failing.'

'Good,' Sig rumbled. 'And I will be happy to tell you my memories of your kin. If we may, I would stay a night or two more, until Hammer is well enough to travel.'

'Perfect,' Nara said, a smile lighting up her serious face.

'And I hope for my huntsman to join me here. He pursued one of the Kadoshim's servants who fled the battle.'

'Yes, to the meat of it, then. Elgin has told me of what happened inside that hill. A dark and dreadful business, and the impudence of that fell creature,' Nara snarled, 'making its lair so close to one of my fortresses. I only wish that I could have been here in time to be a part of your raid.' Her hand slipped to the hilt of her dagger.

I like this queen more and more.

'Elgin was the greatest of help,' Sig said. 'We would not have succeeded without him. And his men fought bravely. It is no easy thing to walk into the darkness, and worse when you know a Kadoshim is lurking there.'

'My men are brave and true,' Nara said with pride. 'Elgin has told me of all that occurred within the creature's lair. The . . . ceremony.'

'Aye,' Sig said. 'It is troubling. The sacrifice, so many acolytes.' She shook her head. 'This is something new.'

'Do you think there are more, like that?'

Sig shrugged. 'I suspect,' she said, 'but there is no proof – yet.'

'I have sent messengers to my lords throughout Ardain, alerting them. We will scour the land.'

'That is good. We must hunt them down and root them out. The Kadoshim are a plague, their deepest desire to drown the world in our blood.'

'If they are here, in Ardain, I will find them,' Nara said.

There was a noise from the far end of the hall, beyond the closed doors. Shouting, and suddenly all were reaching for weapons, Madoc, Nara's first-sword stepping before her, steel glinting. Sig and Cullen strode across the feast-hall, Elgin with them, shouting commands. The doors opened a crack, a warrior's head poked in. He called something out, but then a shape was bursting through above him, a bundle of white feathers.

'*SIG!*' Rab squawked as the warrior stabbed at the white crow with a spear.

'HOLD!' Sig bellowed. Cullen broke into a run.

Rab saw them and flew straight as an arrow towards them, giving the warrior that had tried to skewer him a baleful glare.

'Why are you here?' Sig said, looking at the daylight slanting through high windows. *He's been gone little over half a day.*

Rab fluttered and perched on Cullen's shoulder, hopping agitatedly from one taloned foot to the other.

'*Follow Rab,*' the bird cawed, flapping back up into the air. '*Quickly, quickly. Rab found Keld's hounds.*'

CHAPTER THIRTEEN

BLEDA

Bleda stood in the courtyard of Drassil, waiting. Jin was nearby, and he felt her eyes upon him, though he refused to look. Ever since Israfil had announced that they would be wed she had smiled at him more, touched him more, even if it were just resting a hand upon his shoulder when he made her laugh.

Part of him liked it. It felt agreeable, he had to admit, and started other sensations fluttering in his belly which weren't unpleasant, either. But he was also acutely aware of his mother's presence at Drassil, as well as Old Ellac and a dozen more of his Sirak kin, and they seemed to be watching him all the time. He was straining to keep his cold-face on so much that it was a relief when he lay down in his cot at night and the torches were extinguished. Muscles in his face ached that he hadn't known were there.

Controlling your emotions is a tricky business.

And Jin seems to be getting worse at it, instead of better.

There was the sound of hooves on cobbles and he was grateful for the distraction, though he felt a swell of sadness as well.

His kin were leaving Drassil.

He saw his mother first, riding into the courtyard as if she lived in a saddle, which she mostly did. She had been in Drassil for most of a moon, and yet they had barely talked, and never alone, though the Ben-Elim had been mostly responsible for that. Bleda looked at her now and had no understanding of what she thought of him, whether she was proud or filled with shame. The thought of that gave him too much pain to cope with and he pushed it away quickly, a rapid blinking the only sign that he'd felt anything at all. His mother's eyes touched him, moved to Jin, then on to the great gates and up to the sky, the ever-present shapes of Ben-Elim riding the currents. Close behind her rode Uldin, the Cheren lord and Jin's father. He did not smile at his daughter, either, but he did dip his head to her for a moment as they approached the pair. Then their retinues were clattering into the courtyard behind them; Ellac was there, looking as balanced as the rest of them in his saddle, despite the lack of one hand.

There was a blast of wind and a rustle of feathers as Israfil and Kol landed gracefully either side of Bleda and Jin, waiting for the riders to reach them. Giants, Queen Ethlinn and her father, Balur One-Eye were also standing nearby, and a host of White-Wings lined the courtyard, a sign of respect or a reminder of strength, Bleda was not sure.

Probably both.

Whatever it was, Bleda sensed a tension in the air. The members of his mother's retinue might be skilled in the art of the cold-face, but some were not as adept at keeping their emotions entirely hidden. Bleda noticed white knuckles on reins, strung bows on saddle-pegs, horses with ears back or flicking as their rider's mood was sensed on some level and transferred. And Israfil and Kol either side of him were fidgeting in their tell-tale ways that possibly only Bleda could read, a quiver through their wings, a tightness in their musculature.

Something is wrong.

Erdene and Uldin reined in before Bleda and Jin, Israfil and Kol.

'We will give you your tithe of flesh,' Uldin said, no pre-amble, 'send you warriors from amongst the Sirak and Cheren.'

A silent sigh seemed to ripple through the courtyard, the

change to Israfil and Kol minuscule, but Bleda noticed it: a relaxing in the set of their wings, a slow breath from Kol.

Ah, Mother and Uldin hadn't told them yet, and Israfil thought they would leave without committing to the terms. He would not have allowed that to happen. My mother and the others were no doubt tense because of the shame of it. Another stain as we bend the knee to our new masters. Why could we just not be left to live free. The Sirak are not made for the Ben-Elim's rules and regulations; we are a people of the plain, moving with the seasons and the sun, no yoke or master to bind us in one place.

'When we return to Arcona we shall send a small party, to show our good faith while we select and organize a larger force,' Erdene said. 'First you shall have one hundred riders from the Sirak, one hundred from the Cheren. More shall come later.'

'The Sirak and Cheren are noted for their honour in this,' Israfil said.

Honour? They are forced to bend the knee, something the Sirak have done to no one for as long as the grass wind has blown.

'They will be the honour guard of our heirs. Of Bleda and Jin. A wedding-gift to show our commitment to their forthcoming marriage.'

Even the word *marriage* caused Bleda some significant discomfort and proved difficult to keep from his face.

Our honour guard! Will Israfil allow this? Technically the warriors would not be answerable to any except Jin and me. We would be their lords.

A silence grew, lengthening as Israfil considered this. Just as Bleda thought the time to answer without giving insult had passed, Israfil nodded.

'Of course,' he said.

Erdene nodded, and then she looked at Bleda.

'May your arrow fly true,' she said to him.

'And your horse never stumble,' he gave the response, feeling a joyous warmth spread through him.

She thinks of me as kin.

Uldin said something to Jin, though Bleda did not hear it, his heart still soaring from his mother's acknowledgement, and then Erdene and Uldin were riding away, towards the open gates of Drassil, their retinue following behind. Only Old Ellac looked at Bleda as they rode past.

Before Erdene and Uldin reached the gates, a dozen giants mounted upon bears lumbered out before them, an honour guard to escort the Arcona lords partway along the eastern road.

Bleda and Jin stood watching their kin, giants before them, a handful of Ben-Elim circling the skies above them as they rode a short way along the road of the dead, amongst the field of cairns, before they turned and headed east, moving swiftly out of sight. Bleda wished he could run up the wide stairwell to the battlements and watch them until they faded into the distance.

She is gone, but I have her parting to me. And also those words she whispered in my ear while on the weapons-field, the day that Jin shamed Riv, the trainee White-Wing.

'Well, what are you two doing, standing about?' Kol said to them with an easy smile, glancing up at the sun, which had not long cleared Drassil's high walls. 'You're due at lessons, are you not?'

Bleda and Jin burst into the teaching chamber, a high-vaulted room of stone and wide-arched windows, one long wall filled with shelves full to bursting with scrolls and parchments. It was a room that Bleda was more familiar with than any other part of the fortress, because he had spent such a large portion of his life sitting in there, learning his letters, the histories, the theories of weapon and war, herbs and healing, the ways of earth and sky. And of course, the teachings of Elyon, how to live a life of faith, strength and purity. Of sacrifice, honour and duty.

Though that sounds more like the Ben-Elim than Elyon, to me.

It was fair to say that the Ben-Elim had brought more with them than just rules and an iron-shod foot upon the neck of those who lived and breathed within the Banished Lands. *Though no trade that is forced upon you is a fair trade.*

'Where's Jibril?' Bleda said, skidding to a halt.

A giant stood before one of the long windows. He was leaning over a table, hands resting upon it like two knotted saplings. It was a giant Bleda knew well, or better than most at Drassil, because it was the giant who had plucked him from Israfil's grip that day in Arcona when he had been taken from his people. He had ridden with this giant upon the back of a bear all the long way from Arcona to Drassil, and for a giant he was more talkative than most.

'Alcyon, where is Jibril?' Bleda asked again.

Jibril was their tutor, a dark-haired Ben-Elim who had taught them their histories ever since they had arrived in Drassil, some five years gone. Different Ben-Elim taught different subjects. Bleda suspected it was not because they specialized in different subjects, with some knowing more or less about certain subjects. Bleda believed that all the Ben-Elim were equally knowledgeable, but that they also had their own likes and dislikes, subjects that brought them pleasure and subjects that they disdained.

'Jibril is escorting your kin along the eastern road,' Alcyon said. 'So Israfil asked me to give you your lesson today.'

'You?' Jin said, looking Alcyon up and down.

Much as any other giant, he stood a man and a half tall and was thick with muscle, his face a slab of forehead and angular lines, long moustache hanging and bound with leather. A tattoo of vine and thorn trailed up one arm and partway down the other. The things that were different about him when compared to other giants were his hair and weapons. His hair was shaved from his head, apart from a thick black strip across the centre of his skull, plaited into his warrior braid. And he wielded twin axes, single-bladed rather than one of the double-bladed variety that most giants chose. He usually wore them across his back, but now they were leaning against a wall, long-shafted with hooked, bearded blades.

'Yes, me. I am not Ben-Elim, but I have a little knowledge inside this head of mine.' He prodded his temple with a thick finger.

Jin looked as if she didn't quite believe him.

'What are you looking at?' Bleda asked, moving over to look at the table. A huge parchment was spread out, a map inked upon it. Bleda frowned as he stared at it, for at first it had looked like a map of the Banished Lands, but where the Land of the Faithful now existed, it was divided into different realms. Bleda smiled to see Arcona, a broad expanse to the east of the dark stain that was Forn Forest.

'Isiltir, Carnutan, Helveth, Tenebral,' Bleda read. 'What are these places?' he asked.

'That is the Banished Lands before the Day of Wrath,' Alcyon said. 'There were many realms then.'

'Where have they gone?' Bleda asked.

'They have been welcomed into the Protectorate of the Ben-Elim, become part of the Land of the Faithful,' Alcyon said.

Is this what will happen to Arcona? Bleda thought, a shiver of fear rippling through him, *Absorbed into the Protectorate, as if it had never existed.*

'Sit,' Alcyon said, waving a hand and rolling up the map.

There was a table and bench for their letters, with sheaves of parchment, quills, pots of ink, blotters, a supply of salt and powders of ground cuttlefish. If writing was not required, there were other chairs that they would usually take – more comfortable, covered in leather and fur – usually used when a subject that required a level of deeper thinking was being taught.

Bleda took one look at Alcyon's huge hands and concluded

that he would not be teaching the art of letters, and so sat in a more comfortable chair of leather, draped with fur. Jin followed suit, though she dragged her chair over so that she was much closer to Bleda.

'What are you teaching us, then, with that knowledgeable brain of yours?' Jin asked Alcyon, keeping her face free of the sarcasm Bleda was sure lurked behind her dark eyes. She wiped a stray strand of her jet-black hair from her face, her glance flickering to Bleda, the hint of a smile twitching her lips.

Alcyon walked around the table and sat on the bench, the wood creaking. He smiled and spread his arms wide.

'What would you like me to teach you?'

'Jibril never gives us a choice!' Jin said, surprised.

Bleda shot her a dark look.

'Strategies of war,' Bleda said hurriedly, thinking to make the most of this slip in Ben-Elim discipline.

Alcyon frowned, his massive brow bunching like a storm cloud.

'And how does Jibril teach that?' he rumbled.

'Battles are described, the forces involved, opposing sides. Numbers, styles of combat, strengths, weaknesses. Strategies and tactics,' Bleda said with a wave of his hand. Jin looked at him, a broad smile, smoothed away quickly.

'Ah, I see,' Alcyon said, regarding them both thoughtfully. Bleda thought he'd seen through his plan, but then Alcyon nodded. 'All right then. The Battle of Drassil. Midwinter's Day, the first Year of Lore.'

'We've heard that one so many times,' Bleda said. It was true, they had. All about the Ben-Elim's triumphant entry into the Banished Lands, saving the beleaguered forces of mankind from the overwhelming numbers of Kadoshim and their terrible allies. Jin pulled a bored face.

'What battle, then?' Alcyon said.

'Name some,' Bleda said with a shrug.

'The Battle of Dun Bagul: that one was fought twenty years after Drassil.' He looked at them both.

'Can we hear a few others, then choose?' Jin asked sweetly.

Alcyon shrugged, making his bench creak again. 'The Battle of Haldis, a few years before Drassil. Domhain Pass. Gramm's Hold, Taur—'

'What about the Battle of Varan Falls,' Bleda said.

Alcyon frowned at him. 'How have you heard of that one?' he asked.

'Jibril's mentioned it,' Jin said.

'He has?'

He did, but only to dismiss the idea of ever telling us about it.

'Why would you think he wouldn't?' Bleda asked Alcyon.

'Because that was a bad day for the Ben-Elim, that one.' He paused. 'A grievous day for us all.' Quieter.

'It's important to analyse the defeats, so that they do not happen again, no?' Bleda said.

'True,' Alcyon murmured, rubbing his chin. He stared past them, a far-away look in his eyes. 'Very well, then.'

Alcyon tugged on his moustache.

'First of all, it isn't the Battle of Varan Falls. It's the Battle of Varan's Fall.'

'Oh. I thought it must have taken place close to a waterfall, or something like that,' Jin said.

'Well, it did, which adds to the confusion. It took place in the north-west of Forn Forest. But it was given its name because it was the battle where Varan fell.'

'Varan?'

'A giant, great amongst us,' Alcyon said, a sadness behind his eyes. 'And my friend. He was brave and loyal. Lord of the Jotun Clan for a short time, before he bent the knee to Ethlinn as she united the Clans and we became one; what was left of us.'

A silence fell as Alcyon drifted in thought. Bleda saw the giant differently, then, if only for a few moments. Until now he had only ever thought of the Ben-Elim, the giants and White-Wings as the *Victors*. The triumphant, conquering army that were strangers to loss and defeat. Briefly he saw grief writ across Alcyon's face, in his eyes, and for a few heartbeats felt a sense of kinship with him, a bond created between those who suffered the same pain.

Alcyon shook his head.

'We had information that the Kadoshim were building a fortress, secreted in the north-east of Forn. Our informants spoke of a place built largely beneath the ground, a subterranean structure of labyrinthine tunnels. So, we set out to find it. Giants, Ben-Elim, White-Wings. And we worked with our allies, the Order of the Bright Star.'

'I thought there was bad blood between the Order and Drassil?' Bleda said. 'Aren't they not to be trusted?'

'The Order? I would trust any one of them with my life, and frequently have.' Alcyon shrugged, an acknowledgement. 'There *are* some trust issues, between the Order and the Ben-Elim, aye. But the Kadoshim are enemy of all, and the Order are as fervent in their hatred of the Kadoshim as the Ben-Elim are.'

'But I—' Bleda began, but Alcyon held his hand up.

'If you wish to hear of the Battle of Varan's Fall before horns sound and you're wanted in the prayer-hall, then I suggest you hold your words.'

Bleda and Jin nodded silently.

'A force marched from Drassil, me amongst them. Other giants, Balur leading us. The White-Wings, and Ben-Elim.'

'How many of you?' Bleda asked.

'A thousand, roughly. Half of that White-Wings. Our plan was to meet with a force of the Bright Star, marching east from their fortress of Dun Seren, and assault the Kadoshim's new lair together. We marched north-east, made slow progress the further we travelled. Forn can be a dark and dangerous place, well suited to the hiding of demons, which is why we have spent a hundred years building roads and thinning the trees. But this part of Forn, well, we hadn't given it our attention at that time, so the trees were ancient, their canopy a lattice of limbs wide as my leg, and the paths thick with thorn and vine. And rivers were many, draining from Forn into the Grinding Sea. It was hard going. Until we came to a well-trod path – a road almost, the ground cleared and levelled, wide enough to march upon. We thought it the Kadoshim's, cleared by them as they carried materials for the building of their lair. The Ben-Elim could not scout well, hindered by the dense canopy, but what they saw they deemed safe. We guessed the Kadoshim believed themselves secure that far north, hidden by the warp and weft of Forn.'

His mouth twisted in a snarl.

'We guessed wrong. It was a salmon trap.'

'A what?' Bleda and Jin asked together.

'When you fish for salmon, the easiest way to catch them is you build an easier path for them to follow, steering them into safe waters, or so they think. But it leads to nowhere, and when they are piled up in their road to nowhere like cattle in a pen . . .' He snapped his fingers, a loud crack when it is made by giant fingers.

'We were late to our meeting point, you understand. Which saved us, I don't doubt. We heard the screams, the sound of battle, ringing out through the forest. I ran, because I knew it was the Order, and had both kin and friends amongst them. Balur ran with me, all the giants did, but the Ben-Elim and White-Wings, they were more cautious, fearing an ambush. Sensible, as that's what happened, but sometimes you just listen to your heart. The Ben-Elim were none too happy about that, I heard afterwards.'

'Did the Ben-Elim punish you for your disobedience?' Bleda asked, knowing that Israfil came down like a hammer on the smallest transgressions at Drassil. Part of the Way of Elyon, as were all the imposed rules of the Ben-Elim.

'Disobedience?' Alcyon frowned.

'The Ben-Elim are your masters, and you ran off and abandoned them, disobeyed their order to stay with them.'

'The Ben-Elim are not master to us giants.' Alcyon scowled. 'We are *allies*. Drassil is our home, built by giants. We agreed for the Ben-Elim to reside here. They are our guests.'

'Seems they are the ones giving all of the orders,' Jin said.

'Aye, well, the Ben-Elim like their rules. Ethlinn is a diplomatic woman and so would not speak openly against them, unless she deemed it vital; but we will not be ruled.'

That's interesting. I thought the giants were another conquered people, like my Clan.

'So, the battle,' Jin said. 'You ran off and left the Ben-Elim behind . . .'

'Aye. It was part of the Kadoshim plan, it became clear after the battle, to separate us. The Ben-Elim and White-Wings were attacked separately.'

He sighed, lost in thought again.

'The Order were overrun when we arrived, their backs to a river and waterfall, beset on all other sides by the Kadoshim and their fanatics. From the trees above, from out of the undergrowth, the very air seemed to seethe with them. I saw many comrades already fallen, friends who had fought and survived the darkness that was the Battle of Drassil. My son still stood, thank Elyon above.'

'What about Varan?' Bleda asked. 'Was he with you? Marching from Drassil?'

'Varan? No. He had joined the Order of the Bright Star many years before. We all fight the Kadoshim, just choose who we stand beside when we do it, that's all. Varan was standing with his brother, Gunil. Much younger than Varan, he was, born after the Ben-Elim came, little more than a giantling, really. But he was fierce, a great warrior. The two of them were standing waist-deep in the river, the waterfall roaring at their backs, Kadoshim slain in a heap about them. I ran to them, but it was chaos. Battle always is, once you're in it, and if anyone tells you different they're a liar. It's no clinical act of strategy, then, though that helps to begin with. But when it comes down to it, it's blood, steel and muck, stench and guts and screaming loud enough to burst your head, fear and rage and everything else in between, and you keep swinging your blade at the foe in front of you until your arms are numb and there are no more left, or you die.

'I lost sight of Varan, tried to fight my way to him, though moving in one direction in a battle is a hard enough task. The Ben-Elim finally arrived, the White-Wings with them, blood-ied by another ambush that had been held in reserve for them. By then the Kadoshim knew they were finished and melted away, back into the forest. By then no one was standing in the river, let alone fighting in it. I waded in, the water thick with bodies and blood, and found Varan, floating face-down. Fallen with a host of wounds.'

Alcyon hung his head, and Bleda was shocked to see a tear rolling down the giant's cheek. Jin was staring at him with a look of disgust.

He would be cast out of the Sirak for such a display of weakness; his emotions his master.

'His brother?' Bleda asked, wanting to end this display. It made him feel uncomfortable.

'He fell over the waterfall, I was told,' Alcyon said. 'A long drop, and then the Grinding Sea.' He sniffed and wiped his face. 'So that was Varan's Fall, and a dark day it was, too.'

'What about the Kadoshim's lair?' Jin asked. 'What happened when you got there?

'We never found it. Perhaps it was all a fiction, the intelligence we received false, all of it to lure us to that ambush. If we had entered into that killing ground together, it would have been much worse.'

Alcyon looked at them both.

'So. Analyse,' he said to them. 'Why did we lose? Or at least, why did we not win?'

'Overconfidence,' Bleda said.

'That's right. Good,' Alcyon said. 'Many battles and skirmishes have been fought with the Kadoshim since the Battle of Drassil, scores, and we had never lost a one. Varan's Fall was no crushing defeat, mind; but it was a defeat nonetheless. What else?'

'Planning, scouting, knowing the ground,' Jin said. 'Jibril says they are key steps to victory.'

'Aye, true enough,' Alcyon agreed. 'The Kadoshim were far better prepared than us, that was plain to see. They knew we were coming. Knew we were two forces. Knew the routes we would approach by, and they laid their ambushes well. And we blundered in, expecting to crush them as we had before. Huh.' He wagged a finger at them both. 'Never underestimate your enemy, but especially not the Kadoshim. Their numbers were winnowed on that first day, when Asroth fell, and there are certainly far fewer of them than Ben-Elim, but they are creatures of deep cunning.'

Like their kin, the Ben-Elim.

Horns blew outside, echoing in to them.

'Best be off for prayers,' Alcyon said.

'Are you not coming?' Jin asked.

'Me? No,' Alcyon said, a twist of his lips.

Bleda noted that with interest.

So, giants are not the obedient slaves I thought them.

'Our thanks,' Bleda said. 'You have taught us much today.'

More than old Jibril ever has.

Alcyon waved a hand but had that faraway look again. Bleda and Jin rose and left him to his thoughts.

'See, they are not unbeatable,' Jin said to him as they stepped out into the street. 'Not like the Cheren and Sirak will be when we are wed.'

She squeezed his hand and ran for the prayer-hall looking back to grin at the startled expression that cracked his cold-face.

CHAPTER FOURTEEN

SIG

I should have gone straight after Keld, not sat at Uthandun waiting for him, Sig berated herself, not for the first time, as she ran through the rain, each drop feeling like a chip of ice flung into her face by a spite-filled wind. She'd left Hammer in the stable at Uthandun, her paw not yet recovered enough for a hard run across the wind-blasted hills of Ardain. At the edge of Sig's vision she glimpsed Rab, the albino crow flapping stoically onwards, a white blur amidst the sheeting downpour.

Cullen rode alongside Sig, head down and cloak up against the wind and rain. Sig had thought about ordering him to stay behind, but he was part of her crew. He'd splinted and bound his wounded arm with strips of wood and leather.

Elgin rode at Sig's left, grim-faced, a score of men in column behind them. Nara had wanted to come herself, but Elgin and Sig had convinced the Queen of Ardain to remain at Uthandun. Rab had said that he'd found Keld's hounds, not Keld himself. They'd left as soon as they could after Rab's arrival, making the most of what day remained before nightfall. Since then Sig had hardly shared a word with the white crow, who had led them north-west, past the hill where the Kadoshim had been discovered, on into foothills that had once separated the realms of Narvon and Cambren, long united now by the marriage of Conall and Edana over a hundred years ago.

They'd made camp as darkness fell. Rab had disappeared,

only rejoining them with a screeching admonishment to hurry up as dawn crept unannounced across the land, a grey, rain-soaked shroud. Now Sig guessed it was close to highsun, though that was hard to tell – a diffuse glow only hinting at a sun beyond the leaden sky. They were climbing steadily into the hills, the terrain a bleak mixture of exposed granite and stunted, twisted trees.

'Sets a good pace, that crow of yours,' Elgin said.

'Aye,' grunted Sig, concentrating on the loose rocks and rabbit holes at her feet. To her surprise and anger she was feeling the pace that Rab was setting, lungs burning, legs aching – she, who used to run for a ten-night as easy as rising.

There's a lot to be said for riding bears into battle, but I'm going to have to do something about this.

Ahead, Rab began to circle a spot, spiralling downwards.

Sig wiped rain from her eyes, saw forms materializing upon the path where it narrowed before a sharp turn. To the right was a sheer rock face, to the left a steep drop to a fast-flowing stream. Sig slowed, loosened the sword sheathed across her back, Elgin and Cullen doing the same.

Bodies were scattered across the path, twisted in death. Eight, ten, Sig counted, checking them carefully. Keld was not amongst them, though Sig found his huntsman's axe embedded in the skull of a shaven-haired man. Sig put her foot on the man's head and wrenched the axe free. All of the dead had shaved heads in common, like those they had found at the Kadoshim's lair. Many of the death wounds were ragged tears, flesh torn and ripped. One of Keld's hounds, Hella the brindle bitch, lay strewn across the path, bodies piled around her, a bodiless arm in her mouth, strips of frayed flesh and sinew hanging at the shoulder. A score of puncture wounds crusted dark with blood ranged along the hound's side, her back leg almost chopped clean through.

Sig knelt by the dead hound and put her hand on its head a moment.

'Thank you, Hella, faithful hound, for your sacrifice. You will be avenged.'

'Ach.' Cullen spat. 'Keld will take this hard.'

Aye, if he still lives, Sig thought. *Keld would never have left Hella like this. He's either slain or captured.* She felt a stab of fear for her friend, quickly morphing into a swell of rage.

They will pay for this.

Beyond the dead was a small cabin, situated just around the bend. It looked like a goat-herder's hut. Elgin and a handful of men approached it, Elgin kicking the door down with one booted foot, sticking his head in.

'Empty,' he called over his shoulder.

A squawking drew Sig's attention. She looked around for Rab, couldn't see him at first, then spotted the crow down by the stream at the bottom of the slope.

'Come, come,' Rab was squawking, hopping about upon a rock, bobbing and shaking his head, muttering to himself.

'QUICK!' Rab screeched.

Sig made her way down the slope, skidding and sliding on slick, goat-cropped grass, the sound of others behind her.

Rab had found Keld's other hound, Fen, lying upon the corpse of another shaven-haired man, a long, bloody knife still gripped in the man's fist. His throat was a red, ragged wound.

The hound's hind legs trailed in the stream. He was covered in wounds, one ear missing, but he was still alive, his big chest rising and falling.

'Poor Fen,' Rab croaked mournfully. *'Sig help Fen?'*

'Aye,' Sig grunted, ripping a strip from her cloak and soaking it in the stream, then setting to washing out the hound's wounds, fingers gently probing for broken bones. Footsteps thudded around them as Elgin and a few others joined them.

'Tracks leading on into the hills,' Elgin said. 'My tracker says ten, maybe twelve of them. Looks like your man was still alive then. He tells me they're maybe one day ahead of us, so we've gained on them.' He looked at the big hound, the shallow rise and fall of its chest. 'We should be after them.'

'A few moments,' Sig said. 'Keld will take his axe to me if he hears I left his Fen to die.' She was rummaging through her pack, crushing dried comfrey and lavender in her big fists, drizzling honey into the mix and packing it into the hound's many wounds. Fen whined, lifted his head to look at Sig, then slumped back down. Sig wrapped bandages where she could.

'One man to stay and guard him. Give him water.' Sig unstoppered her brot bottle and poured some into the strip she'd torn from her cloak, squeezed a few drops into Fen's mouth. 'And give him this.'

'One man to guard a dying hound? Can we spare him, not knowing what lies ahead?' Elgin frowned.

'This is no ordinary hound, as you well know. Storm's wolven blood runs in his veins, and Keld will not be best pleased if we abandon him while there's breath in his body.'

'I am not convinced of the wisdom,' Elgin said.

'*Fen one of US!*' Rab squawked, shaking his wings at Elgin.

'Trust me on this, and I'll not forget the favour,' Sig said, holding Elgin's gaze. The battlechief rubbed his bearded jaw, finally nodded and bellowed up the slope to his men.

'Rab, after Keld,' Sig grunted and the crow leaped into the air, flapping and rising. Sig bent and stroked Fen's head. 'Live,' she whispered, 'Keld still needs you.'

The hound whined and then Sig was climbing the slope; Cullen was waiting for her at the top. She handed him Keld's axe. 'Look after this for Keld,' she said. 'He'll be wanting it back.'

'I'll keep it warm for him, maybe crack a few skulls with it before I put it in his hand,' Cullen said.

Sig crawled uphill through the grass, doing all she could to hide her bulk, her breath sounding to her as if it would wake a sleeping draig. Four of Elgin's men were with her, the rest back on the path, waiting for the signal. For three days she'd cursed the rain, but now that it had stopped she wished that it was still falling, knowing it would have served to hide their approach better than the clear sky above her, slipping from blue to purple as the sun sank into the horizon.

Dusk settled about them, that time when shadows were thick as mist, and up ahead Sig saw the darker shape of a cabin, a handful of outbuildings, a pig pen, judging by the smell drifting down the hill to her. Behind and above the cabin on the hilltop there was the silhouette of a large mound, with patches of the sun's last rays gleaming through it.

What is that? An unlit bonfire?

Rab had returned, after scouting ahead, with the news that Keld was only half a league ahead. The crow had seen Keld dragged by his captors into the cabin that stood before Sig now. Sig's first instinct was to charge in, screaming death and murder at her enemies, but she knew Keld would be the first to have his throat cut. So she was hoping stealth would serve them better; Elgin and the others were still mounted and waiting a short distance away for the sound of battle.

What are they doing here? Why is Keld still alive? Why didn't they just kill him back on the path with his hounds?

She crawled closer to the cabin, maybe a hundred of her long strides away, then closer still, grass tickling her nose.

A scream rang out from the cabin, raw and full of pain.

Keld.

Sig was on her feet before she realized it, the others a few heartbeats behind her, and then she was running at the cabin, drawing a knife from its sheath at her belt.

A plan will only take you so far.

The thunder of her iron-shod boots, every breath loud as a drumbeat in her head, behind her Elgin's men, running, steel hissing from scabbards. Another scream, long and lingering. The sound of a door opening on the far side of the cabin, footsteps on wooden boards, then mud. Sig pointed; three of the men with her peeled away to circle the cabin. The drum of hooves, distant.

And then Sig was there, leaping up the wooden steps and kicking at the door. It collapsed inwards, a cloud of dust exploding. As it settled, Sig saw the glow of firelight, faces turned, all staring at her, ten, twelve people, more in the shadows. And Keld, in the centre of the room, strapped to a frame similar to the one Sig had seen inside the Kadoshim's lair, cross-shaped, his wrists and ankles strapped tight, stripped to the waist, drenched in sweat. Fingers were missing from his left hand, blood streaming down his forearm, dripping to the floorboards, pooling. He was spitting curses at his captors, foam flecking his mouth.

The closest shaven-haired man to Keld was standing frozen with mouth open, bloody knife raised.

Sig threw her own knife, the big blade spun, crunched into the man's face, hurling him halfway across the room. A moment's silence, then men were rushing her, swords, knives, axes in fists. Sig's longsword scraped from its scabbard across her back and she snarled a curse at them, striding through the doorway, not waiting for them to reach her.

'TRUTH AND COURAGE,' she bellowed, swinging her sword, a head spinning with her first blow, the body's momentum causing it to stumble on into her. Sig shoved it aside, fouling a man's rush at her, her fist crunching into his mouth, lips mangled, teeth spraying as he dropped on top of the headless corpse. Steel clashed as blows rained upon her, catching some with her blade, others thudding into the shield strapped across her back, or glancing off her chainmail shirt. Then Elgin's men were pounding up the stairs behind her to protect her flanks and rear as she forged into the room, carving her way to Keld.

Vaguely Sig was aware of a door on the far side of the room bursting open: the rest of Elgin's men that had accompanied her storming in, falling upon the shaven-haired acolytes, and beyond the timber walls she heard the thunder of hooves. But it was all as if through mist, her focus on Keld and anyone fool enough to get in her way. She hacked, stabbed and chopped her way through flesh, bone and steel, men hurling themselves at her, one scratching at her face, raking her with blackened nails, teeth snapping at her neck. She headbutted him with her jutting brow, crushing his nose, grabbed a fistful of his cloak's hood and slammed his head into her knee, then cast his limp body aside.

Then she was standing before Keld; his eyes were wild with pain, but he recognized her, mouth moving, words whispered, incoherent at first.

'Forgive me,' Sig finally heard.

'For what?' Sig grunted as she tugged at his bonds. They were tied tight, cutting into his flesh. She sliced through them, taking his weight as he fell onto her.

'Failing you,' he mumbled, spittle and blood hanging from his jaw.

'Ach, my friend,' Sig said, 'it is I who has failed you. I should have been here sooner.'

'Better late, than . . . never,' he said, a twitch of a manic smile. 'My bairns?' Keld growled.

Sig took a deep breath.

'Fen still lives,' she said, 'but Hella is gone.'

Keld's face twisted, a blast of raw grief, then Sig was turning as an acolyte rushed towards her, sword raised high. Keld slumped to his knees. Sig caught the blow on her blade, but before she could retaliate, an axe slammed into the acolyte's head, wrenched free in a spray of bone and gore as the man collapsed, twitching. Cullen stood over the corpse.

'Brought your axe for you,' he said to Keld.

'Good . . . lad,' Keld mumbled. 'The message,' he said, voice trailing off. His head lolled, eyes rolling.

'The message?' Sig prompted as she and Cullen crouched down beside Keld. His eyes snapped back into focus.

'Out there,' Keld said with a nod of his head to the back door. 'He left, just before . . .'

Not again. Sig snarled, remembering the sound of a door opening and footsteps as she'd approached the cabin. 'See to Keld,' she ordered Cullen as she stood and ran for the rear door, bursting out into semi-darkness. A frantic glance. She saw Elgin and his warriors leaping from their horses, the ground churned to thick mud. One rider bearing down upon a fleeing acolyte. Sig's eyes swept further out, the small hold a mass of shadowy buildings. Then movement, higher up the hill. A spark and a torch flared to life.

Sig ran down the mud-churned track that wound through a tangle of outbuildings, ever higher, burst into open ground to see a shaven-haired man shoving his torch deep into the piled bonfire. Smoke bloomed, leaking into the night, the flicker and crackle of flames as wood ignited. Tongues of fire curled sky-wards, an orange glow spreading through the heart of the bonfire. Sig ran at the acolyte, who saw her and drew a sword from his hip with one hand, a short axe with the other, and strode to meet her.

Steel clashed, Sig parrying the sword slashing at her throat, pivoting so that the axe whistled through air a handspan from her head, punched the pommel of her sword into the man's face. He staggered, spitting blood and teeth, and Sig, shoving him hard in the chest, sending him stumbling back, swung her sword in a loop over her head and down low, chopping into his leg just above the knee, shearing clean through flesh and bone, trailing droplets of blood in the air that glistened like a string of red pearls in the bonfire's glare.

The acolyte collapsed screaming, dropped his sword. Sig kicked the axe and fist it was gripped within. Bones snapped and the axe went spinning away.

'What was your message?' Sig snarled, but the acolyte just looked up at her, the bonfire crackling and popping into scorching life, heat rolling off it in waves. The acolyte grinned through bloody lips. Sig put one iron-shod boot upon the man's severed leg and ground her heel, screams ringing out across the hill, louder than the hiss and crackle of flames.

'What was the message?' Sig growled.

The acolyte began to laugh, blood and spittle frothing through his shattered teeth and mangled lips. Sig leaned down and grabbed a fistful of his shirt, hauling him up and shaking him, but he only laughed more wildly.

Footsteps behind her, Cullen supporting Keld, behind them Elgin and a handful of his men. Sig shook the acolyte again, and a scrap of parchment slipped from where it had been stuffed inside his shirt. Sig dropped the acolyte and snatched up the parchment, unfolding and reading by the firelight as Cullen and Keld reached her.

'What does it say?' Elgin asked, as Sig shared a grim look with Cullen and Keld. She showed the message to Elgin – one word scrawled upon it.

Anois.

'What does that mean?' Elgin shouted over the wind and the hungry flames.

Cullen slapped Sig's arm, pointed through the dark. In the distance a pinprick of light appeared, flaring brighter, roaring into crackling life. And then, further away still, another flame flickering, another bonfire igniting. The sensation of creeping dread that had been haunting Sig swelled in her veins, making the hairs on her neck stand on end.

'It is a word from the Old Tongue,' Sig said, not taking her eyes from the string of beacons that were appearing like stars in the darkness. 'And it means: Now.'

CHAPTER FIFTEEN

DREM

Drem woke to his da's boot kicking the wooden leg of his bed.

'It's still dark,' Drem mumbled.

'Things to do,' Olin answered, giving the bed leg another kick for good measure, then turning and leaving Drem's room. For a moment Drem thought about rolling over; the change in routine unsettled him. He liked to see the grey of dawn before he rose.

'Drem,' his da's voice called, insistent.

With a groan, he hauled himself out of bed. It was a painful experience, and not just because the net of sleep still had a few hooks in him. He was battered and bruised all over from his fight in Kergard.

Fight! Beating, more like.

Five nights had passed since the skirmish at Kergard's market. His da had helped Drem to the wain and, with Fritha climbing in as well, they'd returned home as quickly as possible. Before they left town, Calder the smith, one of the original members of Kergard's Assembly, had told them that the trappers Drem had fought with were new to Kergard, having arrived that day. Apparently they were all kin, and were looking to find work and a roof at the new mine on the shore of the Starstone Lake.

'A lot like them coming up from the south,' Calder had said with a grimace. 'They don't like what the Kadoshim are up to, or the Ben-Elim's rules; fair enough,' Calder said, 'but they'll not come up here and act like there are no rules at all.'

Drem pulled his breeches and boots on, wincing as muscles complained and bruises throbbed. His nose was swollen from where he'd been headbutted, and he was still blowing thick clots of blood from it.

This'd better be good, he grumbled to himself as he went in search of his da.

Drem found him sitting on the steps of their cabin, looking out onto the courtyard as dawn leached into the world. His da had been quiet, impenetrably so since the fight. He'd been troubled and withdrawn before that, thinking on the lump of black rock that he'd buried in the paddock, but since the fight Drem had felt as if he was living on his own.

'You all right, Da?' Drem said as he sat down beside him, shivering as a cold wind clawed his skin. His da just pointed into the distance, into the darkness. Drem frowned. There was a light, flickering small and bright in the ink-black of night.

'What?' Drem whispered. 'Is that a fire? In the Bonefells?'

'Would have to be a big fire,' his da said, a frown turning his face into a place of deep-shadowed valleys.

'Don't like the look of that,' Drem muttered. Absently, he pressed fingers to his neck, found the soothing rhythm of his pulse.

'And look, there,' Olin said, twisting to point to the south-west. There was another pinprick of light, smaller and fainter than the first.

They turned back and watched the closer flame in silence as dawn pushed back the night, shadows solidifying, then slowly dissolving as darkness retreated before light, the fire up in the Bonefells dimming with the coming of the sun in a grey, cloud-bloated sky.

Looks like snow, Drem thought, his breath misting.

'All my life I've tried to protect you,' his da said, breaking the silence. 'Ever since your mam . . .' A muscle in his jaw twitched and he pinched his nose. 'I swore to keep you from harm. To keep you from war, from the evil that men do. Not just men – other things.'

Aye, you've watched over me every step. But what is it you're so scared of? What is it you're protecting me from? What does 'other things' mean?

'The Kadoshim?' Drem whispered.

Olin shrugged. 'Aye. And their kin.' A silence settled between them again, Drem's da clearly thinking on the past. Drem wanted to prompt him to speak, but feared to rush him, knew that his da could easily go the other way. He liked to hear him talking like this, so he took a long, steady breath and concentrated on controlling his frustration.

'That's why we have travelled, kept moving, just you and me, Drem,' his da said with a sigh. He reached out a hand and patted his son's knee. 'And it's worked, so far. For sixteen years I've kept us moving, running ahead of the tide. But it's remorseless.'

'What *tide*, Da? Running from what?'

'I've told you,' Olin said, waving his hand vaguely towards the south.

'Never straight, you haven't. More in riddles than facts.'

'Never mind that, now,' his da said, a clear end to that line of conversation. Olin fell silent, eyes distant.

Has he committed a crime, been hunted for something?

Olin shook his head, sucked in a deep breath and looked at Drem. 'You don't like to fight, I saw that in you the other day.'

'I'm sorry, Da,' Drem said. 'I wish I was as brave and—'

'You are brave,' his da interrupted, a fierceness in his voice. 'I asked Fritha what happened. She told me what you did. You, against eight men. Trying to protect the weak, the outnumbered. It reminds me of an oath I once heard . . .' He was silent again. 'Knowing what kind of man you've become, makes me prouder than I can tell you.' He put a hand over his heart, his lips twisted, but no words came out.

Drem wanted to say something in response, but his da's speech had hit him like a hammer, stolen his words and set a lump growing in his throat that words couldn't get past, anyway.

'I wish your mam was here to see you now.'

I wish that, too.

They sat in silence awhile, Drem feeling happier than he could remember.

'You're a good learner, Drem,' his da said. 'You listen; you think things through. Like talking sense to people, showing some kindness, and some manners.'

'Aye, well, I've seen you do it,' Drem said. 'Seen it work.'

'It does, most of the time. But not *all* of the time. Like the other day. Sometimes the only answer is blood and steel.' He sucked in a long, deep breath, back straightening, as if setting his mind to a task. 'I've taught you how to use your fists, if you've needed to, some spear-work, and how to use a knife and axe to defend yourself. But it's time for something more, now. In case that tide that I've kept us running from catches up with us. I've thought we could find peace, you and me. That I could keep us separate from the darkness of this world.' He sighed, rubbing his eyes. 'Looking back on it, I should have taught you a long time ago.'

'What do you mean, Da?'

'This,' his da said. He stood up and strode down the creaking timber steps into their courtyard, the ground frozen hard. Drem followed him and his da turned and threw something to him, Drem instinctively catching it.

It was a wooden sword, long and heavy, and Drem saw his da was holding one, too.

His da had taught him some rudiments with a sword, but it was not a weapon that a trapper required in the same way as axe, knife and spear, so it felt awkward and strange in Drem's hand.

What is it that I need to fight with a sword? Why won't he just tell me?

'Time to learn some real swordcraft,' Olin said, setting his feet and raising his own wooden sword two-handed over his head. 'This is called stooping falcon. It is the first form of the sword dance. A good position for strike and defence. Now, set your feet like mine.'

The sound of hooves, a rumble like distant thunder. Drem's da paused, holding up a hand, head turning, and Drem lowered his practice sword, sweat dripping from his nose. He felt as if every muscle in his body was burning, or weeping. Or begging for mercy. Or all three.

His da strode towards their cabin, held a hand out and Drem threw him his practice sword, then followed. They reached the wooden porch, Olin leaned the swords against a wall and was resting a hand upon the short axe at his belt when riders appeared, cantering on their path and into the courtyard. Ten or twelve men, Ulf the tanner and Calder the smith at their head.

Is this about the fight?

Then Drem saw Fritha amongst them. She was dressed like the rest of them, furs and skins, fur-trimmed boots and woollen breeches. She nodded a greeting to him.

Olin just waited for them to speak.

'Did you see that fire, up in the Bonefells?' Ulf said.

'I did,' Olin replied.

'We're going to have a closer look,' Calder said. 'Thought you might want to come along.'

Drem shared a look with his da.

'Good of you to ask,' Olin said. 'We've missed the Bonefells.'

'Ha, what did I tell you?' Ulf barked a laugh, slapping

Calder across his slab of a shoulder. 'Go saddle a horse, then – we've a lot of ground to travel and not a lot of day to do it in. Don't fancy spending a night out in them hills.'

Mountains, Drem corrected silently, his new strategy to keep his da happy, though he agreed with the principle whole-heartedly. He ran to saddle their horses.

This is not the best way to recover from a beating, Drem concluded to himself. No matter how he shifted in his saddle, there was always an outcry from various parts of his body. Right now the pain was coming from his thighs, which pulsed their throbbing discomfort with every step his horse made.

His da was up ahead, riding with Ulf and Calder, picking a sloping path through rock and pine. The rest of their group, a mix of townsmen and trappers, rode in a loose column. Some spoke in murmured conversation, but Drem kept silent. He was comfortable with his da, but around other people he mostly felt awkward. Never knew what to say, or what he was supposed to say.

Harness jangled behind and Fritha rode up beside him. A couple of knives at her belt. Her jaw still boasted a bruise, mottled and purple as a berry-stain.

'Why are you here?' Drem asked, worried for Fritha, think-ing it was too dangerous, the weather threatening winter, the Wild looming close.

'This is my home, now. Where I come from, we help look after one another. Saw Ulf and Calder, thought an extra spear is never a bad thing.'

'Fair enough,' Drem said.

'I wanted to say thank you,' she said to him, 'for what you did.'

He shrugged, felt heat flush his neck, though he couldn't understand why.

'Anyone would have done the same,' he said.

'I don't think they would have,' Fritha said. She reached out a hand and squeezed his arm. Something about it felt agreeable, though he had to fight the urge to pull away. A smile twitched across Fritha's lips. Drem saw that it made her wince.

'Try a compress of comfrey and witch-hazel for that,' he said, nodding at her bruise.

'Has it helped you?'

'Aye.' He thought about it. 'A little. Not as much as I'd have liked.'

Fritha laughed at that, making her wince again.

'What do you think that fire is?' she asked.

'Don't know,' Drem answered. 'But we'll find out. And it had better be *soon*.' He looked up, the pale glow of daylight shining in fractured beams through the canopy of pine needles above.

'What's wrong?' Fritha asked.

'It's almost highsun,' he said with a shrug. 'If we don't find whatever it is we're searching for soon, we'll be looking at staying a night out under the stars.'

'So?' Fritha said. 'We've furs and blankets. Enough bodies here to keep warm if it gets that cold.' She paused, looked at him a long moment. He felt his neck flush red again, though he still wasn't sure why. He saw that shadow of a smile ghost Fritha's lips.

So speaks a southerner, he thought. *No one who's tasted a winter in the north would say such a thing.*

Something brushed against his face, cold. He blinked, saw a snowflake drift lazily down to the ground, others following, like silent feathers.

'The Bonefells are not the place you want to be sleeping come Crow's Moon,' Drem said.

'Why? Winter is harsh this far north, I imagine. But it's not upon us yet.' She looked at the snowflakes floating about her and shrugged. 'A little snow. It's not a blizzard, and we're only half a day's journey from our holds.'

Not a blizzard yet, he corrected, knowing how quickly winter's caress could turn into a fist.

'I wasn't talking about the snow,' Drem said. 'I was talking about what the snow drives south. Those things that travel out of the north to escape the worst of it. We saw a giant bear, a little west of here; must have come south for a reason. Storms and blizzards are coming.' As if to prove his point, a snowflake landed on his nose. It felt good as it melted, a momentary easing of the pulsing throb where his nose had been broken.

'A bear.' Fritha shrugged.

'And other things. Wolven packs,' Drem said, shivering at the memory of last winter. 'And bats.'

'Bats?'

'Aye.'

'I've heard tales,' Fritha said, a seed of doubt creeping into her voice.

'These are as big as a shield and will suck the blood right out of a person, like they're a skin of mead.' Drem said.

'Thought they were just tall tales,' Fritha muttered.

'No. I've seen what they can do.'

For the first time Fritha didn't look so confident. She eyed the trees suspiciously.

'Best be home before nightfall, then,' she said.

'That'd be best,' Drem agreed. 'I don't think they've come this far south, yet. But I'd rather not put it to the test.'

'Aye.'

They spilt out of the woodland onto an open strip of land, a few hundred paces ahead the slope levelled off. The snow was starting to fall more heavily, the wind swirling it in sweeping eddies. Drem glimpsed his da at the head of the column, saw him ride over the slope onto level ground, Ulf and Calder with him, saw them rein their mounts in and stop, still as the boulders gouged into the land about them.

Drem joined them, their party spread into a loose line along a ridged plateau. The burned-out remains of a huge bonfire lay before them, black and charred, the wind snatching flakes of ash and mixing them with the snow, a dance of black and white. A thin line of smoke still curled from the fire's cooling heart, the lingering glow of a dying ember at its root.

Drem's eyes didn't linger on the bonfire. A body lay spread across a boulder only a dozen paces from the fire. His belly had been slashed open, a ragged mess of torn flesh, his guts pooled around his boots like blue-coiled rope.

Olin was at the man's side, Ulf and Calder a few heartbeats behind him. Drem dismounted and went to help, though there wasn't much he could do. As he drew closer he saw the dead man was old, wisps of white hair frozen to the granite boulder, his face twisted in a grimace of terror and agony. Olin was on one knee beside him, lifting the tatters of his torn clothing to look at the shredded ruin of his abdomen.

'It's Old Bodil,' Calder said, hanging his head.

'What happened here?' Fritha asked, looking from the bonfire to the frozen corpse.

'I reckon Bodil might have met your bear,' Ulf said to Olin.

Drem looked at the ground, already covered in a thin layer of snow. He scraped some away and stamped on the ground beneath, sending a jolt up through his heel into his leg.

Ground's frozen solid.

He still would have expected to see some sign of the bear's presence, the memory of its great bulk vivid in his mind, but the snow was covering all, and there was little point in looking: Old Bodil's wounds told the tale clearly enough.

'Made the fire to scare the beast off,' Calder said, looking from the corpse to the bonfire.

Drem felt himself nodding. That was a tactic that he and his da had used before, against wolven, not bears, but it worked much the same, as long as you kept the fire burning all night.

Didn't work for Old Bodil, though.

'We should raise a cairn over him,' Fritha said.

'Aye,' agreed Olin, still checking over Bodil's wounds.

'Not if we want to be by our hearths by nightfall,' Ulf said. 'Won't be digging any rocks out of this.' He dug a heel into the ice-bitten ground.

'Can't leave him to be gnawed at,' Calder muttered.

'No. A pyre,' Ulf said. 'And quick about it.'

It didn't take them long to gather more dead wood. Drem helped his da, Ulf and a few others carry the frozen corpse to the bonfire. Then flint and tinder were being struck, flames catching in the dry wood despite the falling snow, and soon hungry flames were clawing at the sky, the snow hissing and steaming.

They rode back to their homes in silence, Bodil's pyre roaring and belching flame and smoke behind them. Drem didn't like the smell: flesh sizzling and charring.

Fritha tried to talk to him as they rode through the trees, eerily silent as the snow fell thicker, but he was distracted, preoccupied with his thoughts. He had that anxious feeling he had in his belly when he felt something was wrong, tingling in his blood, all the way to his fingertips. An inexplicable dread.

A bonfire to hold back a bear, maybe, but what about the other fire we saw, in the distance, far to the south-west?

It was a question he wanted answered, but something else was foremost in Drem's mind. He was thinking on the feel of Bodil's corpse in his hands as he'd carried the dead man to his pyre, and the scar he'd seen on Bodil's wrist when Ulf had tripped.

No, not a scar. A fresh wound. As if he'd been bound at the wrist and struggled to break free, like an animal in a wire trap.

CHAPTER SIXTEEN

RIV

Riv hovered at Aphra's shoulder, pouring her more wine as her sister held out her empty cup.

They were in their barrack's feast-hall at Drassil, Aphra's hundred were finishing their evening meal. Once the White-Wings were done, Riv and the other trainee warriors would sit and eat, though usually Aphra was more informal, allowing Riv and the others to sit and eat with them. On occasion some of the Ben-Elim would visit and take their evening meal with Aphra and the White-Wings. This was one of those evenings: white-winged, blond-haired Kol sitting upon the bench beside Aphra, a Ben-Elim named Adonai with him, as perfectly handsome as all the Ben-Elim, a disarming innocence to his smile. A dozen other of their kin were scattered about the feast-hall.

They are not all as aloof as Israfil, Riv observed; the Ben-Elim were looking relaxed, eating, drinking cups of wine and laughing.

'I wish they'd hurry up and go, or finish their meal. I'm starving to death!' Jost whispered to Riv. He stood close by, his broken arm from his failed warrior trial out of its sling now but still bound tight. He was attending to Fia, Aphra's closest friend, and a handful of others, and making a fair job of pouring wine despite his injured arm. Fia was deep in hushed conversation with Aphra. There seemed to be a tension between them, Riv observed. No one else would notice, but Riv

saw something in the set of Aphra's shoulders, the jut of her
jaw.

Aphra held her empty cup out to Riv and she poured some
more wine.

She doesn't usually drink like this.

'What do you make of the news?' Riv said to her sister, as
much to distract her and somehow shift her mood with Fia
as anything else. Aphra looked up at her, an unfocused stare
for a moment, as her mind lingered on whatever she had been
talking about with Fia.

'News? You mean the beacons?'

'Aye.' Riv nodded. Word had reached Drassil, spreading
through the White-Wings faster than fire through a summer-
dry forest, that blazing bonfires had been spied throughout the
Land of the Faithful, and even further afar, in Ardain to the
west, and the Desolation to the north. Rumours of unrest
were spreading along with them. Rumours of human sacrifice,
like the body that Ethlinn and Garidas had discovered in the
Kadoshim lair where they had captured the half-breed.

Aphra shrugged, draining her cup and holding it out for
some more. 'I shall do as a good soldier does, and wait on the
word of my commanders,' she said. 'You could always ask him,
though.' She nodded at Kol, who was sitting beside her, though
he was turned away, his wings taking up a space of their own.
He was laughing good-naturedly with Adonai and one of
Aphra's captains, Estel, blonde-haired and recently promoted.

'Not that he seems too concerned,' Aphra commented.

'These beacons,' Kol said, shifting on his seat to look at
Aphra.

The wine hasn't affected his hearing, then.

'These beacons,' Kol repeated, louder, conversation nearby
stuttering to a halt, silence rippling outwards from him, drawing the attention of the room. 'Whispers and rumours breed
fear and shadows, so I'll not add to them.' He stood, a pulse of
his wings and he was standing upon the table.

'Kadoshim,' he said. '*They* are behind the beacons; that is the information I have been given. What they portend, I do not know.' He shrugged, wings rippling. 'What I do know, though, is that we shall watch, and if the Kadoshim move, we shall be ready. The Ben-Elim and their White-Wings protecting the Faithful, as we have done for over a hundred years.'

A cheer roared out from Aphra's hundred at that, echoing around the vaulted chamber, Riv joining her voice to it. A different sound cut through the roar, closer, higher, a gasp, and Riv saw Estel blinking at Adonai as he whispered in her ear, a shy smile spreading across her blushing face.

Riv frowned; there was something unfitting about the way Adonai lingered too close to Estel.

A memory of the Kadoshim half-breed in the Great Hall, a shiver of revulsion passing through her.

Kol jumped down from his perch on the bench, even that made graceful by the spread of his wings, more glide than crash.

'Some wine, if you please,' he said to Riv with a flourish of his cup. As she poured she felt his eyes upon her.

'Ah, but you've the look of your mother about you,' he said, 'except for her hair.' He brushed a hand across Riv's short-cropped fair hair, still stiff and spiky from sweat and dirt in the weapons-field. 'And you have your sister's eyes, which is a compliment.'

Riv felt herself smiling.

'And her smile,' Kol said, his own eyes shining with mirth.

'Riv's smile and eyes are her own,' Aphra said curtly as Kol sat. 'What else can you tell me about these bonfires or beacons?'

'My thanks,' Kol said for the wine, giving Riv a shrug and a final rueful smile as he turned to talk to Aphra, as if to say he would have liked to talk more with her.

Riv stood back awhile, just watching the meal go on, topping up wine where desired, clearing trenchers.

Aphra talked quietly with Kol for what seemed like half the

evening, and as soon as he left the table Fia leaned close and whispered in Aphra's ear, her jaw tight, which annoyed Riv, because she wanted to talk to Aphra. And she wanted to eat.

Fia sat as still and stiff as stone as Aphra whispered back to her, then gave a curt nod. Riv shuffled closer, trying to pick out Aphra's words, but she heard nothing, and then Fia rose and walked away.

Now's my chance to ask permission to eat! I'm starving!

A loud call, nearby.

Riv ground her teeth.

It was her friend Vald, sitting on a bench with a dozen White-Wings, brandishing his drinking cup, calling loudly for Jost to fill it for him.

He's only a few moons past his Long Night, and before that stood in the line with Jost one side of him and me the other!

Riv eyed Vald with a frown; there was a big grin on her friend's face. She was pleased for him, or more accurately, *had* been pleased for him. But seeing him now, hearing him talking of the White-Wings as if he was a veteran of a hundred missions, all puffed up with his own self-importance, she found herself grinding her teeth.

'You'll do,' Vald said, seeing Riv watching him. 'Some wine over here.' He grinned straight at her. Riv curled a lip and looked purposely away.

'Hey, Fledgling Riv,' Vald called out, using her official and never-used title.

Riv felt her limbs tense.

Just ignore him. He's in his cups, is enjoying the fulfilment of his dream, to become one of the White-Wings. Let him have this moment.

'Do your job,' Vald finished.

Riv spun on her heel and marched straight towards him. Vald was sloshing the dregs of his cup at her, the wide grin still stretched across his face, though with each step she took closer to him the smile seemed to wither a little.

Riv stood over him.

'Your cup,' she said, shaking her wine skin.

Vald's smile returned and he held his cup out for her.

Riv unstoppered the skin and poured the wine over Vald's head.

Laughter rippled along the bench, as well as a warning cry or two. Someone was calling hcr name. Riv heard it as if through fog.

'I'll not be mocked and treated like a slave by anyone, least of all you, you fat pig,' she snarled. 'Want some wine? Pour it yourself.'

He leaped up, spluttering, and pushed Riv in the chest. Vald was as wide as he was tall, and strong as a bull, but Riv was ready for it, had sparred with him many times. She stepped to the left, slapped his hands away and kicked out at him. She must have connected with his stones, because he turned purple and dropped to his knees, hands clutched over his groin, gurgled curses foaming from his mouth. He tried to rise, but didn't quite have the strength for it, instead staggering into Riv, his bulk sending her stumbling back. Her heel hit something and she began to fall, with a moment of perfect clarity knew that they were both headed for the fire-pit where a deer's carcass was turning above the flames, and there was nothing she could do to stop it.

Then she was being yanked by the collar, dragged upwards, a great blast of air beating about her. The flames in the pit hissed and crackled, leaping high.

Riv found herself suspended in the air, Kol's fist bunched in her cloak, feet dangling. Vald hung suspended from Kol's other hand.

Now that is an impressive feat of strength, knowing Vald's bulk.

'We've enemies enough to fight, without starting on one another,' Kol said, throwing them both to the ground. He looked from Riv to Vald, then shook his head.

'You should eat something,' he said to Riv. 'Aphra, you've

kept the fledglings waiting on us too long – they're starving on their feet. And hunger frays tempers, you know. And you,' he said, looking to Vald, who was grunting under the weight of his bulk as he struggled to one knee. 'Perhaps you should consider exercising the humility and honour that befits a White-Wing.'

Vald wobbled to his feet.

'And maybe try eating a little less.'

Laughter rippled around the room, Kol joining in at his own joke.

Riv avoided looking at her sister, knowing the stern glare she'd receive, and made her way to the food bench.

'My thanks,' Riv said to Kol as she sat at the table with a bowl of hot venison stew, fried onions and mushrooms bobbing in the fat-glistening gravy.

Kol drank from his wine cup, only to find it empty and Riv leaned close to fill it for him. He reached out to take the wine skin from her. As he did so, his hand closed around Riv's, big and warm, heat pulsing from it. Riv's instinct was to jerk her hand away, but she resisted, instead looked at him. The ghost of a smile twitched his lips, his eyes sparkling with mirth, and he winked at her, a flicker in the firelight.

'You're welcome,' he said.

Then his hand was gone and he was taking the wine skin and pouring his cup full. Riv went back to her venison stew, not sure what exactly had just happened.

Riv murmured a command and dug her heels into her mount, moving from canter to gallop in the space of a few heartbeats as she leaned forwards, her spear gripped tight, shaft tucked between her arm and torso. Wind whipped her face and dragged tears from her eyes. She wanted to yell for the joy of it, the thundering hooves beating a shuddering time, echoed by the rhythm of her heart.

Her target seemed a long way away, everything around her slow, moving at quarter time. To one side of her, White-Wings were training in the shield wall, on the other side giants were shaking the ground in individual sparring. Closer, she glimpsed Jost, a blur attacking a training mannequin; even with his broken arm still bound he was fast and deadly.

And then, abruptly, her target was close, rushing towards her, the world around her lurching into speed and motion, and everything faded away, the world reduced to the tip of her spear and its target, one seemingly drawn unerringly to the other.

An explosion of straw and she was letting go the shaft, galloping on, leaning back and shifting the pressure on her reins. A spray of turf as her horse slowed and stopped.

Riv looked back to see her spear still juddering in the head of the straw target, felt the thrill of a blow perfectly struck, a grin splitting her face. She saw Jost raise his good arm to her, a salute; the two of them had become closer since their failed attempts at their warrior trial. It still hurt to see her other friends training as White-Wings, although she had a fierce pride in them as well, sword-brothers and sisters whom she had grown up with, trained beside for over three years. Except for Vald. She still felt a simmering resentment for him, though putting her boot in his stones had helped to dim that a little.

Riv patted her horse's neck and praised him as she rode him to the paddocks adjoining the weapons-field. She dismounted and set about removing his tack and rubbing him down before she handed him over to the grooms.

Abruptly, she was stumbling into the fence, a pain shooting through her back, snatching her breath away and turning her legs to porridge. She hung onto the paddock rail, eyes screwed shut as the pain stabbed through her torso, radiating out from her shoulder blades, and then, as quickly as it had come, it was gone, only a dull ache remaining, the faintest echo of the pain.

'You all right?' one of the paddock grooms asked. She stood straight and rolled her shoulders.

'Fine,' she grunted, though she wasn't: an ache in her back

and, come to think of it, in most of her joints as well, a throbbing in her wrists and knees.

I must visit the healers about this. When I have some time.

She headed towards Jost and the training mannequins. Along the way a noise drew her attention, a square of warriors, fledglings from another hundred of White-Wings, training in the shield wall. She stopped and stared at them. There was some kind of disruption going on, voices raised, the shield wall splintering, a figure pushed and falling to the floor, another stepping forwards, standing over the fallen one.

It was Bleda on the floor, the young Sirak. He rose slowly, stumbling over the long wooden shield in his hand. The other lad standing over him was laughing. He pushed Bleda's shield when he was halfway up, sending Bleda rolling to the ground again. He laughed harder and there was more laughter from the rest of the shield wall, about twenty of them. He stopped laughing when Bleda's shield cracked into his ankles, though, sending him howling to the floor.

Bleda was up first, discarding his shield this time, the other lad hobbling to his feet a little more slowly. Bleda flew at him, a flurry of punches and kicks sending the lad reeling backwards.

Others in the group leaped forwards, grabbing Bleda. Five of them, seven, more of them. Riv saw punches flying, and then she was running, the injustice of it sending her blood boiling. She was upon them quickly, though not fast enough to prevent dozens of blows landing upon Bleda. She grabbed one of the fledglings from behind, pulled and threw him, leaving him rolling across the grass. The next one wouldn't come free so easily, so she kicked the back of his leg at his knee joint, sending him crashing to the ground, grabbed his flailing wrist and twisted, heard him scream. The next one saw her, turned and threw a punch at her. She swayed, his knuckles only grazing her cheek, and she punched a fist into his throat, saw him stumble back. Then someone was clutching her leather jerkin and a head was crunching into her nose. She saw an explosion of stars, felt her legs tremble for a moment but, instead of weakness and collapse, the red mist was suddenly there, no creeping growth, just fully formed and filling her; a thunder in her head, her veins, a hot rage pumping strength into her limbs.

'Shouldn't have done that,' she snarled through bloody teeth at the young warrior that had headbutted her.

'Now you've made me *angry*.'

'Riv,' a voice in the darkness. It changed to a red veil, thick and churning, a sea-mist in her head.

'Riv!' Louder, insistent, the voice a pinpoint in the murk, a flaming torch burning away the fog. She blinked. Figures in front of her, someone close.

Jost.

She was standing, but couldn't move. Couldn't quite understand why.

'Aye,' she said, a metallic taste in her mouth. She hawked and spat. Saw blood on the grass. Hers or someone else's, she didn't know – or care.

There were bodies. People. Some sitting, holding bloody heads or mouths. Two unconscious. Others behind Jost standing in a group, the trainee White-Wings, glaring darkly at her.

Bleda was sitting to one side, a giant with him, helping him. There was a lot of blood on his face. His lip split. One eye swollen shut.

'You all right?' Jost said, a strange expression on his face.

'Yes,' she said, the faint anger within her still present enough to make her feel annoyed with him. 'Why?'

'Ha,' a voice barked behind her, deep and grating. Then she realized why she couldn't move.

Someone was holding her.

Thick arms, knotted as rope, hard as iron.

'You can let go, now,' Riv said.

'Your word: no more violence.'

'My word,' Riv said.

Balur One-Eye let her go. 'You are a lot stronger than you look, little girl,' he said, regarding her with his one eye. 'Why did you do it?' he rumbled.

What have I done? At this rate Israfil isn't going to let me take my warrior trial until I'm a hundred and two!

Riv blinked and looked around again, her head clear now, feeling only a residue of shock at the carnage she'd wrought. She could not remember all of it. Only Bleda pushed over, many figures. Someone headbutting her. A berserker rage. Red, red, rage.

'They all attacked him. Ten, twelve of them. More. It wasn't . . . fair.'

'A keen sense of justice, then,' Balur said.

'Maybe a little too keen,' Jost muttered.

Balur looked up, pale blue sky leaking through leafless branches. Riv did too, saw the silhouette of wings spiralling down to them.

Oh no, I will be humiliated and shamed again. A stone in her belly, shame and fear.

'Best if you go,' Balur said to her.

Thank you, Balur. Riv grinned at the giant. She didn't need to be told twice, turning and marching away, feeling a little unbalanced, swaying and light on her feet, as if taking too big a step would result in her floating away.

Thirty, forty strides, and there were footsteps behind her, a hand on her shoulder. She spun around, ready to fight again.

It was Bleda.

'Why?' he said. 'They are your people.' He looked genuinely confused, honestly wanting to understand.

'Because –' Riv shrugged – 'it wasn't fair. Wasn't right. Wasn't honourable.'

He stared at her, head cocked to one side, his face battered and bruised, cut and swollen, but still blank, an unreadable mask.

'My thanks,' he said.

They stared at each other and, then and there, Riv made a decision.

'Tonight, in the forest beyond the field of cairns,' Riv said. 'After the eighth horn.'

Before he had a chance to respond, Riv turned and walked away.

CHAPTER SEVENTEEN

DREM

'Where are we going?' Drem asked his da.

'You'll see,' Olin called over his shoulder as he cantered ahead.

Never a straight answer from that man. Drem bit back his frustration and an angry retort.

He glanced at the sky, the clouds low and heavy, a nimbus glow threatening more snow to come. What was left of the day's veiled winter sun was a faded gleam on the edge of the world. He muttered under his breath and gave his pony some heel, urging it to catch up with his da as he rode out of their court-yard.

Drem had been seeing to their new livestock, chaining the goats in the barn and chasing the chickens in, making sure he did a head count and didn't leave any out by mistake. A night locked out of the barn or stables at this time of year would most likely be a death sentence for any of their animals. This was the Desolation, after all, and there were worse things than foxes that came south from the Bonefells when winter fell like a hammer-blow upon the north.

Hard-frozen snow snapped and crackled under their ponies' hooves as they rode past Fritha's hold, warm firelight flickering through the slats of shuttered windows, looking all the more inviting from this side of the cold. Drem's nose was already tingling, his breath a great mist with every exhalation. Fritha's dog barked as they passed by, tied to a rope and iron ring close to their door.

I told her to bring the hound in at night. Drem frowned. At the thought of Fritha he felt a strange sensation, as if a fluttering moth was trapped in the pit of his belly.

Twilight was as thick as smoke about them when they reached Kergard. Drem was surprised that the gates were still open. A solitary guard was standing beside the gate, cloak hood pulled up over his head, blowing on his hands. Olin reined his horse in and leaned down, taking something from the guard, the rattle of metal. Drem blinked as he caught a glimpse of the face inside the hood. It was Calder the smith.

Without a word, the big man pushed the gates closed and slotted a bar of oak into place, then walked away and faded into the shadows.

'Come on,' Drem's da muttered and clicked his pony on.

The streets of Kergard were empty and still, fat snowflakes falling, silent and soporific, one landing as gentle as a good-night kiss upon Drem's lips. Drem knew where his da was going long before they arrived – he just didn't know why. His da dismounted and walked his mount through an arched gate-way and into a cobbled courtyard situated behind Calder's smithy. Olin unstrapped a package from the back of his saddle and passed his reins to Drem.

'Quick as you can,' his da said, nodding towards the stables, then turned on his heel and strode to the smithy. A jingle of keys and the door was opened, Olin framed for a moment in a red glow. With a sigh, Drem headed for the stables.

'What took you so long?' his da said as Drem entered the forge. He was working a bellows, the suck and heave of air sounding like a diseased giant's lungs, the glow of the forge changing from red to orange, yellow-edged.

'What are we doing here, Da?' Drem asked.

'Here, put this on and keep this going,' Olin said, ignoring the question, shaking a leather apron at him and gesturing for Drem to take over the bellows. Olin wore his own blacksmith's apron, scarred and pitted black.

Drem did, grunting at the weight of the apron. He'd worked a forge before, though it had been a makeshift one his da had built when they lived in Ardain. He'd enjoyed it, finding a deep pleasure in the rhythm of work, whether with bellows or hammer. Drem's thoughts of sleep melted away, along with his irritable mood. Behind him there was the clank and grate of tools pulled from racks, buckets moved, iron shifted through.

The charcoal started to glow yellow, tinged with white.

'Da!' Drem called over his shoulder.

A silence.

'Hotter,' his da said.

Drem scooped more cinder and ash from the ash-pit beneath the forge and banked the fire higher, then set back to work at the bellows.

Olin appeared, put a pile of iron rods on the workbench, and something else, wrapped in sheepskin. The package that had been strapped to his saddle. Almost reverently, Olin unrolled it, revealing the black lump of rock they'd discovered in the foothills of the Bonefells. Drem's sense of worry returned like an avalanche.

'Da, please, what are you doing?'

His da looked up at Drem, as if noticing him for the first time.

'Please, Da, for once, just tell me. I'm not a bairn.'

'I'm making a sword,' Olin said, eyes bright with the forge's glow.

'What? Why?'

'There's nowhere left to run, Drem. Since your mam, we've travelled the Banished Lands, always searching, running, fleeing the tide. Five years since, we settled here, and I thought we'd finally found some peace. And now it's coming here, the curse of the Kadoshim and Ben-Elim polluting everywhere in these Banished Lands. There's nowhere left to go. I'm tired of it, worn out by it.' He went back to his gathering of tools, slipping a bag from his shoulder and rummaging through it. Drem reached out and grabbed his da's wrist, pulling him back to face him.

'Da, you're worrying me.'

Olin sucked in a deep breath, blew out slowly.

'The newcomers in Kergard, the ones you fought. I don't like them.'

'I don't like them either,' Drem said. 'No need to make a sword to kill them with, though.'

A flicker of a smile. 'No, son. I'm not forging a sword to kill *them*. My axe or knife would be good enough for that. No, I mean, there's something wrong about them being here. I feel it. And Old Bodil, supposedly killed by our white bear . . .'

'I've had . . . doubts, over that,' Drem said, frowning, re-membering the strap-mark worn into the flesh of Bodil's wrist. He told his da about it.

His da nodded, giving him a proud look.

'Aye, that's what I'm talking about. Strange things are hap-pening here. The new mine, the miners, men found dead in the Wild, bonfires. Call me suspicious, but I don't like *any* of it.'

I don't like the new miners! Drem thought, thinking of Wispy Beard and the fight near the market.

'And on top of that, the damn Kadoshim are stirring things up in the south – talk of human sacrifice and who knows what – and the Ben-Elim demanding their warrior tithes and taxes. It's their fault, all of it,' Olin snarled, a hint of savagery and rage barely contained. He breathed deep, closed his eyes. 'And I've had enough,' he said with a slow exhalation. 'Something feels wrong, and when I've had this feeling before, we've packed up and left. Moved on. But where else is there to go now?'

Drem shrugged.

'I'm going to end this. All of it.'

Drem didn't like the way his da was acting, the way he was speaking, the look in his eyes, a focus verging on frenzy.

'How? Da, you're not yourself. What do you mean?'

'I'm going to forge a starstone sword and cut Asroth's head off with it.'

Drem felt an overwhelming urge to take his pulse and almost let go of the bellows. There was a long moment of silence between them, even the crackle of fire and charcoal ebbing.

'What?' Drem blurted, incredulous.

Has he lost his mind?

A thousand more questions burst to life in Drem's mind. His da ignored him.

'DA!' Drem shouted, but then his da was moving, all grim focus, and Drem could tell from the look on Olin's face that he wasn't going to do any more talking. With tongs Olin lowered the lump of starstone metal into the forge, laid it into the white heat of the charcoal, so hot the air was a shimmering haze about it.

Drem felt sick, all this talk of running and hiding, of Ben-Elim and Kadoshim. For as long as he could remember, life had been Drem and his da, just the two of them, a solitary existence, but one that Drem was used to and loved. This talk of the world piercing their bubble and crashing into their lives, changing everything, left Drem feeling scared and nauseous.

And he's talking about Asroth? The Demon-Lord of the Kadoshim. But he's dead a hundred years, or alive and sealed in molten rock in Drassil, an eternal gaol. Everyone knows that.

They both stood in silence, looking at the matt black metal. Nothing happened.

'Not hot enough?' Drem said.

Olin stood there, staring at the lump of metal, a dull, impenetrable black, then nodded to himself, drew himself straighter. He unsheathed a knife from his belt and opened his mouth, spoke, but in no language Drem recognized, the words

174

issuing from his throat fluid and unearthly, setting Drem's hairs standing on his arms and the back of his neck, sending an icy chill trickling through his veins, even in the sweat-heat of the forge.

'*Tine agus fola, iarann agus cruach, lann a maraigh an aingeal dorcha,*' his da said, at the same time drawing the knife across his palm, a dark line welling, with a flick of his wrist spattering the blood on the forge and starstone. There was a hissing sound, a sweet smell, and where the droplets of blood hit the starstone the rock began to bubble, rising like blisters, spreading across the dark metal like spilt ink.

'Da,' Drem croaked, his voice dry and cracked. 'You're scaring me.'

The black metal began to glow, red first, shifting to orange and then incandescent white.

'Da!' Drem said, louder.

Olin ignored him, reaching for tongs and hammer.

Dawn was a glow in the east when they left the forge, turning the water of the Starstone Lake to rippling bronze. Snow had fallen during the night, a thick layer fresh upon the ground, but the roof of the world was cloudless now, a pale, fresh blue that felt like it went on forever, the air cold and sharp. Drem found it refreshing after the night of thick heat and hammer blows in the forge.

Drem rode behind his da, staring at his back with a mixture of dread and awe.

What happened last night? A sword forged, my da casting a spell . . .

His mind tried to pick apart the events, to unravel them and piece them back together in a shape that resembled logic. It wasn't working.

Who is my da? It was a terrifying feeling, to realize that he did not know the man he'd spent his whole life with, almost like vertigo, as if the world were shifting beneath his feet.

They had spoken little after Olin had started shaping the white-hot metal, hammering, twisting, cooling, heating and hammering again, dross leaking from the metal like black tears. Drem fed the bellows, between hammering he dipped the shaping sword in water and oil, and towards the end he shared the hammer-work with Olin. The din and smells of the forge filled Drem's senses as he struggled to make sense of what his da had told him. In the end he had become lost in the rhythm and roar of their labour.

Drem's eyes fixed upon the sheepskin bundle that was tied to Olin's saddle, little more than a shadow in dawn's first light.

We'll finish it at home. A handle of ash, bound with leather. Those had been the only words Olin had said as they'd stood and stared at the result of their labour. A long blade, tapered to a fine point, a heavy crosspiece and fuller like a black vein running down the blade's centre.

Kergard's gates were closed when they reached them; Olin frowned at that.

'Calder is supposed to be here,' Olin said, searching the shadows for the big smith, but he was not there. Drem jumped from his horse and hefted the bar across the gates. It was heavier than he'd thought, judging by the way Calder had lifted it last night. The gates opened with a creak, Olin hovering a few more heartbeats, waiting for Calder.

Drem looked at his da enquiringly.

'He's supposed to be here,' Olin muttered again.

He sounds worried.

Olin scanned the streets that converged on the gates. They were silent and still, only melting shadows for company. 'Don't like leaving the gates open and unguarded,' Olin said.

'Guards should be along soon enough,' Drem said.

'Aye,' Olin agreed.

And if we're still here, Da'll have to explain what he's doing.

That thought seemed to have run through Olin's mind, too.

'Can't wait any longer,' Olin said and with a shrug from

Drem they were riding through and breaking into a trot as a world of white opened up before them.

Drem looked at Fritha's hold as they passed it, and he was pleased to see that there was no hound still tied to the rope and ring in the yard. A sound echoed in the distance, from the woodland to the north. Dim and muted. Drem strained to hear it. A crashing, perhaps a roar. He and Olin shared a look.

Wolven bringing down their prey. Something big, anyway.

As they began the long stretch of track to their hold Drem noticed tracks in the snow, following the path they were on, then veering off, towards woodland framed in the distance by the Bonefells. Olin saw them too, reining in his mount.

One man, one hound. Maybe a woman – small feet for a man.

A jolt of worry.

Fritha?

Drem looked up at the sky, heavy with more snow, a strong wind gusting down from the north, bringing with it the taste of ice. Drem looked to his da. At any other time there would have been no question, no hesitation, but Drem knew his da wanted to get the sword home. It was written all across his face.

Drem just waited, knowing what the outcome would be, but letting his da go through the process of it.

'Best go see who those tracks belong to,' Olin said.

'I think we'd better,' Drem agreed.

Drem heard something, away to his left, coming from the scrubland that fringed the wood as it rolled down from the Bonefells.

'You hear that, too?' his da asked him.

A nod, and together they were pulling on reins and riding away from the track, towards the scrub and woodland.

They followed the footprints in the snow, heard a voice calling out, the same word, again and again.

Drem ducked his head under branches heavy with snow, the voice louder now. He recognized it.

'It's Fritha,' he said and urged his horse on. Then he saw her, flitting between the dark trunks of trees, still calling out.

'Surl!' Drem heard her cry.

Her hound.

She saw them, stood and waited.

'It's Surl, he's gone,' she said and pointed at paw tracks in the snow, heading deeper into the woods. She wasn't dressed for the cold, just wearing breeches and boots, a wool shirt and cloak.

Not enough to stop the blood from freezing out here. And no weapon.

'Up with Drem,' Olin said to Fritha and clicked his horse on, Drem taking Fritha's hand and pulling her up into the saddle behind him. She wrapped her arms around his waist.

'How long has the hound been gone?' Drem asked her as he followed his da into the thickening trees.

'Dawn,' Fritha said and he felt her shrug. 'A while. I let him out and he just ran. I followed.'

'Should've brought a spear, and put on some snow-clothes,' Drem said over his shoulder.

'It happened so quickly, I didn't think . . .' Fritha said into the back of his head.

'Not thinking is what gets you killed in the Wild,' Drem muttered, the words drilled into him by his da. There was a pleasure in saying those words, and not being on the receiving end of them.

Fritha said nothing in response.

'There,' Olin said from ahead and Drem spurred his mount on, weaving through the wide-spaced trees, pulling alongside his da, and he saw a dark shape about thirty or forty paces ahead. Fritha's hound, Surl. It was slumped against an ash tree.

Something's not right. Drem frowned. The hound's dun coat appeared much darker, the snow around it serving to intensify the difference in colour: white, unbroken snow almost glowing, the hound dark as night.

Olin reined in his horse, Drem did the same, both of the animals shying and dancing away as the two men slipped from their saddles. Fritha followed and Drem held a hand up, warning her to stay back. Fritha scowled and ignored him.

Closer, Olin and Drem instinctively fanned out, Drem's hand resting on the hilt of his knife, his da slipping a short axe from his belt. Drem saw a splattering across the snow, droplets of blood about the hound, a string of rubies. He scanned the trees around them, widespread, the snow crisp and unbroken.

Nothing and no one hiding close by.

'Surl,' Fritha said, both command and question.

The hound wined, lifting its head from the trunk, seeming as if even that movement took the greatest effort.

Drem stared at the hound's torso, trying to work out what was wrong. He could see the shape of its shoulder, the line of its back, but the colour was wrong, and it looked as if it had been draped with a cloak. A dark and red-veined cloak, the colour of burned charcoal from the forge. Then its body shifted, a ripple from neck to tail and the coal-black shape detached itself from the hound, rising, coalescing into a creature with red eyes set in a bloated, flat-muzzled head and long, needle-like fangs that dripped blood. A tremor pulsed through its body, vellum-like wings undulating, stretching out, twice as wide as the hound, now, snapping taut, a leathery rustle as the creature moved.

'BAT!' Olin yelled, throwing himself to the ground as the bat launched itself at him. It was bigger than a war shield, a high-pitched screeching like grating bones issuing from its mouth, talons raking at Olin's back, his horse behind rearing and screaming, lashing out with hooves. The bat veered away, a shadow in flight, bearing back down upon Olin, who was turning, hampered by the deep snow. The bat landed on his chest, hurling him flat on his back, those long fangs darting down, towards Olin's neck.

Drem flung himself at the creature, a blind rage filling him at the thought of it hurting his da and part-bellow, part-shriek burst from his throat as he slammed into the giant bat, hurling it from Olin, Drem rolling with it in a fountain of snow, wings tangling with his arms, a foul stench of rot and decay mingled with the sickly-sweet tang of fresh blood. Drem came to a halt on his back, grabbed at the bat's wings as fangs snapped a hand-span from his face, a wave of putrescence washing over him, making him gag. He tried to grab the beast by the throat, but its wings were beating a whirlwind in his face. A sharp claw on the spine of a wing slashed his arm, cutting through hide and thick wool to open the flesh beneath, a burning pain and blood-splatter across his face.

Seax on my belt. But he couldn't spare a hand to reach it, tried to roll the creature into the snow but the weight of its body, the jerk and thrust of its muscular neck made it impossible to do anything but hold it, and he wasn't doing that very well.

Fritha appeared above him, swinging a branch at the bat, crunching into its body. With a crack the branch splintered and Fritha grabbed a wing, heaving on it, but the blood-frenzied bat ignored her, jaws snapping closer and closer to Drem's throat.

Another line of raking fire as the wing-talon gouged into his arm again, and then the bat's head lurched forwards, fangs sinking into Drem's shoulder.

He screamed, loud and echoing, new strength fuelling his body, and he ripped the bat from his flesh, blood trailing a crimson arc, the creature frenzied, jaws gnashing, red-lipped, and then, abruptly, its head exploded, blood and bone and rancid skin raining down upon Drem, in his eyes, his mouth, up his nose.

He coughed and spluttered, hurled the bat corpse away, its wings still twitching, wiped clots of blood and bone from his eyes and saw his da standing over him, framed by snow in the canopy above.

Drem rolled onto his side and vomited bile onto the snow, where it steamed in the frost-filled air. A hand under his arm and he was standing, his da checking him over.

'Just my shoulder,' Drem said, shivering at the thought of those long fangs in his flesh. Strangely, it wasn't hurting, even under his da's probing fingers it felt numb, just a faint echo of what he expected.

'Can't feel it,' he mumbled.

'That's the bat's saliva,' his da muttered. 'It numbs, like willow bark or skullcap. They usually attack prey that's sleeping, can drain you dry without you feeling a thing.'

'Is it dangerous?' Drem asked, panic stirring that the numbness would spread, stop his heart and lungs from beating, or that he might die of some infectious disease.

'Let's get you home, clean it out properly.'

'Aye,' Drem agreed enthusiastically.

Fritha was sitting with her hound; the animal was still breathing, its head on her lap.

'Will he live?' Fritha asked, a tear rolling down her cheek.

'Depends how long that thing had been feeding on him,' Olin said, crouching and stroking the hound's neck. 'Get him home, clean his wound, feed him up.' Olin shrugged. Then he looked past Fritha, eyes fixing on something beyond the hound. He stood, walked slowly forwards, examining the ground.

'Get the ponies,' he said over his shoulder. 'We'll see if we can get that hound up across one of their backs.'

Drem turned to find the ponies but had only taken a few steps before he felt a hand upon his arm. It was Fritha.

'Thank you,' she said. He opened his mouth to say something but she leaned forwards and kissed him on the cheek, a gentle brush of lips on skin, a hint of honey on her breath. Compared to the cloying stench of blood that was hovering around his face it was like a whisper of heaven.

'Let's get those ponies,' she said and walked on, leaving him standing there, the beginnings of a smile twitching his lips.

Neither of the ponies had gone far; Drem's was standing and stripping bark from a tree trunk, Olin's remaining almost exactly where it had been to begin with.

'What's that?' Fritha said, pointing at a dark object in the snow.

It was the new-forged sword, lying upon the snow, the tang, cross-guard and a handspan of the black blade poking from its sheepskin wrapping.

'Nothing,' Drem muttered, stooping and scooping it up, hastily pulling the sheepskin up over the tang.

'Drem,' his da shouted, voice muted in the snow-wreathed woods. There was a tone to it that set his skin tingling.

Drem ran, left the ponies, sword gripped tightly under his arm, the crunch of Fritha's feet behind him. They didn't have to go far. The smell hit Drem before he saw.

'Think I've found what brought that hound into the woods,' Olin said, standing and staring as Drem and Fritha stopped either side of him.

'Asroth below,' Fritha breathed.

Before them was a scene of carnage. The ground was stamped and churned, snow and blood mixed to a bloody sludge. Drem saw huge paw-prints amongst the pink mire. Lumps of meat were scattered all about the area. It took Drem a few moments to recognize them as body parts. A hand, half a leg, a shoulder and arm, flesh tattered and torn. A torso and head, the body almost eviscerated, guts strewn about like so much old rope.

'No,' Drem whispered, because the head staring lifelessly into nowhere had belonged to someone he knew, someone his da called friend.

It was Calder the smith.

CHAPTER EIGHTEEN

BLEDA

Bleda walked out through the open gates of Drassil. There were a dozen paces of near-darkness as he made his way through the arched tunnel beneath the battlements and gate-tower, and then he was stepping out into the last rays of daylight, the sun a pale glow above the trees of Forn. Before him spread the field of the dead, a road cutting a line through the cairns that filled the plain. Bleda took a deep breath and marched on.

He'd looked down upon these same cairns from the tops of the battlements many times, knew that they sheltered the fallen from that day that the world changed. The day the Kadoshim and Ben-Elim had broken free from the Otherworld and become flesh.

But those same cairns had looked different when viewed from so high above, like pebbles cast upon a cloth of green fabric. Now, though, they rose to either side of Bleda, tall as him, some taller, looming, filling his world, pressing in upon him.

So many dead! Has there ever been such a battle, with so many killed?

They were covered with moss and lichen, earth filling the gaps between stones, grass and weeds growing, snails and slugs and other things scuttling between the slabs of stone. The wind sighed through them, sounding like a thousand voices, whispering.

And what would the dead tell me, of that dread Day of Wrath?
Deeds of valour, of courage and honour. Of murder and slaughter?

For a moment he remembered another battle, figures on
the ground like ants, the Ben-Elim swooping down upon them,
screams drifting up to a young boy on a hillside. He shook his
head, scattering the memories like flies, returned to the cairns
and their whispers of the Battle of Drassil.

Bleda had heard the tale many times, of how the Ben-Elim's
allies were hard pressed and overwhelmed on the plain by the
greater numbers of the Kadoshim's forces. Led by the black-
hearted King Nathair, if Bleda remembered right. A man who
rode to battle upon the back of a draig, a fearsome beast that
was all but extinct in the Banished Lands now. The Kadoshim
had been the first through the portal from the Otherworld, and
so had filled the skies, diving down upon the beleaguered allies
of the Ben-Elim, a warband from the western realm of Ardan,
wherever that was. All Bleda remembered about them was that
they were led by a beautiful queen, fair as the sun.

Edana.

The Kadoshim had fallen upon them like a plague, spreading their slaughter. But the Ben-Elim had been close behind,
throwing themselves through the portal from the Otherworld, risking all, as Jibril frequently told Bleda and Jin in
their lessons, in a desperate bid to save the good people of the
Banished Lands. Asroth had been defeated, frozen, the Kadoshim routed, their allies slain or scattered, and so had begun the
Age of Lore. The Protectorate of the Ben-Elim.

The reign of the Ben-Elim, whatever they like to call it.

Bleda glanced up at the sky, pale and open now as he moved
beyond the reach of the great tree's canopy, and imagined the
Kadoshim and Ben-Elim up above, blotting out the sun,
swooping and spiralling in aerial combat. He could almost hear
the echo of their battle-cries, their death screams, the explosions of turf as they crashed to the earth in ruin.

It must have been a sight to see.

And then he was through the cairns, the first trees of Forn growing tall either side of the road, thickening as he walked on. The world changed about him in just a few steps, becoming a place of twilight and shadow, of scratching branch, shifting light and rustling leaf. Birds called and insects chittered, wood creaking.

A forest is louder than I ever would have imagined!

He'd rarely set foot outside Drassil. He was allowed to: there were no restrictions upon him as a ward of the Ben-Elim. He was treated as an honoured guest rather than a prisoner, even if Jin said otherwise, so he was at liberty to walk out onto the plains around Drassil, or even into the forest, though he was hesitant to do so. He did not want to do anything that would make the Ben-Elim doubt him, or bring shame on his Clan. Bleda knew that the cords around him were not thick rope or heavy iron. They were bonds of duty and honour and threat, and they bound him more tightly than anything fashioned by man. He knew if he tried to leave, to escape, to flee back to his kin, that he would be responsible for breaking the peace between the Sirak and the Ben-Elim. He would not do something that would shame his kin, or bring the wrath of the Ben-Elim down upon them.

'You must be strong,' his mother had said to him all those years ago. And he had tried to be, every single moment from that day to this one.

Some days that is harder than others, he thought, lifting a hand to his throbbing face. One eye was still closed from his beating, and he could still taste blood. And he was walking with a limp, a pain in his hip. He knew it could have been worse.

Would have been worse, if not for Riv.

He knew her name. A lot of people lived within the walls of Drassil, many thousands, but after five years you tended to know most of the people around you. Especially the ones that spent time on the weapons-field, which he frequented most. He often went there just to watch others train when he was not being taught, or listen to Jin mock them, and he had noticed that Riv seemed to spend more time there than the others. Certainly more than her training regime required her to be there.

She confused him; she was clearly skilled with many weapons.

Though not the bow!

A warrior dedicated to her craft, and brave. But so weak, as well. She had literally no cold-face, didn't even try, and her control over her emotions was obviously just as brittle.

I should be grateful of that weakness today, as she saved me from a worse beating. Maybe even my life.

There had been a long, terrifying moment today when he'd thought that they were going to kill him, as he had fallen to the ground from a dozen blows and felt their boots slamming into him, the weight of them pressing down upon him, suffocating.

And then she had been there: Riv, snarling and spitting like a wolven in a sack.

'Tonight, in the forest beyond the field of cairns,' she had said to him, and so here he was, though he was not quite sure why he'd come. Inquisitiveness, yes, and there had been something in her eyes and voice that suggested this was *important*, somehow.

What does she want with me?

'Over here,' a voice said in the darkness.

Bleda stopped and stared, saw a shadow detach itself from the trunk of a giant oak. It waved an arm at him.

He left the road, skidding down a gentle incline as Riv stepped out into a beam of light. It caught her fair hair, highlighting threads of gold.

'I thought you wouldn't come,' she said, a vulnerability on her face, in her eyes. Her nose was swollen and red, dried blood crusting one nostril. A reminder that she had paid a price for helping him on the weapons-field earlier that day.

'Why would I not?' he asked, frowning. He owed her a debt of thanks.

'Doesn't matter,' she shrugged. 'Here.'

She swung a bag from her back and offered it to him. It was leather, of the kind the White-Wings used to pack their kit in when marching off on a campaign. The shape inside pushed against the leather.

'What?' Bleda said, fighting a frown from his forehead.

'Just take it,' Riv said, shaking it at him.

He did, hesitantly, then opened the drawstring and peered inside. It was hard to see, the shadows of the forest dense and heavy, light shifting about them as branches swayed high above.

'Take it out, then,' Riv said impatiently.

Even her voice betrays her emotions!

Bleda glanced up, saw her studying him with a deep intensity.

He reached his hand into the bag, felt something smooth, a curve. His stomach lurched as within a heartbeat his confusion turned to shock and joy, for he knew in an instant what it was.

A Sirak bow.

He drew it out of the leather bag slowly, disbelievingly, and held it before him in his hands.

Not just a Sirak bow. My bow.

And in his mind he was back in Arcona, nine years old, sitting in an open-fronted ger and watching his brother shape this same bow with a feeling in his belly close to worship.

'*Hand me the sharkskin rasp, little brother,*' Altan had said to him. '*Now the sinew's dry we need to take these rough edges off. Otherwise it can feel like a fistful of thorns, which won't help when you're aiming at a Cheren arse-wipe, eh?*'

Altan had laughed and shown him how to rasp the sinew that had been glued to the bow's back, using sharkskin they'd traded from merchants come up all the long way from Tarbesh, far, far in the hot south. Another world, Bleda had thought back then, his whole existence consisting of Arcona and the Sea of Grass.

He'd loved his brother so deeply, the sudden rush of this

memory so vivid and clear in his mind's eye, that he thought for a moment he could smell his brother's sweat. It was like a punch in his gut. A groan escaped his lips and his vision blurred, tears filling his eyes.

'Are you all right?' Riv asked him.

Bleda blinked, swayed in and out of tree-cast shadows.

'I . . .' he said. 'My bow. How?'

'I saw it in the dirt, that day in Arcona. Just picked it up, I don't know why. I should have given it to you a long time ago, I don't know why I didn't. I just . . .' She looked at him strangely, then shrugged and dropped her head. 'I'm sorry.'

And looking at her, hearing her words, Bleda felt almost overwhelmed by another rush of emotions. Anger, that his bow had been so close, all these years, this physical, touchable link to his brother, to his home, when all else he had was fragile memory, faint and transient as morning mist. But the other emotion surging through him was joy. It was almost like having his brother back, ghost-like memories wreathed about and through this bow like the sturgeon glue they had used to bind it. Joy at seeing his bow, touching it, a feeling of *wholeness* that he had lacked for so long he hadn't realized it was gone. Until now.

Staring at Riv, these two emotions warred within him, back and forth, rage and joy, joy and rage.

Joy won.

'My thanks,' he whispered, and allowed himself the ghost of a smile as he looked upon the bow in his hands, his fingertips moving from the worn, leather-bound grip to the smooth, recurved lines of its limbs, horn on the belly, sinew on the back, all washed in countless coats of lacquer, the last flick of the bone ears where the gut string was attached.

'I've tried to care for it,' Riv mumbled, and Bleda could see that she had. He gave a little tug to the gut string, felt the dryness of it, knew it would fray and snap with much more pressure.

That's simple enough to remedy.

The rest of the bow looked almost the same as it had ever been.

'You have, I can see,' Bleda said. 'It is in fine condition.'

She smiled at him, then, warmth and happiness radiating from her.

She is like the sun when she is happy, like a furnace when she is angry. I have never known anyone so utterly opposite to my people. All seething emotion bound within a sack of skin, blood and bone. Only when alone with our kin or Clan are we Sirak able to be like this. When in front of our enemy the cold-face is king.

There was something appealing about it, almost, if not for the countless years that discipline and control had been drummed into Bleda's every waking moment.

A freedom to being like that, no secrecy, no hiding who you are. And sometimes the effort to keep that control is so exhausting, the sense of failure at just the slightest slip crushing.

'You're pleased, then?' Riv said, frowning.

'I am,' Bleda said, an inner chuckle at the understatement in that.

'Well, you could at least be a little grateful,' Riv said.

'I am,' Bleda said. 'Very grateful.'

'Really? You sure?' Riv said, eyes narrowing.

'Yes. I have never felt more grateful in all my life. Words cannot express my thanks.'

'Well, you don't look it,' Riv said, 'but I'll take your word for it, then.'

'I would do something for you, to repay this debt I now owe you,' Bleda said. He felt immediately and profoundly indebted to Riv, and compelled to try and do something about it. Although by his reckoning nothing could ever repay Riv's act in full.

'Don't worry about it,' Riv said with a shrug. 'Just wish I'd done it sooner, now.'

'There must be something I can do for you,' Bleda said, though in truth he could think of nothing at that moment.

'Is your aim as good as Jin's?' she asked, a gleam coming to her eye.

'Better,' Bleda said, no hint of boast or bluster in his voice, only an utter conviction.

'Teach me, then. To use a bow. I'm not very good.'

'You're not,' Bleda agreed, remembering her efforts that day with Jin. 'I will try, though I cannot promise miracles.'

'Ha.' Riv barked a laugh. 'I'm not expecting any.'

'And I do not know how well I will be able to teach the use of your bows. They are like a giant's club.'

'Well, I'd appreciate any help I can get. Don't want to miss the straw man during my warrior trials. If Israfil ever lets me take another one,' she muttered.

They stood there in silence, then. Bleda unsure what to say. Riv shuffled her feet. The sun was gone now, only different degrees of darkness about them.

'Why did they do that to you,' Riv asked him, touching her lip, 'in the weapons-field?'

'You would have to ask them,' Bleda said. 'I was not very good at your shield wall, slow to manoeuvre. It threw their timing. I kept bumping into Sorch, the one who started . . .' He touched his own lip.

'I know Sorch,' Riv said. 'A high opinion of himself.'

'Pride, that's the first step on the road to defeat,' Bleda quoted from the Sirak code. For a moment he was astride a horse, the wind in his hair, his mother and father either side of him, Altan and Hexa, his brother and sister, riding the wind. He could hear their laughter.

'*Pride, first step to defeat,*' his father had said to him.

'*Emotion, the wild horse that must be tamed,*' his mother had intoned. '*Be the master, not the mastered . . .*'

'Wear courage as a cloak, live free, never bend the knee,' he whispered.

'What?' Riv said.

'Nothing,' Bleda said. 'Sorch. He does not like me. I think it was just because I am Sirak. Not one of them.'

'That's stupid.' Riv shrugged. 'What matter if your eyes are a strange shape, or your skin a different colour? We all come from somewhere else when we start our training. Well, I didn't, but many do. People come from all over the Land of the Faithful to finish their training at Drassil, in the hope of becoming a White-Wing.'

'The White-Wings are fine warriors. Their discipline is to be admired,' Bleda said, and he meant it. He had trained in the weapons-field for many years, but had chosen his preferences. It was only recently that he had lifted a shield and attempted to train in the wall. It was a lot harder than it looked. Not just a case of standing around and pointing your shield one way or another, as Jin always mocked. There was unity of cause about it, a bond forged in shielding your brother-in-arms. There was a whispered appeal there.

'Where were you born, then?' Bleda asked Riv.

I was born into the White-Wings. My mother was a White-Wing, had me while on a campaign. She got back up and went back to her post right after, or so the story goes. Not sure I believe that one, though I wouldn't put it past my mam. She's a tough one.'

'What of your father? A White-Wing also?' Bleda could not recall having ever seen Riv around a man.

'He was. Died on the same campaign where I was born. Fighting Kadoshim in the Agullas Mountains down south, Mam told me. Lasted almost two years, that campaign.'

'I am sorry,' Bleda said.

'I never knew him.' Riv shrugged.

'I, too, have no father. He died in a raid. A rival Clan.'

Jin's Clan.

'I know. That's why they were at war, your Clan and Jin's, when . . . we came to Arcona.'

'Aye,' Bleda grunted.

Another silence grew between them. Bleda ran his hands over his bow once more, then put it back into its leather bag.

'We should be getting back,' Riv said. 'Else I'll miss prayers.'

They turned to walk back to the road, then heard a sound. The pad of footsteps, and instinctively both of them were slipping into the shelter of an oak.

The footsteps grew clearer, more than one person. Two shadows appeared on the road, one tall, one shorter. Starlight silvered them, fractured beams glistening upon the road.

By some mutual consent the two figures stopped and faced one another. Bleda strained to see them, but the starlight was weak and shifting all the time. The taller one was clothed in cloak and furs, seemed dressed for winter travel.

'This is as far as I can come,' the shorter one said, a woman's voice. Bleda heard Riv hiss, her body become tense as a warrior's under inspection. 'You must go on alone, now.'

'I don't want to,' the taller one said. Also a woman.

'I wish I could come further, be with you through—'

'No. I mean, I don't want to do this. Any of it.'

A silence.

'You have to. You have no choice,' the shorter woman said.

'There's always a choice,' the taller one answered, a whisper.

'Aye, and you made yours. Now you must see it through. The bad with the good.'

'What good!' the tall one spat. 'I tell you now, the only reason I'm leaving is because I cannot bear one more day around them. If I am I might . . .' A hand reached to a sword hilt.

'Don't be an idiot,' the shorter one. 'Go. Now.'

A sniffing sound, the taller one wiping at her eyes.

A silence, even Bleda's own breath sounding loud in his ears. He could feel the tension leaking from Riv.

'I don't think I can do this,' the tall one said into the quiet. 'I . . . can't.'

'You must, else you'll kill us all,' the shorter one said, pushing something into the other's hand. They embraced, a whispered goodbye, and then the tall one was striding along the road, turning off a dozen paces on, down the embankment on the far side and breaking into a loping run. Within moments she disappeared into the shadows of Forn Forest.

The shorter one stood still as stone, staring after her companion long after she'd disappeared. Just when Bleda thought he couldn't bear it any longer she turned and marched back down the road, towards Drassil.

'Wait,' Riv whispered, her hand gripping Bleda's wrist. He could feel the strength in her grip, iron-edged.

They stood there a hundred heartbeats. Then another hundred. Finally, Riv breathed out a long sigh and without a word walked back to the road. Bleda followed.

It may have been too dark for me to recognize them, but Riv knew who they were.

CHAPTER NINETEEN

SIG

Sig sat at the end of the Queen's bench in Uthandun's feast-hall, her legs stretched out to the side of the too-low table. A ten-night had passed since the rescue of Keld and the lighting of the beacons. Six days spent travelling back to Uthandun, four more as Sig prepared to leave. Keld had needed time to heal, as had his hound Fen. And although Sig was eager to be gone, she lingered an extra day or two so as to hear news as it trickled in to Queen Nara. Sig hoped for clues as to what the lighting of the beacons signified.

Nara was reading over a newly arrived parchment now, as servants cleared food from the table where they had all gathered to break their fast.

Nara's eyes were narrowing the further she read. She screwed the parchment into a ball and looked up with a glare.

'Attacks on my people, my towns, up and down the long length of Ardain,' she said. 'Kadoshim have been sighted, though from these early reports the bulk by far of the perpetrators are these new acolytes.' She swore in an unqueenly fashion and threw the screwed-up parchment on the floor.

Elgin was sitting beside her, and Madoc, the Queen's first-sword, stood at her shoulder. His eyes tracked the ball of parchment and he bent and picked it up.

'Looks like we were a little late in stamping on the hornets' nest,' Elgin said.

Maybe all I achieved was to kick and stir it up, Sig thought.

'The Order will help you fight this,' Sig growled, feeling a deep anger. The thought of Kadoshim and their servants striking at the people of Ardain like this, a close ally and friend to the Order . . .

She felt her fists bunching.

'I am loath to leave, when my coming may have begun this,' Sig said. 'But I must return to Dun Seren first, tell Byrne of what is happening. There is more to this, I feel it, and I do not like the not knowing. The beacons – I suspect they were not confined to Ardain.'

'No, they were not. My scouts have reported them blazing beyond my borders. Into the Land of the Faithful,' Nara said. 'I wonder what the Ben-Elim will make of this outbreak.'

Sig shrugged. She and her Order were not on the best of terms with the Ben-Elim. They tolerated one another, mostly because they shared a mutual enemy, but there was little trust or friendship between them.

'The Kadoshim are moving, the wheels of some plot turning. I will send aid to you,' Sig said. 'More than one giant, a huntsman and a warrior fresh from his Long Night.'

'We shall fight the Kadoshim together, as we always have,' Nara said. 'And you must feel no guilt in returning to Dun Seren now. From the reports thus far it is nothing Elgin and my warband cannot handle. Night raids, buildings torched, travellers attacked on my roads.' Nara gave a wave of her hand. 'We will bring them to heel. The greatest crime is that you are leaving without telling me your tales of my great-grandparents, something I was deeply looking forward to.'

'When I return,' Sig said, dipping her head at Nara's graciousness. Nara's kin flashed into her mind: Edana, Queen of Ardan and Conall, King of Domhain. They had been a good match, Edana's solid sense and quiet bravery tempering Conall's fiery temper and spontaneity. One other lost friend flickered through her mind, dark-haired, serious faced. A giant. A stab of pain. *Ah, my Gunil. How is it I miss you as much now as I did the day you fell?* With a shudder she pulled her thoughts back to the present.

'By your leave, I shall make for Dun Seren today,' Sig said.

A light rain was falling as Sig pulled herself into Hammer's saddle. The bear gave a low grunt; Sig felt the strength and energy in her, eager to be off and out of the fortress after close to a moon of convalescence in a stable block. Her injured paw seemed fine, scars marking where the Kadoshim's knife had pierced her.

She has her own sgeul, Sig thought, glancing at the fresh tattoos of thorns upon her own arm, marking the lives she'd taken since storming the Kadoshim's lair. The sgeul was the giant's ancient tradition, a tattooed band of thorns to mark every soul they had sent across the bridge of swords.

If I keep on going like this I will need a new arm, soon.

Cullen and Keld led their mounts over to Sig, both of them climbing into their saddles a little clumsily. Keld's left hand was still bandaged around the stumps of his missing fingers, though the wounds were healing as well as could be hoped. There was a new look in Keld's eye since they had found him strapped to the torturer's cross, a barely contained anger, and Sig did not think it was over the loss of his fingers, although that had hit him hard. He was a huntsman, skilled with bow, spear, axe and knife. Sig had known him since he had been a bairn, watched him grow through his training at Dun Seren, always deadliest with two weapons in his hands, preferably axe and knife.

He will have to relearn. He is as strong as an ancient oak. It is losing his hound that has hit him hardest.

Sig looked down, saw Fen padding at Keld's side, the surviving hound's slate-grey fur striped now with thick scars, one ear almost missing, its edge jagged as a broken tooth.

Ach, the blood that has been spilt over the war between Kadoshim and Ben-Elim, and us caught in the middle.

'All right, then?' Cullen said to her. He was looking more himself, his arm out of a splint now, though it was obviously still causing some pain.

'You need some poppy milk before we leave?' Sig asked him.

'No.' Cullen shook his head. 'Pain keeps you sharp.' he grinned.

Sig sighed and shook her head.

There was a flapping of wings and Rab dropped from the sky, alighting on the pommel of Sig's saddle. Hammer looked up over her shoulder and growled.

'She doesn't like uninvited guests,' Sig said.

With a squawk Rab launched into the air.

'You can sit here,' Cullen called out and Rab flew to him and wrapped his talons around his saddle pommel.

'Thank you,' the white crow squawked.

'You're welcome,' Cullen said with a smile.

'Happy,' Rab observed.

'I am,' Cullen replied. 'I've fought Kadoshim, bloodied my sword and spear for the Order. Taken a wound for the Order. And there is more battle to be had out there,' he said with a wave over Uthandun's battlements.

To be young again.

'What more could I ask for?' Cullen finished.

'My Hella back,' Keld snarled. 'My fingers back. Revenge.'

Cullen's smile shrivelled.

An affliction of the young – speaking without thinking.

Sig muttered to Hammer and the bear lurched into motion, across the wide courtyard. The edges were lined with faces, the walls as well. Sig saw Queen Nara standing beside the open gates with Madoc and a handful of shieldmen about her, warriors and townsfolk turned out to bid them farewell, the battlements above crowded, too. There were more riders in the courtyard, forty or so of them gathered in front of a long stable block: those who had volunteered to finish their training in the weapons court at Dun Seren, hoping to join the Order and become men and women of the Bright Star.

They look like bairns, Sig thought, though she knew they were all aged around fifteen summers, a mixture of male and female, all having come through their first year in the weapons court. She stopped in front of them and spent a long, silent moment looking into each one's eyes.

'Long road ahead of us,' she said, 'marching into winter and who knows what else. Kadoshim, maybe. And I'll be travelling fast, need to be in Dun Seren before Midwinter's Day. But if that's too much for you then you'll not last long in the weapons court of Dun Seren. Want to wear this bright star?' She tapped a silver brooch that fastened her cloak about her, saw nods amongst those gathered before her, their eyes bright with dreams of heroism and glory. 'You'll have to earn it, through blood, sweat and most likely a lot of tears.'

She gave them another long look, for the main part liked what she saw and grunted approvingly. Just as she was about to give the order to ride out, a horn blast rang from the gate-tower, a voice shouting, a guard pointing into the sky.

Shapes appeared from out of the rain, winged shapes, flying closer. Sig's hand rose to her sword hilt, thinking it was Kadoshim, but then she saw their wings. They were white-feathered.

A hush fell over the courtyard as the winged warriors grew larger in the sky, a space opening up in the courtyard close to the gate, before Queen Nara. The beating of wings grew louder, three Ben-Elim spiralling down to them, one alighting before the Queen, the other two remaining airborne, looping in slow circles above them.

Hammer growled, deep and rumbling, and Sig rested a hand on the bear's shoulder.

'Greetings,' the Ben-Elim before Nara said with a dip of his head, ignoring the growling bear behind him. He was tall and graceful, as were all Ben-Elim, magnificent wings of white feather furling upon his back, shaking the rain from them. He was dark-haired, wore a dripping coat of scaled-mail, held a long spear in one fist.

Kushiel, Sig thought, knowing him instantly. The arrogance in his stance annoyed her almost immediately.

'Well met, Kushiel,' Queen Nara said to the Ben-Elim. 'It has been many a year since I have had the pleasure of your company. Sadly I have received no word of your coming. I would have prepared a finer greeting for you.'

'There was no time,' Kushiel said. 'I come because of the beacons, have followed their trail. They are lit throughout much of the Land of the Faithful. They have led me here.'

'Only the three of you?' Nara said.

'There are more of us, still on the trail,' Kushiel gestured west. 'But I thought it –' he cocked his head to one side, searching for a word – 'courteous, to inform you of our presence.' Kushiel looked about the walls and courtyard, saw Sig upon her bear. He raised an eyebrow.

'Courtesy would have been to ask leave to cross my borders,' Nara said. 'Before you crossed them.'

Sig stopped a smile from splitting her face.

'We have made the Banished Lands safe, conquered the Kadoshim horde,' Kushiel said. 'All before you were born, I know, but still, I would hope that would count for something, that the passage of time had not dulled our sacrifice for you and your people.'

Be polite, Sig thought, seeing the anger rise in Nara. *Much as I feel the same, this is not the time for a falling-out with the Ben-Elim. Nothing would make the Kadoshim happier.*

'Ardain is aware of all that the Ben-Elim have done for us,' Nara said flatly.

Well done, lassie.

'I will have a room prepared,' Nara continued, 'food and

drink, where I can show you the proper courtesy you deserve. Where we can talk in more comfort. Come, follow me.'

'My thanks. First, one other thing, though. I came here for another reason, also. Israfil has sent me to many places, to many lords throughout the Land of the Faithful with the same request. And finally to you, our ally in Ardain. I would save it for a more private meeting, but . . .' Kushiel's eyes flickered back to Sig and those gathered behind him. 'I do not think it should wait.'

'And what is this reason?' Nara asked.

'Times are dangerous, the Kadoshim treacherous, and as these beacons show, they seem to be stirring.'

'Aye, all this I know,' Nara said.

'We Ben-Elim seek to protect you, the race of men, and giants –' he looked at Sig again – 'from the dread hand of the Kadoshim. But the practicalities. We number only so many, can patrol and protect only so much ground before our watch grows thin. There are many of your kind who . . .' He paused again, thinking on his words. 'Who assist with the practicalities of maintaining the peace. The White-Wings, the giant Clan.'

Not all of the giants.

'But they are not enough. We need more. Those within the borders of our protection give a flesh tithe, as is only right.'

A flesh tithe! Sig frowned at that, felt her hackles rising.

'Israfil has sent me to request a tithe from our neighbours, our allies,' Kushiel continued. 'From you. A tithe of warriors, to fight the good fight. The holy war against the Kadoshim.'

Nara was silent a long moment, quiet settling over the whole courtyard, just the gentle sigh of rain, the pulse of Ben-Elim wings from the two circling overhead.

'I will not order warriors of Ardain to leave their kin and their homes, to leave Ardain against their will,' Nara said.

'Then why do I see two score gathered behind the . . . *representative* of Dun Seren and their Order of the Bright Star?' Kushiel asked, his voice far from polite now. Flat and cold.

'They have chosen – volunteered – to go,' Nara replied calmly. 'And so they have my blessing.'

'Really?' Kushiel asked, his eyebrows rising again. 'Why would they choose *them?* A tower in the north, when they could join the Ben-Elim, the champions and protectors of your race? The Ben-Elim, who defeated the Kadoshim and their allies on that Day of Days—'

'You lie,' a voice said, low, grating, but heard by all in the square. It took Sig a moment to realize that the voice belonged to her.

Kushiel's head turned slowly to glare up at her.

'I was there, too,' Sig said. 'I rode in the charge that broke Asroth's allies on the plain before Drassil's walls. I *know* what Corban did. Fought Asroth, slew Calidus, helped to destroy the Seven Treasures and your gateway to the Otherworld.'

'Enough!' Kushiel snapped.

'Many sacrifices were made that day,' Sig said. 'They will never be forgotten.'

'We will never forget,' Cullen and Keld intoned either side of her, the mantra of their Order.

'And you should take a care,' Cullen said, 'that's my great-grandfather you're belittling. Might be the quickest way for you to go about getting your wings clipped.'

Sig gave a warning growl, at the same time wishing she'd said the same.

Kushiel's eyes blazed.

'Wings clipped?' he hissed, 'You arrogant pup.' He reached for the sword at his hip.

'Not in my realm,' Queen Nara said, a sudden tension in the air.

Kushiel drew in a deep breath and took his hand away from his sword hilt. He stared at Sig, Cullen and Keld, only his eyes hinting at the emotion he controlled within.

'They are free to choose, you say?' he directed at Nara.

'Aye. They are. They have. More than that, they requested the privilege of going to Dun Seren,' Nara said.

'Privilege!' Kushiel muttered. With a pulse of his wings, he lifted into the air and hovered gracefully above the group of volunteers.

'Trainees of Ardain, I speak to you,' Kushiel said. Sig felt Hammer begin to growl, a tremor deep in the bear's belly, vibrating into Sig's boots.

'You have a choice before you,' Kushiel called out. 'Dun Seren or Drassil. The Order of the Bright Star, or the Ben-Elim. Where would you rather complete your training? A crumbling tower filled with a fading order, or the greatest fortress in the world, home to the mightiest warband and warriors the Banished Lands have ever witnessed. What would you rather be part of?'

A silence filled the courtyard, the creak of harness, a horse stamping a hoof.

'Dun Seren for me,' a voice said, high, a tremor running through it. Kushiel's gaze snapped onto the speaker. A girl, dark-haired and gaunt. Despite her trembling voice she held Kushiel's gaze and returned it.

'Me too,' another voice called out. 'Corban was the greatest warrior that's ever lived, and he came from here. From the west.'

'Aye. He was one of us,' someone else called out, 'and he built Dun Seren. That's where I want to be, not Drassil.'

Murmurs rippled through the young warriors.

'I've heard there's wolven-hounds at Dun Seren,' another voice called out, 'big packs of them.' Fen gave a deep-rumbling growl, as if agreeing.

'*And me,*' Rab squawked, making Kushiel blink. '*Rab from Dun Seren, too.*'

Sig twisted in her saddle, looking back at them all.

'Are any of you for Drassil? Speak now, there's no shame or

insult in it. I'll think no worse of you, but it's better to know now, than hold it in.'

A long silence, serious faces looking back at her. All could meet Sig's gaze, none looking away, which held stronger weight to Sig's mind than any spoken word.

Sig nodded to herself and turned back to the Ben-Elim.

'There you are, then,' Sig said to Kushiel. 'You've had your answer.' She sat straight in her saddle. 'Now get out of my way.'

Kushiel hovered in front of Sig a long moment, then his wings beat and he was rising to the battlements.

'Israfil will hear of this,' he said to Nara, then winged higher, joining his kin, and with great beats of their white-feathered wings they were flying away from Uthandun, blurring into the rain-soaked sky.

Sig looked up at Nara and dipped her head to the Queen of Ardain. Then she lifted a fist and uttered a command, Hammer lumbering forwards.

'To Dun Seren,' she called out as she passed through the gates of Uthandun, her voice echoing and booming, and it felt good to hear those words out loud. Cullen and Keld rode either side of her, their small band of would-be warriors cantering in a ragged double column behind them. Sig rode down the long slope towards the Darkwood and onto the wide bridge that crossed the Afren, Fen loping ahead of her and merging with the shadows and murk of the Darkwood. Rab was clinging on to Cullen's saddle as if his life depended upon it, bobbing and swaying with the rhythm of it, wings ruffled and pointing in all directions.

Sig felt her spirits lift at the thought of returning home, but there was a shadow over her soul, the sense of terrors unseen growing ever stronger.

So, the Kadoshim are moving, and now I discover that the Ben-Elim are enforcing a tithe of flesh. Asking for volunteers is one thing, but this! They are enslaving those within their borders to a life of military servitude. This is something else that Byrne must hear about, if she does not know already. How can Ethlinn and Balur One-Eye condone this?

She heard Hammer grumbling beneath her, sensing her mood, and patted her shoulder.

'Dark days ahead, my bad-tempered friend,' she said, 'but we'll face them together.'

CHAPTER TWENTY

DREM

Drem walked back from the paddocks, boots crunching on the fresh snow in his yard, up the steps of his cabin, where he stamped his feet and then into the warmth of home. Heat from the hearth washed his face as he shed his cloak and pulled gloves off with cold-stiff and clumsy hands.

His head felt as if it were packed with wool, so much had happened.

It was highsun now, though the sun wasn't too clear in the sky outside, lurking somewhere behind thickening snow cloud that was rolling down from the north. It had taken almost half a day to deal with Calder's corpse. Drem had taken Fritha and her hound back to their hold, the hound still breathing, last he'd seen it. Hask, Fritha's grandfather, had started squawking at her like an old crow the moment Fritha set foot inside, remonstrating her for leaving without making his porridge.

'Your granddaughter needs some looking after, herself,' Drem had said to the old man. 'She's been through a hard morning. Could do with some care.'

'What have you done to Surl!' Hask had yelled at Drem, as the hound was in his arms at the time, Drem carrying it into their home and laying it upon a fur that Fritha ran and fetched.

'Feed him up: red meat, milk, cheese,' Drem had said to Fritha, choosing to ignore the barrage of abuse and accusations that frothed from Hask's mouth. 'He's a strong animal, got heart to take off into the Wild like he did. And don't listen to him,' Drem had added quietly, a nod at her grandfather.

Sometimes age doesn't mellow and soften, sometimes it twists and toughens, squeezing all the kindness out of a soul.

'He's not always like this,' Fritha had said. 'Worse in the mornings.' She'd paused. 'And the evenings.'

Drem had stood to leave, eager to get back to Olin.

Fritha had held his wrist as he made for the door.

'There's something about you, Drem ben Olin,' she'd said.

'There is?' he'd said, not knowing in the slightest what she meant.

'Yes.' She'd nodded, stepping closer, and suddenly he had been very aware of the sheer blue of her eyes, the scatter of freckles across her cheeks and nose.

'You're different from other men.'

Am I? Is that good? Bad? How?

'There's an innocence to you, nothing asked or expected. And a loyalty.' She had nodded to herself. 'You're a good friend to have, Drem, a rare find, and I'm grateful to you.'

'Well, you're welcome,' Drem had said, feeling his neck flush red. Not knowing what else to say, he'd turned and left, enjoying the pleasant feeling that was fluttering around inside his belly, and then he'd ridden hard for Kergard, seeking out Ulf the tanner and telling him of the grisly find. Drem had returned to his da while Ulf had sought out Hildith and the other Assembly members, promising to gather men and a wain. Olin didn't seem to have done much, bits of Calder were still spread about a wide area, but he was on one knee examining the ground.

'There was a bear here,' Olin had said as Drem dismounted. Bear-prints were all over the area. But Olin had been frowning, studying the ground.

'What's wrong, Da?' Drem had asked.

Then Ulf had arrived, a score of men with him, some Drem recognized, many that he didn't. It hadn't been long before any tracks and clues as to why Calder had been there were trampled away. Drem had stood with Olin as he spoke to Ulf, away from the others as men set to gathering up Calder's scattered remains and loading them into the wain.

'Look at the wounds on Calder's body,' Olin had said to Ulf.

'There's not much left to look at', Ulf had said bitterly. 'We must hunt that bear down.'

'Beneath his ribs there's another wound, doesn't look like a bear's doing, to me. Looks more like a blade,' Olin said. Ulf frowned.

'You must be mistaken,' Ulf had said.

'Just look,' Olin had said, and then he was calling Drem and they were leaving.

And now they were home, Drem feeling his extremities beginning to thaw as the fire crackling in the hearth did its work.

His da was standing with his back to Drem, leaning over a bench in their sparsely furnished room, the black iron of the new sword a dull gleam upon the dark-grained timber. He was riveting a wooden hilt of ash to the tang.

'How's your shoulder?' his da asked him, not looking up from his work.

'I can feel it again,' Drem said. 'Hurts like I've been kicked by a horse.'

'Good,' his da grunted. Drem knew what he meant. It was good that sensation was returning, the anaesthetic of the bat's saliva wearing off. The first thing his da had done upon returning to their hold had been to wash out Drem's wound, finding some usque to boil, letting it cool a little and then pouring it into the torn flesh. Drem had been grateful for the numbness then. After that it had been a poultice of comfrey and honey and then off to the barn to let the livestock out, and the paddocks for their two ponies.

He thought about Calder, could not believe that the big

man was dead. He looked at his da and felt a wave of sympathy for him, knew that he and Calder had been good friends.

And Calder's death. There's something about it that's not right. Another bear attack? And why was he in the woods when he was supposed to be meeting Da at the gates of Kergard? His mind was picking through the threads and tangles of this knot, but he couldn't focus on it, not yet, because there was something else foremost in his mind.

'Da, we need to talk.'

Olin paused in his work, a frozen moment, then he carried on, reaching for a strip of tan leather. Drem watched him as he pinned it close to the cross-guard, then began to wind it tight around the ash hilt, spiralling up towards the pommel.

'We do,' Olin replied. 'You've got questions.'

Da's always been good at understating an issue, but that's the biggest understatement I think I've ever heard.

'Yes,' he answered. 'Last night, the things you did, the things you *said!*'

Drem sucked in a deep breath, condensed all of the spinning questions into one.

'Who are you, Da?' he breathed.

A pause in Olin's work. 'Your father. First, before all other things.'

'I know that.' Drem sighed. *It's like getting a horse to walk where it doesn't want to. Just say it straight.*

'Da, last night, you spoke a spell. In a different language. And it worked! The metal wouldn't soften, even with the white heat of the forge. But then you spoke, and . . .'

And you sprinkled your blood on the fire and metal . . .

But some things he just couldn't say out loud.

'And the metal softened. And now you want to go running off and cut Asroth's head off. I thought Asroth was already dead, and how would you find him, anyway, to get close enough to, you know, chop his head off, and—'

'Stop!' Olin said, turning around. He'd finished wrapping the sword's hilt, was holding it now, blade lowered. There was something about it that drew Drem's eye, even though it was plain and simply bound, no gold or silver wire, no jewels or intricate scroll-work. Shadowed runes were carved into the dark metal of the blade and cross-guard. Drem noticed something else, at the top of the blade; just before it met the guard a small, four-pointed star was carved.

'There's something I need to show you. It will help you understand.' Olin walked away, still gripping the Starstone Sword, out of their shared room into his own bedchamber. He dropped to his knees beside his cot, pulled a pile of furs out of the way and dragged a chest into view. It wasn't particularly big, and about as long as Drem's arm. The wood was plain, old and worn.

'Tell me, Drem. What do you remember?'

'Of what?'

'Of before here. Five years we've lived in the Desolation. Before that, what do you remember?'

'Grass and mountains, Arcona and the mountains to the north.'

'Aye.' Olin nodded. 'I thought we were safe enough there, but then the Horse Clans began to fight and the Ben-Elim came running. Or flying, stamping on any sign of conflict that they hadn't created, enslaving more free people, and too close to us for my comfort. And before that?'

'Travelling, many places. Some hot. I remember a tower that overlooked a bay, the sea blue as the sky. The sound of gulls.'

'Aye, the Tower and Bay of Ripa,' Olin grunted. 'In the Land of the Faithful.'

Now Drem had started, the memories began to come quicker, piling one atop another.

'A black-walled fortress beside a lake, big as a sea.' He closed his eyes, seeing the fortress with its tall tower, looming over a meadow and lake. Ships bobbing, and something in the distance. 'Mountains.'

'Jerolin,' Olin said.

He thought again, enjoying this exercise, though it was getting harder.

'Trees high as the sky, a grey tower. A black river.'

'Brikan, in the fringes of Forn Forest. Before that?'

Drem frowned, screwing his eyes closed. He wasn't sure how long he was silent, sifting through memories. 'Grey hair, a man laughing? It's blurred, like a dream.'

'Aye, that'd be your grandfather,' Olin said, a rare smile ghosting his face.

'Where?' Drem asked.

'Close to Dun Taras, in the far west of Ardain.'

Drem remembered a bleak, rain-soaked land. With the memories came a warm, pleasant sensation in his belly. Then a sour note, an image of packing, running in the dark.

'I liked it there.'

'Aye, you did. I tried to settle there, but . . .'

'But what?' Drem asked.

'Too many people knew me, remembered. So we moved on, after your grandfather died.'

I don't remember him. Or, I do, but only a frozen picture, a sound or two. He felt a flash of anger – at what, he didn't know, just . . . anger.

'You were six summers old when we turned up on your grandfather's doorstep. Eight when we left. And before that?'

Drem rubbed his temples, eyes closed, straining to drag more memories up from the depths of his mind.

'Mam,' he said. 'Her smile.' He shrugged, felt a stinging, burning sensation behind his eyes. He pushed it away, straining to remember. 'Only broken images, really,' he said. 'Mostly of Mam, her eyes, her smile. A tower on a hill. Another woman, blonde-haired and tall, lifting me in her arms.'

Olin raised an eyebrow at that.

'Nothing else,' Drem finished.

'All right,' Olin said. 'This is all that is left of our past, locked away in this chest.' He drew in a deep breath, unclipped the chest and opened the lid. Drem leaned to peer in, saw his da pull out a roll of . . .

What?

Olin shook it out, held it up for Drem to see. A ringmail shirt, well tended, glistening with oil. His da laid it across his cot, then turned back to the chest. He lifted out a sword, sheathed in a plain-tooled scabbard of black leather, a belt wrapped around it. The hilt was leather-bound, worn and salt-stained from use and sweat, a tear in the leather showing a bone hilt beneath.

'What—' Drem started, but his da held up a hand, then lifted out a folded cloak of black wool, sitting upon it a large silver brooch, fashioned into the shape of a four-pointed star. It was beautifully wrought, the silver tarnished and in need of a polish, but still catching a ray of daylight from the shutters and throwing it back.

'I know that,' Drem said, a memory of a banner snapping in a breeze, above a stone keep, above an arched gateway.

'You should,' Olin said, holding the brooch up, catching more rays of light. 'It is the sigil of Dun Seren, Drem, where you were born, where you spent the first five years of your life. Because your mam and me, we belonged to the Order of the Bright Star.'

Drem swayed, felt unsteady for a moment, felt as if the once-solid ground of his life was shifting beneath his feet. He sat on the floor beside his da, blinking.

'Dun Seren. I've heard its name, many times,' Drem said. 'But never from you. People talk of it . . .' He searched for the right word. 'Reverently.'

'Aye,' Olin nodded, 'I suppose some do. Dun Seren guards one of the bridges into the Desolation, but is much more than that. It is the centre of a warrior caste, an order dedicated to learning the arts of combat and healing. Dedicated to hunting down and destroying the Kadoshim.'

Olin fell silent, then, his head drooping.

'That's how Mam died?' Drem whispered.

'Aye. Fighting the Kadoshim. We had received word from the Ben-Elim – never our trusted ally, but we shared a common enemy and so on occasion would share information – your mam and I, many others, rode out. We were ambushed . . .'

'Mam?' Drem asked, though he knew already.

'Aye,' his da said, a crack in his voice. 'She fell. Many fell.' Olin was silent a long time, staring into nowhere. A tear rolled down his cheek, disappeared into his iron-streaked beard. Eventually he sighed and shifted, lifted the sword, turning it to show Drem the hilt.

'I killed the Kadoshim that slew your mam. Took me half a year to hunt it down, but –' he shrugged – 'I took its head, brought it back to Dun Seren. I imagine it's there still. Apart from this piece.' Olin rubbed a finger along the sword hilt, where Drem thought the leather had frayed, revealing the hilt of bone beneath. He looked closer, saw that was not the case. A tooth was set into the hilt, a long, curved fang, the size of a finger.

'That—' Drem began.

'It is the fang of the Kadoshim that slew your mam, aye,' Olin said. 'Couldn't exactly be carrying its head all around the Banished Lands wherever we go, could I? A sword, though.' Olin shrugged. 'And it's yours, now.' He held the sword out for Drem, offering it.

Slowly, hesitantly, Drem reached out and took it, brushed his fingertips across the leather hilt and long tooth, felt a shiver run down his spine at the history within it, the tale it could tell. The pommel was round, engraved with a four-pointed star. He wrapped one fist around the hilt, the other gripping the scabbard, pulled it free. A rasping hiss of steel and leather. It was a long blade, a weight to it, though well balanced, the steel bright and gleaming, signs of notches in the blade worked on with a whetstone.

'About time you had your own blade,' his da said. 'You're making fine progress with the sword dance.'

'Am I?' Drem asked. It hadn't been that long since his da had introduced him to their new morning routine of sword dance and sparring, but Drem felt it was going well. It felt like putting on an old cloak, a bit stiff from lack of use, but fitting well and moulding to him in no time. It felt like coming home.

'Aye,' Olin said. 'But that's no surprise. You were holding a blade at Dun Seren from the age of two, and Sig had to pick you up and sit you on a wall to keep you off the weapons court when we were sparring.'

'Sig?'

'Aye. And you remember her, too, I think. You have just spoken of her. A blonde woman, tall. You're right there, she's a giant.' Olin snorted a laugh, his smile a rare sight. 'She used to pick you up and perch you on a wall while we were doing the sword dance, else you'd run around with your own wooden sword, practising on our shins.'

Drem smiled at that. 'Me?'

'Aye. Sig was my weapons-master. A great warrior.' He was silent a few moments. 'And an even better friend.'

Drem raised his eyebrows.

'Why have you never told me of this before. Any of it?'

So many emotions were coursing through Drem, competing to be heard. He felt hurt, deceived, deemed untrustworthy. And the one constant in his life, the solid rock that he had clung to for every remembered moment, his da, was not the man he had thought he was. He sucked in a deep breath.

'To protect you,' Olin said. 'To keep you safe. And, if the truth be known, because remembering . . . hurts.'

'But, to protect me from what?' As far back as he could remember Drem's memories were of an isolated, solitary existence of travelling, moving, only his da for a companion, working many trades as they travelled, on a farm, elsewhere for a blacksmith, hunting and trapping.

'What exactly were we running from?'

'From the Kadoshim, from war and death,' Olin said. Something about his da's voice was hollow, though. Like when they had been out in the Bonefells being tracked by wolven, and Olin told Drem to go to sleep, that all was well, but really Drem knew it wasn't. He'd awoken to his da stitching a series of wounds on his shoulder and chest, a dead wolven beside him.

'There's more you're not telling. If I lived at Dun Seren, the home of the Order of the Bright Star, home to the greatest warriors that have ever lived if half of what the tales tell is true, why was I not safe there? Surely *leaving* Dun Seren put me in greater danger.'

Olin looked away, could not meet his eyes.

'Please, Da, tell me. I cannot stand the secrets any longer, the not knowing.' He felt a wash of anger. 'I'm a man, fully grown. Stop treating me like a bairn!'

Olin met his gaze, a sadness in his eyes. 'But you're my bairn,' he said. 'And you always will be.'

'It's not fair. I deserve to know,' Drem said. He held his da's gaze until finally Olin sighed.

'I took you from Dun Seren to stop a war.'

'What—'

'Let me tell it,' Olin interrupted, 'and then ask me your questions.'

Drem nodded, gritting his teeth. He felt angry with his da, a rage simmering in his gut.

'Before your mam died, when the Order marched out to battle the Kadoshim, she . . .' Olin paused, eyes distant. He drew in a deep breath. 'She slew a Ben-Elim. It was in Forn Forest. This Ben-Elim was a captain, Galzur was his name. He insulted the Order. When I responded with anger he insulted me and challenged me to a duel. I . . . declined. He struck me.'

Olin stopped, his hand caressing his jaw, as if remembering the blow. 'And your mother slew him.'

He stopped there, rubbed his eyes with the heels of his palms. 'What I'd give to go back to that moment and accept Galzur's challenge. So much would have been different.'

'What happened? I still don't understand?' Drem said.

'The Ben-Elim were outraged, called your mam a murderer and demanded her death. Of course the Order did not see it that way. A decision was made that a trial would be held once the battle with the Kadoshim was resolved. Well, soon after that we fought the Kadoshim. We were ambushed, the Order took great losses – that was where your mam fell – and the Ben-Elim arrived *late*,' his da hissed the last word, a barely contained hatred in his voice. 'After the battle, when we had returned to Dun Seren, the Ben-Elim sent an envoy. Kol, a captain amongst them, bearing a demand from their high captain, Israfil. Lord Protector, they call him.' Olin's lips twisted in a sneer. 'They demanded recompense for the death of Galzur, still claiming that it was murder, and that a blood debt was owed.'

'What recompense?' Drem asked.

Olin looked into his eyes. 'You, Drem. They wanted you, as their ward. They wanted to take you from me and raise you at Drassil. You see, you are more than just mine and your mother's son. Your mam's sister was captain of the Order, still is, as far as I know. Byrne. A good woman. A fine leader. So you would have made a fine hostage, used to manipulate and control the Order of the Bright Star, which has from its beginning answered to no other authority. I was not about to give you up, and neither was Byrne or the Order. We had many friends . . .'

He shook his head. There was a pain in his da's eyes that Drem had never seen before.

'Byrne and the Order said no, and the Ben-Elim said that they would return and take you by force if they had to. Tensions were high. So, in the dead of night I rose, packed our bags and took you from Dun Seren. I have no love for the Ben-Elim, but to see the Order go to war with them, for us – I could almost hear the Kadoshim laughing. It would have been disastrous for the Banished Lands. Whoever the victor would have been, they would have been greatly weakened, ripe for finishing off by the Kadoshim. So . . .' He smiled grimly. 'Here we are.'

Drem looked at his da; Olin's face was lined with age and worry, with the weight of his burden. Drem knew his da loved him.

But the choices he made . . .

And all of a sudden the anger and hurt was gone, melting away, replaced with a wave of sorrow, for his da, for himself, for his mam, for the life they might have had together. His da moved, arms opening; Drem was confused, and then Olin was embracing him, pulling him into a hug that threatened to crack his bones.

'I am sorry,' Olin whispered, and then Drem was wrapping his own arms around his da, clinging onto him like a drowning man, both of them silent, but a thousand words spoken in their embrace.

Eventually Olin stepped away, tears staining his cheeks.

Drem felt as if a weight had been lifted from his shoulders, as he finally *understood*. But this new knowledge birthed so many more questions. He blew out a long breath and gave a hesitant smile.

I have so many new questions to ask! But first, I need some answers to the original ones.

Drem focused, trying to rein in his whirling mind.

'Spells,' he said, remembering the forge and his da's voice, the strange language, the hiss of blood sizzling in the dark and fire glow.

'You learn more than swordcraft at Dun Seren,' Olin said. 'If you're there long enough, and deemed to be trusted. The

Order was founded by Corban, a great warrior and leader. You've heard of him?'

'Aye, of course. Though not from you,' Drem said grudgingly.

'Well, I've avoided the subject. What do you know of Corban?'

'That he founded the Order at Dun Seren,' Drem said, sifting through the myriad legends and fireside tales he'd heard through the years. 'That he had a tame wolven.'

'She wasn't tame,' Olin murmured. 'Go on.'

Drem shrugged. 'That he was involved in the war against the Kadoshim, that he was at the Battle of Drassil, helped the Ben-Elim to defeat the Kadoshim. And that the Order of the Bright Star trains the most feared, skilful warriors who walk the land.'

He looked at his da, the weight of that sinking in.

You are one of those warriors.

'Corban didn't just fight against the Kadoshim,' Olin said, unaware of Drem's gaze upon him. 'He united the Kadoshim's enemies – men and women of all nations, giants, Jehar warriors, all rallied to him, fought for him. They loved him.' Olin shrugged. 'He was beneath a cairn before I joined the Order, but I spoke to some who knew him. A simple man, they said. Humble, quiet. Fiercely loyal to his kin and loved ones. And not bad with a blade in his hand, I'm told. In large part Corban was the reason the Kadoshim were defeated on that Midwinter's Day at Drassil, regardless of what the Ben-Elim will tell you. But he didn't just build a warrior school. It was in memory of two people, two of his most beloved friends who fell in the great battle. A warrior and a healer. Gar and Brina were their names. And Brina was more than a healer. At Dun Seren we are taught that spells are no more evil than a blade is. It is the wielder who makes that choice.'

That made a lot of sense to Drem and he nodded thoughtfully.

'And Asroth's head? I thought you had a fever, or were going mad.'

'Maybe I am,' Olin said, 'but I mean to end this, now. Asroth is encased within a layer of starstone rock, in the Great Hall of Drassil. Alive or dead, frozen or slain, no one knows, though many suspect he still lives. And that is why they are all here: Kadoshim, Ben-Elim. The Kadoshim have been seeking a way to free Asroth since the day of his entombment; he is their only hope of victory against the Ben-Elim, the only one strong enough to stand against them. And the Ben-Elim, they remain to guard him, to ensure that he never walks the earth again.'

'Why haven't they just killed him, then?'

'Because Asroth is encased in starstone rock, and not just a small lump of it like we have discovered. It is the sum total of the Seven Treasures, all of them destroyed and melted to molten slag. Many words of power were worked into them, and they hold a residue of that power still.'

'So how can you hope to kill him, then?'

'Because this is starstone metal,' Olin said, lifting the new blade. 'The only thing on this earth that has the power to pierce Asroth's tomb.'

Olin held Drem's gaze, watched him as the implications of that settled in his mind.

'With Asroth slain, the Kadoshim are finished, defeated for all time,' Olin continued. 'And the Ben-Elim, they would have no cause left to fight for. No reason to scour the land in search of Kadoshim, no reason to control and enslave the people of the Banished Lands. Their great lie would be cast into the light, revealed for what it is.'

'And what is it?' Drem asked.

'An excuse, a ruse fashioned to take and maintain power. Nothing more.'

'Are you sure about that?' Drem asked, frowning.

'With all that I am I believe it to be the truth,' Olin answered.

Drem thought about that a while, following the implications and likely consequences of all his da was telling him. It felt like a great responsibility settling upon them, like the branches in the forest, bowed beneath the weight of snow.

'There's a lot to do, then,' he said, as much to himself as to his da.

Olin laughed at that. 'And you say I understate things.'

'You'll need a scabbard for that,' Drem said, nodding at the starstone blade.

'Aye. It's next on my to-do list. You can help me.' Olin stood, gripping Drem's wrist and pulling him to his feet. 'You should try it on,' he said, pointing at Drem's new sword.

'Are you sure, Da? It doesn't feel right. It's yours.'

'No. It's yours. A gift from father to son. And besides, I've got myself a new sword now.'

'Twenty-one summers, and I have a sword,' Drem mused as he buckled the scabbard-belt about his waist. It fitted well, though the weight of the sword against his hip felt strange.

'I wanted you never to need one,' his da said. 'But I have a bad feeling of late.'

'Maybe I should have a ringmail shirt, as well, then.'

'You probably should,' Olin smiled, 'but that one's likely a little small for you. It wouldn't be a bad idea for you to have one of your own, though. Saved my life a hundred times, that shirt.'

'We'll have to go see—'

Drem stopped. He'd been about to say Calder the smith. But Calder wouldn't be making anyone a ringmail shirt. Or anything else, ever again.

There was the sound of hooves outside, growing louder.

CHAPTER TWENTY-ONE

RIV

Riv concentrated, her entire being focused on drawing her bowstring perfectly. She felt the feather tickle her cheek.

Done it.

'No. You're doing it all wrong,' Bleda said in her ear.

'How?' Riv grunted, trying to keep any hint of the snarl she was feeling out of her voice.

'Start with your bow hand, not the draw hand.' Bleda walked around into her field of vision.

'Firstly. Your knuckles are white. No, no, no. Don't grip the bow in a fist. Now, when you release the shaft and string your fist will twist the bow a fraction, and your aim's thrown. Let the bow rest in your hand, then the string-draw applies the pressure. Understand?'

'Yes,' Riv grunted, feeling a tremor beginning deep in the shoulder muscle of her right arm. Her whole body was aching, the pain worse in her joints. She suspected there was more to it than the drawing of a yew bow, though her wrists and elbows were screaming under the increased pressure.

'Secondly, your arm is straight. This is wrong. I keep telling you, a bend at the elbow of your bow arm, otherwise, when you release, the string will shred your skin. Remember last time?'

Riv did, the throbbing bruise on her arm not letting her forget.

'So,' Bleda continued, 'bow arm bent, *not* straight, bent.' He paused. 'Understand?'

Argh.

'Yes.'

'Release your draw, you cannot hold this small tree at that angle for more than a few moments. It is a poor design.' There was a hint of a smile at the edge of his lips, just for a moment.

Is he enjoying this? Riv clenched her teeth and resisted the urge to throw the bow at Bleda.

'It's worked well enough for our huntsmen,' Riv growled.

'You saw Jin with a bow,' Bleda reminded her.

'Aye,' Riv sighed, a hint of defeat in her voice.

'Do not take too long about any of it,' Bleda said. 'A fight is constant motion, fluid, you moving, your enemy moving. Who has time to stand still for a dozen heartbeats and aim?'

'Show me,' Riv said, holding the bow out to him.

'I don't like these bows, but . . .' He shrugged and took the longbow of yew from her. Riv took a step back, looked at the target and then back at Bleda. The string of his bow was thrumming.

'There,' he said, holding the bow out to her.

'Huh?' Riv grunted. She looked back to the target, saw an arrow in the target's head, just about where an eye socket would be found.

'The eye is a more certain kill if your foe is wearing a cuirass and chainmail. Depending on the distance,' Bleda said.

'That is amazing,' Riv said.

'Pah,' Bleda said. 'From horseback, against a mounted foe. That is where skill *really* starts to tell. But you will never shoot from horseback with a bow like this,' he said, giving Riv back her bow. 'Too long, too hard to draw. Which is why in Arcona we have bows like this.' He patted his recurve bow, sitting in a case on his hip. He never seemed to be parted from it these days.

'Do not be dejected,' Bleda told her. 'Before too long I will have you loosing three shafts before the first hits your target.'

You have greater faith in me than I do.

Footsteps, a tap on Riv's shoulder.

It was Vald, her friend.

My once-friend, she corrected herself. *Strangely, since I kicked him in the stones we have not been so close.*

'Can we talk?' Vald said to her. Riv realized that she was looking him in the eye.

I thought he was taller than me.

He was still broader, covered in a sheen of sweat, muscles bulging after his training session in the weapons-field.

He looks tense.

'Aye,' Riv said.

'Somewhere private,' Vald said, not able to meet her eyes.

Riv felt her anger stirring, remembering him treating her like a servant, in front of the whole hundred. Warriors she had lived amongst all her life.

'Whatever it is, you can say it here. And if you're about to ask me to clean your boots, you'd better bid a final farewell to your stones.'

A moment's pause, pride warring with something else across his face.

Shame?

Vald sighed, blowing out his cheeks. 'I just wanted to say . . .' Vald looked about, saw Bleda standing nearby, outwardly appearing calm and controlled as always, but nevertheless there was something about the way he was looking at Vald. A threat in his eyes. Vald returned his gaze, then looked back to Riv.

'I wanted to say, I am sorry. I should not have treated you like that. We have been friends for many years, trained together, guarded each other's backs.' He shrugged. 'What can I say? I'm an idiot when I drink.'

Riv felt her anger melt away, replaced with a pleasant glow. She grinned at him.

'It's forgotten,' she said easily. Vald gave her a huge grin, relief rolling off him in waves, and offered her the warrior grip, which technically was reserved for those who had passed their warrior trial. Riv appreciated the gesture and took his arm.

A noise drew their attention, the blowing of horns.

The three of them looked at one another.

'Too early for prayers,' Vald said.

'It's the Lore-Giving,' Bleda said.

'Aye,' Riv agreed. People were beginning to leave the weapons-field, heading towards Drassil's Great Hall.

'Come on,' Riv said, and with a shrug of her shoulders she led them off the field.

The last time this happened a half-breed Kadoshim tried to slay Israfil before every eye in Drassil.

She quickened her pace.

As they followed the crowds hurrying through Drassil's wide streets Riv saw her sister, Aphra. She hurried over to her.

Because the two women she'd seen on the road, that night with Bleda, had been her sister and Fia, and since then Fia had disappeared from their barrack, had not been seen at Drassil. Aphra had been difficult to pin down every time Riv had approached her.

They stood in the midst of the crowds hastening to the Lore-Giving summons, a rock amidst a fast-flowing river.

Aphra blinked. 'There's no time for this.' She scowled, waving a hand at the air. 'The summons.'

Riv grabbed her arm, holding her fast. 'I saw you,' she said in a low voice, urgently, 'on the road with Fia. Where is she?'

A flash of concern, then anger.

Aphra tugged free of her grip and strode on with the fast-flowing crowd, leaving Riv wondering what it was her sister was hiding.

The Great Hall thrummed with murmured conversation, full to the brim with Drassil's residents. The tiered steps were not enough to contain everyone, crowds standing pressed close together in stairwells around the room. In the chamber's heights Ben-Elim flew in lazy circles. They raised horns to their lips as a door opened and Israfil, the Lord Protector, strode into the room, a procession of Ben-Elim behind him. Golden-haired Kol was first amongst them, a score more, spread in two wide columns, and between them walked two figures. One Ben-Elim, one a woman in the training livery of a White-Wing.

Israfil stopped on the dais, standing before the figures of Asroth and Meical, giant guards looming behind him.

'Faith, Strength and Purity,' Israfil said, shouting passion-ately, far from the monotone recitation that was the normal way of speaking Elyon's Lore. His eyes were blazing, wings twitching with pent-up anger.

'For that is the Way of Elyon,' Riv muttered along with the rest of the chamber, though she was unsettled by Israfil's demeanour.

'A crime has been committed, here at Drassil,' Israfil's voice boomed, a hush falling over the chamber.

Riv could see the two figures escorted in the midst of the Ben-Elim. One was the Ben-Elim Adonai, the friend of Kol. He had feasted with Aphra's hundred the night Riv had kicked Vald in the stones, been seated on the table of honour, along-side Aphra. His skin was pale as milk, eyes dark hollows. The warrior beside him lifted her head. It was Estel, who had been sitting on the bench beside him the same night. Her eyes were red for weeping, face twisted with shame.

'They are accused of improper relations,' Israfil continued, 'of behaving in a manner which has been deemed unaccceptable between a Ben-Elim and a mortal of the Banished Lands.'

Whispered murmurs rippled around the chamber. Riv felt herself lurch in her seat, the horror of Israfil's statement like a blow.

'Elyon the Maker created us all,' Israfil continued, 'but the Ben-Elim he created as beings of spirit, without the desires of the flesh. We have become flesh now, as you humans are flesh, but that does not mean he created Ben-Elim and humans to lie one with the other. We Ben-Elim are the Sons of the Mighty, the Separate Ones, that is how Elyon made us, and that is how we shall remain!' He held a hand up as shouts rang out. 'These two have not committed that foul act, or their lives would be forfeit. But they have acted improperly, one with the other, and committed acts which if left unpunished may lead to the Great Transgression. To mix the blood of eternal with mortal.' He paused there, his eyes blazing with wrath. 'We are Ben-Elim, separate, pure, created so by Elyon. Our blood cannot become diluted, mutated. And that truth is the same for the mortals of these Banished Lands, whether mankind or giant.' He paused, looking down contemptuously upon Adonai. 'You would make us *less*, your thoughtless act threatening to bring upon this earth a new, tainted breed, corrupted by the weakness of human emotion, ruled by the desires of the flesh, rather than Elyon's Lore. You would make us too weak to enforce the Lore of Elyon.' He almost spat those last words, took a long, trembling breath to compose himself. 'We were created separate, and our blood must remain so. The Lore demands it. By pain of death.'

He turned to the Ben-Elim flanking Adonai and nodded to them, at the same time drawing his sword.

The Ben-Elim gripped Adonai and forced him to his knees.

A hush fell across the chamber, across the whole of Drassil, it felt to Riv.

Adonai looked up at Israfil as he approached.

'Don't do this,' Adonai whispered, though his voice carried across the crowds. 'We are all Elyon's creation.' His eyes flickered to the Ben-Elim standing guard about him, lingering for a moment upon Kol. He stared back at Adonai with hard eyes.

'Be silent, Lore-breaker,' Israfil roared as he stood before Adonai.

'Adonai of the Ben-Elim, I judge you guilty of breaking our Holy Lore,' Israfil cried out as he raised his sword, 'and in judgement I take your wings.' The sword sliced down, a sound like soft wood splitting, an explosion of white feathers as the wings were sheared away, followed by a piercing scream, ringing out, another heaped upon another, seeming to Riv that they would never end, fading slowly to a piteous whimper as Adonai slumped in the grip of the Ben-Elim to either side of him. His two white wings lay in the dirt, speckled with crimson as blood pumped sluggishly from the two stumps upon his back.

Israfil and the Ben-Elim guards stared down at Adonai. Riv glimpsed a ripple of emotion on Kol's face, something between pity and shame.

Israfil turned to Estel.

To Riv's surprise the woman did not cry or whimper, but instead stood and returned Israfil's gaze with a silent courage.

Like a White-Wing, Riv thought.

'You, Estel ap Toril, are stripped of your rank and position in the White-Wings. You are banished, from this moment forth, from Drassil and the Land of the Faithful. You have two moons allotted to you to vacate this realm, after which, if you are discovered within our borders, you will be executed without trial.'

He glared down upon her, his sword still dripping with Adonai's blood.

A white feather drifted down to the ground between them.

He stepped forwards and grabbed the White-Wing emblem sewn upon the shoulder of her training vest, ripped it off and threw it to the stone floor.

'Do you understand your punishment?' Israfil said.

Estel did not answer, just stared at Israfil.

'Estel ap Toril, do you understand your punishment?' Israfil repeated, quieter, yet more terrifying.

'I do,' Estel said, bowing her head, a sob rippling through her, quickly controlled.

'Get them out of my sight,' Israfil snarled and strode from the Great Hall.

CHAPTER TWENTY-TWO

DREM

Drem opened the door, looking out and along the track that led to their hold. Riders were approaching. Lots of them.

'Da,' Drem said, stepping out onto the porch. His da followed, moved in front of him, wrapping a cloak about his shoulders and slipping the Starstone Sword inside it.

Riders cantered into their courtyard, ten, twelve, sixteen men, more still coming. Drem felt a leaden weight shift in his belly, because he recognized some amongst them. The man at their head was shaven-haired and had a scar running from mouth to jaw, and behind him rode a man with a wispy red beard. He had a new bruise that covered half his face, one eye purpled and swollen.

Has he been fighting someone else?

As they reined their mounts in before the cabin, Drem recognized more of them: one had a splinted forearm, and another splint upon his hand, where Drem had crushed it and broken finger bones. Others gathered behind, an aura of bad intentions radiating from them. Drem was used to living amongst trappers and men who existed on the fringes of civilization, men who lived by their own laws, or none at all. But there was something different about these men, something worse, as if there was a stain upon their souls.

'What do you want?' Olin said to the bald one with the scar, who still seemed to be their leader. 'Why are you here?'

'We're here to hang the murderers of Calder the smith,' the bald man said as he dismounted, 'and then I'm going to strip your hold of anything worth a coin and burn the rest, leave you two swinging from a beam.' He grinned at them both as he unstrapped a long thick rope from his saddle and strode towards the cabin, men swarming behind him.

'What are you talking about?' Drem said. 'Murderers?'

'Don't deny it,' the bald man said. 'Ulf's saying Calder was stabbed and left in the woods for a bear to maul. Everyone knows you were in Calder's forge all night long – robbing him, no doubt. There's witnesses. The town guards saw you leaving Kergard at dawn, and your hold is the closest to where he was found.'

He put a boot on the first step to the cabin, men either side of him.

Drem felt a jolt of panic ripple through him. He opened his mouth to protest, to point out that their logic was flawed: how could they have murdered Calder and left him in the woods if witnesses had sighted them in Kergard at dawn? But he knew it would be futile.

These men mean to see us dead and just want an excuse to make it happen, and there's near enough a score of them! Not even Da's weapons-skill and magic can fix this!

'Drem,' his da said, a hissed whisper. One look at him and Drem knew he'd reached the same conclusion. 'Back inside, through the cabin and out the back window.'

For a moment Drem almost did it, so used was he to following his da's instructions. Then he realized his da did not intend to follow him. Fingers to his throat, counting the beat of his heart. It was a lot faster than normal.

'No,' Drem said, stepping forwards to stand beside his father.

Olin glanced at him, saw the resolve in Drem's face and gave a curt nod.

'We're innocent of Calder's death,' Olin shouted, 'but

another step closer and I'll have *your* blood on my conscience, and not lose a single night's sleep over it.' He shrugged his cloak from his shoulder, freeing his sword arm, and raised his black blade, high, two-handed, over his head.

The bald man hesitated on the steps, whether at Olin's words or at the sword in Olin's hands, Drem did not know, but his eyes were fixed on the blade of the black sword.

Others around and behind the bald man pressed forwards, though, and, for Drem, everything slowed. He saw Wispy Beard climbing the steps, a spear in his hand, a frenzied grin splitting his face, realized the man had shaved his head.

He must be cold. An impractical act for one who is wintering in the north.

Then someone was stabbing a spear at Olin, blade aimed at his da's gut. Olin just seemed to shuffle his feet and then the spear was stabbing past him, through thin air, at the same time Olin's black sword was chopping down, cutting into the man's head, just behind his ear. There was a wet cracking sound, and what looked like a burst of flames around the starstone blade and the man's head, except that the flames were black and sulphurous, and then the sword was shearing out through the bottom of the man's jaw, the front of his face falling to the step with a slap, blood and bone and brains splattering those either side of him. Olin kicked the still-standing corpse back into those behind, men falling, tangled.

Drem fought the urge to vomit. The sight of a man swinging a sword at him helped him to get that under control. He stumbled back a step, felt the hiss of air past his face as the sword missed by a handspan.

How can this be happening? I just watched my da kill a man, while others are baying for our blood. Can I do this? Can I take another's life?

He felt sick, wished for a moment he'd taken his da's advice and run for the back window, though he wouldn't have left without his da.

What do I do? Stand and fight? Kill or be killed?

A glance at his da, who was holding the top of the stairs, chopping through a spear shaft, splintering it like kindling, back-swinging across someone's eyes, a spray of blood as they fell away.

And then the decision was taken from Drem. As more men pressed onto the steps to the cabin, the man with the sword who'd just tried to carve a slice from Drem's face was pushed forwards, and without thinking Drem stepped in to meet him, slipping past his sword, slashing with his bone-handled seax across the man's arm, chopping with his axe between neck and shoulder. The man screamed, blood bubbling in a fountain as he collapsed, tripping the man behind him.

Pain lanced across Drem's arm, a spear-thrust grazing him, a hand gripping his axehaft, pulling him forwards. He slashed and stabbed wildly with his seax, heard a scream, the grip on his axe pulling him off balance. He stumbled, dropped to one knee, something hard glancing off his head, white lights exploding in his vision as he stabbed blindly, felt his blade punch into something, the resistance of flesh, the grate of bone.

His vision cleared and he was still on one knee, his knife blade stuck to the hilt in the thigh of the man who had gripped his axe haft. More bodies were pressed behind him, men shouting, yelling, reaching for him. He tried to see his da, but there was a crush about him, no sign of Olin, though he did hear a man scream, which was encouraging – meant that fighting was still going on, just as long as the one screaming wasn't his da.

Drem twisted his blade inside the man's leg, heard a corresponding scream, rising in pitch and felt the grip on his axe disappear. He wrenched his seax free of the man's thigh, a gush of hot blood over his hand, and he tried to stagger to his feet. More blows, hands grabbing him, dragging him in all directions, and he was lurching forwards, then his feet were leaving the ground and he was being carried, passed down the steps of the cabin and into a courtyard. The noose of a rope was slipped around his neck, yanked tight; it was Drem's turn to scream, fear erupting in his belly, gave his limbs strength and he kicked and stabbed and hacked. There was a sharp pain in his left arm and his axe was gone, hands holding his other arm, pinning him, twisting and then his seax was gone, too.

'DREM.' He heard his da roar, 'DREM.'

'Da,' he tried to yell back, but the noose around his neck was too tight to flex his vocal cords fully. He saw branches overhead, a rope hurled across them, hands grabbing it, and the pressure about his neck was growing and he was being hoisted upright, his feet dangling and men were shouting and jeering and he couldn't breathe, his hands grasping at the rope around his throat.

It's too thick, too tight, and a blind terror gripped him, his lungs burning, screaming for a breath, everything about him fading as the instinct to live, to breathe, consumed him. Black spots blurred his vision, joining like spilt ink, blotting out the world.

Another sound, merging with the frantic drumbeat of his heart, drowned out the roar of the baying mob about him, a rhythmic thunder. Voices, shouting, louder, and then he was spinning, someone grabbing him, lifting his legs and abruptly he could breathe, only a trickle as if through a reed, a gasping burn but nevertheless sweet, glorious relief. A jerk on the rope, realized someone had cut it. A voice close by and his vision was returning, blurred, focusing slowly.

'What's that Olin feeding you?' the voice said and he saw Hildith, owner of the mead-hall, sitting upon a horse. One of her burly guards had hold of Drem. Another guard cut the rope above him and he was dumped unceremoniously onto the ground.

'My thanks,' Drem managed to rasp and Hildith nodded to him.

'Gather them up,' Hildith shouted, more of her guardsmen appearing and rounding up the men who had tried to lynch

Drem. Ulf appeared in the courtyard, riding at the head of a dozen men. He looked around wildly and then saw Drem, dismounted and hurried over.

'Da,' Drem croaked.

'Your da's fine,' Ulf said. 'Least, I don't think any of the blood he's covered in belongs to him.'

Ulf began to laugh, a baritone chuckle that soon turned into something that resembled the braying of a donkey. Then Drem's vision blurred again, the darkness swooping in from the edge of his vision. His last sensation was that of weightlessness, of falling.

Drem jerked upright, coughing and spluttering. His throat felt as if it was on fire, and that air was trickling through a hole the size of a needle.

They're killing me, hanging me.

'Easy, son,' a voice said close by, his da, instantly soothing him, and he calmed.

'Keep breathing, nice and slow. You're fine.'

Drem did and, opening his eyes, saw his da leaning over him, that anxious look on his face.

'Ah, my boy, I thought I'd lost you, for a few moments back there,' Olin said. He cupped Drem's cheek. 'My wonderful, wonderful boy,' he whispered, a smile softening his eyes. Blood-spatter freckled his face and his clothes.

All of him, Drem realized as he sat up, taking his time, his da offering him a ladle of water.

The first sip felt like knives slipping down his throat, but after that he started breathing more easily, drinking more normally.

'What happened?' Drem croaked, his voice grating like rusty hinges.

'Hildith and Ulf arrived, with half of Kergard, it looks like.'

Drem looked about, saw he'd been carried back to the

porch and was sitting up now on a bench under a window. His back was wet from snow-melt.

'What're they doing here?'

'They're leading a bear-hunt; thought we might like to join them. Arrived just in time.'

'I'm in definite agreement there,' Drem said, touching his throat. The skin was raw, weeping in places from rope-burn. 'Are you all right?'

'Aye,' his da said, 'though I wouldn't have been if Hildith had arrived a hundred heartbeats later.'

'And the others, those trappers and miners?'

'They're still here. Ulf has threatened them, and there's more swords at his back than there are behind Burg.'

'Who?'

'Their leader. The bald one with the scar. So they'll abide by Ulf's word. For now.'

'For now,' Drem muttered, sitting up, rising slowly. He looked about, saw men and horses milling about their court-yard, a few braces of hounds baying excitedly. Wispy Beard was giving him a dark look. Drem looked away, saw a row of bodies stretched out upon the porch, seven of them with cloaks wrapped about them.

'There's blood feud now,' Olin said. 'This will only get worse.' He lowered his voice, handing Drem back his seax and axe. 'It's time for us to leave the north.'

'Couldn't agree more,' Drem said, the thought of getting away from this murderous bunch a happy thought, though oddly his next thought was of Fritha kissing his cheek beneath snow-heavy boughs.

Maybe she could come with us. Don't like the thought of leaving her here with the likes of them about.

He shot Burg and Wispy and their crew a dark look as he slipped his weapons back into their sheaths and loops at his belt. As he did so, he felt the hilt of his new sword, realized he hadn't even thought of using it during the fight.

'Habit.' His da shrugged, seeing his look. 'Besides, it was close-quarter fighting, you made a good choice.'

'Did I?'

'You're still breathing, but there's two down there that aren't, and that's because of you.'

Drem felt that like a punch, somewhere deep inside. Two lives, gone, because of him. He looked at the shape of their bodies beneath their cloaks, once men who laughed, loved, smiled, swore, now reduced to sacks of meat and bone.

'Would you rather it was you down there, instead of them?' his da said, watching his face closely.

'No,' Drem said, no hesitation there.

'That's all there is to it,' his da said. 'You didn't go looking for blood, didn't make this happen. Sometimes you can only respond, and sometimes the only answer is—'

'Blood and steel,' Drem finished.

'Aye. Sig taught me that.' Olin smiled, a hesitant twitch of his lips. 'Ah, but it feels good to be able to talk to you of her. To talk of the past. I feel like a weight has been lifted. I should have told you sooner.'

Aye, you should.

The thud of footsteps: Hildith and Ulf thumping up the stairs to them, Ulf favouring his injured leg, Asger the market trader at his side.

'You all right, lad?' Hildith asked Drem.

'Thanks to you.' Drem nodded.

'Might have to agree with you,' she said, grinning. 'Think you might owe me one, there.'

'I do,' Drem said.

'We both do,' Olin added. 'All of you.' He looked to Ulf and Asger.

'You should come with us,' Ulf said. 'On this bear-hunt. So I can keep an eye on you. And you're not bad when it comes to tracking, I've heard . . .'

'What about them?' Olin nodded at the group of trappers who had tried to hang them.

'They're coming too. We'll have a line, you at one end, them at the other, me, Hildith and our lads in between. You'll never be closer than half a league.' Ulf tugged on his greying beard, looking around the hold. 'Don't like the thought of you two here, alone.'

Neither do I, thought Drem. *Don't really like the thought of wandering around in a forest with them, either. But sometimes it's safer when you can see your enemy.*

Olin frowned. 'We'll come,' he said.

'And when we get back,' Hildith said, 'we do need to ask you two some questions about Calder. You were seen at his forge through the dead of night, seen leaving Kergard at dawn.'

'I paid Calder to use his forge,' Olin said. 'Had some iron-work to do. He was supposed to meet us at Kergard's gates at dawn. He wasn't there, we left.' Olin shrugged.

'Huh,' Ulf grunted. 'Doesn't explain what he was doing out here in the arse-end of the Wild, though.'

'Or what looks like a knife-wound in his corpse,' Hildith added.

'That's jumping to conclusions,' Ulf said. 'Calder could have fallen on something sharp, even his own blade if he was trying to defend himself.' Ulf shrugged. 'There's questions, and there'll be plenty of time to answer them, but for now we know a bear's out there, and we need to kill it, before it attacks again. So, we'll get that job done first, eh?'

'Agreed,' Hildith grunted.

Ulf winked at Drem and then he was turning, shouting commands, and men were climbing into saddles. Drem was running to the paddocks, his da fetching saddles and tack. It wasn't long before they were all riding along the track that led from Drem and Olin's hold, back towards the spot where they'd followed Fritha's tracks. The plan was to return to the location that Calder's body had been discovered and begin their search from there.

Drem and his da were riding at the head of the column, their numbers more like a small warband.

Calder was well liked by all in Kergard. If we find that bear, it won't be walking away from this lot.

Drem glanced towards Fritha's hold as they reached the spot where they'd seen her tracks that morning. He frowned and reined his horse in. Stared.

'Oh no.'

'What?' Olin grunted beside him, followed his look.

Drem spurred his mount on, tugging on the reins, reached a gallop in a score of heartbeats. He heard hooves behind him, voices shouting, but he didn't stop or even slow, dug his heels in his pony's ribs as they approached the fence and his mount was leaping, flying through air, the fence passing beneath them, hooves thudding, snow exploding, galloping on. Drem reined in as they drew near to the timber cabin, a spray of snow, and he was leaping from his mount's back, drawing his sword this time, and running up timber steps to the door.

It had been smashed in, the frame and wall around it a splintered wreck, wide enough for two horses abreast to ride through. Blood was smeared on the floorboards.

'Drem, wait,' he heard his da shouting behind him, but he ignored it and stepped inside the cabin.

He had to wait a moment for his eyes to adjust, no fire or torches burning, just shadow, pierced by beams of daylight that flooded through a huge hole in the side of the cabin. Then Drem saw a shape, gouts of dark blood pooled on the floor about it, and he rushed forwards.

It was Surl, the hound, its belly and flank opened by raking claws. Drem put fingers in the blood. There was an echo of warmth, faint as dawn's first kiss. There was blood on the hound's teeth, too, some flesh and fur, what looked like a shred of leather.

Brave hound, gave some back before the end, then, Drem thought, patting the animal's head.

Fritha, where are you? Please, be alive.

He stood, continued searching as his da's silhouette was framed in the smashed doorway.

A denser shadow in the darkness, a body. Drem felt his heart lurch as he approached it, slowly this time, trying to prepare himself to see Fritha's blonde hair, the pale, fine-freckled beauty of her face. He stood over the body. It was turned away from him, half-buried beneath the shattered door. He crouched down, put a hand on its shoulder and turned it towards him.

It was Hask, Fritha's grandfather. Eyes and mouth wide open, shock and horror mingled, a huge, ragged wound across his chest, flecks of bone in the torn flesh. Drem heard his da going through the debris, searching meticulously, the consummate tracker.

Drem strode to the hole in the wall, saw a bloody bear-print, the timber floor claw-gouged. More blood.

But no Fritha.

CHAPTER TWENTY-THREE

RIV

Riv sat in her barrack's feast-hall, picking at a plate of boar ribs and sweet parsnips. Jost and Vald were with her, sitting beside each other. At any other time the sight of them would have made her chuckle, Jost slim and tall as a sapling, looking as if he was all sinew and bone, and Vald, so muscled that his linen shirt and leather vest were straining to contain him, making him appear squat, which he wasn't, being taller than Riv.

No, not taller than me now. I must have grown, and quickly. Is that normal?

It was quiet in the feast-hall. Aphra and her captains had been summoned to a meeting with Israfil and the Lord Protector's council.

That's not the only reason it's quiet in here, though.

The mood amongst Aphra's hundred had been subdued and sombre ever since the afternoon's judgement in Drassil's Great Hall had taken place.

Poor Estel, having your wings torn from you – something you have worked and trained your whole life to achieve – and then exiled. No kin, no friends, having to start all over again. And where would she go? Ardain, Tarbesh, Arcona, the Desolation? Where else is there?

Riv sighed, prodding her food with a knife. She knew what Estel and Adonai had done was wrong, an act that disobeyed the greatest of Elyon's Lores that forbade the Great Transgression.

But they did not actually do that. What were they caught doing? Kissing, in an embrace? Flirting? Riv had seen them at Aphra's table, thought they were too close, a touch lingering too long, and she'd felt the wrongness of it then.

But does that deserve so great a punishment? Adonai's wings cut from his back. Estel exiled . . .

She felt confused, and guilty, too, for even questioning Israfil's judgement.

She could still see the deep crimson of Adonai's blood, dripping onto his severed wings as they lay in the dirt.

To have flight taken away from you. It must be like losing your legs.

I should have told Aphra, when I saw them. She would have known what to do.

'Don't want that? I'll finish it for you,' Vald said, eyeing up her plate while mopping up the last of his gravy with a thick slice of black bread. The wooden plate looked so clean, as if it hadn't been eaten from.

'Have it,' Riv said, pushing her unfinished food towards Vald.

'I'd have had that!' Jost exclaimed, eyes bulging in his gaunt face. He ate almost as much as Vald, not that you'd know it to look at him, the two of them often arguing over food.

'Too slow.' Vald winked at Jost.

How can they joke at a time like this?

She spied her mam sitting in a shadowed corner of the feast-hall and stood.

'Going to see my mam,' she said to Jost and Vald, scooping up a skin of wine and two cups, and left them bickering over her half-eaten plate of food.

Riv had felt deeply moved by the judgement upon Adonai and Estel, still did, her feelings swinging from judgemental to pity every few heartbeats.

As her mam looked up at Riv she thought how much she looked like an older version of Aphra, creases around her eyes

and mouth, the streaks of grey in her hair spreading – there was
more than black, now. It struck her that she herself looked very
little like them, her hair fair where theirs was dark, her features
finer where her mam's and Aphra's were stronger.

*Aphra is so like Mam. I must resemble our father, instead. I wish
he were here, that I had known him. Is my temper his legacy, as well?
Because I see none of it in Aphra or Mam.*

Dalmae gave Riv a wan smile that shifted partway through
into resolute, but couldn't quite conceal the worry that lurked
behind her eyes.

'What is it, Mam? Upset about Adonai and Estel?' Riv said
as she sat, pulling the stopper from the wine skin with her teeth
and pouring wine glugging into the two cups.

'Aye,' her mam said, 'a terrible thing.' She sighed. 'And I
am worried about Aphra,' she added.

'Worried about Aphra?' Her sister was always so capable,
the perfect disciple of Elyon's Lore. Disciplined, calm, a consummate warrior and leader, and devout, embodying Riv's idea
of what Faith, Strength and Purity were in reality. And yet now
she agreed with her mam. Aphra had been acting out of char-
acter, ever since the night Riv had seen her with Fia. 'I was
going to ask you about her. She's been . . . strange, lately.'

'You think so, too?' Dalmae asked. 'How so?'

'Bad-tempered, not interested in anything I have to say to
her.'

'Leading is hard, sometimes,' her mam said, squeezing Riv's
hand. 'All the time,' she corrected herself. 'And these are dark
days – the beacons, rumours of the Kadoshim moving. Estel.'

'Aye,' Riv said as she took a long sip from her cup.

Truth be told, Riv didn't spend much time thinking about
the difficulties and stresses of leading the hundred. Only the
glory of it. The pride and respect she felt for her sister, and for
her mam, who had accomplished the same task before Aphra.
And an ever-growing pressure upon her own shoulders, made
all the worse by the thought that she might not actually ever

become a White-Wing, let alone rising through their ranks into a position of leadership.

'What do you think Israfil's meeting's all about? It's late to call it, eh?' she asked her mam, wanting to steer herself away from that uncomfortable thought.

'It is,' Dalmae said with a slow, deliberate nod. 'Whatever it is, it must be important.'

Riv's mam had led the hundred for many years, only stepping down when the combined effect of age and cumulative injuries made the decision for her. If anyone understood the pressures and politics of leadership within the hundred, it was her.

'Maybe these beacons,' Riv said.

'Maybe.' Her mam leaned close to her. 'Don't let Aphra's moods trouble you. She has her own pressures, and sometimes we take them out on those that we are closest to.'

'So it's a compliment, then.' Riv snorted, smiling.

'Aye, you could say that.' Her mam laughed.

'Doesn't much feel like one.'

'No, I'm sure it doesn't, but Aphra will deal with her concerns, sooner or later. And then you'll enjoy her apology, no doubt.'

'Aye, that I will,' Riv agreed. 'I'd just like it to be sooner, not later.'

'What about you?' her mam said. 'How are you doing?'

'Me? I feel a bit, heavy-hearted,' Riv said, a whisper, as if even speaking of it was wrong, a betrayal to the Ben-Elim and the hundred. 'This afternoon,' she said with a wave of her hand as explanation. Every time she closed her eyes she saw Adonai's wings tumbling to the dirt, heard his screams. She almost had sympathy pains for him, her back aching between her shoulder blades.

If these pains had only just started, I'd have believed that.

'Part of me understands. The Lore says what they did was wrong, so it is wrong.'

Though I am not really sure what they did. Improper relations? What does that even mean?

'There is only one path to Elyon, and that is Faith, Strength and Purity,' Dalmae intoned from the Book of the Faithful. 'The Lore cannot be broken, and if it is, those who broke it must be punished, else the Lore is made to appear meaningless,' her mam said.

'I know. But part of me . . .' Riv shook her head. 'They have lost so much. Their lives, almost.'

'Sometimes the heart leads us down a path that the head would avoid,' her mam said. 'That is why a warrior must learn to master their emotions. Self-control can save your life, whereas lack of control . . . It can make it feel as if nothing exists except the *now*. And that the future –' she shrugged – 'fades in the mind.'

Riv could understand that, remembering how Israfil's goading during her warrior trial had led her anger to explode. It had controlled her, no, *consumed* her. One moment she'd been aware of the consequences, the next, she had not cared.

I gave no thought to the future at all.

'But we are not beasts,' her mam said, 'which is why we train so hard. Discipline, of body and mind, regimentation, endurance, it all teaches control, which leads to purity.' She gave a self-deprecating smile. 'But that's all very well for me to say, sitting in the safety and calm of our feast-hall, a cup of wine in my hand, my beautiful daughter by my side. I'm glad you feel compassion for Estel and Adonai. You have a big heart, Riv. And an . . . emotional one.'

Riv smiled ruefully.

My temper. Always, my temper.

'Am I ever going to become a White-Wing, Mam?'

'Of course you are,' Dalmae said firmly, cupping Riv's cheek with her palm. It was cool to the touch, hard-skinned from decades of weapons-work. 'Next time, just refrain from punching the Lord Protector in the face.'

'Good advice,' Riv muttered. Her mam smiled and poured her another cup of wine.

The barrack doors creaked open, a cold wind swirling through, raising goosebumps on Riv's arms. Aphra strode through the doors, her unit captains behind her. They marched to the fire-pit, all eyes upon them.

'Make sure your kit-bags are packed and your weapons polished,' Aphra said. 'We're marching out at dawn.'

'Why?' Riv called out before she could rein in her tongue.

Aphra stared at Riv a long moment, silence settling in the hall.

'We're going to Oriens, a town on the east road, about a ten-night's march. Israfil has received strange reports. Screams heard by travellers on the road. No word from there since.' Aphra looked around the whole hall, her gaze finally coming back to rest upon Riv and her mam.

'Israfil fears the Kadoshim are behind it.'

CHAPTER TWENTY-FOUR

DREM

Hildith, Ulf and their riders were arriving as Drem stepped into the yard, through the huge hole in the building's side. It had exploded outwards, splintered wood sprayed about the yard, littering the ground, spiking up through the snow, like the skeleton of a leviathan in a white sea.

Except for the blood.

Droplets speckled the ground, no death wound, but injuries, nevertheless.

Is the bear wounded? From Surl as the hound put up a fight? Or is it Fritha's blood, spilt as it crushed her in its jaws?

He didn't like that thought and pushed it away.

His da appeared by his side.

'You like this girl, don't you?'

'I do,' Drem muttered, only admitting the thought to himself at the same time as he did to his da. At that internal and external confession he felt a rush of fear and dread at what might have happened to her. The thought of life without her sky-blue eyes and freckles.

'We'd best be getting after her, then,' Olin said.

Drem nodded.

'Why's the bear taken her?' Olin muttered.

'Bears do that, take their kill to a den where they can eat in peace,' Drem said. 'The white bear did it with our elk, remember?' He thought his da was being kindly, telling him that, even though they both knew that Fritha, despite not being here, was most likely dead.

'Why did it leave Hask and the hound?' Olin muttered, quieter, more to himself than to Drem.

For the first time in his life Drem didn't want to ask questions. He felt frantic with worry for Fritha, desperate to find or avenge her.

'Now's the time to hunt, Da,' Drem said.

Olin looked up at him and nodded.

Drem sat silently upon his mount, snowflakes falling steadily about him, gusts of wind catching and swirling them into twisting, spiralling patterns, like a kaleidoscope of white butterflies. His da was beside him, Hildith and Ulf just ahead.

We are wasting time. Let's get on with it, Drem thought, knuckles white as he gripped his reins.

Ulf raised a horn to his lips and gave a great, ringing blast. Hounds were released from their leashes and bounded baying into the gloom, noses to the ground. From left and right answering horn calls echoed out, dull, distant things in the snow-shrouded woods. They had followed the bear tracks in the snow from Fritha's hold back to the woods and then formed a long line through the trees, over a hundred men wide, far wider than Drem could see, long enough, he hoped, to catch any sneaky creature that thought to circle around the hounds on its trail, as a beast at bay is likely to do. With a stuttering shudder, Drem lurched into motion, following Ulf and the hounds-men who led the way, following the blood-spattered bear-prints into the wooded murk of shadow and thorn.

Drem saw his da glance skyward, searching for any sign of the sun's position through the snow curtain beyond the branches above. It was hard to tell, but Drem guessed it was closer to sunset than highsun.

Not the best time for a bear-hunt. It should really be starting with dawn on the morrow.

But then Fritha would be gone another day. The cold will have killed her even if the bear hasn't.

A branch slapped into Drem's face, sharp fingers raking his cheek. The trees were growing thicker about them, branches lower, men ducking in their saddles. They'd made the decision to stay mounted for as long as possible, just to use every moment of extra speed to close the gap between them and their quarry, but the time to dismount and leave the horses behind was rapidly approaching.

The line of hunters grew fractured, the thickening trees and dense scrub a barrier that sent horses searching for easier paths. A horn blast, and then they were dismounting, Ulf choosing a score of his followers to stay with the mounts, the rest of them reforming as best they could and marching on.

Hounds bayed somewhere ahead of Drem, a fresh excitement in their barking. His da was beside him, the next hunter a vague shadow slipping in and out of view.

'Do you think they've found it?' Drem asked his da, a hand reaching for his sword.

Should have brought a spear.

His throat still hurt, inside and outside, his cloak rubbing against the rope-burn, his voice grating raw when he spoke.

'No,' Olin said. 'They'd be making a different sound entirely if they had. More like dying.' He looked at Drem's face, saw the worry in his eyes. 'They might be getting closer, though, the scent stronger.'

'That's what I thought,' Drem muttered.

Snow was falling thick about them, swirling with gusts and eddies into banks at their feet.

If it's this thick inside this wood, what is it like beyond it? We'll be needing to dig through snowbanks to get in our front door.

A hand closed around his wrist.

'Drem,' his da said, leaning close, 'we should leave.'

'What!'

I can't. Fritha.

Olin saw Drem's expression, but continued anyway.

'We should go, now. While we have a chance.'

'Da, how can you say this?'

'Drem, you're usually the practical one. Think. I've told you what I plan to do.' He put a hand to the sword that was hanging through a leather thong at his hip, the blade wrapped in leather and sheepskin.

Asroth. Drassil. With us being attacked, Fritha taken, I'd almost forgotten my da plans on slaying a demon-lord.

'Hildith and Ulf have told us we are involved in this investigation into Calder's death. Do you think we'll just be allowed to leave? And now there's blood feud against us. A whole town of miners and trappers out for our blood. I've told you: something is wrong here, and we need to be away, before it's too late. This is the perfect opportunity, while the townsfolk, and the men who wish us dead, are stumbling snow-blind amongst these woods. We could just turn around and go back, and no one would know for a good while. We could get a day's head start. We should go.'

He let go of Drem's wrist, just held his gaze. His looked grieved to say it, clearly knew the turmoil Drem was feeling over Fritha.

'You're right,' Drem said, 'it is logical. It does make sense. But . . . Fritha . . .' He trailed off, unsure of what he meant or wanted, just knowing that he felt torn, emotions running through him that he was unable to put into words. He looked at his da, feeling as miserable and conflicted as he could ever remember.

His da sighed, nodded.

'We'll see this through,' he said, 'find Fritha . . .'

Alive or dead, Drem finished his da's sentence.

'And then we'll be away, quick and quiet as we can,' Olin added.

'Thank you, Da,' Drem said, relief washing through him. To give up on her now would feel wrong.

Olin took the lead, pushing on through the deepening snow. The hounds were silent now, and Drem could see no one to the left or right, only the snow, the constant flutter of it in his face. Olin's eyes were on the foliage about them, branch and bush. He paused once, lifting leaves that had been snapped, scraped past; he marched on more quickly.

And then somewhere up ahead hounds were barking, a raucous baying, close, much closer than Drem would have thought, and he felt his heart lurch in his chest. He broke into a run, past his da, the sound of the hounds growing ever louder, deafening now, and changing, snarling, growling, snapping, a yelp and whine. Drem burst into a clearing, or, at least it was a clearing now, as a giant white bear had snapped branches, torn bushes up and uprooted trees in its violence against the hounds that had tracked it and brought it to bay.

There was blood on the snow, a hound crawling, whining, its back legs not working, another hound lying as still as stone, head twisted at a sickening angle. Others were circling the bear, snarling and snapping as the great beast growled and swiped at them with its huge scythe-like claws.

Where's Fritha? Drem thought, looking about frantically for her, but he could see no sign of her. Hope drained from him.

It wouldn't have left her alive in its den, or anywhere else. Dead and stored, more likely. He'd seen predators do it many times, hide their kill until they felt it was safe to retrieve it. He felt a rush of anger, rage like he'd never felt before.

I will kill you, bear, for what you've done.

Ulf burst into the clearing, a handful of men about him, all of them pausing for a frozen moment, staring at the white beast in astonished wonder. Then a man was charging it, a spear levelled at the bear's chest, stabbing through fur and flesh, the bear bellowing its pain, a shrug of its shoulder and claws splintered the spear shaft, another swipe and the man was spinning through the air, an arc of blood trailing him. He crashed to the ground, rolled, didn't move again.

As if breaking a spell, the first man's ruin released the others from their frozen stupefaction, Ulf bellowing, the others rushing forwards, spreading about the bear, jabbing at it with their weapons. Drem charged with them, Olin following more cautiously, unsheathing their own blades. Drem heard the distinct sound of sizzling, saw snowflakes melting to steam where they touched his da's black sword. Then they were part of the net closing on the white bear, Drem stabbing when it slashed or bit in another direction, jumping back when it cast its baleful attention in his direction.

That's definitely the one from the elk pit, Drem thought as he saw its right paw, one long claw clearly missing.

Just need to carve the rest of you up, now.

Red lines appeared on the beast, blood leaking into its fur, and more men died, those too slow or too foolhardy. In a few hundred heartbeats five men lay bleeding into the forest litter, only two dogs still standing, but a handful of new men had trickled into the clearing, one of them, Drem noted, was Wispy Beard.

The bear lunged forwards, caught a warrior's thigh with its claws as he tried to jump away, sent him crashing to the ground, and the bear's head darted forwards on its long, powerful neck, its jaws crunching about the man's torso, lifting him into the air and shaking him like a terrier with a rat. Blood sprayed in fountains, the man's screams rising in pitch, abruptly silent as bones snapped. Olin danced into the rear of the bear and slashed two-handed at the beast, carving a red gash down the bear's flank and leg, the stench of meat burning, flesh and fat hissing. It bellowed in pain, dropping the dead man, and surged forwards, straight at Drem, fleeing this new agony. It slammed into him and the bulk of men about Drem, sending them spinning, flying through the air like so many twigs. Drem crashed to the ground, air forced from his lungs. He tried to move, hand grasping for the hilt of his blade, and then a clawed paw thumped into the ground by his head and the bear's jaws filled his vision. It stood over him, looking down at him, saliva dripping from one long tooth to land on Drem's forehead.

It sniffed him, opened its jaws and let out a great roar, then exploded away from him and went crashing into the undergrowth, disappearing into the twilight.

Only Olin was still standing, a handful of others groaning as they tried to rise. Olin ran to Drem and helped him back to his feet, put his sword back in his hand.

'I'm all right,' Drem said to his da's worried look.

I should be dead. It didn't kill me.

Drem shared a look with his da and they followed the bear, moving quickly, not quite a run, the sounds of it crashing ahead making it easy for them to track the beast.

The noise of the bear slowly faded, despite Drem and Olin picking up their pace, a sense of despair settling in Drem's chest. Eventually Olin stopped, twilight thick about him.

'We'll not catch it in a sprint,' his da said. 'And anyway, it doesn't have Fritha, you saw. It might have dropped or discarded her somewhere in the forest. Best thing to do is retrace its steps. And then . . .'

We'll find Fritha's dead body in the snow and forest litter, Drem thought morosely.

'She may have escaped the bear of her own accord,' Olin said. 'She may still live.' Drem could tell that his da didn't believe that, though. And neither did he.

Drem nodded, admitting defeat, the forest silent about them now, draped with shadow, snow still falling, though he could feel it more than see it, twilight masking the world in grey. A voice in the distance, a horn call, faint and far.

'Ulf and Hildith, regrouping. Might be better to camp out here as a group than try and walk home,' Olin said.

'I think you're right and it's time to leave, Da,' Drem said, 'in the dark, where we won't be missed. Fritha must be dead, though I dearly wish she were not.'

Olin looked at him.

'Only if you're sure, son. She means much to you; we'll stay and search until you're ready.'

Drem nodded, then froze, cocking his head to one side.

A sound, to their right, deep in the undergrowth. His da heard it, too, both of them staring, alert. And slowly something formed in the shadows, the darkness deepening, a shifting of muscle and bulk, a low rumbling growl.

'RUN!' Olin yelled, shoving Drem back the way they had come as the undergrowth exploded outwards, snapping and shattering in a burst of snow and leaves, a deafening roar blasting them, filling Drem's head as he stumbled to the ground. He glimpsed his da setting his feet, lifting his blade, heard the crash and growl of the bear as it surged from the shadows.

It came back. How did it flank us so quietly?

His da's voice was raised in a battle-cry and there was a roaring bellow of pain from the bear. Drem pushed himself up to his knees, grasping for his sword, then something slammed into the back of his head. There was a bright explosion of light behind his eyes, quickly followed by darkness as he crashed to the ground, consciousness fluttering away.

A gasp of air, ragged, pain in his throat, in his head, everywhere, it felt, his whole world a vault of pain. He opened his mouth, tasted snow and dirt, and with a grunt pushed himself over onto his back, then just lay there gasping for a few moments.

Above him the scrape and rasp of leafless branches stirred by the sighing wind, boughs sagging with snow. Snowflakes landed on his face, tingling.

Then he remembered.

The bear.

'Da,' he rasped, a whisper, his bruised throat raw and on fire. He rolled, pushed himself to hands and knees, then upright, ignoring the pain, spiked explosions pulsing out from the base of his skull. He stood. Looked frantically about.

There was still a dim light in the twilight world, a faint

glow from the snow on the ground. He looked at a hole the size of a barn, a blackness amidst the undergrowth and trees, branches and bushes snapped and torn where the bear had charged them.

'Da,' Drem said louder, a stone of dread dropping in his belly; with every heartbeat of silence the dread growing, becoming worse.

'Drem,' a whispered breath that made his heart leap, and he saw him, a dark, still figure lying on the ground. Drem stumbled to his da, dropped to his knees, at the same time heard voices in the distance behind him, heard men calling, recognized Ulf's voice.

His da was pale and blood-drenched, and this time Drem knew it was not the blood of his enemies. He was lying upon his back, one leg twisted at a strange angle, his torso looking like one big wound. Blood pulsed sluggishly from long gashes that started at his shoulder and ended at his hip. Between them the flesh was torn and ragged, flecks of bone amidst the crimson.

'Oh, Da,' Drem whispered, the breath hitching in his chest, something cold clenching in his belly, squeezing his heart. He'd seen wounds like this, not in a man, but knew what it meant, something in him refusing to accept it. Couldn't bear to accept it.

Olin's eyes were distant but, at Drem's presence, he blinked and lifted his head.

'Lie still, Da, Ulf's coming,' Drem said desperately, stroking sweat-soaked hair from his da's forehead. All that he had been consumed with – finding Fritha, killing the white bear – all of it evaporated as his whole world constricted down to this moment. His da, the only person in his life who truly mattered. His blinked tears from his eyes.

Olin shifted, his mouth moving. A trickle of blood dribbled over his lips, a whisper of air.

'Sword,' he said.

He wants to hold his sword in his hand. He thinks he's going to die, going to cross the bridge of swords.

Drem looked about frantically for the black sword, could not see it anywhere, though the ground was churned and covered in bits of tree and bushes. He couldn't bear to leave his da's side to search more thoroughly, so Drem drew his own blade and put the hilt in his hand, closing his fingers about it. Olin's gaze flickered down to it, then pushed the blade away.

'Starstone,' Olin wheezed.

'I can't see it, Da,' Drem said, lifting his da's hand and kissing it, felt his da's fingers twitch and he put them to his cheek, as his da had done to him so many, many times before.

'My . . . boy,' Olin whispered, a bubbling rattle. 'I was . . . wrong.' Olin jerked then, his other arm rising, palm upon Drem's chest, fingers clenching, gripping onto the bear claw about Drem's neck. One long, slow exhalation that seemed as if it would never end, his eyes fixed onto Drem's with a burning gaze and then Olin was still, the light in his eyes fading, glazing over.

'No, Da, no,' Drem breathed, his vision blurring with tears as Olin's fingers slipped from the claw about his neck.

CHAPTER TWENTY-FIVE

SIG

Sig crested a low rise in the land and, with a word and a touch of her heels, reined Hammer in. Somewhere behind she heard Keld shout a command, the drum of hooves as their loose column drew close. But Sig only had eyes for the view on the horizon before her.

Dun Seren.

It was highsun, a pale sun suspended like a marker in the sky above the fortress of grey stone. It was standing upon a gentle hill, a keep and tower silhouetted on the horizon. Around it dark walls circled the hill, the hint of myriad buildings contained within. Another wall had been raised closer and wider still, upon the flatter meadows that surrounded Dun Seren's hill. Sig had been there when the decision to build it had been made. The Order had grown beyond its founder's wildest expectations, the twin arts of weapons-craft and healing drawing so many to their halls. Corban, the creator of the Order, had been grey-haired then, and he had smiled to see how the seed of his dream had flourished into something far greater than he had ever imagined.

Staring at it now, a kaleidoscope of memories flashed through Sig's mind, more than a hundred years' worth of remembrance condensed into a handful of heartbeats, of weapons training, pain, sweat, broken bones, battle and loss. But far greater than that were the memories of song and laughter, a bond of friendship forged with men and giants that she had never believed possible. A host of names and faces hovered in her mind's eye: Corban, Gunil, Varan, Coralen, Veradis, Cywen, Dath, Kulla, Farrell, Storm, so many, many more.

And so many of them gone, now. But their memory lives on.

We shall never forget.

'We shall never forget,' Keld murmured beside her, and she looked down at him to see him staring at Dun Seren's walls with a faraway look in his eyes.

'Come on,' Cullen cried out, all excitement and passion. 'What are we waiting for? Let's go home!'

Home.

'*Home,*' squawked Rab as he alighted on Cullen's shoulder, the young warrior wincing as crow talons flexed.

And in good time. Still a ten-night to go before Midwinter's Day.

She glanced behind her, saw expressions of wonder and awe spread upon the faces of the young recruits from Ardain, and then Sig was spurring Hammer on, the bear roaring as it ran lumbering down the rise, Keld, Cullen and their recruits from Ardain cantering behind, Fen the wolven-hound a grey blur ahead of them.

The scrape of Hammer's claws and the clatter of hooves echoed as they passed through the arched gate of Dun Seren's inner wall and into the courtyard before the grey keep. Above the gatehouse a banner of a bright star upon a black field snapped and rippled in the cold wind that was blowing hard from the north. Sig tasted a hint of snow upon it. Warriors lined the walls, horns ringing out and voices cheering Sig's return, sword-brothers and sisters, a smattering of giants as well, and Sig smiled to see them, raising her hand in greeting. Cullen grinned and waved as if he was a returning hero, though Keld was more contained beside him, still raw with the loss of his wolven-hound, Hella.

A statue loomed before them, dominating the centre of the

courtyard, twice the height of Sig upon her bear's back. Two figures carved from dark stone, pale veins running through it. One a man, handsome and serious, broad-chested and thick-armed, his hair tied into a thick warrior braid that coiled across one shoulder. He was dressed as a warrior, wearing a shirt of mail and leather surcoat, breeches and boots, a round shield slung across his back. A torc sat about his neck, snarling wolven heads at either end, with an arm ring spiralling about one bicep, two more wolven heads at beginning and end. One hand held a naked sword, the tip resting upon the ground, its pommel another wolven head, this one raised with jaws open, howling.

The warrior's other hand rested upon the neck of a wolven, broad and muscular, standing almost as tall as the warrior's chest. Its teeth were bared in a snarl, long canines curved, scars latticing its body.

'Behold Corban, the Bright Star, founder of this Order,' Sig bellowed. 'And Storm, his faithful companion.'

'Told you he had a pet wolven,' someone said.

'Storm was no *pet*,' Sig growled at them.

A figure stepped out from the fire glow of the keep behind the statue, the jut of a curved sword sheathed across its back. Byrne, the high captain of their Order. A giant walked beside her, the outline of a crow upon the giant's shoulder. Sig raised her hand to them, saw Byrne raise hers in return, then turn and walk back into the keep.

Sig led their party through the courtyard towards the main stable block, a word to Hammer and the bear was slowing to a halt as stablehands swarmed to meet them.

'Back to your tower and report to the crow master,' Sig said to Rab, who was still clinging determinedly to Cullen's shoulder. The white crow looked up at her from its human perch, appeared to sigh – a rise and slump of its wings, if that was possible for a crow – and then winged into the air, spiralling slowly upwards, circling the tower that loomed behind the keep. Other dark-winged shapes appeared from the tower, a raucous cawing drifting down from them.

'Hope they're nice to him,' Cullen muttered beside Sig.

Sig just shook her head.

'See to your mount, greet your kin, and then meet me in the High Captain's chamber,' Sig said to Cullen and Keld, 'I'll see that our new recruits are looked after.' They nodded to her and dismounted, leading their horses to the stables.

Sig turned to look at the two score young warriors behind her.

'Welcome to Dun Seren,' she said.

'Welcome home,' Byrne said with a warm smile as Sig stepped into the High Captain's chambers, Cullen and Keld either side of her. Fen the wolven-hound was with them, slinking towards a fire that blazed in a hearth almost the size of one wall. He flopped down in front of it with a satisfied sigh.

I'm glad Dun Seren was built by giants, Sig thought. *At least I don't have to lower my head entering every chamber, or risk smashing any chair I sit in.*

Byrne looked older. Sig had been gone from Dun Seren less than six moons, but the lines in Byrne's face were deeper, and there was more silver creeping through her once-black hair.

'Did you miss me, cousin?' Cullen said, all smiles and swagger, the returning hero, his sleeves rolled up to show his new-earned scar, a white slash through the centre of his left bicep.

Fool boy. There'll come a time when he wishes for fewer scars, and the ache they give him.

'Whisht,' Sig said to him with a scowl.

Byrne raised an eyebrow at him.

Cullen's smile shrivelled.

Byrne raised her other eyebrow, continued to scold him with her gaze.

'Sorry, High Captain,' he mumbled.

*Ach, but she looks like her great-grandmother when she pulls
that face.*

Byrne was descended from Cywen, the sister of Corban,
who had founded the healers' element of Dun Seren, teaching
and pioneering new methods of the healing art, of herbs and
remedies and medical procedures. All who came to Dun Seren,
who dreamed of becoming warriors of the Bright Star, were
educated in the art of healing as much as developing skill at
arms. It was the same in reverse: any who came with a passion
for healing would be taught with just as much rigour how to
fight, how to kill. And Byrne had excelled at both, from a bairn
Sig had noticed the talent in her. It had fairly glowed.

Sig had once seen Byrne drill a small hole through a fallen
comrade's skull to relieve swelling and pressure upon the
man's brain, the result of a heavy blow from a sword-pommel.
A difficult procedure at the best of times, but this had been
knee-deep in an ambush, Kadoshim and their servants all
about. Sig had stood over her, trying to guard her back while
she did it.

*It's no wonder she rose to the position of high captain of the Order.
And she's a good friend.*

'It's good to be back,' Sig said. She threw a leather bag onto
a wide desk, where it landed with a heavy thud, its contents
spilling out, rolling a half-circle. It was the severed head of the
Kadoshim from Ardain, flesh rotting and peeling, stinking,
the long fangs in its mouth accentuated by the decomposing
lips, pulled tight and slimy with putrefaction.

'Do you know its name?'

'Rimmon,' Sig said.

Byrne nodded, her lips a tight line. She opened a large
leather-bound book upon her desk, dipped a quill in ink and
wrote upon a page. Sig leaned over, saw Byrne write *Rimmon* at
the bottom of a list, pages long. Above it were the names
Charun, Malek, Balam, Dramal, many, many more.

I know. It's always good to see a dead Kadoshim, a new name on the list. But it would be better if it was Gulla, the self-called New Lord of the Kadoshim.

'The rumours were true, then,' Byrne said, bending closer to study the Kadoshim's features, her expression clinical and detached as only a healer could be.

There was a knock at the chamber door, Cullen rising from the seat he was lounging in to go and open it. Byrne did not have servants.

A giant walked in, taller than Sig, though not as broad, dark-haired as she was fair, his hair wild, poking in all directions, apart from the warrior braid that coiled across one shoulder.

'Well met, Tain,' Sig said to him, and he beamed to see her, a broad smile that seemed to take over most of his face. It was unusual to see a giant smile, never mind a smile so huge or teeth so bright they could dazzle a charging warband.

'I am glad you are returned to us safely,' Tain said, looking from Sig to her companions. He was the crow master of Dun Seren, overseeing the care of the birds like Rab that nested in Crow Tower, a few score rare and gifted crows that had mastered the art of speech. They were born and bred from Crow Tower, their talent passed on to them by their sire, who at this moment was sitting upon Tain's other shoulder.

Half of the crow's feathers were missing, patches of pink skin flaking, his beak long and curved, old beyond years. The crow regarded Sig and her companions with bright, intelligent eyes, though, undimmed by his age. Those eyes swivelled to the Kadoshim's head upon Byrne's desk, and he squawked and bobbed, excited.

No. Pleased with himself.

'Well met, Craf,' Sig said, keeping the fondness she felt for the old crow from her voice. It did not do any good to show the crow that kind of kindness, he was notorious for exploiting it, as Tain, the giant he was perched upon, would readily testify.

'*Craf right then,*' the bird squawked, '*Kadoshim in Ardan.*'

'It's called Ardain, now, but yes, Craf,' Byrne said.

'*Ardain, Ardan,*' Craf grumbled.

The world has changed much since you were hatched, old crow, Sig thought. *Realms come and gone. Ardan, Domhain, Narvon and Cambren in the west becoming one realm, Ardain. And the Land of the Faithful, ruled by the Ben-Elim. Once the realms of Tenebral, Helveth, Carnutan, Tarbesh and Isiltir. And still the Ben-Elim spread their influence ever wider.*

'Though, to be fair, we all thought it so, and sent Sig based on that decision,' Byrne pointed out to Craf.

'*Craf's fledgling bairns first to tell,*' Craf said, flapping his wings in annoyance, a black feather drifting to the ground. Craf watched it fall with a beady eye.

Now look what made Craf do,' he muttered. '*Cold enough, now one less feather.*'

'I'll fetch a blanket for you after,' Tain said quietly.

'*Kind Tain,*' Craf crooned.

Crow master we named him, but it's more like crow servant, Sig thought, keeping the smile from touching her lips.

'So there's one fewer Kadoshim in Ardain,' Byrne said, bringing their attention back to the severed head upon her desk.

'Aye,' Sig said, 'though there was more to it than we would ever have expected. There is much to tell you, of acolytes, of sacrifice and incantations. Of a new strategy amongst the Kadoshim. The slumbering beast stirs,' Sig said ominously. 'Something dread is afoot.'

'Tell me,' Byrne said.

So they did.

Sig told most of it, how they had hunted the Kadoshim to its lair, enlisted the aid of Elgin, Battlechief of Ardain, and then attacked the Kadoshim's den. Of the numbers of acolytes, the human sacrifice and spells, the escaped messenger. Keld hung his head – in shame or grief, Sig did not know – when she told of his capture and the death of his wolven-hound, Hella. At the mention of her name Fen lifted his head from the fire and whined. Craf cawed softly, the sound somehow full of melancholy.

And Sig told of Rab's arrival at Uthandun, the white crow's help in Keld's rescue. Craf bobbed his head at that, clacking his beak loudly. Sig ignored him and carried on, telling them of the lit beacon in the rain-soaked hills of Ardain, the other beacons lit in response. Of the note that simply said: *Now*. And finally of the recruits Queen Nara had sent north with them, and of the Ben-Elim, Kushiel's visit to Uthandun as Sig was preparing to leave.

All of it Sig told in a flat, inexpressive voice, as if she were recounting a morning's sparring on the weapons court, giving an analysis of the strengths and weaknesses of a student of the Order. Apart from when she spoke of Keld and Cullen, of Rab and Fen and Hammer. Those she praised.

Cullen beamed as if it was his name-day. Keld sat there grim and dour, a scowl looking to have been etched through his face with a plough.

When Sig finished, a silence settled upon them all, only the fire crackling in its great hearth, the snoring of Fen as he slept in front of it.

'There is more news from the Nest,' Tain said, meaning Crow Tower, 'that makes more sense, now we have heard Sig's tale.'

'Go on, then,' Byrne prompted.

'Frick has returned from Jerolin,' Tain said. 'The poor lad; it's a long way to fly, he's fair shattered, he is—'

'*Tell them, tell them,*' Craf squawked impatiently in Tain's ear, making him jump.

'Beacons, springing up all across what once was Tenebral, now the southern reaches of the Land of the Faithful. And attacks. Much the same as you have described in Ardain. Holds burned, merchants and travellers attacked upon the road. Some villages. No organized assault on what you would call a military strength, though. Or at least, that's what Frick has heard.'

'Thank you, Tain,' Byrne said with a dip of her head.

'There was no way of bringing this Kadoshim back alive, head still attached to its body?' Byrne said, her dark eyes fixing Sig. Even though Byrne was little more than half Sig's height she still managed to hold her with that gaze. 'It would have been helpful if we could have asked a question or two. And, as I remember, that was your task. To find it, and bring it here.'

'Aye, well, the Kadoshim was not for cooperating,' Sig said. 'I tried, had it in my net, even. And to be fair, it wasn't me that killed the beast.'

Sig felt disloyal, informing on Hammer, but Byrne somehow had that effect on people. She could suck the truth from a stone and Sig had long come to the conclusion that there was no point fighting it.

'Hammer killed it.'

She's a bear, she's got broad shoulders.

A raised eyebrow from Byrne. Surprisingly effective at eliciting an urge in Sig to provide further information.

'The Kadoshim stabbed her in the paw.'

'Ahh,' Byrne and Tain said together.

'No matter,' Craf cawed. *'Only good Kadoshim is a dead Kadoshim.'*

'Well, what's done is done,' Byrne said. 'No point wishing it were not so. But I think you are right, Sig, this heralds something new. Not just another skirmish in the endless war. A new strategy. But what are they up to, and why?'

'Craf will think on it,' the crow squawked, as if they could all stop worrying now. Craf fell from Tain's shoulder, spread his wings and glided to Byrne's desk, where he hopped over to the Kadoshim's head. He stabbed his beak down, came back up with a long strip of decaying flesh.

'Ugh!' Cullen groaned. 'That'll make you gut-sick, that will!'

'Dead is dead, meat is meat,' Craf squawked as he swallowed noisily, *'and Craf not fussy.'*

Clearly not.

Even Byrne pulled a disgusted face.

'We must talk more on this,' she said, turning her back on Craf, though that didn't blot out the wet, disgusting sounds of his feast. She spoke louder. 'The Captains of Kill and Cure must be told. We'll hold a meeting on the morrow, with all the captains and masters of Dun Seren. And Tain, word must be sent to our outposts at Brikan and Balara.' She pursed her lips, thinking. 'And we should tell the Ben-Elim. This is bigger than our . . . differences. Choose a bird and send word to your father at Drassil.'

Tain nodded.

'I urge you all,' Byrne said, worry creasing her eyes. 'Think hard on this. I have a feeling in my gut; the Kadoshim are coming out from the shadows, attacking for the first time in a quarter of a century. The question is: why? To what end? we must solve this riddle, before it is too late.'

'What feeling?' Cullen asked. 'In your gut, I mean.'

'Dread,' Byrne said, and Sig nodded her agreement, for she felt it, too.

CHAPTER TWENTY-SIX

DREM

Drem sat in the darkness of his cabin, staring at nothing. Two fingers were pressed to the pulse in his neck as he rocked gently back and forth, counting.

It was the third day since his da had died. Or at least, that was what he thought, but he couldn't be sure. It had taken a day to get back home, after Ulf and Hildith had gathered their scattered hunting party back to them, he was sure of that. He strained to remember, a wave of fresh pain crashing over him with the coming of memories, making him wince and groan. They'd camped in the forest that night, lit blazing fires, and wrapped the dead in cloaks. It was not only his da who had fallen to the white bear. The next day had been a sombre procession back through the forest, carrying litters fashioned from spears and cloaks, Drem carrying his da. He'd been aware of men around him, Ulf offering his sympathy, others like Wispy Beard and Burg saying nothing to him, and for the most part Drem had been unaware of anyone else's existence. All he could think of was his da, the fact that he was gone now feeling like when the giant bat had sunk its fangs into his shoulder. Sharp, excruciating pain, followed by a numbness to all else, then a memory surfacing through the fog that would drag him back to the pain, followed by the numbing sensation again, over and over.

They had reached his hold on the evening of the first day,

bringing his da's body into the cabin. On the second day Ulf and Hildith had returned with half a dozen men and they had carried Olin's body into the paddocks and there helped Drem to raise a cairn. Words had been spoken, by Ulf, and Drem remembered even saying something himself, though he could not remember what he'd said. More vivid was the pain in his knees where he had dropped to the ground in his grief. His breeches still bore the snow-salt and grass stains as a reminder.

And now it was the third day since his da had died.

I think.

His stomach growled, but he ignored it, the thought of putting food in his mouth making him feel sick.

Or is it the fourth day? How long have I been sitting here?

He didn't know.

A shiver rippled through him, his body telling him he was cold, but he didn't care. He was close to the hearth, though no fire burned in it; only cold ash and black embers filled it. Blinking, he looked at the shuttered windows, realized that it was getting lighter outside, faint beams of light stretching through the slats.

The fourth day, then.

What does it matter?

Da's gone.

I'm alone.

No one and nothing to live for.

He felt so alone, a depth to the feeling that the word couldn't hope to contain, and he felt lost, like a broken compass with the needle spinning wildly. His da had been his compass, his lodestone, his north star, and now he was gone.

He realized he had something in his hands, looked down as the daylight washed over it, a gleam of silver.

Da's silver cloak-brooch.

Sunlight reflected from the four points of the star on it.

The Order of the Bright Star. My da was a warrior, fought for a cause.

But he walked away from it, turned his back on it.

Aye, for me. To protect me, and to avert a war.

That's what he was doing, even to the end. Telling me to run, standing before me, protecting me. He was only there, in that forest, for me. Because I wanted to find Fritha. And she's gone too.

Tears came then, not the first time he'd shed them since his da had fallen, but this time they came as great, racking sobs, heaving out of him, his whole body convulsing, his voice and throat a raw, wounded howl. At the end of it he sat there, rocking back and forth, his arms wrapped around his knees. The brooch glinted on the floor where he'd dropped it, and, not knowing why, he bent and picked it back up, wiping tears and snot from his face.

He was a warrior, and even though he walked away from the Order he never turned his back on me.

One of the few things that Drem did remember clearly from those tangled moments when the bear attacked was the sight of his da setting his feet and raising his sword, and the battle-cry that had issued from his lips.

Truth and Courage.

Why that?

Hooves drummed in the courtyard, one horse, no more, the sound of someone dismounting, feet thudding up the steps. A knock at the door.

'Drem?'

The handle turned, the door opening slowly, a creak of hinges, light flooding in. A silhouetted figure stepped in, opening the door wider.

'There you are, lad,' the figure said, turning now so the daylight washed his face. It was Asger, the market-stall holder. He had been on the hunt, Drem remembered, and been one of those who had helped raise a cairn over his da.

Asger looked at Drem, then about the room, finally at the hearth, and went to work. He threw the shutters open, letting in a blast of cold air and daylight, the sky a pale blue beyond the window frame. He scraped the hearth clean of ash and cinder, found a pile of split logs, a basket of kindling, and started a fire, then went to searching in the kitchen. It wasn't long before an iron pot was hanging over a fire crackling in the hearth, the smell of porridge wafting about the room as Asger stirred it with a wooden spoon. To Drem's surprise, when his stomach rumbled this time he didn't feel immediately sick, as he had the last time.

'It's a hard thing, what's happened to you,' Asger said to Drem as he passed him a bowl of porridge and scooped one for himself. He pulled up a stool and sat with Drem.

'No words that'll make it go away, no deed, either.' Asger looked hard at Drem, who had been staring into his porridge bowl. Drem stirred it with his spoon, then took a mouthful.

'I wanted to talk to you about something,' Asger continued. 'I'm leaving; me, my wife and bairns. We're packing up and leaving Kergard, heading back south. Don't much like the way things are going up here. Don't much like the new crowd, either. All together it leaves a sour taste in my mouth.'

He spooned a mouthful of porridge while he waited a few moments for a response from Drem, but didn't get one.

'So I'm leaving on the morrow. And I was wondering if you might like to come with me.' He held a hand up. 'It's not charity, though maybe there is a bit of kindness in it. But I need some help with the stall, and my bairns are too young to give it. I'd pay you fair, feed you, put a roof over your head.'

He shrugged, coming abruptly to the end of his speech, and went to finishing off his bowl of porridge. Then he stood, washed it clean and left it in the kitchen, came back.

'Ulf will be leading a fresh hunt out after that white bear, in a few days, he says. Guess you may have a mind to stay and have some revenge. I'd understand that, though revenge won't bring your da back.' He shrugged. 'It's up to you. Just wanted you to know, the offer's there if you want it. I'm leaving at dawn on the morrow. You know where to find me.' He stood in front of Drem a while longer, then made for the door.

'My thanks,' Drem said hoarsely and Asger stopped and looked back.

'You're welcome, lad. Your da was a good man. And so are you.'

'Can I ask you a question?' Drem said, looking up at him.

'Course you can. I might not have the answer, but asking never hurt nobody.'

'Truth and Courage. Have you ever heard that before?'

Asger snorted. 'Not heard it used, but I know where it's from. Thought everyone did.'

Drem just looked at him.

'It's the battle-cry of them at Dun Seren. The Order of the Bright Star.'

Drem nodded, feeling something shift inside him.

Drem shovelled the steps to his cabin free of snow, piling it in banks to either side, then scraped the last of the ice clear. Once it was done he sat on the steps.

After Asger had left he'd felt a little life return to him; maybe it was the porridge, or the fact that another human being had cared enough to come and find him, he didn't know. He still had that weight of grief in his heart and belly, like a cold, hard stone, but he didn't feel incapacitated by it, at least, not for the moment. He'd finished his porridge, got up and let the goats and chickens out, checked on the horses in the stables, stood by his da's cairn, rested a hand upon it and shed some more tears, and now he was here. Thinking.

He was grateful for Asger's visit, grateful for the act of kindness in it, though it was a dim, distant gratitude, his grief too raw and potent a thing for other emotions to make any kind of lasting impression. And he was considering Asger's offer. Leaving was what he and his da had been about to do, after all. Though Drem knew that his da had a different destination in mind.

But Drem liked Asger, had always thought well of him, and the offer was a good one. A new life. A fresh start. Just the thought of some kindness and company was a tempting enough reason to go, without the fact that there were men not so far away with a blood feud against him. That wasn't going to go away, either. And, as much as he felt like his heart was broken, that all of the colour of life had just drained away, the thought of being skewered upon the end of Burg's or Wispy's blades was still not an appealing one.

And he'd been thinking on other things, too. Things that he needed to sift through first, before he fully faced up to Asger's offer. He'd been thinking on his da's last words. His cry of Truth and Courage, how that had still been so much a part of him, even after sixteen years of living a new life with Drem, that it had burst from his lips at such a telling moment.

A life-or-death moment.

And then, when he was dying, when he knew he was dying, he'd asked for his sword. The Starstone Sword.

Drem had not been able to search for it as he'd sat with his da, not while his da still had breath in his body, and every breath and moment had been precious. But after, Drem had searched everywhere, all the more desperate to find it because his da had asked for it.

But Drem had not found it.

Maybe I just missed it. It was dark. I was wounded and grief-stricken.

No. He knew how methodical he was, even in anxious, stressful times.

Then where is the sword?

He moved to his da's very last words.

I was wrong.

What did he mean?

It could have meant so many things. Wrong to walk away

from the Order of the Bright Star. Wrong to think he could protect Drem. Wrong to go after the bear. Wrong to give in to Drem's desire to find Fritha, even when they both knew she was most likely dead and that they were wasting their best opportunity of leaving without being noticed.

But none of those options rang true with Drem.

I was wrong.

There's more, I know it. Think back further.

Fritha's cabin. Da was concerned, then.

Drem closed his eyes, seeing the cabin, the destruction and bodies. He remembered his da crouching by the hound, then moving on to Hask's body, lifting a piece of timber.

Part of the door.

Maybe he wasn't as concerned by the need to leave as he was about what he saw in the cabin.

And that wasn't the first time da had been troubled lately. Think back, further.

He remembered their night at Calder's forge, sifted through their snatches of conversation over or between the din of hammer blows.

We spoke of Bodil, how we were both troubled by the death-scene. No tracks. And the strap-marks torn into his wrist, like an animal caught in a snare. And Da said that Calder's corpse bore a knife-wound.

Drem stored this information away, a nagging voice telling him he was missing something. He felt as if he was sitting at a loom, staring at the threads of a tapestry but not quite seeing the picture.

And then, finally, he forced himself to think of the scene in the woods, amidst twilight and snow, where his da had died. A shivering breath threatened to overwhelm him again, a blur of tears and pain in his chest, but he took a few long moments and breathed deep as his da had taught him when he was worried or anxious, and slowly the sensation subsided. Not gone, but it became a calm sea of grief, not a great wave.

The white bear, sounds of it fading. A conversation – what to do.

He realized he was standing, physically re-enacting the moments and steps with his da.

Pursue. Stay. Go. That's what we talked about. I said it was time to leave. If only I'd said that before the bear had been brought to bay. Da would still be here.

The ocean of his grief threatened to rise up at that, and for a while Drem stood there with fresh tears rolling down his cheeks. After a while he gave a shuddering sigh and wiped them away. Forced his mind to return to the scene of his da's death.

The bear. We both heard it. To our right.

He turned, staring to his right, eyes screwed shut as he remembered.

How did it flank us so quietly, when it had been crashing through the forest so recently?

No answer would come for that, so he moved on.

Da telling me to run. Me falling. Snatched glimpses. Da's battle-cry.

He was on the ground in his yard now, the snow cold, exhilarating.

Me trying to get up.

On his knees in the courtyard, pushing to stand.

An explosion in the back of my head.

Dropping back into the snow.

Waking, pain, turning, standing.

He re-enacted it all, just as he remembered and saw it in his mind's eye.

The blow to my head? What was it? Not the bear – its claws would have carved me like a melon. And besides, it came from the wrong direction.

He spun on his feet, looking accusingly about his yard for the hidden culprit, but only one of his goats looked back at him, chewing.

A branch, maybe, sent flying through the air by the bear's attack.

He moved on to the last moments when he held his da, spoke to him. First the sword. Then . . .

I was wrong.

The goats bleated, the second one there too now. Both of them watching him.

He felt frustrated because he was still not understanding. His hand rose up to the bear claw about his neck, the bloodstains still upon his shirt from where his da had gripped it.

I was wrong.

And then Drem was breaking into a run, past the barn and stables and into the paddock, crunching, almost wading through the deep snow until he was standing before his da's cairn. He stopped then, breathed in deep, long breaths, as if he'd been running half a day, the thought of what he intended to do stopping him, holding him in a grip of iron.

I can't do it.

You have to. It's the only way to know.

Another deep-tremored breath.

I can't.

You must. Da would want you to, if it leads to the truth. To an answer.

With an act of will he reached out and grabbed one of the stones upon the cairn, covered in a thick skin of snow and ice, and pulled it off. It resisted a moment, its mortar of rime binding it, but then with a crack it was free. He turned and placed the stone carefully upon the ground. Then another, and another. Soon sweat drenched him as he laboured, removing rock after rock, until he saw a hint of wool and a gleam of pallid flesh. He stopped then, a groan escaping his lips. But he was committed to the act, now, and must see it through.

Until, finally, his da's body was exposed to the light. A faint smell of damp and rot drifted up to him, though thankfully the snow and ice had made that far better than it otherwise would have been. His hand shaking, Drem reached out and pulled back the cloak, revealing his da's head and torso. He let out a strangled sob, took another handful of moments to catch his breath and hold his courage. He had cleaned his da as best he could, that night in the forest. His da's face was a bloodless grey, now, pale as winter's morning. Drem ripped his eyes away, looking to his task, and gazed at the wounds raked across his da's chest. He lifted his right hand, fingers curled like a claw, and in slow motion followed the path of the wounds upon his da. One terrible claw swipe, from right to left, high to low, starting at his da's left shoulder, ending at his right hip, destroying everything in between. Drem paused, thinking, tried the same motion in reverse, up from the hip to shoulder.

No. Not that. It couldn't have been that. The flesh is tattered and torn in the other direction. It must have been its right paw, slashing down, from right to left.

He stared at it.

And then he lifted a hand to the claw about his own neck, gripping it tight and he swayed a little as the truth hit him.

Because the wound upon his da's chest was given by a bear with five claws, and the white bear only had four.

Drem reined in his horse before Asger's house. It was on the outskirts of Kergard, a sturdy cottage of wattle and daub with a grass-sod roof, a side gate and track running between house and barn. Drem heard the creak and roll of wheels and saw Asger emerge from the barn, sitting upon the bench of a heavily loaded wain, reins in hand, his wife and bairns snuggled up close to him. There could have been a dozen more of them wrapped beneath the folds of blankets and furs they were buried beneath, guarding them against the dawn cold.

Asger smiled when he saw him, reining in the two sturdy ponies that were pulling the wain.

'I'm glad to see you,' Asger said. 'You're coming with us, then?'

'No,' Drem said, dismounting from his pony. 'But I wanted

to give you my thanks, for your offer. It was a kind thing you did.'

'Ach, lad, it was more to save my failing back!' Asger grunted, though Drem saw his wife dig him with an elbow and heard the giggle of bairns somewhere beneath all the furs.

'And maybe a hint of kindness,' Asger admitted.

'More than a hint,' Drem said. 'And I'll not be forgetting it. Ever. When you came to see me yesterday, I thought I had nothing left to live for, and now I have two. You have a friend in me, Asger. For life.' He looked the trader in the eye, as his da had often told him to do when you mean what you say, and Asger nodded.

'Sure you want to stay?' Asger said. 'Kergard's not what it was, and I think it's only going to get worse.'

'I'm sure you're right, but I have some things to do. Have to do,' Drem said. 'But, there is one favour you could do for me. I'd be grateful.'

'I'll tell you when I know what this favour is,' Asger said, a suspicious twist of his eyebrow.

Drem reached into a saddle bag and pulled out a package. It was about the size of a plate, wrapped tight in a cloak of black wool, tied with twine. Drem held it out, but Asger didn't take it, just stared at it.

'And where would you like me to be delivering this package of yours?' Asger asked.

'If you're travelling south, you'll most likely be passing their door,' Drem said, his eyes earnest and hopeful.

'Where?' Asger repeated.

'To Dun Seren. It is to be given into the hands of a warrior of their order. She goes by the name of Sig.'

CHAPTER TWENTY-SEVEN

RIV

Riv felt a jolt of fear and excitement with every marched step along the eastern road. She'd gone on plenty of patrols with Aphra's hundred before, protecting a merchant convoy here, escorting state ambassadors there, even to restore peace where some dispute or other had turned bloody between villages or towns, like the incident between Bleda's Clan and Jin's. But this . . .

Kadoshim!

They might be fighting them, and soon. It was everything she'd trained for. Her whole purpose in becoming a White-Wing. It felt like some kind of lifetime fulfilment.

And, truth be told, it was good to be away from Drassil. After what had happened to Estel and Adonai, the fortress had felt different, dour and cold – something she'd never felt about the place she'd been born and raised before. Every day away from Drassil and Riv had felt her spirits lift, and the spirits of their company, as well, it seemed. Three units of White-Wings were marching down the Arcona road, the first hundred led by Aphra, the second by Garidas, ever earnest and devout, the third by a stern-faced woman named Lorina.

Riv was situated at the rear of the column, part of the retinue that travelled with Aphra's hundred White-Wings as assistants, most of them fledgling warriors within a year of their warrior trials. In reality they performed the bulk of tasks required for a warband on the move. Making camp, digging trenches and latrines, collecting wood and building fires, securing fresh water and filling hundreds of water skins. And then seeing to the needs of whichever warrior they were assigned to, in Riv's case her sister, Aphra, which included keeping her weapons and armour maintained, clean and polished.

Behind her rolled two dozen wains pulled by big-boned horses, the wains full of the camp supplies. And behind them two score giants marched rear-guard at the back of the column, Balur One-Eye leading them, the white-haired giant dressed for war in ringmail and leather, his great war-hammer slung across his back.

The iron-shod boots of the Hundred cracked a rhythm on the flagstones of the eastern road. An embankment fell to either side, the land stripped of trees for a good hundred paces, a task that never ended, having to be performed every year, as the forest was ever trying to reclaim what it had lost. Beyond the cleared space Forn reared tall and brooding, a wall of twisted bark and rustling leaves.

They could be in there, right now. Watching us.

It was sections of the forest like this that were dangerous, where Forn Forest had still to be thinned and searched, declared free of Kadoshim and made safe.

The sky was clear and blue up above, like a bright road between the arching canopy. Silhouettes of Ben-Elim flew weightless circles, guarding above, patrolling ahead, searching.

Wish I could fly, she thought. *The sense of freedom, seeing so much, so far . . .*

Golden-haired Kol led the Ben-Elim, fifty or sixty of the white-winged warriors scattered across the sky.

'Do you think we're nearly there yet?' Jost said beside her.

'I don't know,' Riv muttered.

I swear, if he asks me that one more time . . .

A horn blast drifted down to them from above, and suddenly Ben-Elim were swooping low over the column, shouting orders. Riv almost felt feathers brush her upturned face as a Ben-Elim skimmed above her. It was Kol, grinning and whooping. Riv smiled at his exuberance.

He and Israfil could not be more different.

More horns blew and the column rippled to a halt, Riv and those with her running to their allocated warriors. She glimpsed Ben-Elim flying ahead, twelve of them shaped like an arrowhead in the sky.

'I don't need you,' her sister Aphra said as Riv handed her a water skin. She drank deep. 'I want you at the back of the column. Protect the wains.'

'But . . .' Riv said, looking beyond Aphra and the White-Wings to the outline of walls and buildings up ahead.

'Now!' her sister snapped, voice cold and hard, no give in it.

No changing her mind when she's in this mood.

Riv's shoulders slumped and she turned to go.

'Stay close to One-Eye,' her sister called after her. Riv didn't answer, a petty last victory and protest.

Riv stomped back down the line, saw Vald checking the straps of his shield and setting himself in line with other White-Wings. He nodded to her and flashed an adrenalin-fuelled grin. She tried to return it, but knew it was weak and forced, her shame at not being part of this, at being relegated to the safe place, again . . .

Horns sounded and shields came together with a crack, making Riv's heart leap. She loved that sound, though she preferred it when she was in the thick of a shield wall herself.

Resignedly, she found Jost waiting for her with the others, gathered about and amongst the wains. Behind them, and curling around the flanks like a protective hand, were Balur and his giants, all with their axes or war-hammers in their hands, their eyes fixed on the walls of the town that the White-Wings were approaching.

It was named Oriens, a way-point upon the eastern road for those travelling to or from Arcona. Since the Ben-Elim had put down the seeds of civil war between the Sirak and Cheren, trade with the east had flourished. Oriens had grown, from not much more than a feast-hall for travellers and a few wattle-and-daub buildings, into a thriving walled town. Reports had reached Drassil that something was wrong, that travellers had heard screaming and the sounds of battle and slaughter echoing from the walls and instead of stopping had galloped on past. Ben-Elim had made aerial assessments but seen no signs of movement. Something was wrong, and they had decided against entering the town's walls until they had ground support from the White-Wings. They had learned their lesson after the Battle of Varan's Fall, where many had died because they had rushed blindly into an ambush.

Aphra and her hundred had been told little more than that, although the word *Kadoshim* had been whispered.

Riv watched as Aphra led her hundred White-Wings out. They marched down the wide road towards the town, keeping their ranks as they trod the sloping embankment and on across open ground towards Oriens' open gates. No one manned the town's walls, no curls of smoke marked the air where there should have been many cook-fires burning. All was still, tension hovering like a thick mist.

Something's wrong.

More horn blasts and shouted orders, and Garidas' second hundred rippled into motion, the crack of their iron-shod boots setting a drumbeat for Riv's heart. Lorina's hundred waited in reserve as Aphra's White-Wings marched through Oriens' open gates, Ben-Elim swooping low over the walls, one alighting above the gates. Riv's flesh goosebumped, felt like spiders skittering across her skin.

Aphra is in there, maybe risking her life. I should be there, too.

She felt the familiar tingle of anger stirring in her veins, making her bounce on her toes, clenching and unclenching her fists.

The last of Garidas' White-Wings marched through Oriens' gates, disappearing into shadow. Still there was only silence from the town, pulsing in almost palpable waves. A creak of leather and rattle of chainmail behind her; giants were slipping between the wains, Balur striding past Riv as they approached the town.

And they waited, and waited . . . silence radiating from the town like heat from a fire-pit. Riv's anxiety mounted with each passing moment as she stared fixedly at the walls, images of Aphra walking into an ambush flooding her mind. Her fingers clenched white around the hilt of her dagger at her belt.

Worry, fear, shifting into anger at being left behind, at the way Aphra was treating her, her emotions bubbling away inside her.

As usual the anger burned all else away. Common sense. Her sister's orders. Thoughts of consequences. Riv could almost feel it spreading through her veins, like ink through water, seeping into her head, whispering to her.

You should be a White-Wing already, inside those walls with the other warriors, not out here with unproven, untested fledglings. You're as good as any of them with a blade, better than most, and they only give you a knife!

Before Riv realized what she was doing, she was running. Not towards the town, because that would take her through Balur and his giants, and even when she was rage-blind she wasn't that much of a fool. She skidded down the embankment and sprinted across the open space towards the trees of Forn Forest. Dimly she heard a voice behind her, Jost hissing her name, didn't think to look, and then she was amongst the trees, in an instant moving from bright day to a world of twilight, shadows shifting, branches swaying, vine snagging at her feet.

She ran on, hardly breaking her stride, flitting through the forest, around trees, becoming one of the shadows herself. Even sound was different within the forest, noise magnified, the crackle of forest litter beneath her feet, the scratching rustle of branches overhead. Her own breath in her head, a drum keeping time.

Looking to her right, she saw the shadow of walls beyond the trees, veered towards them and burst out into a strip of cleared meadow between the forest and Oriens' walls. This north-facing wall was not as well tended as the western gates: Riv saw patches of the timber wall covered in great swathes of vine, and further on a giant oak spread a gnarled branch over the town's wall.

She sprinted towards the oak, hardly breaking her stride as she reached the twisted trunk of the ancient tree, running up thick roots, gripping ridged bark, clinging like a lizard to a sun-baked wall. A contraction and extension of muscle in calf and thigh and she was leaping, almost felt like she was flying, grinning with the joy of it, and then her hands were clamping around the branch, pulling herself up, getting her feet set and she was upright, running along it, arms spread wide for balance. In heartbeats she had crossed over the wall and was jumping down from the oak onto a wooden walkway.

She paused and looked around, chest heaving. The town spread before her, a patchwork of thatch and timber. There was a flash of movement to the west and her eyes were drawn to the higher roof and long structure of a feast-hall, what looked like a town square before it. She heard marching feet, rising from a main road that cut from the gates to the town square.

Aphra's hundred.

A shadow flitted across the ground.

Ben-Elim. Or Kadoshim?

Without thinking she sprinted down a stairwell and carried on running, into a wide street, then zigzagging into a smaller one. She threw herself against a shadowed wall and twisted her head to look up, searching the skies, but whatever had made the shadow was out of sight.

What am I doing here? What have I done?

She stood there, breathing heavily. The thought of going

back crossed her mind, but the red mist was still making a fog out of everything; the idea of her sister walking into danger without her was a wildfire fuel. She ran on, through smaller dirt-packed roads, searching for Aphra, thinking she could check on her, ensure her safety and then maybe head back to the wains. The town was eerily silent, shuttered windows dark with shadow, doors closed, dew-filled cobwebs latticed across them. And then the shadow was flashing across the ground again and Riv glanced up, saw the dark outline of wings haloed by the sun. She ran on.

She burst into an open space, the town square, the long feast-hall of timber and thatch before her. Skidding to a halt, churned mud spraying, legs scrambling, arms windmilling desperately to stop, she just stood there for a frozen moment staring at the scene before her in horror.

In the centre of the square, placed immediately before the steps to the feast-hall, stood a mountain of severed heads, steaming in the winter's cold.

CHAPTER TWENTY-EIGHT

SIG

Sig swung her weapon, a swooping curve, from high to low that arced around her opponent's attempt at a parry. Too late he tried to dance back out of reach, but the length of Sig's arm with a blade was too far for any man to evade in half a heartbeat. Her weapon crunched into his leg, just below the knee, lifting him from the ground and spinning him a full circle in the air before he crashed to the hard-frozen grass, flat on his back, the air leaving his lungs in one massive *whoosh*.

The scuff of feet behind her and, without a second's thought, Sig spun on her heel, parrying the axe blow aimed at her head, flinging it high and stepping in close to stab her sword-point into the chest of the giant before her. As he stumbled back, dropping to one knee, Sig ducked, air hissing over her head as she spun again, this time chopping her blade two-handed into the waist of another giant, seeing him sway and slowly topple to the ground. Sig took a step forwards, standing over him, sword-tip at his throat.

The giant on the ground looked up at her, then swore.

'Ach, you're just showing off for the new bairns,' he said gruffly.

'Give me your hand,' Sig replied, lifting her wooden practice blade away from Tain's throat.

He smiled then, that infectious grin, even as he was wincing with the pain of moving as his waist twisted and bruised ribs contracted.

'I'm going back to my Crow Tower,' Tain said with a mock groan, 'it's safer up there.'

'Not by the looks of your cloak,' Sig commented, looking at what was once a black bearskin cloak, now streaked and strained with the arse-end of crows.

'That I can live with, pain's a much deeper issue,' Tain grunted.

Behind her Fachen, another giant warrior of the Order, was climbing to his feet.

'You all right?' Sig asked.

He raised a hand to Sig, nodded.

'You're slowing down,' he grunted.

Sig breathed in a long, deep breath, enjoying the sensation of the cold as it seeped into her lungs. They'd already had some light snow, and more on the way, by the smell of it. She was glad to be back. Even though that sense of dread that Byrne had spoken about had not gone, it had faded, and Sig was home in time for Midwinter's Day. It was a holy day for the Order of the Bright Star, a day of remembrance, for it was on Midwinter's Day that the Battle of Drassil had been fought, the Kadoshim and Ben-Elim unleashed upon the Banished Lands. The Kadoshim had been defeated, driven from the field, and Asroth sealed within his cage of molten stone. Corban the Bright Star had been central to those events, and it had been on that day that his dear friends, Gar and Brina, had fallen in the great battle. It was also the day when Corban had resolved to create the Order of the Bright Star, both as a legacy to Gar and Brina, and also to continue the fight against the Kadoshim. The festival was on the morrow, a day of sombre remembrance, and in the evening they would feast in the grey keep and drink to fallen comrades. It was important to Sig that they were remembered, honoured for their sacrifice. On the morrow they would gather before the Stone of Heroes, bow their heads and think of their fallen sword-brothers and sisters . . .

They were upon Dun Seren's weapons-field: a huge expanse contained between the inner and outer walls of the fortress. Warriors were hard at combat in various sections of the field, training. Some were mounted upon horseback, giants upon bears, elsewhere a hundred or so formed up in the shield wall. The Order of the Bright Star used round shields in their wall, unlike the rectangular ones favoured by the White-Wings of Drassil. That was because, to become a warrior of the Bright Star, a novice had to master all of the disciplines, be able to fight in the shield wall, or upon horseback, or upon their feet all alone, and a rectangular shield was impractical upon a horse or in individual combat. A round shield was more adaptable across the disciplines, and so that was what they used.

Sig heard a distant shouted command and the front row of shields dropped as warriors hurled javelins skywards, the iron-tipped shafts arcing high, then thudding to the earth. Sig could almost see the imagined Kadoshim ripped from the sky, imagined the ruin of their fall, the shield wall marching forwards, short-swords stabbing down to finish any survivors as they trampled over the dead and injured.

Much stays the same, and yet much has changed, since that day at Drassil. Heart and courage, iron and blood is as old as the hills, but we are ever finding new ways to kill our foe. The worry is that they are just as diligent at finding new ways to kill us.

Sig turned, looking closer to home, and saw a knot of people staring at her: the two score new recruits from Ardain. Mouths were open, expressions a blend of shock and awe.

They'd been at Dun Seren almost a ten-night now, but this was the first morning that Sig had resumed her duties as sword master of the fortress. The captains of each discipline rotated, so that some would train the warriors at the fortress, while others would lead missions and campaigns out into the Banished Lands against the Kadoshim. It had worked well enough for the past hundred years, keeping all warriors sharp in both training and experience, whether captain, veteran or newcomer.

'Help . . . me,' a thin, reedy voice wheezed.

It was Cullen, still flat on his back from where Sig had spun him through the air and winded him.

'You did ask to join in,' Sig said as she stood over him.

'Thought Tain and Fachen were enough to take the sting out of you,' he gasped. He tried to sit up, grunted with pain. 'I was wrong.'

He tried to sit again, winced again.

'I think you've broken my back.'

'Nonsense,' said Sig, 'stop making such a fuss.' She grabbed hold of his leather jerkin and hoisted him unceremoniously to his feet. He whimpered.

'Bruised a little, maybe,' Sig conceded.

'Bruised a lot, more like.' Cullen rubbed his back, then hoisted his wooden practice sword and brandished it at her.

'Again?' He grinned at her.

Sig shook her head, hiding a smile.

He has a death-wish.

A murmur behind them, and Sig saw heads turning amongst the new recruits as Byrne approached, dressed in her training leathers, dull and scuffed, sweat-stained from years of use.

'A fine display,' Byrne said to Sig. 'Glad to see half a year on the road hasn't dulled your skills.'

Fighting Kadoshim tends to keep you sharp.

They were standing on the part of the field where individual sparring took place, with all manner of weapons. Byrne approached a weapons rack and sifted through the wooden replicas on offer. They were dull edged, of course, but every weapon had been hollowed out and filled with iron, making it heavy. Heavier than the weapons they were fashioned to represent, usually, unless it was a giant's war-hammer or battle-axe, but Sig thought that was a good thing, forging strength in muscle and tendon and sinew, so that when a warrior came to use the sharp steel version, it felt light and responsive in their hands.

Byrne selected a curved sword with a two-handed grip, the wooden likeness of the blade that she usually wore slung across her back. All who came to Dun Seren were trained in a multitude of martial disciplines: sword, spear, axe, hammer, bow; shield-work, knife-fighting, axe-throwing; the shield wall. Various swords – short-swords, longswords, curved swords, single grip, one-and-a-half hand, double grip. Blade-work on foot and mounted. Horsemanship, tracking and hunting. Everything imaginable, and all had to master each discipline. Most had a preference, though, a weapon or combination of weapons that they gravitated towards, a style of fighting, and they were free to choose it, once they'd mastered all of the disciplines and proved it in their warrior trial and Long Night. Sig preferred her longsword, loved the simplicity and elegance of it. Byrne had always been drawn to the curved blade of the Jehar, warriors from the east that had dedicated themselves fanatically to Corban. Gar, the man in whose honour Corban had built the weapons school, had been such a warrior.

'Anyone?' Byrne said as she walked into an open space. Sig grinned and took a step, remembering a thousand hours they had sparred together through the years, but before she could stand in front of Byrne another figure jumped before the High Captain of the Order.

Cullen, his wooden sword resting across one shoulder.

He's a glutton for punishment, Sig thought, stepping back and leaning against a weapons rack, folding her arms.

Byrne dipped her head, raised her sword, not taking her eyes off Cullen, and that was a good job, for he darted in, sword a blur, stabbing straight at Byrne's heart. The crack of wood, Cullen's blade was slapped away and he was spinning, a horizontal chop at Byrne's waist was again blocked, almost casually, as Byrne shifted her feet, not wasting her energy on a counter-strike as Cullen was already out of range, dancing away and back in again, a combination of blows this time, chops, stabs and lunges, all met by Byrne's blade, a discordant rhythm cracking out the timing of their battle as Byrne became the calm centre of Cullen's storm.

Sore back, my arse, Sig thought.

'Is his tactic to wear her out?' a voice said beside Sig. Keld was there, silent as only a master huntsman could be. His dark mood had lifted a little in the last few weeks, Dun Seren a tonic to him as it was to Sig.

Sig shrugged. 'If it is, he should be the one standing still, not dancing around Byrne like he's had a barrel of mead on Midwinter's Eve.'

'I was thinking the very same thing,' Keld said. 'Mind you, he's wearing me out just watching him. Maybe that's his thinking.'

Sig snorted.

Despite their gentle mocking, Sig knew that Cullen was good. More than that, he was exceptional. But he was not the only exceptional warrior at Dun Seren. It took a large dose of exceptional to become high captain of the Order, as well as a significant portion of wisdom.

And it might be the wisdom that Cullen's lacking at the moment, while the stuff fair leaks from Byrne.

And, as if to prove Sig's point, Cullen was abruptly flat on his back, rolling to avoid Byrne's economical chops, spraying turf where his body had been a heartbeat before. Somehow Cullen managed to make it back to his feet, circling Byrne as she resumed stooping falcon, sword high above her head, and waited for him to launch himself at her again.

'Now, I've given you a chance,' Cullen said breathlessly, 'but I'm getting hungry now so it's time to end this.' He lunged in again, laughter rippling around the spectators.

'Do you think he's got a chance of even touching her with his blade?' Keld asked.

Sig had drawn breath for seven hundred years and was

considered past her prime and slipping into old age by giant reckoning, and in that time she had fought all manner of foes. Only three people had ever defeated her in combat: Corban, his wife Coralen, and a man named Veradis, who had been one of the masters at Dun Seren, teaching the shield wall. He too had been exceptional with a blade, preferring the short-sword used by warriors of the wall. And he was Byrne's great-grandfather, for he had wed Cywen, Corban's sister. As Sig watched Byrne spar now she saw Veradis in her, not her physical appearance, which was all Cywen, but in her demeanour, the economy of movement and tactical brain, the way she would calmly weather any storm of blades and wait for her moment. And when she saw it, she would not hesitate.

As if that was her cue, Byrne began to move, not a whirling storm like Cullen, but a steady progress forwards, pushing Cullen back, containing him, restricting him. Her blade hit his arm, then stabbed his thigh, came around high and chopped into his shoulder, making Cullen yelp and Keld laugh, and then Cullen had his back to the weapons rack and Byrne's sword against his throat.

He stood there, breathing heavily.

A horn blast called time to move to a new weapon in the field.

'All right, then, we can stop now if you like,' Cullen said. 'Call it a draw, and count yourself lucky.'

Byrne just stared at him. Sig thought that he'd finally gone too far and that Byrne would give him a week of kitchen duty, but instead a smile split her face.

'Get on with you,' she said.

'He's not right in the head, that one,' Keld said to Sig.

'I know, it's part of what will make him great. If he lives long enough, that is.'

'Got to love him for it, though I often want to strangle him for it, too.'

Sig noticed a man approach Byrne. It was Odras, a fine

healer, and warrior besides. He was the chief quartermaster of the keep, with a talent for keeping supplies flowing and the barns and grain stores full. He spoke in Byrne's ear, and she turned, beckoning Sig over to her.

'A visitor to see us,' Byrne said with a frown.

'Who?'

'A merchant from the north, Odras says. And they have asked to see you. I think I'll come along, though. I'm curious as to who would visit the ill-tempered Sig!'

They left the weapons-field together, leaving a few hundred warriors-in-training behind them. As they stepped from the field onto a wide street, Sig paused beside a great slab of rock that rose from the ground, taller and wider than she was. The Stone of Heroes, it was called, a host of names carved into it. Sig ran her fingertips over some of them.

Gar and Brina were the first names, carved large at the top of the stone, and beneath them many hundreds more. Sig whispered some of them to the sky.

'Dath, Akar, Kulla, Farrell, Veradis, Corban, Coralen,' she breathed. As she said their names their faces formed in her mind's eye, so many, many more, the names of those who had given their lives to the Order, whether they'd fallen in battle or to time and age, if they had served the Order, their names were honoured.

Her eyes came to rest upon one last name, her fingertips tracing the rune-work carved into the stone.

'Gunil,' she whispered, just the sound of his name bringing back so many emotions, a gossamer web spiralling through her veins, about her heart.

Sig shook her head.

A hand touching her – Byrne, a small comfort.

'We will never forget,' Byrne murmured beside her, then turned and walked away.

No, Gunil, I will never forget you. With a sigh Sig followed after Byrne.

The merchant was waiting in a chamber of the keep, sitting at a table with a platter of food and a cup of wine poured for him. A barrel-chested man with thick-muscled arms, more hair on them than there was on his head. He stood as Byrne and Sig entered the room, a mouth full of crumbling cheese, his eyes widening as they took in Sig's size and musculature, hovering on the sword hilt that jutted over her shoulder.

'When he said *warrior*, what he meant was *monstrous killing machine*,' the man muttered.

Sig frowned. *Is he touched in the head?*

After the merchant had recovered from the general shock of meeting Sig, the sight of a warrior giant seeming to unman him for a moment, and then the added shock of being introduced to Byrne, leader of the fabled Order of the Bright Star, he announced himself as Asger, a merchant trader recently from Kergard, the most northern outpost of the Desolation.

'There was nothing there but ash and rock when last I travelled the Desolation,' Sig rumbled. She looked out of the window at the far end of the chamber, which opened out onto a view of the north. The fortress spilt down the hill towards the river Elv, dark and wide, as it curved sluggishly around the hill that Dun Seren was built upon, a hundred quays and jetties jutting out into its waters. A bridge of stone arched over the river, leading into the Desolation, now more green than the grey it had been when Sig had dwelt there. In the distance leaden clouds were massing, creeping their way south.

And bringing snow with them, no doubt.

'It is thriving now,' Asger said, still eyeing Sig dubiously. 'Kergard, I mean. Since the crater became a lake the land has become green again. There are fields and farms, a wealth of furs and skins to be had from the Wild. A good life to be had, if you're not afraid of some hard graft, and the cold, of course. Or at least, it was a good life . . .'

'What do you mean?'

'Things have turned, sour,' he said. 'New folks, bad folks, fleeing the goings-on down south.'

'Then why are you coming south, marching into these troubles?' Byrne asked him.

'There's trouble all over, seems to me,' Asger muttered, 'but I didn't like what I was seeing. Fights in the streets, friends killed, giant bear running amok. Lynchings. It all started with that bonfire in the Bonefells, and Old Bodil's death.' He stopped.

'Bonfire? Like a beacon?' Sig asked him.

'Aye, you could say that,' Asger said. 'But I didn't come here to tell you the troubles of the north; I'm sure you have enough troubles of your own to be dealing with.'

'The Kadoshim are our trouble,' Byrne said. 'And they would be your trouble as much as ours, if we were not the shield that seeks to protect you from them.'

'I'm sure,' Asger said, though he looked as if he was thinking he'd never once seen a Kadoshim, and hoped he never would.

'Least you don't charge a flesh tithe for the service, like the Ben-Elim,' he said, then shook his head. 'I didn't come here to grumble and complain. I was asked to deliver a package. To you,' he added, looking at Sig. He bent down and rummaged in a bag at his feet, straightened with a package in his hand, about the size of a wooden plate, bound with twine, and held it out to her.

Sig turned it in her hands, saw it was some kind of spun wool, dyed black, though faded. With big fingers she undid the twine and let it fall away, unfolding the cloth. She stood there a moment, just staring.

Sig trod the spiral stairs of Crow Tower, torchlight flickering, her shadow stretching before and behind her. The cawing of crows grew louder, and then she was stepping into the chamber, a high-roofed room with a tree growing at its centre, spreading wide branches that were full of dark-shadowed nests.

'*Sig, Sig, Sig,*' a crow squawked, others joining until her name was ringing out like a manic battle-cry, Sig fighting the urge to cover her ears.

'All right!' she yelled and the crows fell silent.

She scanned the nests in the tree, saw black-feathered heads and glistening eyes staring down at her, eventually found what she was looking for. A gleam of white feathers in the highest reaches of the chamber, Rab peering out of a nest that teetered on the thinnest of branches. He puffed his feathers out, pleased to see her.

Tain was standing below a branch, having a conversation with a crow perched above him. Craf was sitting upon a table, one scabby wing over his head, sleeping. Sig thought she could hear snoring. Tain saw Sig and raised a hand, then came over.

'Sten's back from the east. More beacons and unrest,' Tain said. He paused, looking at Sig's face. 'What's wrong?'

'I need to speak to Rab, and I've a message I'd like you to send to your da in Drassil.'

'Cullen,' Sig said, standing over the young warrior in the feast-hall. A dark-haired woman was draped across his lap and he was curling ringlets in her hair with a finger, his other hand emptying a horn of mead down his throat. Sig recognized the woman as one of Tain's helpers from Crow Tower.

Ah, now that would explain why Cullen knows so much about the behaviour of crows.

'Eh? What?' Cullen said as his eyes focused on Sig.

She turned and walked away. When she heard Cullen swear and stumble to his feet, the slap of boots as he ran after her, she nodded to herself.

The kennels were quiet and warm, more like stables than kennels, a long, stone-built building, straw thick on the ground. Broad, furry heads lifted, over a score of amber eyes and fangs glistening in the torchlight as Sig and Cullen strode through them. Two hounds growled, one of them only for a few moments before it caught their scent. All of the wolven-hounds of Dun Seren knew the warriors of the Order by scent. The other hound that had growled was separated in a stable of its own, because it had just whelped eight pups and would happily tear the face off any living thing that stepped within a dozen paces of its pups. As the visitors put some distance between them and the newborn pups the growling subsided.

They found Keld playing knuckle-bones with half a dozen others. By the look on the faces of those around Keld he was winning. He saw Sig's expression and left the game.

'Somewhere private,' Sig said, and Keld led them to the far end of the kennels, into an empty stable that was used as a storeroom. Cullen flopped down on a sack of bones with a huge sigh.

'This better be good,' he said. 'I was enjoying the celebrations.'

Keld leaned against the quartered carcass of a boar, both of them staring at Sig.

She took the package Asger had given to her from a pocket in her cloak.

'A merchant from Kergard delivered this to me today,' she said. She opened it, unfolding black-spun wool to reveal a silver cloak-brooch, fashioned in the shape of a four-pointed star. Cullen and Keld knew it instantly for one of their Order; they wore the same, as did Sig.

Beneath the brooch was a folded sheaf of parchment. Sig opened it and began to read.

'*This message is for the eyes of Sig, and for Byrne, of the Order of the Bright Star. If either of you still live. I am Drem, son of Olin, who was once a warrior of your Order. I have only discovered this recently, and also that I am blood-kin to Byrne. I am writing to tell you both that my father, Olin, is dead. I suspect he was murdered, and I don't know what to do. Strange things.*' Sig paused there, looking up at them. 'The word *strange* has been scored through here, replaced with *sinister*,' she said, then looked back to the parchment.

'*Sinister things are happening. Men and women abducted, bound and slain, a great bonfire. Newcomers with murder in their hearts. I don't know what to do. I know that my da was part of your Order, once, though he walked away a long time ago, and he has spoken to me of you, Byrne, and you, Sig, with great affection. If that counts for anything, after so many years have passed, then I would ask for your help. I would ask you to help me bring my da justice. I have thought on leaving Kergard and coming to you in person, but my heart will not let me leave while my da is unavenged.*'

Sig looked up, feeling her blood stir, a cold anger, a white flame in her belly. A silence filled the stable.

'Little Drem,' Keld whispered, 'Byrne's nephew. The Ben-Elim wanted him as a ward, and Byrne said no. You used to sit him on the Stone of Heroes so that he'd stop chopping at your shins while you were teaching sword-skills.'

'Aye.' Sig smiled at the memory.

'What do you want to do?' Cullen asked.

'I'm going to do as he asks,' Sig said, 'Byrne wants her nephew back – I've had to talk her out of coming with me. She's needed here with all that's happening. It sounds as if the Kadoshim are moving in the Desolation as well, so I'm going to poke a nose in and see what I can find. And more than that, I'm going to find some justice for my sword-brother and friend, Olin, and I'm going to bring Drem back to Dun Seren. He's one of us. Was born here. This is his home.' She looked at them both. 'I'm asking you both to come with me. You're my crew.' She shrugged. 'You don't have to. I know what the morrow is, would not think less of either of you for wanting to stay.'

'Of course I'm coming,' Keld said, tightening his belt and looking for a cloak, as if he were going to walk out and head north right then and there.

'But, what about Midwinter's Day? The Remembrance? The feast. The drinking!' Cullen said.

'We'll leave on the morrow, stay for the Naming, be away right after, long before highsun.'

'But, the evening feast, the toast to the fallen,' Cullen said. He knew the weight that Sig put upon honouring their fallen sword-kin, but Sig suspected he also looked forward to the evening feast for his own reasons.

'It is good and right to honour the dead,' Sig said. 'But I'll not turn my back on a brother that needs us.'

CHAPTER TWENTY-NINE

RIV

Crows lurched into the air at Riv's arrival in the town square, squawking a raucous protest as they abandoned their grisly feast. A choked cry escaped from Riv's lips as she stared at the mound of heads. It stood twice as tall as her, wide at the base, steam curling up in clouds from the rotting skulls. Most had red holes for eyes, flesh ripped and torn into tatters, the dull gleam of bone beneath. A stench of decay and putrefaction rolled out from the mound clawing into Riv's nose and mouth like rotting fingers. She retched, turned away and vomited onto the dirt.

There was the sound of marching footsteps, growing louder, and somewhere above and behind her the rush of air, the beating of wings. The scrape of a sword drawn from its scabbard.

'Turn around, slowly,' a voice said behind her, calm and cold. 'Reach for your blade and you'll die.'

A jolt of fear like bright sunlight burned through the red haze that had been driving her feet and fogging her head. Suddenly cold to her toes, Riv turned slowly, making sure her hands stayed well away from her belt and the hilt of her dagger.

Kol was staring at her, white wings flexed, ready for flight, a bright sword levelled at her chest.

'Riv!' he said, a frown marring his scarred face. 'You shouldn't be here.'

What have I done? Think I'm going to save Aphra all on my own. Think I'm the hero of every story, she berated herself. *I'm just an idiot girl who's ruled by her childish temper. Israfil is never going to allow me to pass my warrior trial.*

'What are you doing here?' the Ben-Elim asked suspiciously.

'Being an idiot,' Riv muttered. 'I was worried about Aphra,' she added, fully aware of how stupid she sounded.

'You were given orders,' Kol said.

'Aye,' Riv said. 'I broke them.'

A silence, Kol's gaze intense, boring into her.

'Rules are not iron, and breaking them not always a sin,' he said.

Riv blinked at that. It was not the answer she'd been expecting from a Ben-Elim.

The noise of the approaching White-Wings filled the town square, almost upon them now. Kol's eyes twitched from Riv to the street the White-Wings were advancing from, then back to Riv.

'Get out of here,' Kol said, jerking his head towards the street she'd run through to get here. 'Quickly; if you're seen, I can't help you.'

Riv didn't need any more encouragement. She leaped forwards, sprinting out of sight just as the first row of the White-Wings' shield wall entered the courtyard. Slamming herself against a wall, she looked back, saw Kol give a beat of his wings and glide twenty paces towards the skulls. The White-Wings spread into the town square, scouts breaking off to search buildings, looking for any potential ambush, and other Ben-Elim dropped down from the skies.

Aphra appeared with her guard; orders were given, smaller units of tens breaking away, marching to the outskirts of the square, setting secure perimeters while Aphra, weapons drawn and prepared for battle, led her warriors past the mound of heads, their booted feet thudding on the timber steps of the feast-hall. Then she was disappearing into the shadowed doors, Riv straining her ears, heart beating heavy as a drum in her head.

Be safe, be safe, Riv pleaded, eyes flitting back to the mound of heads.

Whoever, or whatever, did this might still be here, might be waiting in the shadows of that feast-hall.

Aphra appeared in the doorway, sheathing her sword, and signalled that the building was clear. Riv released the breath she hadn't realized she'd been holding.

There was the sound of more feet as the second hundred of White-Wings marched into the courtyard, led by Garidas. They split into smaller units, continuing the search of buildings and alleys around the courtyard, moving on towards the far end, and to where Riv was lurking.

Time to go.

Riv turned and ran back towards where she determined the main gates were. As she drew close she heard familiar voices, saw Jost and the other helpers moving into the town now that perimeters were set. She made her way as close as she could to them, always hugging the shadows, light and silent on her feet. As they passed her by, she stepped out and rejoined them. Jost pulled a relieved face.

'Thank Elyon you're back,' he whispered. 'There's only so long I can tell people you're on a latrine break.'

'Thanks,' she said and grinned at him.

Riv sat close to Aphra, who was engaged in deep conversation with Garidas, Lorina and Kol.

They were sitting around a fire-pit dug into the meadow that surrounded the town of Oriens.

All around the meadow fire-pits crackled, small oases of light in night's darkness. White-Wings were sitting and taking their meals, giants and Ben-Elim spread amongst them, the Ben-Elim looking as relaxed as she had ever seen them. It reminded her of the night in her own feast-hall back in Drassil, when she had seen Adonai with Estel. Something twisted in

Riv's stomach, a sour taste in her mouth, and she pushed the memory away.

There's enough darkness in this very day, without searching old memories to find it.

Guards patrolled the line between meadow and forest, and above her Riv occasionally heard the whisper of wings, hoped that it was Ben-Elim, and not one of the huge blood-sucking bats that dwelt within the gloom of Forn.

Or Kadoshim.

Riv glanced at the walled town, silent and still. There was plenty of room in there for the warriors, and the walls and roofs would have offered protection against the predators of the forest. But no one wanted to sleep within the walls of Oriens. The mound of heads had made an impression upon all of them. It was clearly the townsfolk, not just warriors or men who had taken up arms against a raider. Men, women, bairns, all were amongst the macabre, blood-soaked mound.

Kol had ordered the mound dismantled, in itself a grisly act, as a search for the bodies had been made, but none had been found before light had begun to fade. So a deep pit had been dug, Riv's hands blistered by the hard shovel work, and the heads were buried. Kol had spoken words from the Book of the Faithful over them.

'The unjust will laugh and mock the righteous, they may outlive their dark deeds by a day or a year, but the righteous will find them, and when they do, the unjust will tremble.'

Voices had called out agreement, oaths made to avenge the slain.

'Who would do such a thing?' Jost whispered to Riv.

'Kadoshim,' Riv breathed back to him.

Must be. Who else would murder innocents, mutilate children and babies?

The smell came back to Riv unbidden, a vision of a tiny skull, red holes for eyes. She breathed deep and slow, controlling the lurching of her stomach.

'Ask Aphra,' Jost urged her.

She looked at her sister, who was staring into the flames of the fire-pit, not involved in the conversation between Kol and Lorina. Garidas was silent, too, though his eyes were on Aphra, not the flames. Riv had long thought that he had more than a warrior's respect for her sister.

'Go on.' Jost nudged Riv with his elbow.

'Is it Kadoshim?' Riv leaned close and whispered in Aphra's ear.

Her sister jumped as if stabbed, staring at Riv.

'I don't know, Riv. We found only the dead in Oriens,' Aphra said, her voice clipped, as if she were straining to hold the rest in.

Kol glanced between Aphra and Riv.

'It's a dark, grievous thing that has been done here,' Kol said, standing; others turned to listen. He looked at the faces about the fire-pit, all staring at him, washed in a blood-red flicker.

'Was it the Kadoshim?' a voice asked. Jost.

Kol looked at Jost, the fledgling White-Wing standing still as stone, all sinew, stretched muscle and tendon. He looked ten shades of uncomfortable under the scrutiny of so many eyes.

'I don't know. This could well be the work of the Kadoshim,' Kol said, a snarl twisting his features, his golden stubble glinting in the firelight. 'I can think of no other that would perform an atrocity such as this.'

That's what I thought.

'Whoever they are, we will find them,' Garidas spoke up. He was a fine warrior, and a respected leader, though Riv considered him to be too serious, too obsessed with following the Lore's every dictate, and that was saying something, because she took the Way of Elyon more earnestly than most. As Riv watched him, his gaze flickered beyond Kol's wings to Aphra.

'As to the how of it,' Kol continued. 'When the sun rises we search, we scour this place for tracks, signs as to who did this.

Then we hunt them down. There will be a reckoning.' He shrugged, his wings a rippled sigh with the motion, then strode into the darkness.

'There's your answer, then,' Aphra said with a weary sigh to Riv.

'What's wrong with you?' Riv said, sitting next to her sister. 'Is it something I've done?'

Aphra gave her a long look. 'No,' she said eventually.

'Then wha—'

'Leave it,' Aphra snapped, quiet and cold. 'The world does not revolve around you and your woes, Riv. Shocking as it may seem, people have troubles of their own.'

Riv stared at her, then stood and marched off.

Sick of being Aphra's training post. Thinks she can take out her anger on me!

She heard footsteps behind her, hoped it was Aphra following her. She didn't like how cold and distant her sister had become, wanted her to go back to normal.

I suppose Mam is right, though. Leading is hard. Especially at times like this.

She looked back over her shoulder and saw Jost hurrying up behind her, felt a rush of disappointment that it wasn't her sister.

'What do you want?' she said to Jost, more curtly than she meant it to sound.

'Shouldn't be walking around on your own,' Jost said stoutly. 'Orders. Safety in numbers, those giant bats of Forn . . .'

Riv knew that. 'Orders aren't iron,' she said, though, and stalked on.

The camp was contained to the meadow and road, neatly ordered rows of tents, a paddock roped off for the horses, wains on the raised embankment of the road. Riv was stomping along close to the paddocks, only a few hundred paces from the trees of Forn which loomed like dark cliffs.

Riv knew Jost was right, and she had no intention of wandering off alone into the dark. The mound of heads in Oriens had left its mark. And she was glad of Jost's company, at least it meant he cared whether Riv lived or died. She rolled her shoulders, trying to shift a dull ache in her back, high, between her shoulder blades.

Must've pulled a muscle climbing that tree.

They walked past a group of White-Wings gathered around a fire – the paddock guards, part of Lorina's hundred. Some of them were singing; one invited them over, but Riv walked on.

'Hold,' a voice rang out before them; two figures stepped out of the darkness, spears in their fists. Two White-Wings standing guard duty. One of them was Vald. He looked tense, his eyes constantly scanning the gloom and shifting shadows within the forest.

'Don't stray so close to the trees,' the other one said, an older warrior from Garidas' hundred.

'They're all right,' Vald said.

'Aye. Of course they are, they're going to be White-Wings. Won't stop them being eaten by one of Forn's hungry mouths, though, or snatched by a Kadoshim, or whatever it was did that to those in the town.' He looked pointedly at Riv and Jost. 'Back to the meadow, eh?'

'As you asked so nicely,' Riv said, and they started back, soon reaching the road guards. They were still in their cups, songs louder and more slurred.

'Aren't they the two fledglings that failed their warrior trial?' a slurring voice said.

'Ignore them,' Jost whispered.

'Run back to your sister's apron strings,' one of them said, pointing at Riv, then he fell over, laughing.

Riv scowled at the warriors, a mixture of young and old. The one who'd fallen over climbed back to his feet, only a few years older than her. Jost was pulling on her arm and she gave a frustrated sigh, stamping down the ever-present rage that had begun to burn again. She turned away with Jost and began to walk away.

'Fly along, little fledglings,' another guard said, making a flapping motion. 'Get back to Big Sister before it's too late.' The one who had fallen over laughed so hard it sounded like he was crying.

Riv twisted on her heel and marched towards them, the rage descending like a red mist again.

'What?' Jost said. 'Riv, what're you doing? Riv, no, come back, Riv. Riv, please.' He hurried after her, snatched at her arm but she pulled it away.

'So, which one of you arse-wipes wants to go first?' Riv asked, glaring at them all.

'Eh?'

'Just ignore her,' Jost said, pulling at Riv's arm.

'Listen to your friend,' one of the other guards, a sharp-nosed man, less in his cups than the others.

'Aye, listen to that bag of string and run along,' said another, a woman, a scar running from eye to jaw. 'No doubt you'll be a White-Wing soon enough – your sister will make sure of that, even though you don't deserve it.' She looked Jost up and down. 'What is he, anyway? Your guard-stick?'

'Bag of string? Guard-stick?' Jost said.

'You first, then,' Riv said and leaped at the woman.

She crashed into the warrior, the two of them rolling together, Riv throwing punches and using elbows all the while. Someone grabbed her collar, hoisting her away. A glimpse of Jost punching someone flush on the chin.

He has long arms, as they're finding out, Riv thought, feeling a rush of joy sweep through her, a grin splitting her face as she let the frustrations in her bubble over into a physical release of violence. She twisted in the grip about her neck, knee lashing out, connecting with something soft. There was a whoosh of air and a gurgled groan and she was no longer being held.

People all around her, faces, limbs, all one long, furious, blurred drunken dance. She threw punches and kicks, felt some land, dimly, through her euphoria, saw a flash of a face that looked like Vald.

Couldn't have been.

And then, abruptly, she was airborne, weightless, legs kicking, the snarl of bodies below her stopping in mid-punch or kick. She saw Jost upon the floor, someone's arm around his neck, but he had another's leg in his grip, his mouth open to bite their calf.

The rushing of air about her, a sound. She looked up, saw broad white wings beating, Kol's grim face looking down at her.

Dawn was close, a grey stain seeping across the horizon, turning the solid black of night into shifting shadows. Riv's mouth throbbed, pains everywhere clamouring for her attention and she put a hand to her face, felt a cut on her lip, a loose tooth.

She was in a wain with the baggage train, her head on a grain sack, peering out through a slot in the wain's tall sides. It was the closest to an isolation cell that Kol had been able to find at short notice. Jost and Vald had their very own wains a few score of paces away. Riv could hear Vald snoring, could hear the rhythmic shaking and rattling of his wain's brackets as if they were in a storm.

It *had* been Vald's face she'd seen in fight last night. He'd seen what had happened and come rushing, diving bodily into the melee.

He's a good friend, coming to help like that. And now he's in isolation for deserting his post!

Must control my temper, must control my temper, Riv recited to herself, over and over.

If I don't get my temper under control I'll never get to pass my warrior trial. I'll never even get to take it. When Israfil hears about this . . .

She punched the side of the wain, hissed a string of curses and then sighed, setting about removing the splinters from her knuckles.

A whisper of wings, a silhouette blotting out the grey of dawn, and then Kol was alighting inside the wain, sitting down so that he was hidden from view from outside the wain, his great wings wrapping around him. He stared at Riv, his dark eyes fixing her, golden hair shimmering in the first glow of the sun.

'Disobeying orders and sneaking into Oriens. Fighting guards. Let's go back a little. Fighting on the weapons-field. Further. Fighting in the feast-hall, kicking your friend in the stones. Back further. You *punch* Israfil, the Lord Protector of the Ben-Elim, Overseer of the Land of the Faithful, in the face.' His lips twitched at the last. 'It would seem you have anger issues, Riv.' He shook his head. 'What am I to do with you?'

A silence settled between them, just his stare.

'Was that a rhetorical question?' she eventually asked, uncomfortable, 'or do you want me to answer?'

Kol snorted a laugh at that. He laughed a lot, judging by the creases at his eyes.

'I can only help you so much – like today in the market square. You must help yourself.'

'Why do you care?' Riv grunted. She knew it was churlish as soon as she said it, but she seemed to be doing a lot of things like that lately. Acting, speaking, doing, before thinking.

'I like you, Riv.' Kol shrugged. 'You have spirit. I can see your mam in you, and your sister, and that is no insult. But keep on like this and you'll never make the White-Wings.'

'I know,' said Riv with a frustrated sigh. 'And that is my greatest, my *only* wish.'

'Then let me help you make it come true,' he whispered.

'You would help me?'

'Yes. If I can. But you must help yourself, too. Start by stopping your brawling. It won't do. It's spoiling your looks.' He smiled then, a flash of white teeth and Riv felt herself blushing. Starlight highlighted the arch of his eyebrows and cheekbones, making the scar that ran from forehead to chin a dark valley. Somehow it made his face more handsome, different from the Ben-Elim's perfection. And fierce. She was glad the sun hadn't risen so far that Kol could see her blush. He reached a hand out, fingers brushing the cut on her lip. Riv fought the instinct to pull away, would have, if not for the wain's board behind her head. Something about his touch sent a shiver through her.

'You are so different from Israfil,' she whispered, scared by his touch, the smile in his eyes, enjoying it, too.

'He is too serious,' Kol whispered, fingertips still brushing her cut lip. 'This life of flesh, there is so much more to it than his constant frowning and his fixation with the Lore.'

Riv smiled, snorted a shocked laugh.

'I thought the Lore was everything,' she said.

'Is it?' Kol said. 'The Kadoshim must be exterminated, it is the only way to fulfil our Holy Calling, to protect mankind. But as for the rest . . .' He shrugged, a ripple of his wings. His fingers moved away from her lip, a caress on her cheek.

Footsteps, soft, a shape looming over the wain's side.

'Riv—' her sister said as she looked into the wain, then froze, stared from Riv to Kol.

'No,' she said, a quiet voice, cold as winter, face hard and flat, but Riv could see the sudden fury in her eyes. 'No,' she repeated, some of that fury leaking into her voice.

Kol smiled at Aphra as he stood, stretched luxuriously. With a beat of his wings he was airborne, a silhouette against the rising sun.

Aphra stared at Riv, her mouth twitching, though nothing came out.

Horns sounded, announcing the change of guard and the coming of morning.

It's Midwinter's Day, Riv realized.

*

Trees blotted out the day as Riv entered Forn. It was close to highsun, and she was marching in formation with the other fledglings of Aphra's hundred, all of them equipped with shield and spear.

Scouts had worked through Oriens and out onto the surrounding area as soon as dawn had arrived and, not long after, evidence of a trail had been discovered on the north-eastern side of the town, leading into Forn Forest. Kol had sent two score White-Wings in to scout the path while the rest of the three contingents prepared to march.

As they did, Kol had alighted on the wall of Oriens and addressed them all, a stirring speech of justice for the slain, of Elyon's judgement upon the murderers. He quoted from the Book of the Faithful again, more about the iniquities of the Fallen catching up with them, of justice and blood. Then he ordered that the fledglings be equipped for battle and accompany the search into Forn. Riv had seen Aphra's frown, but not known whether it was from worry for Riv's safety, or for some other reason.

And now they were marching into Forn, shadow and leaf all about.

Has Kol done this for me? Is this what he meant, when he said he would try to make my dream come true?

It was like a dream, a thrill coursing through her as she'd stepped into line and lifted her shield, Jost beside her. To her left there was a loud crack as a branch snapped, a giant appearing between trees. They were spread to either side of the White-Wings' ragged column, impossible to keep tightly regimented in this terrain.

And on they marched, deeper into Forn.

Something changed about them. Riv was at first unsure what the change was. Then she realized.

It had become silent.

No birdsong, no insects. And with it, a tension in the air, thick and stifling.

A horn blast, the front of the column halting, the rest rippling to a stop behind.

'What's happening?' Jost said, peering along the line.

'You're taller than me,' Riv said. 'All I can see is someone's back. And Jost, I wanted to give you my thanks, for last night.'

'You're my sword-kin, what are friends for, eh?' he said, smiling, one eye half-closed, a purple bruise circling it.

'Your poor eye,' she said.

'Ah, it's not so bad. I'd rather that than wake up this morning with teeth marks in my ankle, like one of their lot has had to do.'

They both laughed at that, receiving strict looks from a White-Wing in the ranks ahead.

Another horn blast and then the column was moving on again. Suddenly, Riv saw what had caused them to stop.

They had found the bodies of the townsfolk. From an overhanging tree branch hung a body. A noose about one ankle, it was headless, skinned and gutted like a boar ready for the spit. Riv had to force herself to look away as they marched beneath it and on into the forest.

As they pushed on, more bodies were visible, hanging from branches, swaying, dangling, chewed upon by things that flew or climbed.

They are like markers showing the way.

Which is worrying. Is this an ambush? Are we marching to our slaughter?

Riv felt fear tingling through her veins, but also excitement, the thought that she might finally fight the Kadoshim. She felt as if she were born to do that. The one thing that she existed to do.

And then they found them.

Bodies in a small clearing, hundreds upon hundreds heaped upon each other in a tangled, stinking pile. Crows and flies rose in a buzzing, croaking cloud, the stench of rot rolling out from the dead like a wave. Jost was not the only one to empty his guts into a bush.

Orders were barked, Balur One-Eye appearing out of the gloom. All were mindful of an ambush, eyeing the trees suspiciously, horns blowing and the White-Wings splitting, some moving to help Balur and his giants as they went about setting up a perimeter, giants hacking at thinner trees, White-Wings using machetes and axes to chop at vine and brush, pushing the forest back a little, clearing a defensible space. The other White-Wings and fledglings merged into a circular defensive formation, weapons bristling outwards, while Kol and his captains stood and consulted near the pile of the dead.

Riv scanned the forest, her spear clutched ready, her eyes drifting higher, aware that Kadoshim could strike from any angle, any direction. She saw a Ben-Elim swooping through branches high above. The more she stared, the more she thought.

There's no one here, except the dead.

It doesn't seem right, Riv thought. *For whoever it is to do this, even to go as far as marking the way to this spot. The trail of bodies. Why go to all this trouble? It must be an ambush. Why else would we have been lured out here.*

Why else would they want us here.

And then it hit her.

So far away from Drassil.

CHAPTER THIRTY

BLEDA

Bleda's eyes snapped open.

Something's wrong.

It was dark, his eyes taking a while to adjust, some instinct telling him it was the small hours between midnight and dawn, though he could not be sure. And his head hurt.

Too much wine.

But it has been Midwinter's Day.

Then he heard it. Faint cries.

What?

He swung his legs out of bed, feet cold on the stone floor. Embers still glowed in his fire-pit, a half-light that he dressed by, swiftly pulling on breeches and boots, a wool tunic, reaching instinctively for his belt with his bow-case and quiver of arrows.

I feel like someone made anew, since Riv returned my bow to me.

Just at the thought of it he felt a tremor of emotion that threatened to undo his cold-face. It took a few moments to master it.

More cries, louder. Boots thudding on stone.

He padded to his window and opened the shutter, shivered at a blast of frost-filled air and looked out into the starlit street. White-Wings were running, still in loose formation, but running.

They never run. They march everywhere. Even to bed, most likely.

Screams on the night air. The clash of steel. Bleda felt a jolt of fear, a shock.

Death, battle, in unassailable Drassil, heart of the Ben-Elim.

He left his chamber, his heart thumping in his chest, and found Jin standing in the doorway of their shared house. Their guards, usually half a dozen White-Wings that dwelt in the same building, were nowhere to be seen.

'They ran off, towards the gates,' Jin hissed, an answer to his look at the empty guard room where water in an iron pot was bubbling over flames in the hearth. 'What's happening?'

'We're being attacked,' Bleda said.

'Who?'

He just shrugged.

A raid? A full-on assault?

'Let's go find out,' Jin said, stepping into the street, breath misting in the starlit night. She looked excited by the prospect, one hand resting on the hilt of a long dagger sheathed at her belt. Bleda followed, as it was exactly what he had intended to do, anyway.

They slipped through the darkness of Drassil, the ancient trees' branches swaying high above, sending shadows shifting across the flagstoned streets. The clamour of battle rose in volume, and then they were at the courtyard before Drassil's gates. Bleda pulled Jin into a darkened alcove.

Before them was a scene of chaos.

The gates were open, flames flaring high from one of the oil-filled braziers that burned day and night, and smoke and flame crackled and spilt from one of the stables edging the courtyard. Horses screamed within.

Combat ranged about the courtyard, steel clanging. Shapes of men silhouetted by flame were fighting, wrestling, as a wave of dark-cloaked figures surged through the open gates, hundreds, it seemed to Bleda, though it was hard to tell through the smoke and flame. White-Wings were forming their shield wall, more shields locking into place with every moment, and then a horn blast and they were slipping fluidly into movement, pressing towards the gates, the dark-cloaked enemy falling before their short stabbing blades.

Two figures crashed into a wall nearby, came careening towards them, a White-Wing and a Dark-Cloak. There was a wet, punching noise and the White-Wing fell at their feet, blood bursting from his mouth, black in the starlight. The Dark-Cloak stood over his enemy, his hood fallen away to reveal a pale-faced man, shaven-haired and wild-eyed. He looked about for more White-Wings to kill and threw himself back into the battle.

'Stay back,' Bleda hissed at Jin when she took a step forwards, 'you've only got a knife.'

'And you've your present, I see,' Jin said, not able to hide an edge of venom from her voice as she glanced at the bow in his hand.

Jin had been awestruck when she saw Bleda's bow, a little less so when she'd heard where it had come from.

'All these years she's kept it from you,' Jin had said.

'She has,' Bleda had agreed. *'But she has given it to me now.'* And Jin had seen something in his eyes then that she hadn't liked. Not one little bit. Ever since then Jin had hidden it well, but whenever he used his bow or spoke of it her voice had been gilded with spite, veiled threads of jealousy leaking from her.

Jealous of his bow, or of Riv, he did not know.

'Don't worry for my safety,' Jin said as she stood over the dead White-Wing, turning the fallen man's head with her foot. 'I just wanted to make sure he's dead. I have no intention of getting involved. Let them kill each other, what do I care? Good, I say. The world is better for fewer Ben-Elim and White-Wings.'

A short while ago and Bleda would have agreed without thought, but now, at Jin's words the first image to flash into his mind was Riv.

A fledgling White-Wing.

He had missed her since she'd been gone, over a ten-night, which had surprised him, but now he just felt a sense of relief that she was not here, was not fighting, risking death in this courtyard.

Though she may be no safer, wherever she is.

He pushed the thought away, brought back to the present by another death-scream.

How did they get in here? Get the gates open, take Drassil by surprise? And where are the Ben-Elim?

As if answering his thoughts, he felt the air shift above him, saw shadows flitting across the sky.

But they weren't Ben-Elim.

Bleda knew it in a moment. The shape of them was different, their outline – silvered by starlight above, red-flamed glow from below – looked wrong, somehow. Their wings were ragged and thin, like wind-torn clouds after a storm, and they were edged in sharp-curved talons.

Kadoshim!

Even as he thought it, one of the winged figures was descending to the ground, only fifteen, twenty paces from Bleda and Jin. And it was carrying something in its long arms, another figure that it as good as hurled into a knot of White-Wings who were forming a small shield wall of a dozen men, calling others to them.

The figure thrown into their midst scattered them like kindling, roaring a battle-cry as the White-Wings scrambled to their feet. Its arms swung, some kind of sickle-like blade in its hand, and a head was spinning through the air. Then it leaped at two more White-Wings, the three of them crashing to the ground in a roaring tangle of limbs.

The Kadoshim alighted between them and Bleda, its wings furling behind it with a snap, a rush of air that tasted of the grave, of rot and decay. Bleda and Jin just stood and stared at the creature. All his life Bleda had heard of the Kadoshim, dread foes of the Ben-Elim, their opposite in every way. But no tale had prepared him for the sight of one in the flesh, living, breathing, stinking, just ten paces away. It was taller than a man, black eyes set in a reptilian face, fixing upon him, dark veins cobwebbing its pallid flesh. Its face shifted, smile or snarl, Bleda was unsure, revealing white, pointed teeth, and it strode towards them, drawing a sword from its scabbard, dark wings framing it like a cloak.

'Kill it!' Jin hissed beside him, but Bleda was frozen, those black eyes burning into him. He felt the closeness of death, a cold breath down the back of his neck. He fumbled desperately with the arrows in his grip, dropped them clattering about his feet, beside him Jin moved into a fighting stance, knees bent, her knife gleaming in her fist.

The Kadoshim raised its sword.

Bleda nocked an arrow to his bow, fingers feeling numb, swollen, like when he'd been stung by a bee. He tried to draw his arrow, aim, knew he was too slow, too late, the Kadoshim's shadow falling across him, the stench of its breath filling his senses, and all Bleda could do was stare into its pale-as-death face.

Jin stepped forwards, crouched, knife levelled. She hissed a challenge.

An axe slammed into the Kadoshim's skull, its head gone in a heartbeat, an explosion of blood and bone and brains, the axe continuing its descent, carving down deeper, through clavicle bone, sternum and ribs, on and into its chest cavity. Then the axe-blade was being ripped free, the Kadoshim collapsing to the ground with a wet slap, blood steaming. A figure appeared in its place.

Alcyon, covered in blood.

'Get out of here,' the giant shouted at him, gesturing for Bleda and Jin to flee. Then he was turning and wading into the fight, other giants appearing, Ethlinn striding into the court-yard wearing a gleaming coat of mail, a long spear in her fists.

The air above was suddenly full of movement, more

Kadoshim winging overhead. And other shapes, winged, but their outlines shorter and less reptilian, more human.

Like the half-breed that attacked Israfil.

The pale gleam of white feathers reflected starlight as Ben-Elim appeared, the din of steel clashing, shapes swirling, Ben-Elim and Kadoshim spiralled through the night sky, stabbing and chopping and screaming at each other.

Bleda felt overwhelmed, chaos, confusion and death a whirling maelstrom all about. He felt he couldn't breathe.

He turned and ran from the courtyard a dozen paces, a score, two score, the tumult receding quickly behind him. He paused, hands on his knees, sucking in deep breaths.

'What are you doing?' Jin said behind him. 'Don't leave, I want to watch!'

He felt better now, his head clearing, angry with himself. Ashamed of his fear.

The whisper of wings overhead, a swift shadow, and Bleda looked up, glimpsed a Kadoshim flying deeper into Drassil, carrying a figure in its arms, more of them, too dark to count.

Where are they going?

'Get Alcyon,' he said to Jin and ran off after the disappearing Kadoshim.

Within moments the streets were silent, the battle seemingly focused and contained within the courtyard. Bleda caught a glimpse of dull metal up above, more Kadoshim and half-breeds flying overhead, all clutching a warrior-passenger in their arms, moving in the same direction as he'd guessed the other ones to be flying. Deeper into the fortress.

Where?

And then he knew, as he ran skidding into another courtyard, this one all but empty, the huge domed walls of Drassil's great keep rising before him. Bodies lay scattered upon the steps, a Kadoshim or two, some Dark-Cloaks, and White-Wings. Blood steamed, clouds of it in the cold night air.

And from out of the open doors echoed the sounds of battle.

Asroth.

Bleda had visited Drassil's Great Hall on his very first day with Israfil. The Ben-Elim had shown him the iron-clad Asroth and Meical upon their dais before the trunk of the great tree. He had stood quietly and listened as Israfil told the story of the Seven Treasures, how both Asroth and Meical were encased by some dread spell during the Battle of Drassil, maybe alive, maybe dead, forever imprisoned, and under eternal guard. It had just seemed like a faery tale to him, an excuse for the Ben-Elim to enslave the people of the Banished Lands.

Until now.

Abruptly, terrifyingly, he entertained the thought that it was all true. That Asroth was *real*.

And the Kadoshim are here to free him.

Bleda ran, then, leaping up the wide stone steps, over the dead. At the open gates he stopped and peered in. The floor of the Great Hall was lit by huge iron braziers, blue flame blazing from giant oil, giving the chamber an eerie, dreamlike quality.

There was a guard of giants about the statues within, a score of them in ringmail, wielding war-hammers and axes, ranged in a half-circle before the dais upon which stood the statues of Asroth and Meical, and they were beset by Kadoshim, half-breeds, Dark-Cloaks, and . . . other things.

Some were men, shaven-haired warriors, fighting with a frenzied, heedless energy. But there were also human-like creatures, shambling and disjointed, arms too long for their bodies, nails curved and long as claws. Bleda saw three of them attacking a giant, acting like a pack of wolves, darting in and out with tooth and claw, hamstringing the giant and then ripping at his throat with their claws. As the giant fell, one of them raised his head and howled.

In the air of the great dome Ben-Elim flew, a dozen of them at least, though they were falling even as Bleda looked on, outnumbered and locked in swooping, spiralling aerial combat with Kadoshim.

Fear breathed upon his neck once more, a cold fist contracting in his belly.

This is not your fight. Kadoshim, Ben-Elim, they do not belong here. Let them kill each other, as Jin said, and rejoice in it.

It is not your fight.

He looked at the splayed corpse of a Kadoshim close to his feet, dead eyes staring, dark veins mapping its face and arms.

The Ben-Elim are bad, but these Kadoshim . . .

They are worse!

In his mind's eye he saw the one in the courtyard, sword raised high, malice radiating from its every pore like mist. The thought of them setting Asroth free, of what they would do if they won against the Ben-Elim, sent shivers down his spine.

He looked over his shoulder, hoping to see Alcyon leading a host of giants and White-Wings into the courtyard. But there was only stillness and silence.

He reached into his quiver, pulled out three arrows and stepped into Drassil's Great Hall.

On the floor below, many of the giants were down, the survivors drawing tighter about the iron-black statues of Asroth and Meical, Dark-Cloaks and the things with them throwing themselves at the giants, Kadoshim swooping down from above.

Bleda raised his bow, nocked and loosed without thinking; a Kadoshim shrieked, arching in mid-air, then tumbling, limbs loose, crashing to the stone floor. He paused, realizing it was the first time he had shot at a living foe, the first enemy life he had taken. The weight of that shivered through him.

Screams drew him back to himself. He shook his head and focused. Nocked an arrow and loosed again, a Dark-Cloak stumbling and falling, another arrow, another Dark-Cloak down.

More arrows from his quiver as he padded down the wide steps that led to the chamber's floor. Another Dark-Cloak falling with an arrow in his back. Then a Kadoshim saw him, shrieking a warning, and some of the Dark-Cloaks on the ground looked up at him.

Half a dozen of them, more, turned and ran at him, the Dark-Cloaks screeching battle-cries, the beasts with them disturbingly silent.

Breathe. Don't panic. It's like shooting rats in the salt gorge.

Nock, draw, release. Nock, draw, release.

A Dark-Cloak down in a spray of blood. Another doubling over, an arrow in the gut.

Easier when they're running straight at me.

Nock, draw, release.

Sparks as an arrowhead crunched into stone, his first miss.

Though the fact they're coming to kill me isn't helpful for my concentration.

An arrow thumping into a shoulder, spinning a Dark-Cloak.

Nock, draw, release. Nock, draw, release.

One of the shambling creatures dropped to one knee, Bleda's arrow lodged in the meat between neck and shoulder. Another arrow skittering on stone, his second miss.

Jin would laugh to see those shots.

There was a slap of wind in his face and he instinctively ducked, a Kadoshim's sword from above just missing where his head had been. He fell, rolling, dropping arrows, desperately clutching his bow. Gasping, he regained his feet and leaped away, running a dozen paces down the tiered steps as the Kadoshim came after him. He tugged an arrow from his belt-quiver, loosing wildly, the Kadoshim veering away, the arrow piercing its leathery wing. Bleda was dimly aware of the surviving Dark-Cloaks and their companions still charging at him. Much closer now. Grabbing at the remaining arrows in his quiver, only a few left, he backed away, pausing to nock and aim, loosing, one shot slamming into a Dark-Cloak's chest, hurling him to the ground.

Two figures were still running at him, only twenty paces

away, the shambling, loping *things* the Kadoshim had flown across Drassil's walls. Bleda starred into the face of the wild-eyed man, if you could call him that. There was a feral, soulless cast to him, teeth bared in a snarl, canines worryingly sharp, nails grown long and black, thicker than they should be, limbs having a stretched appearance, running in a loping, shambling gait, as if its bones had grown overnight.

Bleda readied himself, nocked and aimed, put an arrow into the man's chest, at less than twenty paces, the force of it hurling him backwards, head over feet, down the wide steps. Bleda had another arrow nocked and was aiming at the last Feral when he saw the first one rise, stagger to his feet, shake himself like a wounded hound, and then the eyes were fixing onto him. It sent a jolt of fear lancing through Bleda.

That should have killed him. What are they?

He adjusted his aim, away from the closer attacker, back to this difficult-to-kill creature, loosed, his arrow leaping from the bow. Bleda knew it was good without needing to see it land, shuffling back to make time for the last Feral.

His arrow punched into the first creature's eye, sending it tumbling, limbs boneless. This time, to his relief, it didn't get back up.

He nocked another arrow quickly, shifting to aim at the last Feral, but too late. It was upon him, a crunching impact, launching him through the air with a moment's weightlessness, then a bone-jarring impact as his shoulder slammed into stone. Breathless, he lost his grip on the bow, then the man-beast was on top of him, claws reaching for his throat, scouring his chest, pain erupting like lines of fire; hot, fetid breath in his face as far-too-long teeth snapped a handspan from his jaw. He kicked and punched, pain lancing up his shoulder, writhed and bucked in the thing's grip, felt those long claws seeking out his throat, moving inexorably closer.

I will not die like this!

His grasping hands made contact with a loose arrow on the

floor and he grabbed for it desperately, punched it into the side of the creature's head, into its cheek, ripped it out, stabbed again, saw teeth through the gash. The creature barely seemed to notice. He stabbed again and again before it howled, jaws open wide, its red maw of a mouth all jagged teeth, and bit into his shoulder.

The pain was shocking, a burning, tearing agony . . .

Then large hands were around his attacker's neck, hauling it off, the creature tearing chunks of flesh from his shoulder, as Alcyon held the spitting, snarling thing in the air then hurled it away. It hit stone, rolled, scrambled to its feet far too agilely and then it was running at them. Alcyon stepped in front of Bleda with a roar, his twin axes windmilling, hacking into the creature's shoulder and waist. It collapsed, howling, Alcyon putting a boot onto its head to wrench his blades free. The thing on the ground twisted, tried to bite into his foot, somehow still refusing to die.

Another axe blow and it spasmed, one foot drumming, then was finally still.

Behind Alcyon Ben-Elim were sweeping through the wide-open doors, White-Wings beneath them in a shield wall, marching out of the darkness of the courtyard, down the stone steps into the blue-flicker madness of the Great Hall.

'Here, lad,' Alcyon said, offering the blood-soaked shaft of one of his axes for Bleda to pull himself upright. His shoulder was screaming its pain at him, nausea lurching in his belly, but all he could think of was his bow. He'd dropped it, had glimpsed it skittering across stone.

There.

He stumbled down a dozen steps, over halfway to the chamber floor now, and swept it up.

Someone grabbed his arm, spun him around.

'You could have died!' Jin said to him furiously, looking as if she wanted to slap him.

'Still could,' he muttered, pulling his arm free, the battle din echoing loud and furious.

The new wave of White-Wings, giants and Ben-Elim had hit the battle on the chamber floor, and though the fighting was fierce, it did not look as if it would last long, the Dark-Cloaks and their Feral companions outnumbered and flanked now. Although, even as Bleda stared, he saw the shrinking line of giant guards around the statue of Asroth and Meical fracture and break apart into islands of melee-like combat.

One figure drew his eye. A tall Dark-Cloak, hood falling back as he leaped onto the dais. Slim and athletic, fair hair shaved to stubble on his head. He drew a sword from a scabbard; something about it was strange, the metal a dull, sheen-less black. The warrior strode to the figure of Asroth and lifted the blade. His lips moved, the clamour in the chamber was too great to hear anything, but again, there was something *wrong* about it.

No!

Bleda reached inside his quiver, only one arrow left, and nocked it. Drew it, an explosion of pain in his shoulder where the Feral had bitten him.

Black smoke hissed from the sword.

Bleda gritted his teeth, drew and loosed, hoped his aim was good.

A moment as he held his breath.

The arrow struck the man in his shoulder, staggering him, dropping the sword.

Bleda grinned.

A Kadoshim alighted beside the shaven-haired man, this one standing out from the others, bigger, a greater sense of menace and power about it. It hauled the warrior Bleda had shot back to his feet, and together they gripped the black sword's hilt and touched its blade against the starstone metal that encased Asroth and Meical. Then they began to chant.

'*Cumhacht cloch star, a rugadh ar an domhan eile, a leagtar aingeal dorcha saor in aisce.*' Though Bleda did not understand their words they chilled his blood. The chanting continued, rising in volume over the din of battle, the same phrase, again and again.

And then the black sword began to glow, tendrils of red veins spiralling through it, up, seeping into the starstone metal that encased Asroth and Meical.

'*AINGEAL DUBH*,' a voice bellowed, Ethlinn striding into the chamber, spear in her hand. '*Ar ais go dtí an dorchadas, cumhacht réalta cloiche*,' the Queen of the Giants cried, and Bleda swore that for a heartbeat her eyes glowed, a bright flash.

The Kadoshim and the shaven-haired acolyte swayed, the red seams in Asroth's tomb retreating, shrinking back into the black sword.

They redoubled their chanting, the red veins grew again.

Israfil flew into the chamber, alighting beside Ethlinn, taking up her chant, power emanating from them like a heat haze. The red threads dwindled.

The Kadoshim snarled, releasing the sword, turning and hurling a spear at Israfil. Ethlinn deflected it with her own spear, sent it skittering across stone.

The acolyte with the black sword glanced around, saw their war party dwindling, Ethlinn and Israfil marching towards them.

They are beaten, and they know it.

Bleda saw something pass across his face, a shouted word to the Kadoshim, who leaped into the air, powerful wings taking it higher. The acolyte swept up the black sword in both hands and raised it high. Brought it down onto Asroth's arm.

There was a moment when all sound seemed to be sucked from the room, like an indrawn breath, and then a huge noise, like a tree splintering, followed immediately by a detonation of air that exploded outwards from the dais in an ever-expanding ring, knocking all in its way flat. Bleda had a half-moment to feel fear, and then the wall of air was crashing into him, hurling him from his feet, his back slamming into stone. He saw Jin thrown to the floor as the explosion hit her, heard Alcyon grunt somewhere further up the stairs.

He scrambled to his knees, just staring at the dais.

A cloud of dust slowly settled, revealing the two black-iron statues still there, though something had changed. Red veins now ran through the iron, like seams of gold, and for a heart-beat the iron casing seemed to ripple and swell. Bleda thought he saw Asroth move. A twitch of his head, a flare of light at his eyes. Then the red veins faded, retracting through the figures, drawing in to a focal point. Asroth's right fist. Or, to be exact, where his right fist had been. Now there was a stump, a bright forge glow about it, quickly fading.

The shaven-haired warrior with the black sword was on his feet again, the snapped shaft of Bleda's arrow still protruding from his back. He bent and picked something up, black and heavy, put it inside a leather bag.

Others were climbing to their feet, giants and White-Wings, half-breeds, Ferals and Dark-Cloaks. A Kadoshim screeched and swept down from high in the chamber's roof, swooping low, skimming heads. The man on the dais lifted an arm and the Kadoshim grabbed hold of him, swinging him around so that he straddled its back between its wings, and then it was banking left, turning a tight circle, wings beating and it pow-ered for the chamber doors, other Kadoshim and half-breeds falling in about it, others snatching up surviving Dark-Cloaks and Ferals, and then they were flying out of the chamber doors like the north wind. Ethlinn threw her spear at one, skewered it through the chest, hurling it against one of the chamber doors, the blade driving deep into wood, thrumming, the Kadoshim slumped, pinned. Ben-Elim swept after the disap-pearing Kadoshim, a storm of wings.

Bleda looked back to the statues, the chamber floor littered and strewn with the dead and dying, screams, groans echoing, survivors climbing slowly to their feet.

Asroth and Meical were in the same positions they had ever been, Meical on his knees, grasping at Asroth, whose wings were spread, trying to lift free, one hand around Meical's throat, the other drawn back into a fist.

Except that the fist was gone.

There was no fire glow now, just a stump at the wrist, the black iron back to the matt-dull that it had always been. No hint of life in Asroth's eyes.

CHAPTER THIRTY-ONE

DREM

Drem strode to the centre of his yard and drew his da's sword.

My sword, he reminded himself. *Da gave it to me, before he died.*

He raised it over his head, gripping it two-handed.

Stooping falcon, he recited to himself, holding the pose, counting his heartbeats, feeling the slow burn beginning in his wrists, in his part-bent thighs.

Ninety-nine, one hundred, and then he was chopping down, right to left in one smooth, fluid movement, a hiss of air as the blade passed through it. 'Lightning strike,' he murmured, holding that for another count of a hundred, then a powerful stab up with boar's tusk, into his imaginary foe's belly, holding that, then slowly, methodically moving through the forms of the sword dance that his da had taught him, muscles and tendons shifting gradually from burning to trembling to exhaustion, sweat beading his brow amidst the snow and ice, his breath a mist about him.

When he'd finished, he practised sheathing his sword in one move, so far proving harder to master than most forms in the dance. He swore as he cut his thumb, again, and looked around to see not only the two goats but also the chickens standing around the yard, staring at him.

'Not funny,' he muttered at them, then, at the rumble of

hooves, shifted his gaze to look out of his hold's gates, seeing riders approaching down the track.

'We're going to kill that white bear,' Ulf said, looking down at Drem from the back of his horse. Hildith and a score of her lads were with her.

'If you're wanting some payback for your da, you're welcome to join us,' she said to him, sympathy in her eyes softening the hardness in her face.

Drem rubbed his chin, surprised at how long his stubble of beard had grown. He'd already gone to Ulf and told him that the white bear had not killed his da, that it had been a different bear.

Ulf hadn't believed him.

'We all saw the bear, lad. We fought it in that glade,' Ulf had said to him. *'Many didn't leave the glade breathing because of it. Of course it was the white bear that killed your da.'*

Drem had told Ulf his reasoning, but Ulf had baulked at the idea of digging up Olin's body and inspecting his wounds.

'Disrespectful,' he'd said, looking at Drem with a little horror and a lot of disgust in his eyes. *'Don't need to go digging up a corpse that's been buried a ten-night, anyhow. Think about it. A swipe with the other paw, a different angle than you remember in your mind.'* Ulf shrugged. *'It was fast, confusing, and you had a crack on your head, Drem. Easy to make a mistake. Now stop spouting your nonsense theory like it's fact, and go sharpen your spear. We'll hunt that white bear down soon enough.'*

Drem had known better than to argue, knowing how men got that look in their eyes and tilt to their head when a discussion had gone past the facts and somehow turned in their minds into a question of who was cleverest, wisest, strongest, most skilled, whatever.

So Drem had just sighed and left.

'Drem, we're talking to you,' Ulf said to him now.

Drem blinked and focused back on Ulf, Hildith.

'You coming or not?'

Out of the corner of his eye he saw the goats, standing and staring. Heads swivelling from Ulf to Drem, as if they were waiting for his answer.

'No,' Drem said.

'All right then. Too painful. It'll bring it all back, I understand.' Ulf nodded, turning his horse in a circle. 'Wanted to make the offer, though. I'll bring you a set of claws to match the one round your neck.'

Drem didn't say anything to that and after a moment's silence Ulf clicked his horse on, back to the gates and track. Hildith hovered a moment, then dipped her head to Drem and followed.

Drem waited until they had faded from sight, the track empty, just churned snow and ice and sentinel trees. He drew in a deep breath and sighed.

'Best be on with it, then.'

Drem stopped at the gates to Fritha's hold and stared at the wreck of her cabin. A cairn stood to one side, between the cabin and some stables.

Drem had returned to the cabin the same day as he'd given Asger his package. He'd found it exactly the same as the last time he'd seen it – no kin or friends of Fritha and Hask to raise a cairn over the body.

Apart from me, he'd thought. So he'd carried Hask's corpse out into the yard, and the hound's, too, laying Hask and Surl side by side, and then gathered rocks from the field behind the cabin, loading them in a wain he found in the barn, and bringing them back to pile over the two bodies. When it had come to saying some words for the dead he'd stood there silent a while, thinking with sadness that Hask's only mourner was a stranger who knew almost nothing about him.

I knew his granddaughter, though. And to have raised a woman so fine and brave and kind – well, he must have done something right.

And so Drem had said so, spoken words out loud to the stones and snow, adding something about the hound's loyalty and Hask's spirit.

He waved a spear at my da, that was spirit enough!

Then he'd left.

But before carrying the bodies into the yard and raising a cairn over them, Drem had spent half a day going over the destruction of the cabin; every splinter of wood, every hand-span of the room, the floor, the walls, the gaping entry and exit holes, meticulously checking both bodies, their wounds, finger-nails, teeth, claws. Everything. It hadn't been pleasant, limbs part-frozen with the cold, blood congealed and black.

Now, as he thought of what he'd found, his hand drifted down to a pouch at his belt, fingertips through his gloves brushing it. Then he turned and looked to the snow-heaped forest, saw the track Hildith and Ulf's hunting party had made through the snow, and followed after them.

Drem stood in the woodland twilight, looking at the trampled ground. Searching. He found the buckle from his da's belt, amidst forest litter and something darker. He didn't want to look too close, didn't need to. Ahead of him lay the path the white bear had trampled, the one he and his da had been following it along, branches splintered to ruin, bushes and undergrowth trampled and torn. And to Drem's right lay another path, the destruction that the other 'bear' had caused in its attack, leaping out from the darkness. Drem stared into it, all shifting shadows and the rare glitter of daylight on ice.

Behind him he heard the distant baying of hounds, some-where north and west of him, Ulf's hunt picking up the scent of the white bear. He kept his back to it.

That is nothing to me.

He thought of his da then, an act of choice, of will, basked in the memory of him, felt the grief stir in his belly, and some-thing else, anger, fire in his veins. He thought of the decision he'd made when he declined Asger's offer to leave Kergard and travel south, and the reasons why.

Two reasons to live, I said to Asger, though I didn't tell him what they were. One, to finish Da's quest. To go to Drassil and cut Asroth's head from his shoulders. But I need the Starstone Sword to do that.

And the second reason, to see justice done for my da.

He tugged off a glove with his teeth and reached down to the pouch at his waist, pulled out a cloth and opened it carefully, revealing a few strips of torn, tattered leather. He'd found them within the jaws of Surl, Fritha's hound, and another strip hanging from one of the hound's paws. They hadn't matched any item of clothing within the cabin.

If I find the Starstone Sword I will find the answer to who killed my da. A bear, yes, though not a white one with only four claws on its right paw. And it wasn't alone. Bears don't pick up swords and walk off with them, and nor do they wear leather clothing. It wasn't the bear that struck me on the head, but a person. Whoever or whatever it was, it played a role in my da's death, and now has the Starstone Sword.

Drem wrapped the strips of leather back up and placed them in his pouch, then methodically went over his kit. A skin of water across one shoulder. A bag slung across his back, full with essential gear: tinder and kindling, flint and striking iron, fish-hooks and animal gut for the stitching of wounds, a roll of linen for bandages. Medicinal herbs – honey, sorrel, yarrow, comfrey, skullcap, seed of the poppy. Oats for porridge and strips of salted pork. A slab of cheese. And a pot. He wore layers of clothes, linen, wool, leather and fur, his bone-handled seax and his da's axe at his belt, as well as his sword, and a thick-shafted spear in his fist.

And courage in my heart, and vengeance on my mind.

Drem breathed deep, his back straightening, and then he stepped off the path and into the splintered gloom made by his father's killers.

CHAPTER THIRTY-TWO

RIV

Riv approached the walls of Drassil. They rose tall and forbidding before her.

They had marched back from Oriens as fast as the White-Wings could travel. Riv had rushed to Kol, Aphra and the other captains in that grisly glade deep within Forn Forest, telling them of her suspicion that they had been lured from Drassil for a reason. At first Aphra would not entertain the thought, instead had ordered her to leave, to get back into rank before she was punished for more insubordination and rule-breaking. But Kol had called her back and questioned her rationale behind the suspicion. Meanwhile scouts were sent out into the forest, reconnoitring deeper to search for any signs of recent life or the vaguest hint of a trap.

They had come back shaking their heads.

Kol had ordered horns blown and an organized retreat. Then they had turned around and marched as fast as they could physically manage for Drassil. Kol had led many of the Ben-Elim ahead, and he had returned to their column on the east road two days ago, announcing the dark news that Kadoshim had indeed raided Drassil, a bold attempt to set Asroth free from his gaol of iron. Many had fallen, he reported, but the Kadoshim's plan had been thwarted.

Riv's first thought had been for her mam, and for Bleda.

She had asked Kol, who said that they were both alive, easing her mind.

After that the horror of Kol's news had seeped into her. Just the brazenness of the attack had shocked Riv deeply.

A hundred and thirty-seven years since the Battle of Drassil, and never once have the Kadoshim attacked this fortress, whether in raid or assault.

Why now?

And how would they free Asroth from a cage forged from star-stone? I thought that was impossible.

She wanted to ask Aphra, to talk about the possibilities, but her sister had been consistently tight-mouthed and aloof with her since Oriens.

What is wrong with her? She has never been so unkind and bad-tempered before.

Then they were marching out onto the plain that surrounded Drassil, Riv's heart leaping at the sight of her home, the white-winged banner snapping in a cold wind above the gates. She looked closer and forgot all about Aphra for a short while.

New cairns had been raised in the plain before Drassil's walls, the reality of the tragedy that had befallen their home, their friends and kin, hit her, all of them, a silence falling over the White-Wings and giants as they marched past in sombre mood.

The carcass of a Kadoshim was nailed to the battlements above the great gates; Riv was not the only one who stared up at it as she passed through the gateway. Its head lolled between wide, leathery wings, eye-sockets dark holes excavated by crows.

Further above on the battlements she glimpsed a dark-skinned face, staring down at her, and she felt some warmth spark into life in her belly, welcome after the unsettling anger that was lurking in her veins.

It was Bleda.

The flagstones of the courtyard were stained with blood, even though eight nights had passed since the attack. The stains were faint, just an echo of what it must have been like, but Riv saw them.

Blood always leaves a stain.

It felt good to walk into her barrack, the fire-pit roaring, a deer turning on the spit, fat sizzling and crackling in the flames. A dash up to her chamber and it did not take long for Riv to unpack her and her sister's kit, all of it already shining spotless, as Riv had tended to it each night on the road. When she finished, Jost and Vald tried to tempt her with a cup of wine in the feast-hall, but she felt the call of the weapons-field. As she stepped onto the turf she saw Bleda on the field, where he usually was, at the archery range. Riv felt a little flutter in her belly and increased her pace, only for it to drop like a stone as she saw Jin appear from behind him.

'Well met,' Bleda said to Riv as she approached them, and she thought she saw the hint of a smile ghost his lips, just for a moment. His hair was longer than she remembered, no longer close-cropped like the White-Wings, as it had been for so many years. It stuck out at angles, giving him a scruffy appearance. Riv supressed the urge to smooth an unruly tuft behind his ear.

Bleda gripped his double-curved bow, a quiver of arrows at his belt. And he had a bandage wrapped around his shoulder.

'You were injured in the attack?' Riv said, hurrying forwards and reaching a hand out to Bleda's injury.

'Aye.' he nodded, his serious face back in place.

'Bleda fought,' Jin said proudly. 'It was he who realized the Kadoshim's plan. He fought in the Great Hall, slew many Kadoshim and their Dark-Cloaks and Feral beasts. And he foiled the plot, put an arrow in the black sword.'

Dark-Cloaks and Ferals?

'Black Sword?'

'The warrior with the Starstone Blade, who tried to set Asroth free,' Jin said. 'My *betrothed* is the hero of Drassil.'

Riv blinked, looking from Jin's proud face to Bleda's embarrassed one, both of them seeming to have lost the ability to maintain a cold-face.

Bleda is a hero!

A rush of pride made her grin.

Betrothed!

She felt something else at hearing that word, but chose to push it away into some dark corner, not even acknowledging it.

'Your mission?' Bleda asked her, shifting his feet.

'A ruse, to lure us far from Drassil and weaken the defences here. Or so we suspect, anyway.'

'So you have not fought, then?' Jin said. The words were spoken flat, no intonation, but Riv felt the insult in them.

Please don't make me angry.

'No. I did not fight.'

Not the enemy, at least.

'The bait to lure us from Drassil was a terrible thing,' Riv said, trying to ignore Jin.

She told Bleda of their discoveries at the town of Oriens, Jin moving closer to hear properly. Riv was still talking when a Ben-Elim alighted close beside them, the only warning a blast of air.

'The Lord Protector wishes to speak with you,' the Ben-Elim said to Riv.

Oh dear. Riv gulped. *Has he heard of my fighting at Oriens already?*

She took a resolute step.

'And you,' the Ben-Elim said to Bleda.

'Not you,' he said to Jin as she made to walk with Riv and Bleda.

The only thing that made the thought of the dressing-down

she was no doubt going to receive from the Lord Protector bearable was the look on Jin's face as they left her behind.

Riv and Bleda sat in the entrance hall of Israfil's chambers.

'You are a hero, then,' Riv said to Bleda as they sat waiting.

'No,' Bleda said, sounding very certain of the fact. After a few moments of staring straight ahead he looked at her, more emotion in his face than she had ever seen. 'I would like to tell you something,' he said. 'I could not tell anyone else.'

'Not even Jin?'

'No. *Especially* not her.'

She felt a warm glow at that.

'Of course you can, Bleda. You can tell me anything, we are friends.'

'I was terrified,' he said, looking down at his clasped hands.

'What?'

'During the battle. In the courtyard, a Kadoshim attacked us. Me and Jin. I dropped my arrows, fumbled my bow. I am surprised I did not soil myself. I froze with terror.'

'You're alive, though?'

'Alcyon chopped it to tiny pieces.'

'He's good at that, I've heard,' Riv said. 'And what about these acts of bravery, the Kadoshim you slew?'

'That happened later. In the great chamber. With my bow.' A brief flicker of a smile.

He does love that bow.

'So let me get this right. You were attacked by a Kadoshim, and you felt scared—'

'Terrified,' Bleda corrected.

'Terrified. And then, soon after, you killed Kadoshim and their servants in the Great Hall. And wrestled some man-beast *thing* that chewed your shoulder to pulp.'

'Aye. And then Alcyon saved me. Again.'

'Bleda, that is the definition of courage. Or so Balur One-

Eye has told me, and if you want to argue with him, well, that doesn't make you brave, that makes you stupid.'

'What do you mean?' Bleda said.

'You cannot be truly brave unless you feel truly afraid. That's what courage *is*. Doing it anyway, even though you're scared. Sorry, terrified. And you did. You chose to fight. To step into that furnace of blood and madness and pain, and fight. Despite your fear.'

She watched him, saw his face shift in ways she'd never seen it move before as her words settled into him. He sighed at the end, a relief.

'My mother said something like that to me, a long time ago. I'd forgotten, until you said those words.'

He has fine eyes, she thought. Almond-shaped, a deep brown.

'You fight all the time,' he said to her. 'Is that what you feel?'

She thought about that, her frown deepening.

I don't ever remember feeling scared. Mostly just angry. No. Only ever angry.

And even more so recently.

'Tell me of your mother, your home,' Riv asked him, avoiding answering his question.

'My mother,' he said, leaning back, a slight frown creasing his forehead. 'She is strong, brave, wise. A respected leader of the Sirak.'

'I know that already, tell me something different about her.'

Bleda thought about that a moment.

'Her laugh,' he said. 'When she laughs, really laughs, she snorts like a pig. My brother, Altan, he could always make her laugh, with just a look, a raised eyebrow. And once my mother started laughing – like a pig – then we would all be laughing.' Riv was amazed to see a smile spread across his face, deep and genuine, muscles relaxing. He looked at her. 'Thank you,' he said. 'It is like a gift, a forgotten memory. Ah, to be Sirak again, to live free, travelling with the seasons, dismantling and rolling the gers, herding flocks of goats, hunting with my father, with hawk and spear. The freedom of the Grass Sea . . .'

I believe in the Way of Elyon with all my heart, and pray every day for his Lore to spread throughout the Banished Lands, to bring peace and harmony, but, listening to Bleda . . . She sighed. *Life does not sound so bad, the Sirak don't seem in any great need of saving or protecting.*

'Bleda,' a voice said, and they looked up together, saw Israfil standing in an open doorway.

'Come in,' Israfil said, and Bleda's cold-face slipped back over his smile, like a mask. He rose and entered the Lord Protector's chamber. The door closed, voices muffled. Riv could only stand being able to hear their voices but not the words for so long. Then she stood and crept oh so quietly across the flagstoned floor to the closed door.

'. . . proud of you, Bleda,' Israfil was saying. 'You fought for us. For the people of the Faithful. I wanted to give you my gratitude, not just for the act that you did. Stopping the foul deed that could well have freed Asroth from his prison, but also for the principle of what you did. Of making a stand. Of fighting for us. A selfless act against our common enemy. I knew my faith in you was well placed, just as I know that you will make a fine leader of your people. We will accomplish great things together, when you are lord of the Arcona.'

'The Sirak, you mean.'

'The Sirak and Cheren will become one, when you and Jin are wed. One people, working with us, driving the Kadoshim from the land.'

'The Kadoshim, they are terrible,' Bleda said. 'I could see their hatred, taste it.'

'They are,' Israfil agreed.

'But I do not think I stopped them . . .'

There was a pause.

'What do you mean?' Israfil said.

'I think they *wanted* Asroth's hand. Or part of him.'

Footsteps echoed in the corridor beyond the entrance chamber and Riv ran to her seat, only to hear the footsteps pass the door and fade. She thought about going back to eavesdrop at Israfil's door again, but then it opened and Bleda came out.

'Riv,' Israfil said sternly, and she rose and entered the chamber, giving Bleda a little smile as they passed each other. He didn't acknowledge her, looked distracted.

'Close the door behind you,' Israfil said, walking away to stand before an open window, his chamber looking out over Drassil and the plain beyond.

'Sit,' Israfil said, gesturing to a chair, his back to her.

Riv did, nervously, wood scraping on stone.

'I am worried for you,' Israfil said, turning to face her.

She didn't say anything, had done so many things of late that she wasn't sure what Israfil was referring to, and didn't want to incriminate herself any further.

'Fighting, with White-Wings, while on a mission.'

Kol has told him.

She dipped her head with a sigh. 'I am very sorry, Lord Protector,' she said.

'I have watched you on the weapons-field. You have the potential to become an *exceptional* warrior, Riv. One of the most skilled I have seen come up through the ranks of Drassil since the Ben-Elim have dwelt in this world. But more than that, there is a fire in you, a purity of dedication to our cause. You hate the Kadoshim, long to take your place in the ranks in this holy war.'

'I do.' Riv breathed, looking up now, meeting Israfil's gaze.

How can he know me so well?

'But there is something else in you. An anger that cannot be quenched.'

'Yes,' she admitted.

'What I said to you, during your warrior trial. You remember?'

About my father. About my pride. About needing to prove myself. That I am shallow and brittle. Out of control . . .

Even at the memory of Israfil's words Riv felt her blood stirring, her anger flexing.

'Aye.'

'It was not true. It was a test, designed to provoke, to push, to *strengthen* your control, your ability to weather any storm.'

It's as Aphra told me, then. And I failed.

'Aye.'

'You are the first person that I have told this truth to, before they have passed. All go through it unknowing. It is a hard test.'

She nodded grimly.

'I want you to pass your warrior trial, Riv. And soon. Dark times are ahead, I feel it. Your sword arm and fervour will be needed.'

'There is nothing I long for more.'

'You shall retake your warrior trial soon. So master your anger.'

'Yes, Lord Protector.'

'There are other things that I wanted to talk to you about.' Israfil fell silent, just staring at Riv, a level of sternness in his gaze that she had not seen before.

Oh no. He knows about all of the fights.

'The other fights,' Riv said, then paused. Israfil was frowning. 'What did Kol tell you?' she asked.

'Kol? No, it was not Kol that told me of your altercation at Oriens. It was Aphra.'

What! My own sister! How could she?

Riv did feel her anger stir then, a snake uncoiling, hissing and rearing, fangs bared.

'Riv!' A hand slapping on his desk, a loud crack. 'You remember that last command. To master your anger. I suggest you start right now. I can see it in you.'

It's getting worse. I can feel it there all the time, like a deep ocean, any insult or injury, the wind that whips it into a storm.

'Please, help me,' Riv said, fighting back a sob. 'I can feel it, moving through me.' She rubbed her temples. 'It is like a drug in my blood. Like when you drink wine, I feel it in my belly, a warmth, a glow. Then it is in my veins, spreading through me, seeping through every part of me, into my fists, making them clench, and into my head, like a mist, fogging all thought. And then . . .' She shrugged. 'Then it is just me, and I am it.'

'A dark affliction, it sounds.'

'It can be,' Riv nodded. 'And it can move from the belly glow to the head mist in a few heartbeats. No slow process, no time to fight it.'

'Perhaps *fight it* is the wrong phrase. Control is what you need. To harness that rage, and use it. You would be formidable.' Israfil stared at her a long time. 'Maybe some time at Dun Seren would help you,' he said, sounding as if he was talking to himself rather than Riv.

'I thought things were not good between us and Dun Seren,' Riv said.

'Oh, there has always been a tension,' Israfil said with a wave of his hand. 'Their founder, Corban, took issue with our tactics from the very first day. Overly emotional and sentimental, I always thought him. Unable to see the greater good. Always obsessed with notions of kin and friendship and loyalty. Leaders must act for the greater good.' He shrugged. 'But they are the enemy of the Kadoshim, as are we. And of a time we will share information. I only think of them now because Balur and Alcyon speak of their training with much respect.'

'I train hard, none harder,' Riv said, 'and no warriors train harder than the White-Wings.'

'So quick to judge, when you have not seen,' Israfil said, raising an eyebrow.

That is a fair point.

'I understand, you are defending the pride and honour of your people, the White-Wings,' Israfil said. 'But do not let that sentiment cloud your vision, or your understanding. A warrior sees to the heart of his enemy, sees strengths and weaknesses honestly, dispassionately. And casts the same gaze upon himself. Or herself. That is purity of mind, what the Lore demands we strive for. Removing the ego.' He paused, a slight smile. 'My apologies, this was not supposed to be a lesson on the philosophies of combat.'

'I like it,' Riv said with a shrug.

'Another time, then. As for your sister, do not be so hard with her. She did tell me of your misdemeanour at Oriens. She also told me that it was you who first saw through the Kadoshim ruse; that Oriens was a lure.'

Oh. There is some pleasantness left in her still, then.

'Now, on to the other matter I wished to speak of with you. It is a grave matter, and its possible consequences far-reaching.'

'If I can help in any way, Lord Protector, I will.'

'Adonai and Estel,' Israfil said, and suddenly Riv's head was full of blood and feathers, of Estel's White-Wings insignia torn and stamped upon on the flagstoned floor. 'You know of what I speak.'

It was not a question.

'Improper relations,' Riv murmured, remembering Israfil's words in the Great Hall.

'Yes. I am hearing rumours. That this *behaviour* . . .' He paused, face twisting with uncommon passion. 'This sin is more widespread than I would have hoped. That Adonai was not the only Ben-Elim, Estel not the only mortal engaged in these . . . practices.'

Riv felt a heat flush through her, as if she were racked with guilt.

But I have done nothing wrong.

And then she thought of Kol, on that moonlit night beyond Oriens. His smile, the touch of his fingertips against her lips. The shiver it had stirred in her.

'Do you know of any such conduct?' Israfil asked her.

She gulped. 'Me, I, no. No, Lord Protector.'

He regarded her a long moment, then nodded slowly.

'It may be that I am wrong. But, if it is happening, it must be stamped out, quickly and ruthlessly, before it spreads. It is wrong, and it would destroy us.'

Riv nodded, though again she got the feeling that Israfil was talking to himself more than to her.

'I am gathering a small group about me,' Israfil said, definitely talking to Riv now, as he pinned her with his gaze. 'A few that I trust. You are one of them, Riv, because I see your passion and dedication to the cause, despite your, *issues*. I am placing my trust in you, even talking to you of this. But I would ask more. I would ask you to be my eyes and ears.'

He is asking me to spy on my own. But he is the Lord Protector, the highest power in my world. How can I refuse him?

'Of course, Lord Protector,' she heard herself say.

There was a knock at the door, making Riv jump.

Israfil took a long moment, eyes fixed on Riv. 'My thanks,' he said to her. Then. 'Enter.'

Ethlinn walked in, Balur One-Eye at her shoulder.

'We've had news from our scouts tracking the Kadoshim,' Ethlinn said. She saw Riv sitting before Israfil, raised an eyebrow, but continued.

'Has one of my Ben-Elim returned?' Israfil asked.

'*No,*' a croaking voice came from the unshuttered window, and a big black crow flew into the room, flying around and then landing on the arm of Riv's chair. It looked up at her with one beady eye.

'Our friends from Dun Seren have sent help,' Ethlinn said, a twitch of a smile on her lips.

'*Flick,*' the bird croaked.

Riv had heard of the talking crows of Dun Seren, but never seen one in the flesh. She'd always thought it would be amusing to meet one, but now that it was sitting a handspan from her and regarding her with all too much intelligence, the whole experience felt far more like unnerving, rather than amusing.

'Is Flick your name?' Riv said, feeling strangely uncomfortable.

'*Yes. You?*'

'My name is Riv,' Riv said.

'*Well met,*' the crow rasped.

'Yes, this is all very polite,' Israfil interrupted. 'But do you have news of the Kadoshim force that attacked Drassil?'

'*They scattered, fled in many directions, lost in Forn,*' the crow squawked, its talons clenching alarmingly with each syllable. *One group, largest, went to Varan's Fall. Grinding Sea.*'

Israfil looked to Ethlinn. 'What do you make of that?'

'There is nothing there, only sea.'

'*Boats,*' Flick croaked.

'The ground is marked with boats that had been moored on the shore,' Balur said, his voice a deep growl. 'They rowed away.'

'Where to?' Israfil mused. 'It is a clever move, making them untrackable. What options are there for their destination?'

'The coast runs west to east. East is a few hundred leagues of Forn Forest, then mountains, then Arcona.'

'So, unlikely they would go that way. West?'

'Is Dun Seren and the Desolation.'

'Dun Seren is as unlikely a destination as I can think of,' Balur rumbled. Riv realized that he was laughing.

'And north?' Israfil asked.

'The Grinding Sea,' Ethlinn said, open handed.

Riv had felt uncomfortable, initially, as if she wasn't supposed to be involved in this meeting, and not enjoying the way the crow seemed to be sidling its way closer to her arm. But now she was engrossed in the conversation.

'So,' Israfil said. 'Unless there is some hidden location in the Grinding Sea, the logical conclusion is that our enemy have fled to the Desolation.'

CHAPTER THIRTY-THREE

DREM

Not the best time of year to decide to go camping in the Desolation, Drem thought, not for the first time, as he woke to find ice in his growing beard. He cracked it free and scraped more ice from his eyebrows, then crawled from his makeshift tent, a bearskin propped up by branches, only to see that it was covered in another layer of fresh-fallen snow. He regarded the sky through a canopy of pines, saw a clear bright blue far above. Breaking camp was a swift affair, Drem taking comfort in the routine of it, all the little practices that his da had drummed into him over countless years. Soon his bag was across his shoulder and his thick-shafted spear in his fist and he was walking on through the snow.

He'd been following the trail of the bear that killed his da for over a ten-night, now. Twice he had lost its tracks completely, fresh snow masking everything, and he'd had to retrace his steps, searching not just the ground but all that grew, shrubs and bushes and trees, until he'd found the bear's trail again. And once he'd seen two sets of boot-prints, one uncommonly large, but it could have been a big man wearing snow-boots.

The trail had led northwards, into the foothills of the Bonefells, though in a looping arc, and Drem had found a number of pits and traps along the trail, as if the bear followed a trapper's trail, returning to collect its prey. And now the trail was circling back, southwards. Drem paused as he stepped onto a plateau, open and free of pine trees. He walked to the edge, stood on a ridge and looked south onto a world of white that seemed to go on forever. The only blemishes were Starstone Lake, directly south of him, its waters dark and glittering in a winter's sun, and Kergard, further west and south.

And that, he thought, eyes narrowing. A few leagues ahead of him, beyond the tiered roll of foothills and forest, there was a small village, smoke rising from hearths and fire-pits. It was built upon the edge of Starstone Lake, a pier jutting into the dark waters.

'The mine,' he said to himself, feeling something shift in his gut.

Somehow he knew, sensed, this was the place he would find his answers. His hand rested on the hilt of his sword as he stared. Then he gripped his spear and walked on.

Drem crept through the last patch of bush and scrub and crouched in the snow.

It was twilight, the sky a mixture of purples and pinks, and he was situated at the top of a gentle slope, looking down upon the mine spread before him, a squat, sprawling mess of buildings. Even from this distance Drem knew something was wrong about the place. Barns, huts and barrack-like cabins were scattered around the enclosure with no seeming logic to their positioning. All of it was ringed by a palisaded wall that curled around to the lakeshore, gates on every side. And most of it was in darkness, a few torches belching smoke on the wall, some lights flickering inside huts. He could see no signs of life, no movement on the walls, no voices, singing, not even the rhythmic crack and crunch of miners at work, carving their living from the rock.

Then an animal noise rose up, part roar, part mournful howl, and ice skittered through Drem's veins.

He'd spent many years in the Wild, hunting, trapping, and

thought he'd heard all there was to hear from an animal's throat, but this sound . . .

Drem sat and waited, watched as the sun became a thin line on the horizon. He shrugged off his kit bag, pulled out a roll of rope and hooked it on his belt, and then he stood and sprinted, bent low, straight towards the wall. His heart pounded in his head, waiting, *expecting* a voice or horn to ring out the alarm.

Thirty paces left, he looked up, saw the wall was empty.

Fifteen paces. Ten.

And then he was there, back against the timber, sucking in air.

He was close to a large, double gateway, a smaller, single door beside it, a simple latch on the door. He'd planned to loop his rope around one of the timber beams of the palisade and haul himself up, but thought he might as well try the latch first.

The door opened.

He slipped through, closed it behind him, and moved along the wall. It was near dark, now, the solid buildings and shadows in between merging. Stars flickered into life. He looked about, unsure what to do, where to go.

What am I doing here?

A pang of fear, threatening to overwhelm him. He took a moment to remember.

The bear. My father's killer. The Starstone Sword.

He took a deep breath, focused on those three things, stiffening his resolve, and moved on. Ran across the gap between wall and a building, slipping deeper into the enclosure.

Then the smell hit him. First the clear smell of animal dung, but there was more to it, not sweet-scented like a horse, something acrid in it.

A meat-eater.

Voices. He followed the sound, found himself in an alley between two long buildings, what looked like sleeping barracks, and beyond them a larger building, longer and wider, timber-walled with a grass-sod roof. Lights flickering in shuttered windows, the murmur of voices. One man's rising in laughter.

He moved close to a shuttered window and carefully peered in.

A long table, a score of shaven-haired men around it, a wooden board, one man standing, grinning as he tossed the bones onto the board, watching them roll.

Playing knuckle-bone.

The man barked a laugh, punching the air, turning so that Drem could see his face.

It was Wispy Beard.

Conflicting emotions at seeing him, anger and fear mixed as he remembered the noose around his neck, being hoisted into the air. Wispy laughing.

Drem scanned the others, recognized some, though he didn't see Burg there, the leader with the scar on his face. In the gloom someone else sat, the firelight and darkness making him look too big, longer and wider than a man, legs outstretched as he leaned back in his chair, arms folded, seemingly asleep.

The animal-roar again, a sad thing, closer, louder, vibrating through the snow-slush and into the soles of Drem's boots. Most in the room ignored it, the big man's legs twitching, but nobody moved to tend whatever it was that made such a sound. The stench of excrement was stronger, too, insinuating itself into the back of Drem's throat.

He moved on, a lifetime of trapping having taught him silence and patience. He knew instinctively when to wait, when to move, and how to tread as silent as a fox. But there was no light-footed trick in the world that could avoid footprints in snow. He tried to follow well-used tracks, his footprints mixing with a stream of others.

A stable block stood before him, a torch burning outside it, fixed atop a post. Drem froze in the shadow of a building and stared. In time a head loomed over the stable-door, but it was no horse. A bear, dark-furred, huge, its eyes baleful. It opened its jaws and let out a sound closer to groan than growl.

Is that the bear that killed my da?

Drem's fist tightened on his spear, the urge to run over and plunge it into the creature's chest sweeping him.

Wait. The hunter is patient.

In answer to its mournful groaning another sound echoed around the encampment, a chorus of howls and whines.

'Shut your row,' a voice called out. Drem's head snapped around to a dark hollow, dense and thick behind the bear pen. He crept along the building's wall to get a better view and saw an open space, a long table set within it, legs of timber thick as trunks. Shapes were scattered upon the table, unclear in the darkness.

Strange, a table out in the open.

Behind it was a huge boulder, rising like a cliff face. As Drem moved to get a clearer view, the stench grew worse, fetid and cloying.

A man stood in the boulder's shadow, wrapped in furs and cloak, a spear in his hand that he rattled against the rock, clanging on iron, and Drem saw darker shapes in the boulder, iron bars slatted across them.

Cells, dug into the rock face, iron-barred gates.

'Shut your row,' the guard shouted again as strange howls and whines echoed out from many cells, haunting, chilling Drem's blood.

As Drem watched, the man walked a dozen paces, turned to face the wall, his back to Drem, and urinated up the rock face. Drem hurried across the open space, long legs speeding him, the man hearing him at the last moment, turning, urine steaming in the icy cold, but not quick enough to avoid Drem's spear-butt in the head. He dropped with a grunt, cloak hood falling away. Another shaven-haired man.

Drem hit him again, just to be sure.

A sound in the cell closest to him and he approached it, saw only darkness inside, a form moving, deep at the back. A warning growl.

Drem bumped into the table, turned and looked at it.

Tools were scattered across its surface, saws and knives, a butcher's cleaver chopped into the wood. Thick iron rings were set deep into the timber, chains hanging from them. Then Drem realized what the lumps he'd seen spread upon the table were.

Body parts.

Some animal, some human. Arms, legs, torsos. A wolven head, a furry shoulder and leg, its paw as big as a plate. A bat like the one that he'd seen feasting on Fritha's hound was pinned to the table with a spike through its chest, wings spread wide, pierced with iron nails. It tried to flap its wings, a feeble movement, head swivelling to regard him with its red eyes. On the table beside it was a human hand, an iron rod jammed into the gaping wound of its wrist, tendons somehow attached. Other things, unrecognizable. A wooden frame, some kind of fabric stretched across it. Drem peered closer.

Skin! It's flayed skin!

'Help . . . me,' a voice whispered, Drem leaping around, spear pointing. A shape moved in one of the cells, a dark shadow shifting.

'Please,' the voice whispered, slurring, as if drunken or broken-jawed.

There were rush torches set in holders about the table, some blackened, burned-out stumps, others still fresh. Drem took his fire iron from his belt pouch and struck sparks, a torch flaring to life. He knew how dangerous it was, here in the middle of this place, enemies all around – but that voice. He recognized it.

'Sten?' he said, holding the torch up, approaching the boulder. Darkness retreated, orange glow washing the rock face, shadows flickering and dancing, the cells looking like myriad dark eyes staring back at him, silent as secrets. 'Sten?' Drem said again.

Sten was one of the trappers from Kergard who had not returned from the Bonefells, along with his partner, Vidar. Drem remembered Ulf telling him and his da over a skin of mead and a warm fire. That seemed like so long ago.

Light from Drem's torch pushed back the darkness in the cell, a figure slowly emerging, a man, stooped and hunched, shambling forwards, dragging one foot that was twisted at an odd angle.

'Stennnn,' the figure whispered, finally looking up at Drem.

He almost dropped the torch.

It was Sten, but not as Drem remembered him. His lower jaw was distended, looking too big for his head and hanging open, sharp teeth rowed within red, swollen gums, and his eyes were yellow. His hands were curled, as if sore and swollen, nails grown long and black.

'Sten, what have they done to you?' Drem whispered.

'Killll me,' the thing that had been Sten breathed.

'Vidar; where's Vidar?' Drem asked, stepping close to the iron bars. Sten twisted his head, bones clicking. Muscles bunched in his shoulders and back, unnaturally large between shoulder and neck, taut as knotted rope.

'Vidarrrrr gone,' Sten groaned, eyes flitting to the table behind Drem. He slumped, like a sail with no wind, then suddenly grew, swelling, and hurled himself at the iron bars of his cage, clawed hands clutching at Drem, snagging in his torch, his cloak. Drem leaped backwards, stumbling and falling into the snow. Sten pounded and snarled and smashed at the iron bars, a feral fury sending an explosion of dust and fragments of stone from where they were buried into the rock face.

All along the boulder things swarmed to their cell bars, crouched things, things on all fours, looking like huge, mutated wolven, bears, badgers, other creatures of the Wild. And then there were things that stood like men, or half-men, bodies unnaturally muscled, furred in parts, bones elongated. At one cage a bairn stumbled forwards, feet stretched and clawed. It wrapped its too-long jaws around an iron bar and shook it, saliva and blood dripping down the iron in long streaks.

Drem staggered to his feet, backing away, spear levelled at the cages as his torch sputtered and went out. His hands shook. Horror and fear swept through him, threatened to overwhelm him.

Behind him the bear roared in its pen, the door rattling, a loud crack as it swiped a paw at the lock. Voices shouted. The guard groaned in the snow.

A horn blew, further away, faint and distant. Beyond the enclosure, from the direction of the lake.

Drem ran, blindly, no destination in mind, just away from these creatures of nightmare. He kicked the rousing guard in the head as he raced past, then rushed into the darkness. In moments he was at the encampment wall, felt a wild moment of panic, feeling trapped, knew that if he was found he'd be thrown to those *things* in the cells, or worse, turned into one of them. He saw a set of stairs that climbed the palisade and sprinted up them, slipped on half-frozen snow, righted himself and reached the top.

He turned and stared back into the compound, saw figures holding torches running to the boulder, one thrusting his burning torch into a cell, a high-pitched scream rang out. Something else moved close to the bear pen, a tall figure, wreathed in shadow.

Too tall, can't be a man.

He felt sick, his stomach threatening to empty itself, cold wind snatching at him. He put a hand to his neck, found that his cloak and undergarments were torn, right down to his bare skin.

Sten's claws.

He shivered.

Movement elsewhere caught Drem's eye, the horn he'd

heard still ringing out, and he saw activity towards the southern end of the encampment: figures hurrying onto the pier. Further out, shapes emerged from the darkness, two boats, bristling with oars, rowing steadily for the dock. And in the dark skies above them a shape flew, two more appearing, dark shadows skimming the water, a shimmer in the starlight.

Too big for birds, Drem frowned. Then he saw one alight on the pier, a winged man in chainmail shirt. Shaven-haired warriors fell to their knees, bowing.

A rush of ice swept through his veins, a new level of fear.

It cannot be! Kadoshim.

He felt his legs turn to water, had to hold on to the timber struts of the wall to keep himself upright.

But of course it can be. Look at what I've just seen in those cages, twisted by Elyon knows what foul magic and dark practices. Oh, Da, you were right. There's nowhere left to run from this.

Drem leaped over the wall, weightless for a moment before he fell crunching into a bank of snow and scrambled to his feet. Then he was running for the trees.

CHAPTER THIRTY-FOUR

BLEDA

Bleda stood in Drassil's courtyard, stamping his feet against the cold.

'Why are we here?' he said to Jin, who was standing beside him, somehow managing to look far less cold than he felt.

'I don't know.' She shrugged. 'Kol asked me to be here by highsun, and he asked that I bring you.'

'Kol. You friendly with Ben-Elim, all of a sudden?' Bleda asked her.

'Not as friendly as you are with the Lord Protector,' she shot back at him. It was said harmlessly enough, but Bleda knew there was an edge to Jin's words. A confusion, and a suspicion.

I understand that, because I am confused about it myself.

It had been two days since he had been summoned to Israfil's room, since he had been commended for making a stand, for fighting the Kadoshim. He could not lie, it had felt good to be praised like that. And there was much truth in it. He *had* chosen to fight the Kadoshim, rather than watch them and the Ben-Elim kill one another.

And I am still not completely sure why.

A good part of it had been seeing the Kadoshim. Never had he imagined such malice made flesh. Politics, border disputes, even blood feuds he understood. But at the sight of the Kadoshim all of that had faded.

*It was evil. I saw evil, poured into a form of blood and bone.
That's why I fought.*

But was that the only reason?

And being commended by Israfil had felt wrong, not just
because he had come to see Israfil as the personification of all
that he stood against, the empire that would subjugate his
people, *had* subjugated his people.

And now he is proclaiming me as a hero of the Faithful.

'I'm not friendly with Israfil,' he muttered.

'Then tell me what he said to you,' Jin said.

Bleda just looked at her, could see in her eyes the desire to
understand him, wanting him to allay her suspicions.

'He thanked me for what I did in the attack.' Bleda shrugged,
looking away.

Jin nodded, but her eyes still watched him closely.

'Your hair is longer,' she said, brushing a strand from his
face.

'It is,' he agreed. He'd been growing it since the day his
mother had visited, when he'd felt shame at what she must think
of his appearance. It had grown to the point that he needed to
tie it back, now, into a knot, but it was not long enough that
all of his hair was cooperative enough to stay where he put it.
It was annoying.

Figures marched into the courtyard, giants riding upon
bears. Bleda was glad of the distraction. Ethlinn was at their
head, a cloak of white fur draped about her shoulders, dark
warrior braid coiled about one shoulder. A spear was couched
in a saddle holster, resting loosely in the crook of her arm.
Balur One-Eye strode at her side, white hair spilling over a black
cloak, the opposite of his daughter and queen. A war-hammer
was slung across his shoulder, body wrapped in leather, a
breastplate and shoulder-guard of steel. Other giants followed,
a score, two score, three score, all mounted. Bleda saw Alcyon
amongst their ranks; the giant saw him and nodded a greeting,
a broad grin splitting his face.

That giant is uncommonly good-humoured, Bleda thought, dipping his head in answer. Alcyon had saved his life, after all, and Bleda was keenly aware of that debt.

Ethlinn led them out through the gates of Drassil, the column turning north and disappearing from view.

There was a beating of wings and Bleda looked up to see a Ben-Elim alighting beside them: Kol with his golden hair and his easy smile.

'We have come as you asked,' Jin said to him.

'My thanks,' Kol said, stepping close to her and resting a hand upon her shoulder. Bleda was surprised that she did not pull away.

'Though if it was to watch giants riding off into the distance,' Bleda said, eyes still fixed on Kol's hand upon Jin's shoulder, 'I'd rather have heard about it while sat beside a firepit.'

'Them? No, I did not ask you here to watch Ethlinn ride out,' Kol said, finally stepping away from Jin. 'Better to watch tar dry, I think.' He grinned, and Jin half laughed.

'Where are they going, though?' Bleda said. 'That must be every last giant in Drassil.'

'Do not fear for your safety, you are well guarded by my Ben-Elim and White-Wings,' Kol said, his tone and smile softening the insult in his words, but Bleda still bridled.

'I am *not* afraid,' he managed to say through the thin line of his lips.

'Of course you aren't,' Kol said. 'A poor jest, I apologize. To answer your question, they are going to Dun Seren. These are dark times, and the enemies of the Kadoshim must unite against them. Ethlinn and Balur have a better relationship with the Order of the Bright Star than we Ben-Elim do, and so they are better placed to speak with them, to share information and come away with an agreed plan of attack against the Kadoshim.'

'We will attack the Kadoshim, then?' Bleda asked. A shiver

of fear ran through him at that prospect, but a fresh under-standing of its importance, as well.

'Oh, aye, if we can find them,' Kol said, no smile now, just a cold hatred radiating from his eyes. 'When we find them.'

The sound of a horn echoed down from the battlements over the gates.

'Ah, here they are,' Kol said, smiling again, emotions shift-ing like the breeze.

'Here who are?' Bleda asked.

A rumble, low and distant, quickly growing. Jin heard it, too, cocking her head.

'Hooves. Many riders,' Bleda said.

'Aye,' Kol agreed easily. 'About two hundred, I think.'

The rumble grew to a roar and then riders were pouring through Drassil's gates, and Bleda's heart was soaring, because he saw the banner of a white horse upon a green field above them, Sirak warriors in their deels of grey pouring through the gates, heads shaved, warrior braids tugged by the wind, and behind them more riders, a blue banner with a stooping hawk upon it.

'Our honour guard,' Jin breathed, a grin slipping through her control, a hand reaching out to squeeze Bleda's.

The Sirak and Cheren riders swept into the courtyard of Drassil, two hundred of them, the riders merging, grey of Sirak and blue of Cheren a blurred whirlwind galloping around the courtyard's edge. Then they were separating, regrouping, Bleda and Jin staring in unadulterated joy, cold-faces forgotten for a few glorious heartbeats, and then the riders were slowing, forming up before Bleda and Jin.

Bleda forced his cold-face back into place, even though his heart was pounding with the joy of seeing his kin, a fierce pride at the mounted skill of Sirak warriors. One of them drew up before him, face a map of deep lines, and Bleda breathed deep to hold back the smile that wanted to spill onto his own face.

Old Ellac upon a black horse, the rest of Bleda's honour guard falling into place behind the old warrior.

And then the courtyard was still, dust settling, a horse whickering.

Ellac dismounted, behind him a hundred others did the same, and those gathered before Jin followed suit. And then they were all dropping to their knees, heads bowing to touch the cold stone of the courtyard.

Bleda just stood and stared at them, not knowing what to say, a storm of emotions swirling through him.

'Welcome to Drassil,' Kol shouted, spreading arms and wings wide in greeting.

CHAPTER THIRTY-FIVE

Drem

Drem stumbled into his yard, feet and hands half-numb, still clutching his spear with frozen fingers, his vision blurred, body drenched with sweat, yet it was cold enough that he felt ice crackling in his hair.

A day and a half he'd run, expecting at any moment to hear the roar of a giant bear behind him, or the whisper of wings above, or the eerie howling of twisted, mutated *things*. His blind terror had lasted a good while but, by the coming of the first dawn, exhaustion had finally driven it off, and even as he forced his legs to keep moving, trudging through snow and ice, he had started to think. First and foremost, how to survive, how to get home, and he had used every trick and tactic his da had taught him in their years in the Wild to hide his tracks from an unwanted follower. He'd splashed up streams and down streams, entering at one point and exiting half a league north or south, doing the same at half a dozen streams that fed into Starstone Lake from the Bonefells. He'd climbed trees that grew tight and close, shuffling along branches onto a neighbouring tree, then onto the next, and the next, and the next, eventually climbing down and running on. He'd come across a fox's den and taken his hatchet to a pile of frozen dung, smearing the softer faeces inside all over himself, to cover his scent from anything that might track him with its nose. He'd sought out higher ground forested by pine, where the snow-cover was

357

thin upon the ground, the forest litter thick with spongy pine needles that sprang back and hid his tracks far better than ankle-deep snow.

And now, against all expectations, he was home.

He didn't bother entering his cabin, just staggered into his barn, was greeted by goats and chickens that he'd locked up and left with enough food to feed them for a whole moon. He broke the ice in the water barrel and drank deep, found some eggs, cracked them and swallowed them raw, then locked the barn back up and set about saddling a horse in the stables.

'Get on, girl,' he said and touched his heels to his mare's ribs, and then she was cantering from the yard onto the track that led to Kergard.

On the meadow before Kergard a great space had been cleared, tents and a roped ring set up, and beyond them the bars of what appeared to be an iron cage rearing high. Drem barely glanced at any of it, his eyes fixed on his path.

'Ulf?' he asked the gate guards.

'An Assembly meeting, at his yard,' one said, looking him up and down and wrinkling his nose.

Drem rode on, through Kergard's streets, people staring strangely at him as he passed, until he was clattering into Ulf's tanning yard, the caustic smells of lime water and animal fat hardly affecting him at all. A handful of men were there: Hildith's guards and others. They stared at him as he slid from his mount and staggered through Ulf's doorway. He stumbled on, almost falling through another set of doors into a large room, half a dozen people sitting round a table. Ulf was there, and Hildith, some others Drem recognized, and some he didn't.

Ulf was speaking when Drem burst in, but paused when he saw Drem, frowning as if at a stranger. Recognition dawned.

'Good grief, lad, what's happened to you? We're but soon back from a seven-day bear-hunt and by the looks of it we feel a damn sight better than you!'

Drem swayed and Ulf jumped from his chair, catching Drem.

'Sound the alarm, the call to arms,' Drem said, his voice cracked and trembling from lack of use.

'Fetch the lad a drink, and something to eat,' Ulf yelled out, easing Drem into a seat close to a crackling hearth. He sniffed. 'By Asroth's stones, but you don't smell so good, lad. Now, what are you saying? Call to arms? No need, we've caught your white bear. Don't need to worry, it's caged up on the meadows.' He frowned, put a hand to Drem's forehead. 'Have you got a fever, lad? Having fever dreams?'

'No,' Drem said, leaning away from Ulf. 'I'm not talking about the white bear. There's worse things out there than that bear.'

Faces round the table moved in and out of focus, all of them staring at him.

An Assembly meeting. Good, I can tell them all.

'Drem, you're not making any sense,' Hildith said. 'We came out to your hold when we got back with the bear, wanted to tell you. But you weren't there, didn't look like you'd been there for a while. Where've you been?'

'The mine, on Starstone Lake,' Drem said. The warmth of Ulf's fire was seeping into him, setting his fingers and toes tingling. Instead of waking him up, making his mind sharper, it was dulling his senses, a fog settling upon him. Someone appeared and thrust a cup of something warm into his hands and he sipped. It was like warm honey, soothing his throat, warming his belly.

'What about the mine?' Ulf said. 'Come, have some stew. He put a bowl in front of Drem, gravy and onions, chunks of beef floating in it. The aroma set Drem's stomach churning. Before he knew what he was doing, he was spooning it into his mouth, blowing on it, gravy in his beard.

'Slow down, lad, you'll give yourself gut-ache. When was the last time you ate anything?'

'Two days,' Drem mumbled. 'Three?'

'I think you need some rest, lad,' Hildith said, 'and someone to watch over you.'

'Aye,' Ulf agreed. 'You can stay here, if you like. My lot'll make some room for you.'

'No,' Drem said, putting the bowl of stew down. 'Thank you,' he added, remembering his da's constant expounding on the benefits of good manners. 'No, I can't stay,' Drem said, 'though I'm grateful for the offer, and the kindness behind it.' He drew in a deep breath. 'I have something important to tell you all.'

How do I say this, without sounding insane?

'The mine at Starstone Lake. It is not what it seems. The missing people; they are there, have been abducted. They've been . . . changed.'

Gasps and hissed breath. Someone laughed.

'What do you mean, lad?' Ulf said.

'They've been experimented upon. Foul acts of sorcery. Turned into half-men, feral, beast-like.' He looked Ulf in the eye. 'And Kadoshim are there.'

Ulf blinked. Sat back, blinked some more, a frown creasing his face. He shook his head.

'Lad, you've lost me.'

'There are Kadoshim and worse up at that mine. Plain enough for you?'

Ulf smiled gently, shaking his head. He shared a look with Hildith.

'Drem, there's no Kadoshim up this way. All that trouble's down south. That's why we're all here. Why so many more have come north this year.'

'They're here,' Drem said, insistent. 'And they're killing your townsfolk. Or making them into something new. Into killers themselves.' He looked into Ulf's eyes, saw only worry and sympathy mingled. Not even an ounce of belief of fear.

Hildith stared at him, a frown creasing her face. Others whispered to one another.

'I could take a ride out there, if that'd make you feel any better,' Ulf said.

'Only if you take *every* man that can hold a spear with you,' Drem said.

'Don't think that's going to happen, Drem. I'm only offering to ease your mind a bit. And I'd like to have a nose around that mine.'

Murmurs of agreement at that.

The memory of the cages in the rock face came back to him, of the boats on the lake, men kneeling to the Kadoshim on the pier. He looked at Ulf, saw that he didn't believe a word of what Drem was telling him.

'Can we get on with our business?' a man at the table said, heavily muscled, bald with a grey-braided beard. Drem didn't recognize him.

'Hold a moment, Ridav,' Hildith said.

'Aye, the lad's recently lost his da,' Ulf said.

'And he has my sympathy,' Ridav said, 'but he's clearly exhausted and delusional. Give him a bed and a jug of mead, and we can get on with our business.'

'I'll take a few of my boys and ride up to the mine for you, Drem,' Ulf said, 'but it won't be for a few days.'

Ulf going up to the mine not believing me and unprepared would be like sending him to slaughter.

Sometimes there's no getting through to a man. And sometimes the only answer is blood and steel.

With a sigh Drem stood. 'My thanks for the stew and drink, Ulf,' he said.

'Stay, lad,' Ulf said. 'You'll want to see the bear-baiting on the morrow, and a day of rest and some of my Tyna's cooking, you'll be feeling better about all this . . .' He waved a hand. 'Business.'

'Bear-baiting?' Drem said.

'Aye. We trapped it in a gorge, gave it a boar's leg full of enough valerian to kill a horse, chained it and dragged it back.'

'Why?'

'There's a lot of people in this town that lost kin to that bear. Seems like a way to give them some justice. And people always like bear-baiting. Set the hounds on it, bet a few coin. It'll be a right good day. Just what we all need.'

'There's not enough hounds in all of the north to bring that white bear down,' Drem said.

'Might have to bleed it a bit first, or give it some more valerian to slow it down,' Hildith said. 'Either way, it'll be a show and a crowd-pleaser. You should stay. It killed your da.'

'It *didn't* kill my da,' Drem said, his hand instinctively going to the bear claw around his neck. He was surprised to find it was gone, his cloak and shirt torn, the claw and leather cord gone.

When Sten tried to grab me.

'It did kill your da, lad,' Ulf said soothingly. 'You're just a bit mixed up in the head. You should stay with us a day or two.'

'You're a kind man, Ulf. My da always liked you,' Drem said. 'I hope the Kadoshim don't kill you.' He walked out of the hold with Ulf and the rest of the Assembly staring at him open-mouthed.

As he rode out of the gates of Kergard he reined in and stopped. He looked to the south, thought of the message he had sent with Asger. Then he looked north, to his hold, then past it, east, to Starstone Lake and the mine.

I don't know what to do. I should run. They will come for me eventually. No matter how well I hid my tracks, they will find them in the end. I could go to Dun Seren, tell them what I have found. They need to know.

He sucked in a deep breath and looked to the south, a white landscape undulating into the distance. Exhaustion swept over him again, and he knew that he could not outrun any pursuit over fifty leagues of the Desolation.

And what of my oath. Vengeance for my da, and the fulfilment of his last wish. To take Asroth's head? How will I accomplish that if I run? The sword must be at the mine, in the hands of the Kadoshim.

He heard a deep roar, making his stomach lurch, then realized it was not coming from the north, but west, from the meadow in front of him.

The white bear.

Without really knowing why, he clicked his tongue and guided his horse down the slope towards the meadow. He passed holds, more like one big hold, a score of homes merging into a village on Kergard's doorstep, children laughing amidst the snow, throwing snowballs, a big hound barking, jumping and snapping snowballs from the air.

He rode out onto open meadow, carpeted in white, and saw the cage. It was huge, a gaol of iron bars. Inside it the white bear was motionless, blending with the snow. Only as Drem approached did it move, lifting its big head and regarding him, or maybe his horse. One guard was sitting upon a stool a distance from the cage, a fire burning, pot bubbling over it. Drem knew him – Aed, one of Calder's sons.

'Not too close,' Aed said to him as Drem rode up. His horse whinnied, ears back at the scent and sight of the bear, danced on the spot, not happy about going on. Drem dismounted, not even looking at Aed, and walked to the cage.

The iron bars were as thick as Drem's arm, and he could see where the bear had vented its fury upon them, scratches and gouges in the metal, though not even the white bear's strength or bulk could break these bonds.

A rumbling growl, deep in the bear's belly. Drem saw the scars and scabs that crisscrossed the beast's body, the claw missing from its right paw. He felt a wave of sympathy for it.

You are caged, going to be torn piece from piece on the morrow, a crowd watching and cheering and laughing as it happens. All for acts that you have not committed.

'Going to be a good show on the morrow,' Aed said behind him.

The bear lurched upright, shockingly fast, and then its head was a handspan from the bars, on a level with Drem, staring at him. Aed stumbled back a few paces.

'Careful, Drem,' Aed said.

The bear leaned forwards, muzzle pressing against the iron bars, and it took in a great breath, sniffing in Drem's scent, a snorting breath out, misting in the cold.

Drem stared into the bear's eyes, seeing defiance, an animal's strength and spirit. Unbowed. Indomitable. It would never give in.

Like my da.

And confusion, at a world suddenly turned upside down, inside out. He remembered lying flat on his back in the forest, the white bear looking down at him, then fleeing into the undergrowth.

You spared my life.

'You didn't do it,' Drem said sadly, 'you don't deserve any of this.'

And I owe you.

In a fluid motion Drem drew his short axe from his belt, raised it two-handed and brought it down upon the lock and chain wrapped around the iron-barred gate. An explosion of sparks, links falling away.

'What are you doing?' Aed shouted.

The axe rose and fell again, and then the chain fell away, unravelling to the ground in a long, sinuous coil.

'What have you done?' Aed whispered.

Drem grabbed the cage door and threw it open.

'I think you should run,' he said to Aed as he walked calmly back to his horse.

'WARE!' Aed screamed as the white bear burst from the cage, head high, sniffing the air. It roared, a great, defiant bellow that rattled the iron bars of its cage, looked about, taking in Aed, Drem swinging back into his saddle, and the open spread of meadow that led to woodland and the Bonefells.

It's not a mankiller; it proved that in the forest when it left me alive and chose to run.

Another roar and it shambled away, breaking into a ponderous run, snow spraying as it aimed straight as an arrow for the trees and mountains.

Your home. Drem thought. *And I should do the same.*

With a touch to reins and heels to his horse, he urged his mount to a canter across the white meadow, heading northeast.

Heading home.

Exhaustion was heavy upon him when he rode back into his yard, but he knew he could not rest yet.

Men or worse from the mine will be coming for me, soon enough. Later today, maybe on the morrow. I've not the energy or will to run any further, and even if I did, they would catch up with me, out in the Wild where I would be defenceless. They won't expect me to make a stand, and, besides, this is my home, where I spent the last five years with my da. As good a place to make a stand as any.

He stabled his horse, let the livestock out, and looked up at the sky. It was well past highsun, edging towards sunset.

Still time enough.

And he went to work.

Later that night he finally collapsed onto a makeshift bed of hemp sacks stuffed with hay. His weapons were still buckled around his waist, sword, axe, his bone-handled seax, more axes and knives in a bundle on the ground, and his spear leaned against the wall by his head. It was dark, the wind whistling around the hold as exhaustion finally claimed Drem.

I've done all I can do. You never know, I might just make it through this. Depends how many are tracking me.

The last thing he remembered before he fell into the black well of sleep was the sound of a goat bleating close to his ear.

CHAPTER THIRTY-SIX

RIV

Riv gazed in awe at Bleda and a dozen of his honour guard. They were galloping across the weapons-field in an arrowhead formation, leaning low in their saddles, bows drawn, two or three more arrows gripped in the same fist that held their bows. Without any obvious sign that Riv could tell, they loosed their bows together, arrows flying at the straw targets before them; within heartbeats they had drawn and loosed another shaft, then were thundering past their pin-cushioned targets, twisting in their saddles to shoot one last arrow into the back of the straw men.

Just in case two arrows in the face isn't enough to put your enemy down.

Riv whooped her approval as the riders curled around the field, slowing to a canter, and another dozen rode at the straw targets.

'Have to admit, that's an impressive party trick,' Jost said beside her.

'Aye. How can Bleda still do that, after five years away from it?' Riv said.

'It's like riding a horse,' a voice said behind her, and she turned to see Jin, sat upon a mount of her own, a curved bow in her hand. 'Once you learn the skill of it, you never forget.' She shrugged. 'It may take a while to come back, like knocking the rust from a blade left untended, but the iron and steel is still beneath.'

'Wise words,' Jost said.

'Huh,' Riv grunted. She didn't much care for Jin, had always found her abrupt, rude. And now that she had an honour guard of a hundred warriors, there was a new level of arrogance in her, the way she spoke, even the way she walked was irritating Riv.

'It's about discipline, self-control, focus,' Jin said as she rode past them. She looked down and met Riv's eyes flatly. 'Something *you'd* know very little about.'

'What's that supposed to mean?' Riv said, a seam of anger heating in her veins. She felt Jost's hand upon her arm, heard his voice. Ignored it.

'You know exactly what it means,' Jin said. 'I saw your warrior trial. You have no discipline, no control.' She snorted a laugh. 'What kind of warrior are you? The answer is: none at all. I doubt you will ever pass your warrior trial, will always be wishing, hoping, dreaming. As you dream of *other* things.'

Riv opened her mouth, but only a strangled hiss came out.

'I see the way you look at my betrothed. Bleda is mine. Betrothed to *me*. We shall rule Arcona together, while *you* are still polishing warriors' boots and dreaming of being one.'

Jin kicked her horse on. Riv snarled, clenching her fists, and started after her. Jost was hanging on to her, pleading for her to calm down, to see sense, though she was dragging him across the grass. But the anger had total control again, was putting a fire in her limbs and, even as she knew she shouldn't be doing this, should be mastering her emotions, she couldn't. Part of her didn't even want to try, there was something bittersweet about the surrender, relinquishing the need to think, instead just *doing*.

A great gust of wind, and a Ben-Elim was alighting between Riv and the shrinking backside of Jin and her horse.

It was Kol, all gleaming mail, golden hair and white teeth.

'Here,' he said, throwing something through the air at Riv.

Instinctively she caught it, a practice sword. She looked up and saw Kol coming at her with a weapon raised high, whistling towards her head. Without thinking, she blocked it, rotated her wrist and shoulder, sending it wide, knocking her opponent off balance, and she was swinging her blade at him, all the rage she'd felt a moment ago still there, coursing through her, just focused on something else now. With a savage fury she attacked Kol, chopping, stabbing, lunging, feinting, stabbing again. Her blade connected more times than she missed, hard blows that would leave a tale of bruises, Kol grunting with the pain of them, though he kept grinning the whole time.

'Feels good, doesn't it?' he whispered as she lunged in close, seeking to skewer him, but he stepped to one side, their bodies crashing together.

'What does?' she snarled up at him.

'Letting go,' he breathed, pushed her with his empty hand and swept his wooden blade at her neck, a blow that would have decapitated her if it were sharp steel.

If it touched me.

Riv ducked, spun away, set her feet.

Kol followed her, their battle resuming, a blur of blows. He landed a few of his own strikes, though with less power than Riv, just letting her know that he could. She shrugged them off, attacking like a force of nature, swirling around Kol, sweat stinging her eyes.

Dimly, Riv became aware of a circle forming around them: Ben-Elim, white-feathered wings and mail shirts bright in the winter sun. She ignored them, continued to batter, spin and hack at Kol, surrendering totally to the emotion that was coursing through her, allowing her anger to have free rein, like a stallion galloping freely, and for a while her anger led her and she allowed her body to follow blindly.

Eventually the red mist began to fade, and she saw an opening against Kol, swung low, her blade catching him in the ankles, and then he was falling, Riv ready to step in and put her blade to his throat, but he did not end up on the ground, instead with a pulse of his wings he was rising, turning in the air, suddenly behind her as she stepped forwards, off balance. His sword blade pressed against her throat, his other hand about her waist, body pressed tight against her back.

'I win,' he whispered in her ear, so close Riv wasn't sure if it was the touch of his breath or lips upon her neck. Whichever one it was it made her skin gooseflesh, a shudder of warmth rippling through her body. Then Kol was stepping away, leaving her standing there, breathing heavily, heart thumping in her head like a drum.

She became aware of the Ben-Elim ringed around her, fifty, sixty of them, maybe more, recognized many of them as those that Kol had taken with him on the mission to Oriens. They all stared at her, their bodies and wings blotting out the rest of the field.

A figure pushed through them, smaller, dark-haired. Aphra.

Riv took a step towards her sister, felt dizzy, a sequence of pains shuddering through her body. In her belly, lower, but overwhelming them all a sudden pain stabbing in her back, between her shoulder blades, as if Kol had pierced her with his sword. She grunted, and then she was falling, the ground rushing up to meet her.

Voices, blurred, as if heard through water.

'. . . so worried about her, I cannot think,' someone said.

Aphra?

'She has her blood, is becoming a woman, and she has a fever. She will recover.'

'It's not just a fever, Mam, *is it?* What about her *back?!*'

Water, Riv said, or tried to, unsure whether the word actually left her lips.

She was lying face-down, the pillow beneath her face wet, which was uncomfortable. She tasted salt.

My own sweat, she realized, which was strange, as she was so cold.

Freezing! Why don't they put a blanket on me? She tried to move, to speak, but didn't think even a finger or toe twitched. A pain, deep in her belly, feeling like her insides were falling out, and her back . . .

Dear Elyon, the pain.

Perhaps she gasped, for there was a hand upon her back, a wet cloth, feeling like heaven.

'What's happening to her?' Aphra said, and Riv felt a tugging sensation across her back, like when she had sat out too long in the sun and a few days later was peeling strips of sunburned skin from her shoulders and arms.

Footsteps, a shadow, Riv's eye open a crack. Her mam stood before her. Behind her a stone wall, not her barrack room.

Where am I?

'I don't know,' her mam said. A silence. 'We may have to get her out of Drassil.'

And then sleep was pressing in upon her again, Riv fighting it, but her mam and sister's voices faded . . .

CHAPTER THIRTY-SEVEN

DREM

Drem woke with a start. A beam of daylight pierced a gap in the wall of the barn where he'd slept, motes of dust floating in the sunlight. A goat was nibbling at his breeches.

'Off,' he breathed, pushing it away.

Outside there were the sounds of splintering ice, the crunch of snow. Voices, whispered.

Drem's eyes snapped open, fully awake now, and he eased himself up to a sitting position, clamping back the groan that wanted to escape his mouth.

They're here.

He gripped his spear and levered himself stiffly to his feet, picked up his bundle of weapons and crept to the barn door.

Figures were in his yard, wrapped in fur, heads close together, whispering, the glint of steel in their hands. Other shadows moved at the edges of the yard, creeping around the sides of his cabin. Someone's back shifted along the barn door, pressed against the crack he was peering through, cutting off his vision.

Counted eighteen. Heard more. That's not good.

He thought about tiptoeing out the back of the barn, hiding, fleeing. He recognized the fear jolting through him that prompted these thoughts, thrusting them to the foremost of his mind. The logical voice in his mind managed to see them for what they were. A knee-jerk reaction. One that he would not listen to.

He'd made his decision. To stay and fight. If he'd run for Dun Seren, they would have caught up with him in the Wild, and he'd have less chance there than he had here. He thought of his da, closed his eyes a moment, breathed in long and deep, then blew it out slowly.

The figure moved away from the door and he saw Wispy Beard, head freshly shaved, though he hadn't done a very good job of it, clumps of red stubble catching the sun. He signalled with a hand motion, sent three men towards the front door of Drem's cabin, others spreading loosely through the yard.

Wispy's in charge, then. No Burg or Kadoshim. That part of my gamble's paid off. Just wish he hadn't brought so many with him.

A scream rang out, distant, from the back of the cabin.

Drem smiled.

Nails and old knife blades frozen into the window frames.

A splintering crunch, yells, changing to thuds and screams. Much closer than the first ones, and higher pitched, communicating a much greater degree of pain.

Drem peered through the crack in the barn door, saw the three men Wispy had sent to his front door had disappeared, a great big hole in front of the steps to his cabin porch.

Hardest elk pit I've ever dug. And the first one I've set spears into.

All the men in the yard were alert now, anxious, weapons gripped tight, staring at Drem's cabin. Two men climbed over the railings to either side of the steps. The crunch of the snow that Drem had decided to leave thick on the porch. A different type of crunch as one of the men trod on a bear trap, iron jaws snapping shut, shredding flesh and breaking bone.

Another ear-splitting shriek.

The last man at the door, kicking it open. Wood splintering.

The creak of rope, and then the man in the doorway was flying through the air, a wooden post the size of a tree trunk swinging in the open door.

Time to move.

Drem slipped the bolts on the barn door, padded back behind the baggage ponies he'd brought in from the stables. With a great shout, he slapped one on the rump, another and another, sent them neighing and bursting through the barn doors as they exploded outwards into the yard, men turning, yelling, leaping out of the way, slipping, sliding, falling in the snow and ice.

Men went down, trampled, the sound of screams, bones splintering, the horses bolting left and right, some to the paddock, some for the yard's gate and the track away from Drem's hold.

Men were groaning, rising from the snow, others turning to stare at the barn. One at least lay motionless in the courtyard. Drem stood just inside, set his feet and hurled his spear, saw it punch into a man's chest, hurling him onto his back, an eruption of blood, bright on the snow.

Men shouted, saw him. Started to move.

Still too many.

Drem reached to his bundle of weapons set on a crate beside him, gripped a short axe, hefted its weight and threw it. A man went down in a spray of teeth and blood.

He gripped a knife handle, again taking a moment to gauge its weight, then hurled it at the men crowding the open gateway. A scream, a man stumbling, another axe and knife hefted and thrown. Then they were too close and Drem was running towards the back of the barn, stopped by a barrel of lime water that had been left from tanning last year's furs, swept up his fire iron and struck sparks.

A *WHUMPH* as the barrel ignited and he kicked it over, hairs singeing, the men behind him skidding, one pushed by those behind him into the flames, screeching in agony, and Drem was running on, grabbing the reins of the pony he'd left saddled and tethered at the back of the barn and kicking at the boards he'd cut partway through last evening. He crashed out into bright daylight and snow, his pony only too eager to follow and escape from the flames and screams. Drem clambered onto his mount, dragging on the reins and cantered round the side of the barn to the front of his yard. Shouts behind him, the crunch of footsteps in snow told him there were at least some that still chased him.

A handful of men were still in the yard, three or four. More staggering out from the barn. One of them was on fire, a human torch.

Six still standing in the yard, at least, and more behind me, and I'm out of tricks. Too many for me to take. Time to ride for Kergard, and get this lot to chase me. If I make it, then Ulf, Hildith and the Assembly will have to get involved, will have to protect me. It could lead to them doing something about the mine.

He put his heels to his pony and she neighed and leaped forwards, a dozen strides and she was close to a gallop, wind ripping tears from Drem's eyes, the gateway of his courtyard looming closer.

An impact, a scream from his mount and he was falling, threw himself clear and grunted as he hit the snow, saw his pony rolling, a spear protruding from her chest. She screamed again, tried to regain her feet, but her strength was failing her, blood staining the snow pink.

Drem staggered to his feet, looked about wildly, saw Wispy and a handful of men running at him, the sound of men behind.

Some detached, analytical part of Drem's mind hoped that the goats and chickens were all right, that they'd escaped from the fire that was now blazing through the barn, black smoke belching into the sky.

Almost made it.

He drew his sword, felt a comfort in the knowledge he'd put up a good fight, more than good. Enough to make his da proud. He just wanted to take Wispy Beard with him now. Wispy was running towards Drem, sword in his fist, screaming orders, spittle flying, almost incoherent.

'Why don't you come and kill me yourself?' Drem shouted, surprising himself with the passion he felt, and he strode towards Wispy. Was pleased to see a flicker of fear in the man's eyes. But then others were flanking him, spreading into a half-circle about Drem.

He didn't wait for them, instead hurled himself at Wispy, startling him, slicing down with his sword as he ran. Wispy shuffled back, more stumble than swordcraft, managed to raise his own sword, deflecting Drem's blade, though it still cut a red line into Wispy's arm through his fur cloak. Drem swung again, a wild blow, his momentum carrying him on, his blade chopping into Wispy's torso, leather and fur deflecting the blade, but Drem heard the distinct sound of ribs breaking, and then Drem was crashing into the man, both of them stumbling, falling to the ground, limbs tangled, Drem's sword spinning away. Wispy cursed and spat, tried to headbutt Drem, failed, tried to bite him instead, managed to latch onto his ear. Drem felt the pain, but as a distant thing, utterly focused on inflicting as much damage upon this man as was possible before he ran out of time. He managed to connect a punch to the back of Wispy's bald head, felt him loosen for a moment, teeth dropping away from his ear, and Drem pulled free, climbed to his feet.

Something clubbed him across the shoulders and he collapsed back on top of Wispy, felt his strength leaking away, but still managed to put a knee in Wispy's groin and rolled away as the club came down again, missing him and driving into Wispy's gut. Drem remembered his bone-handled knife, still sheathed at his belt, wrapped a fist around it, slashed across someone's leg planted in the snow before his eyes, saw a spurt of blood, swung his seax wildly about him as he tried to scramble to his feet, slipping in the snow-churned mush.

A boot in his gut drove the air from him, sending him crashing back down. There was a thud in the small of his back, the worst pain so far, and he gasped, not enough air to scream. Slashed with his seax again, someone crying out, a shouted oath, a boot stamping on his forearm, his grip abruptly empty. Blinding pain in his wrist, a scream this time, breath or no breath. Kicked in the mouth, the taste of blood, kicked again in the chest, rolled onto his back. Something cold and sharp at his throat. Opening his eyes to silhouettes against the bright sky.

'Get him up,' a voice snarled. Wispy, he guessed. Drem didn't care, was in a place beyond caring, he'd done his best, slain more than he believed possible. Smoke billowed in the sky above him, and Drem saw a shape highlighted by the black clouds.

A white bird, circling.

Is that death, come for my spirit? What form of bird does death take? That looks like a crow!

He heard it cawing, a raucous squawking.

Then he was being hauled to his feet, a noose wrapped around his neck.

Not this again.

He found the strength to scream, even knowing that it would not do him the slightest bit of good.

CHAPTER THIRTY-EIGHT

SIG

Sig saw the smoke first, grunting at Cullen and pointing. Keld was somewhere in the woods to the north, only the flash of fur showing that he and Fen were close. They'd just passed a derelict hold on their right, the main cabin with two splintered holes in it, a cairn in the yard. Sig would have stopped, but something whispered to her of haste. They'd planned to stop at Kergard, but the place had been heaving like a kicked nest of wasps and so Sig had made the decision to ride on in a wide half-circle around the town, so as not to be seen. The trader Asger had given clear directions to Olin and Drem's hold anyway, and after almost two ten-nights of travelling ever deeper into the ice and snow, Sig was eager to be at her journey's end.

'I don't like the look of that smoke,' Sig said.

'Isn't that close to where we are heading?' Cullen asked.

'Aye,' Sig grunted. 'Some speed, I think, and loosen your blades. The frost—'

'I know,' Cullen said, checking his sword and knife in their scabbards, 'it can make the blade stick.'

'You've learned something, then,' Sig said, muttering to Hammer beneath her, the bear shifting from a lumbering walk to a lumbering run.

'Oh aye,' Cullen nodded, touching his heels to his horse's ribs. 'Maybe because I've been told the same fact five times a day, every single day since we left Dun Seren.'

'Well, it gets—'

'Cold in the north. I *know*.'

For once Cullen sounded short of humour.

A shape appeared in the sky: Rab, flapping towards them at great speed.

They're going to kill him!' the crow squawked, turning in a tight spiralling circle about Sig and Cullen.

'How many?' Cullen called up to the bird.

'Ten, twelve. Lots dead already,' Rab cawed down at them.

'Tell Keld,' Sig said, snapping a command to Hammer, who leaped forwards with a ground-shaking growl. Sig shrugged her cloak from one arm and drew her longsword as Rab bolted towards the snow-laden trees.

A fence and open gateway appeared at the end of the track they were speeding down, black clouds of smoke billowing in the wind. Sig saw figures in a courtyard, growing larger by the heartbeat as Hammer's loping run ate up the ground.

Flames crackled up into the sky, a barn engulfed, roaring, and there were men gathered beneath the branches of a tree, hoisting on a rope that had been thrown over a branch, a figure dangling on the end of it, fingers clawing at the noose about its neck, feet kicking.

Sig was almost at the gates when the first man heard her. She guided Hammer off the track, cutting across deep snow, saw a man turn and look straight at her just before Hammer smashed through the post-and-rail fence that enclosed the yard. He was shaven-haired, a vicious smile on his face from laughing at the man at the end of the rope.

The fence fractured with a deafening crack, an explosion of splinters, one piercing the man staring at her, straight through his eye. He dropped like a puppet with its strings cut. Others ducked or leaped away from the noise. Hammer smashed straight into those that remained, a boulder amongst twigs. Bones snapped, flesh tore, men screamed and died, flying through the air in myriad directions. Sig swung her sword, cutting the rope, the man at its end dropping to the ground. He coughed and heaved, body convulsing, hands ripping the noose free from about his neck.

Good, he lives.

There was movement to Sig's right and she swung her sword, took the head from a man attempting to stick his spear in Hammer's flank, saw it fly spinning through the air, the man's body stumbling on a few paces before it collapsed. Another ran screaming at them and Hammer split him open with one swipe of her paw, claws raking him into bloody strips of meat and bone. Hooves drummed, and Sig twisted in her saddle to see Cullen ride into the yard, his spear skewering a man brandishing a sword at him. Cullen left the spear in the dying man, drew his sword and then rode at two more shaven-haired men who were hovering between fight and flight. His mount crashed into them, sent one spinning to the ground, the other swinging his sword at Cullen's legs, but Sig knew that Cullen was more than their match.

She looked about, assessing for more danger.

None stood before her or close to the tree. Three figures were sprinting away from her and the courtyard, northwards towards the treeline that edged the hold. Rab flapped and landed on a branch before them, dislodging snow in a heap upon the head of one of the men. He looked up and opened his mouth to curse, but then a shape was bursting from the shadows of the trees, a huge, grey-streaked hound, thickly muscled, jaws gaping wide. Fen slammed into the man, teeth clamping around his face and throat, the momentum of his leap sending them both crashing to the ground, rolling in a spray of snow. The man was screaming, battering at the hound as their roll slowed and came to a halt, Fen scrambling on top. A savage wrench of his head, as if it were shaking a caught rabbit, a spray of blood, and the man was abruptly silent.

The other two men had paused a moment, but they were running now.

One collapsed, falling back into the snow, clutching at an axe that suddenly sprouted from his chest. Bloody froth bubbled from his mouth. Keld emerged from the trees, running, another axe in one hand. His eyes fixed on the last man standing.

He was a shaven-haired warrior, sword in hand, a wispy red beard growing from his chin. He knew he had no chance of out-running Keld, so accepted his only option and swung his sword at the onrushing huntsman. Keld caught the blade with his axe, twisted, and the man was crying out, his blade falling from his grip.

'I want him alive,' Sig bellowed, Keld swirling round the red-haired man, his arm already moving, whole body committed to his blow. Sig saw him try to check it, but there was only half a heartbeat to do it in, the axe shifting its angle a fraction, the blow chopping into the base of his neck instead of his skull, and judging by the way the man screamed as he collapsed, there would be no coming back for him.

Too late.

Keld looked at Sig and shrugged, mouthed *Sorry.* Then the huntsman chopped his axe into the man's head, silencing the screams.

Sig slipped from Hammer's back, patting the bear's neck, and strode to the man on the ground. He was sitting up now, just staring at her.

'You must be Sig,' he croaked.

'Aye,' Sig said, feeling the grin split her face, for she recognized this man before her, could still see the shape of the boy in the sharp lines of his face, echoes of his mam and da, too.

'Well met, Drem ben Olin,' she said, crouching and giving him her hand.

CHAPTER THIRTY-NINE

RIV

Riv lay in a cot, slowly realizing that she was awake. She had been dreaming, strange, unsettling dreams of steel and blood, of Bleda, Aphra and Kol. Of Jin opening her mouth, a snake emerging instead of words, long and sinuous, jaws opening to reveal fangs dripping with poison. Of a mountain of heads with eyes that watched her every move. She was glad to be awake, though her throat felt blistered and raw, and she was still cold. Oh so very cold.

She opened her eyes, only a crack, but it felt as if it took more energy than a morning's training on the weapons-field. A figure, just an outline, stood with its back to her, before an open window, moonlight pouring through it. Aphra. A torch burned, flame flickering, shadows dancing on a curved stone wall.

This isn't my room.

The flames hurt Riv's eyes and she closed them.

A beating of wings, the moonlight veiled, a figure at the window. The soft slither of leather on stone, the rustle of wings furled.

'My thanks,' a voice said, deep and warm.

Kol.

'What is it that you want?' Aphra's voice, cold and weary.

'I need to speak with you. Alone.'

'Well, I am here,' Aphra said.

'I have to ask a question, need to know – *must* know – the answer—' An indrawn breath. 'I said, *alone*,' Kol hissed.

'I'm *not* leaving her. If you wish to speak to me, it's here or not at all.'

'Who is it?'

'It's Riv. And you have nothing to fear. She cannot hear us.'

'Why?

'She is in the grip of a fever. Has been hallucinating for two days. The worst has broken, and now she sleeps like the dead.'

'Are you sure?'

'Yes, look.' Footsteps, a hand clapping over Riv's head. She didn't have the energy to open her eyelids, let alone anything else.

'Why are you here?' Aphra, a coldness in her voice Riv had never heard before.

'There is a question that I must ask you.' A deep sigh, a protracted silence.

'Ask it, then,' Aphra said.

'A storm is coming,' Kol said. 'I feel it.'

'No.' Aphra said, a denial.

'You must choose a side.'

'No. It won't happen.'

'He is searching, snooping ever deeper,' Kol said, the hint of things unsaid in his voice. Agitation, laced with anger. 'You saw what he did to them, and they were only caught *kissing!* If he only knew the half of it.' A pause, footsteps pacing. 'Can you imagine what he would do?'

'He is the Lord Protector. He will do what he judges to be right,' Aphra said.

'Yes, he will. And that's exactly what I'm worried about,' Kol said.

'The almighty Kol, scared?'

'Yes, I am.' A silence. 'And so should you be. Do not think that the passage of time destroys all things, or even softens them. *Time is a healer*, you mortals say. Not to us Ben-Elim. A crime is a crime, a grudge a grudge, until the end of days. Blood feud will last an eternity. Israfil is immortal, he sees things differently to you. And he takes his job far too seriously. He is dogmatic, as uncompromising and inflexible as the day Elyon created him. He is very . . . rigid, in his ways, and not afraid to pass judgments with violent ends. To him a sin is a sin; the older it is, the deeper the stain. Do you really think he will view the sins of the past any differently to the sins of the present? Do you?'

A sigh, Aphra shifting.

'No,' she said.

'So, I need to know. When the storm breaks—'

'*If* it breaks,' Aphra said.

'All right. *If* the storm breaks; are you with me?'

More pacing. This time a softer footfall, coming to rest beside Riv. A hand upon her brow, gently stroking damp hair from Riv's face.

'Leave Riv alone,' Aphra said.

'What?'

'I've seen you. I know what you're doing.'

A gentle laugh.

'I would deny it, but not to you. None could claim to know me better,' Kol said, a new tone in his voice. Playful. Mocking.

'Leave her alone,' Aphra repeated.

'You never complained.'

'I was young.'

'Yes, you were. And beautiful. As is she. And spirited, full of fire. Bursting with it.'

'Leave her alone.'

'I need to know. Are you with me?'

'Swear, on your precious Elyon. You will leave Riv alone.' Iron in Aphra's voice now.

Footsteps, Kol stepping close to Aphra, almost touching.

'I swear it,' he growled.

A long, indrawn breath.

'Then I am with you.'

No words, just the rustle and snap of wings unfurled, the rush of air in this confined space, then gone as Kol leaped from the window into the darkness.

CHAPTER FORTY

DREM

Drem woke, his neck throbbing, a burning sensation that was none too pleasant. And his ear hurt; he lifted a hand to feel scabs.

Wispy bit me.

Many pains demanded his attention, but a thought still managed to push past them. He did not feel immediately concerned for his life.

That's a new sensation, of late, and a pleasant one.

Probably because there is a giant the size of a tree sitting at my hearth. A bear as big as my barn in the yard, two men that seem to be able to kill their enemies at will, while tying their bootlaces, and a hound that looks more like a wolven. And rips my enemies' throats open.

And a talking crow standing watch.

Things had worked out a lot better than Drem had expected, although as he'd imagined death was his only option, his expectations hadn't been that high.

Still, alive and safe is good. Or as safe as I can be, with Kadoshim and feral men who want to see me dead less than a day's ride away.

He rolled out of bed, saw that his boots were still on, all of his clothes, in fact. His weapons-belt was draped over a chair, his sword, axe and seax all back in their various sheaths. He stretched and clicked his neck, buckled the belt on, liking the familiar weight.

When did that start to become comforting?

Then he walked out into the main room of his cabin. It was empty, apart from a pot bubbling over the hearth.

'Morning,' a rough voice croaked at him, making him jump.

Drem looked about, saw the white crow perched on a roof-beam, sitting directly above the steam that was rising from the pot. Its head was tucked under one wing, one red eye regarding him.

'Morning . . .' he said, remembering his da's admonishments to always be polite, though he felt a little strange, talking to a crow.

'Rab,' the white crow cawed. *'Name is Rab.'*

'Morning, Rab,' Drem said. Then he frowned. 'I thought you were on watch duty?'

'Rab cold,' the bird said, giving his best impression of a shiver to reinforce his point, feathers puffing up and sticking out in odd directions.

'No fears, Fen prowling.'

'The others?'

'Outside,' Rab squawked, poking his beak at the open doorway and yard beyond.

He saw it was only a little past dawn as he stepped out of his doorway, the sun a heatless glow clawing its way up over the edge of the world.

What happened to yesterday? I remember Sig cutting me down from the tree, the others. Telling them about the Kadoshim. He frowned, the rest of it a blurred jumble.

In the yard Sig, Keld and Cullen were standing, swords in their fists, shields slung across their backs, performing the sword dance. Drem recognized it instantly from what his da had taught him, though watching these three perform it made him feel like a clumsy oaf in comparison.

They made it look beautiful. And deadly.

Nevertheless, he felt drawn to join them, his hand settling upon his sword hilt. On the porch to his right the snow was bloodstained, the bear trap closed and put to one side. Drem didn't know what had been done with the body they'd found in the trap, bled out by the time they'd gone to check. Then he saw a row of boots and legs sticking out from around the side of his cabin, remembered Sig and the other two heaving the dead around there.

A board had been nailed onto the splintered doorframe overnight to keep out some of the chill, but now it was laid across the elk pit Drem had dug. He walked carefully down the steps of his porch and across the wooden board, slightly concerned when it creaked under his weight.

His barn was nothing more than a smoking ruin, charred stumps of timber and the iron parts of his wain making up most of what had survived the fire.

Hope the goats and chickens survived. Though not sure they'd be safe around here with a bear and a wolven-hound.

He saw a goat poking out from the stables and smiled.

He joined Sig and the other two, drew his sword and moved with them, stepping from iron gate into scorpion's tail. He saw Cullen's eyes flicker to him, but Sig and Keld took no notice, and before long he was lost in each moment of the dance.

Sig's sword snapped back into its scabbard, Keld and Cullen sheathed their blades without any noticeable or conscious thought. Drem felt blood well on his thumb as he cut it, trying and failing to sheathe his own sword without looking at it.

'Need to work on that,' Sig said as she cuffed sweat from her brow.

'Here, use your thumb as a guide, not like a vegetable you're slicing for the pot; like this,' Cullen said, stepping next to Drem and breaking the move down into smaller pieces. Drem watched, the individual parts clicking into place in his head, and he managed to perform it correctly on his third try.

'Well done, Drem, my lad. We have a fast learner, here,' Cullen called up the steps, slapping him on the back. 'But you are my cousin, after all, so I'm not surprised.'

Cousin? I've never been spoken of as kin to anyone before, except my da.

'Cousin,' Drem repeated, liking the sound of it.

'Blood doesn't help in the sword dance,' Sig said, 'there are no short cuts; it's dedication, day in, day out. That's all.'

Drem had snatched memories of Cullen riding into the yard with a spear in his fist, the clash of steel as he fought. He was shorter than Drem, slimmer-framed, though Drem recognized the whip-cord strength in him that he often saw in trappers.

Living in the Wild bones a man, his da had often said to him. *Body and mind.*

Living at Dun Seren must do something similar, then.

'Ignore her,' Cullen whispered, 'she's too serious by far. You are Byrne's sister son, descended from Cywen, sister to Corban, so you have royal blood in your veins.'

Drem paused on the step at that. His da had never told him of his lineage past his mam, only that he was blood-related to Byrne.

'Royal?'

'Well, as good as, if you're a resident of Dun Seren.'

'And who are you descended from, to be my cousin?'

Cullen's chest swelled a little. 'Corban and Coralen are my great-grandparents,' he said.

Drem blinked at that.

Corban. He looked at Cullen with fresh eyes.

'Enough of that,' Sig said from Drem's smashed doorway. 'We need to talk.'

They all settled onto stools or chairs around Drem's hearth. Sig sat on the floor, her legs taking up half the room.

'We came because of your message,' Sig said to him once

Cullen had put hot bowls of porridge and steaming tea in all their hands.

'You asked me to come, if my friendship with Olin meant anything to me after so many years. A fair question. And here is your answer,' she said, spreading her hands, as if to say: *We came.*

'First I must tell you that Byrne wishes she were here. She very nearly came, it was I and her captains who dissuaded her of it. Strange things are happening in the Banished Lands, the scent of war with the Kadoshim in the air and Byrne is the high captain of the Order of the Bright Star. She could not abandon her post at such a dangerous time. But she asked me to tell you that she has thought of you every single day, from the moment that Olin took you from Dun Seren until now, that she searched for you and would have fought the Ben-Elim to keep you free.'

'My da knew that,' Drem said, 'which is why he took me. To avert a war.'

'Aye,' Sig said, 'we knew that, and loved him for it. But we would rather the both of you had stayed with us.' Sig dipped her head a moment. 'One last thing Byrne asked me to tell you. That Dun Seren is your home. It always has been, and always will be, if you so wish it.'

Home. That was a strange concept to Drem. Home had always been at his da's side.

'And I would say,' Sig continued, 'that you are not just Byrne's kin, but kin to all of us. We of the Order have a bond that cannot be broken, and you were born there, spent your first four years amongst us. Olin was my sword-brother. He was my friend, and that's more than enough for me, whether you are Byrne's kin or no.'

Drem felt his chest swell at that, a surge of emotion. He had felt nothing but alone since his da's death, and to hear Sig's words felt as if a door had been unlocked in his heart. Tears glistened his eyes.

'My heart breaks for Olin,' Sig said. 'He was brother to us all, and dearly missed these past years.' She bowed her head, Keld and Cullen following suit, even the white crow. Drem was deeply touched by the small display of respect.

'He spoke of you,' Drem said when Sig looked up. 'Though not until a moon or two ago. Until then I knew nothing of his past, or the Order of the Bright Star. He said you were friends.'

'Aye, though friends is too small a word for it,' Sig said. 'And I knew your mother, Neve. We were all close, closer than kin. And you. You gave my shins more than one bashing with your wooden sword. I was not surprised to see you join us in the sword dance just now, as we could hardly keep you from it as a bairn. You showed great promise on the weapons-field.'

'I did? I don't remember.'

There were fractured, lightning flashes, more of frozen images and moments. A huge tower upon a hill. A stone, words carved upon it, smooth under Drem's fingers. A fair-haired woman, laughing as she admonished him.

Sig!

'Little Drem.' Keld chuckled, shaking his head. Somehow Drem thought a smile on the man's face was a rare thing.

'There's more to tell you, that I've discovered since I wrote the letter to you,' Drem said, desperate to hear more of his past, of his mam and da, but he knew the knowledge he had was momentous.

'You said something last night. About Kadoshim, but you were delirious by that point,' Keld said.

'Aye, you were off with the faeries.' Cullen grinned.

Three days and nights of no sleep and then being hanged, again, will do that to a man.

'And Asger told us of a great bonfire in the Bonefells.'

'Aye,' Drem said. 'What of it?'

'There have been bonfires, beacons, lit throughout the Banished Lands. We know it is some kind of signal amongst the Kadoshim. Which is another reason for my presence. It is a hint that the Kadoshim are here, this far north, and if they are, the Order must know.'

'They are,' Drem said. 'The Kadoshim. I saw them. Only half a day's ride from here.' He gestured vaguely north-east.

'They?' Cullen asked. 'More than one?'

'Aye.' Drem nodded.

The three newcomers shared a look.

'How many?' Sig asked Drem.

Drem closed his eyes, remembering those moments when he'd stood on the palisade and stared out over Starstone Lake.

'I saw three, at least,' he said at last. 'It was night, there could have been more.'

He saw the questions forming on all their lips and held a hand up. 'But before that, I must tell you this. My da found a lump of the Starstone, and he fashioned a sword from it.'

'What?' Sig, Keld and Cullen said in unison. Rab squawked above them.

'Why?' Sig said. 'The man I knew would not have done something so rash, not without good reason.'

'He wanted to end it all. The war between Kadoshim and Ben-Elim, wanted them gone from the Banished Lands.'

'And how was he going to accomplish that with one sword?' Cullen said. 'Even if it was a magic one.'

'He planned to cut Asroth's head from his shoulders.'

A silence, Sig and Keld sharing a long glance.

Cullen whistled.

'Well, that would probably do it,' Keld said.

'And who has this sword, now?' Sig asked.

'The Kadoshim must. My da's killer took it from him.'

Sig looked at him pointedly.

'Tell us everything you know.'

So Drem did, beginning with the clues he'd discovered that pointed to another bear and person being his da's killers, and ending with the nightmare scenes he'd stumbled upon at the mine. The boats returning, Kadoshim in the air. The desperate, exhausted run through the forest.

'And then you all arrived, saved me,' Drem said with a shrug.

'To be fair, you did a large part of that job for us,' Keld said. 'We've counted the dead. You must have put fifteen of them down before we got here.'

'Sixteen,' Cullen said.

'Olin would have been proud of you,' Keld said.

'The question,' Sig rumbled, 'is what are they doing at that mine, and why?'

'They're making monsters,' Drem said. 'Feral beast-men, strong, fast, and they want to rip your throat out with their claws and teeth!'

'That's not the worst trait to have,' Keld said. 'Though I'd prefer it if it stayed with my hounds.'

'But it sounds as if they're experimenting,' Cullen said, brows bunching. 'That whatever they're trying to create, they haven't perfected it, yet.'

Aye. The things I saw were as much crippled as they were killing machines.

'It sounds to me as if the Kadoshim are making weapons,' Sig said. 'Which would make a good deal of sense. They have their acolytes, and a lot more of them than we thought, but they still lack the numbers to win this war. They need something to tip the balance in their favour.' She looked at them all. 'During the War of Treasures, the first war of the Starstone, when the Seven Treasures were forged from it, the giant Clans did something similar. They bred new species: wolven. White wyrms. Draigs. Living beasts, but they were also weapons of war, used in battle. The Kadoshim are doing the same, but taking it a hundred steps further, using dark magic and evil intentions to create mutated half-breeds.'

'Why here?' Drem asked.

'Because it's the Desolation, free of the Ben-Elim's rule, and their watchful eye,' Keld said.

'Aye, and do you think it's a coincidence that this is happening where the Starstone fell?' Cullen asked. 'I don't. That's why they've built a mine. They've been searching for a stray bit of starstone. They know the only way to free Asroth from his gaol is with the Starstone.'

'And my da gave it to them,' Drem whispered.

'No, lad,' Sig rumbled. 'He was murdered, and had it stolen from him. That's a different thing entirely. And one that requires vengeance.'

Drem liked the way Sig said that. Not just as if she meant it, but as if it had already happened, was inevitable, and it was just the doing of it that was left to happen.

'There's just one other thing I need to ask you about,' Sig said. 'You saw a giant bear, stabled at this mine. And you think it's the one that killed Olin.'

'Aye,' Drem nodded.

'And you saw a figure, like a man, but bigger. As big as me?'

Drem looked her up and down, closed his eyes, remembering the shadowed figure in the feast-room of the mine.

'Maybe,' he nodded.

'They have a rogue giant?' Keld said.

'Sounds like it,' Sig growled. 'Perhaps it was him, or her, who hit Drem when Olin was killed. And then took the Starstone Sword.'

Drem nodded thoughtfully.

That would make sense of the abductions, the bear killings and sacrifices. Bear, giant and Kadoshim, all working together.

A thought hit him.

Fritha's hold, smashed by a bear, and leather in the hound's jaws. Surl the hound bit the giant, which killed it and old Hask, and abducted Fritha to take her back there, to the mine, to be experimented upon. She is one of their Feral things, now. It could have been

her body parts upon that table, or she may have been one of the things
that threw itself at the cage bars.

The thought of it made him feel physically sick. Beautiful,
kind Fritha, reduced to some creature consumed with blood-
lust and used as a weapon.

'So, what now, chief?' Keld said to Sig.

'We go kill them,' Cullen said. 'What else?'

'No,' Sig said. 'We take Drem back to Dun Seren and
report to Byrne.'

'But we're so close,' Cullen said. 'And what about these
Ferals, and a Starstone Sword? How can we just walk away
from that?'

'You remember Ardain?' Sig said. 'Where we attacked one
Kadoshim and its coven. We had the Battlechief of Ardain at
our back with a few score of his best shieldmen, and it was still
a hard fight.'

'It was nothing,' Cullen said, 'we barely worked up a sweat.'

'That scar on your arm says different,' Keld said.

'Aye, well, I've matured since then.'

Rab squawked.

'Three Kadoshim together,' Sig muttered. 'And what if
each of their covens are with them? That is the most Kadoshim
sighted together since the Battle of Varan's Fall. Where your
mother fell.' She nodded to Drem.

'Da told me only a little of it,' Drem said.

'I will tell you of it. Of her. Songs are sung of her that day.'

'I would like to hear that,' Drem said quietly.

'How many acolytes?' Sig asked him.

'Acolytes?'

'The shaven-haired warriors.'

'Many,' Drem said. 'Two boatloads, and others already at
the compound.'

'And these creatures, these Ferals?'

'In cages. It could be ten, could be fifty. A hundred. I'm

guessing at much of this, you understand?' Drem said. 'It was dark. I was terrified.'

'*Poor Drem,*' Rab cawed from above them.

'Aye. Approximate numbers, but the result is the same. A lot. Too many, and at least three Kadoshim. One Kadoshim is hard enough to kill.' She looked at Keld and Cullen. 'I've much faith in you two, in Hammer and Fen. And my own sword arm. But—'

'*And me. And Drem,*' Rab squawked.

'Aye, even you, Rab,' Sig said. 'And Drem, but we've no right to ask him to go into any battle with us, let alone one where we are so heavily outnumbered. And Byrne needs to know of this. We should go back to Dun Seren, come back with a few hundred swords.'

'Ach, we didn't come all this way for nothing,' Cullen said.

'We've achieved much already,' Sig said, frowning at him. 'We've saved our long-lost brother, for one. And his information is more valuable than gold, for two.' Even so, Drem could see it pained her even to consider walking away from this fight. But it was the logical thing to do.

'You said I was your brother, your kin?' Drem said.

'Aye, that you are, Drem,' Sig said. 'I have told you, you are kin to me. As much a part of us as Olin was, and know this: if you have need, I – we – will be there, at your side. We are bonded, we few of the Order of the Bright Star, a bond of blood and friendship, unto death.'

She held his gaze a long moment, giving her words time to settle into him.

'Then I shall go where you go. Fight or freedom, either way.' he shrugged. 'Though freedom is the logical choice.'

Sig smiled at him.

'To ask you to walk back to that hell-hole, quite possibly to fight and die.' She thought about that and shrugged. 'Probably, not possibly. No, I will not ask you to do that. We came to help you, not march you to your grave.'

'I could scout this mine out, with Fen,' Keld said. 'Don't doubt Drem's account, but some eyes on the place in daylight would give us a better idea, more solid ground for Byrne to make a decision on.'

Sig looked at him thoughtfully.

'I could send Drem back with Cullen and Rab,' Sig said, 'and come with you.'

'You'll not get to have all the fun while I walk back to Dun Seren,' Cullen muttered sullenly.

That mine is not what I call fun.

There was the sound of hooves in the yard, all of them standing, reaching for weapons, then a strangled cry, high-pitched, a woman.

Drem burst onto the porch behind Sig and Keld, saw a woman upon a dun horse. She was as pale as death, staring wide-eyed at the bear Hammer as it lumbered out of the trees to the north.

'Dear Elyon above, it's going to eat us!' the woman shrieked.

'Hold, Hammer,' Sig shouted and the bear stopped.

Drem ran forwards, recognizing the woman as Tyna, Ulf the tanner's wife. She looked as if she was going to faint at the sight of Sig.

'What is it, Tyna?' Drem asked. 'What's wrong?' Why are you here?'

'I'm worried about my Ulf,' she said. 'Listening to you and your talk of Kadoshim, I told him he should have a look at that mine, just for some piece of mind.'

'He didn't go, did he?' Drem asked.

'Of course he did, and he took my three boys with him, amongst a dozen others. Went off yesterday morning, and he's still not back.'

Drem shared a look with Sig, Keld and Cullen.

More fodder for the Kadoshim to mutilate and transform. Not Ulf.

'We'll go and take a look.' Sig nodded.

'Well, it would have been a shame to come such a long way for just one little fight,' Cullen said.

CHAPTER FORTY-ONE

RIV

'Water,' Riv whispered, breath like a rasp in her throat, scraping her flesh raw. It was dark, the sound of rain, pounding and hissing against stone, a torch flaring bright, though she could just about manage to keep her eyes open now without the sensation of sharp, sliver-thin knives stabbing into the back of her brain and scraping upon the inside of her skull.

That's progress.

Fractured memories slipped through her mind. Sparring with Kol on the weapons-field. His arm tight around her, his breath on her neck. Collapsing, a kaleidoscope of images in this room. Aphra, her mam, Kol. A whispered meeting in the dark.

There was a dark shape over her, a hand behind her head, helping her sit. Water, oh blessed, sweet, heaven-sent water, a trickle on her lips, over her swollen tongue and down her red-raw throat.

'Slowly,' Aphra said as Riv tried to tip more water into her mouth.

'Where am I?' Riv croaked, looking around. The room was circular, one long window starting from the floor and ending with an arched top, tall and wide enough for a giant to walk through. Darkness, wind and rain leaked in, pressing upon the torchlight, making it swirl and hiss. Something about the way the wind whistled through the window whispered to Riv of height.

'A tower room,' Aphra said, 'above our barrack.'

Never knew this was here!

'It's my solitude room,' Aphra said with a sad smile. 'How do you feel?'

Riv wasn't sure. She felt as if her body had been put through a mangle, aching and entirely lacking in anything resembling energy. Keeping her eyes open and looking around seemed to be taxing enough.

'Weak,' she breathed. 'Cold.' She shivered, trying to shrug the woollen blanket tighter around her. She frowned at the open window.

A shutter would help.

'Your fever is returning,' Aphra said with a frown, her hand on Riv's brow. 'This is the third time. Twice I thought it had broken and you were healing.'

'How long?'

'Half a ten-night.'

'What! Is that how long I've been . . . ?' She didn't know what to call it. 'Unwell?'

'Aye.' Aphra nodded. 'Since you collapsed on the weapons-field.'

Riv drank some more water, managed to blink and roll her neck without feeling as if she'd spent a morning in the shield wall. Her back ached, a dull throb of pain, pulsing out from her shoulder blades.

'Back,' she said, trying to roll her shoulders. She felt different, somehow. As if she'd grown. 'It hurts.' She shifted, feeling muscle move that hadn't been there when last she checked.

'Your back. Well, I'm not surprised it's hurting.'

'Why?' Riv said, not liking the sound of that, or the look on Aphra's face. Not just worry. Something more. Something far greater than worry.

Aphra held up a strip of something that looked like parchment, crinkled and opaque.

'What's that?' Riv pulled a face.

'Your skin. It's been peeling from your back for half a ten-night.'

'Ugh!'

'And there's plenty more where that came from.'

What's happening to me? Have I caught some disease from the mission to Oriens and into Forn? Some plant spore that has infected me? I've heard tell of warriors breathing spores or seeds into their lungs, their stomachs, and fungus growing inside them, eating its way out!

'Am I going to die?'

Riv found the fact that Aphra didn't immediately discard that option deeply worrying.

'No,' Aphra eventually said. 'But I think we're going to have to get you out of Drassil.'

'What! Why?'

'Riv, you're growing. You have new muscle forming—'

'I can feel it,' Riv said, flexing her shoulders, feeling muscle bunch between her shoulder and neck. It was an odd sensation.

'This must be how Vald feels,' she said.

'You're starting to look like him,' Aphra agreed with a wry smile. She stroked Riv's face. 'I'm sorry,' she whispered.

'Why?' Riv said. 'What for?'

'So many things. For the way I've been, with you. I've had my own troubles, but that is no excuse. You are my blood, the most important thing to me in all the world, and I have neglected you, let you down.' A fat tear rolled down Aphra's cheek.

Riv looked up at her, a whole host of emotions whirling through her. She tried to find words, but they wouldn't come, so she settled for a smile.

The latch on the door rattled. Riv jumped, twisting to look and immediately regretting that, a wave of dizziness.

A figure entered. Aphra was standing, a hand on her sword hilt, stepping between Riv and the door. She relaxed when she saw who it was.

'Mam, you startled me.'

'How is she?' Riv's mam said.

Aphra stepped out of the way.

'Hello, Mam,' Riv said.

'Oh, my darling,' Dalmae said, crouching down beside Riv, stroking her face.

'Nice to see you,' Riv whispered, feeling an edge of delirium starting to fog her brain again.

'It's nice to see you, too,' her mam said, a half-laugh. Riv was surprised to see tears in her mam's eyes. She wasn't much of a crier. Riv was also surprised to see that beneath her cloak her mam was dressed in her old White-Wing uniform, a short-sword hanging from her belt.

'What's going on?' Riv asked, brow wrinkling, her sense for danger tingling, a faint echo in her head.

'The fortress is on alert,' Aphra said, her eyes flickering to their mam. 'Word of a possible Kadoshim attack.'

'I'd better—' Riv started, struggling to rise, though too quickly, a new wave of dizziness and she blinked and found herself lying in her cot again.

Try again, slower this time.

'Garidas is downstairs, asking for you,' her mam said to Aphra. 'He's not alone. A score of his hundred in the barracks. More outside.' There was meaning in the words that Riv didn't understand.

'What did you tell him?' Aphra asked.

'That he cannot see you. That you are indisposed at present.'

'Do you think he will settle for that?'

The sound of footsteps on a stairwell. A knock at their door. A silence.

'There's your answer,' Dalmae whispered.

'Aphra. Aphra, it is I, Garidas. If you are in there, I *must* speak with you.'

A shared look between Aphra and her mam.

'Enter,' Aphra said, her mam slipping back into the shadows behind the door as it opened.

Garidas walked in, Riv, trying to sit up again, was abruptly aware that she had little in the way of clothes on. She pulled the woollen blanket higher, saw her clothes at the bottom of the bed.

Garidas' eyes took in Riv, a look of concern. Genuine.

Riv liked Garidas. He had always seemed straight and kind, if a little pompous. She could see that kindness in his eyes now.

'Are you well?' he asked Riv.

'No,' Riv said, feeling honesty was more appropriate than politeness, and she didn't have the energy for any social niceties, anyway.

'I am sorry if I am interrupting something,' Garidas said, looking to Aphra, 'but I need to speak with you. It is most urgent.'

'My sister is unwell,' Aphra said. 'This is not a good time.' Her eyes glanced to the dark window, looking out, beyond, though all Riv could see was the blackness of night, hear the rattle of rain on stone and the wild gusts of wind through the great tree's branches high above.

'I will be quick,' Garidas said, something about him making it clear he would not leave until he had said what he came to say.

'Go on, then,' Aphra said, a sigh, a hint of resignation in her voice.

'You must leave Drassil,' Garidas said. 'Tonight. Now.'

Aphra did not answer, just stared at him. There was clearly more to come.

'You're in danger.' He opened his mouth, closed it, pinched his nose. 'You know I think highly of you. I hoped that one day . . .'

He paused, the words seeming to stick in his throat, and took a deep breath.

'Kol is finished. His transgressions are uncovered. I know

that you have been . . . *involved* with him, in the past. But not for many years. I would not see you torn down and destroyed with him in his ruin.'

A long silence, emotions playing across Aphra's face.

Kol and Aphra, like Adonai and Estel! Riv felt as if she was experiencing it all through a veil, like a secret observer. As if it were all a dream, just another of the many lurid, irrational, sometimes insane dreams she'd experienced lately.

No, I am here. It is the fever in my body making it feel like this.

'What do you mean, *finished*?' Aphra said.

'My men have taken Kol into custody, are taking him to Israfil as we speak.'

'Who else knows?' Aphra asked.

'That does not matter,' Garidas snapped. 'The whole sordid tale will be spilling from Kol's lips soon. His confession is only a formality. Israfil already knows, and he will carve a confession from him, if needs be. Go, now, before it is too late. Once this is settled and over, you will be able to return—'

'That will be impossible,' Aphra said. 'Lorina? Does she know?'

'Not of Kol's arrest, no.' Garidas scowled. 'She is in league with him. Did you not know?'

'I suspected,' Aphra said.

'We are wasting too much time. You have to leave, now, or it will be too late. I have horses ready for you, a wain if you need it. Come.' He held out an arm to Aphra, stood there long moments as she hesitated.

'Please,' Garidas said.

A creak of leather behind him, a familiar hiss, one they all knew instantly. The sound of a sword being drawn.

Garidas turned, hand on his sword hilt, drawing his blade as he moved.

A sword punched into his belly, low, beneath the line of his cuirass, and he gasped, slumped forwards onto his killer, rested his head upon her shoulder, as if she were his lover.

'I am sorry, my sword-brother,' Dalmae said as she pushed him away, pulling her sword free, the splash of blood on stone, and he fell backwards, clutching his gut, staring up at her. He cried out, loud, wordless betrayal, full of pain, and Riv heard an answering call below. Dalmae stepped forwards and stabbed him in the throat.

CHAPTER FORTY-TWO

SIG

'We'd best leave the track, now,' Drem said beside Sig. After hearing the news from Ulf's wife they had ridden hard from Drem's hold, using a well-worn path that hugged the fringes of the northern woodland. To their right was the Starstone Lake, dark and still, and in the distance Sig saw the outline of a stockade wall, buildings rearing within. A pier jutted into the lake with boats moored along it.

Sig looked up at the sun, veiled behind fraying louds, saw it was a little past highsun. She grunted an agreement with Drem and barked a command, the four of them riding into the eaves of the wood, Hammer ploughing a way through the snow that as good as made a new track, the others falling in behind. Every now and then Sig saw the grey streak of Fen shadowing them.

After a while the woodland grew too close and dense and they dismounted, Drem taking the lead, as he told them he knew the ground a little, which was a lot more than them.

'Five years my da has taught me to track, hunt and trap in this northern Wild,' he said, 'and for a good while before that further south. If I can't do a job, or someone can do it better than me, I'll tell you.' He looked at Keld. 'He's as much a hunter as his wolven-hound, and far better at it than me, but I know this ground. Know where I'm leading you.'

Sig glanced at Keld, always her first port of call, and he nodded.

'He knows what he's doing,' Keld said. 'I'm happy to follow him.' He'd told Sig of the number of traps and work he'd found around Drem's hold, his preparation for the coming of the Kadoshim's acolytes. Keld had laughed, he'd been so impressed.

'He dug an elk pit. In the heart of winter, and then sank a dozen spears into it. And that wasn't all. A nail trap, a bear trap, a mini-stampede, and he blew the barn up. On purpose.'

Sig liked what she saw in Drem. There seemed to be no falsity to him, no bluster or hidden ways. He spoke the truth as he saw it and displayed very little bravado.

Which is good, as I have enough of that to put up with in Cullen. Though he's a good lad, too, just trying to live up to his heritage. One day soon he'll realize it's more about what he does than what he says. I think he and Drem could work well together.

Sig was already beginning to form plans on how her small crew would be changing once they got back to Dun Seren.

Best not get ahead of myself. If Drem's right, there are Kadoshim and a host of enemies out there. Getting back to Dun Seren alive is going to be task enough.

There was a flapping above and behind. Rab appeared, blending with the snow-glow.

'Done it,' he squawked, alighting on Cullen's shoulder. The young warrior scratched his neck.

Sig had been loath to walk into such a dangerous situation, knew the perils around them and feared that if things went sour Byrne would never hear of the Kadoshim and their dark goings-on in the north, so she had inked a letter on a scroll of parchment at Drem's hold. She could not spare Rab to fly the parchment all the way back to Dun Seren, as she needed his eyes here, but Drem had told her of a woman at Kergard whom he trusted, whom he believed would make sure the scroll reached Dun Seren. It was not as reliable an option as Sig would have liked, but assessing the situation, she could think of no other way to get word to Byrne.

'You're sure you gave the parchment to the right woman?'
Sig asked.

'*Hildith, Hildith,*' Rab squawked.

'What did she look like?' Drem asked.

'*Stern. Big men with her. Smelled of mead.*'

'That's her,' said Drem.

'Good enough.' Sig nodded. 'Well done, Rab.'

Rab bobbed his head and puffed his feathers out.

Welcome,' he croaked.

'Now, would you fly ahead and have a look at this mine for
us?' Sig asked.

'*Course,*' Rab squawked and then he was flapping away.

Drem led them on.

'How did my mam die?' a voice said. Sig looked down to
see Drem walking beside her, leading his horse by its reins.
Hammer was following at her own pace, treading her own path
at the edge of Sig's vision.

'She was slain by a Kadoshim, at the Battle of Varan's Fall,'
Sig said, a rush of memory flooding her mind. Of trees and
Kadoshim and blood.

'I know that,' Drem said. 'I have the Kadoshim's tooth.' He
drew his sword and showed Sig the hilt of his father's blade.

'I remember,' Sig said. 'I helped your father hunt the beast.
Moloch was its name. It was the Kadoshim that struck your
mam down. Olin made it scream when finally we brought it to
bay. It was not a quick death.'

Drem nodded, looked as if he was storing that piece of
knowledge deep inside.

'Varan's Fall?' Drem said. 'My da said it was an ambush.'

'Aye. In the north of Forn Forest. We were after the
Kadoshim's captain, second only to Asroth. His name is Gulla.
But we were over-confident, did not scout ahead properly.
Dead Kadoshim were heaped around your mam in piles that
day. She and your da fought back to back, but were cut off from

the rest of us for a while. Many of our sword-kin fell that day. Gunil,' she whispered, then fell silent, remembering the others who had been cut off and slain. Brave, noble Varan. And his brother . . .

Gunil. How I miss you. A memory of his smile filled her mind, the way it would start in his eyes.

'Gunil?' Drem said.

His ears are good.

'A giant,' Sig said. 'A friend.'

More than a friend.

'You were close?'

'Aye,' Sig sighed.

I have never spoken of Gunil to anyone before. There is something about this lad, a goodness in him.

'Death and heartache are all about,' Drem said quietly. He looked up at Sig. 'So, Gulla was responsible for my mam's death, then. He did not strike the blow, but he led the attack.'

'Aye, you could say that.' Sig nodded.

'And responsible for your Gunil's death, too.'

Sig regarded him a long moment.

'Aye,' she growled.

Rab flapped and threaded through a gap in the canopy above.

'It's close,' the crow squawked. *'Buildings, torches burning.'*

'There it is,' Drem said, though the place hardly needed pointing out.

They were standing to the north of the mine, behind a cluster of boulders and hawthorn, Drem having led them in a wide circle around the encampment, all of them of the opinion that any watch would be focused more to the west and the road to Kergard. It was sunset, the sky above a dull orange, shifting towards pinks and purples.

'Looks quiet,' Cullen observed.

'Aye, it does,' Keld agreed. 'Could be an ambush.'

'I hope it's an ambush,' Cullen said, his fingertips brushing his sword hilt.

Sig sighed.

'Is he always like this?' Drem asked.

'Like what?' Cullen frowned.

'So keen for bloodshed.'

'Yes,' Sig and Keld said together.

Rab flapped down and landed on a hawthorn branch.

'Only a few on walls. Something happening inside. A meeting. Bad smell.'

'What's the plan, chief?' Keld asked her.

Are we to storm a fortified position with unknown numbers of our enemy inside, with just the four of us, and a bear, a hound and a crow?

Keld is right, we need solid information to take back to Byrne.

But townsfolk from Kergard are in there, Drem's friend amongst them. More innocents likely to be slaughtered by the Kadoshim scum.

She thought of the Order's oath, to protect the weak, to fight for them. Looked at her palm, the scar a silver line where she had sealed it with her own blood.

She knew they should already be on their way back to Dun Seren.

But if I leave now, innocents will die. And what of this Starstone Sword? Can I just walk away and leave it in the hands of the Kadoshim, to do Elyon knows what kind of evil. If we can get that, I'm guessing we'll stop a world of hurt from happening.

Sig looked at the sky.

'We'll wait for twilight,' she said, feeling her blood stir, a snarl twitching her lips at the thought of Kadoshim so close. 'And I'm thinking Hammer should be dressed for the occasion.' Then she drew a knife from her belt and tested its edge with her thumb.

Just enough time for a shave. She smiled at Cullen.

'What?' Cullen said suspiciously.

*

'Give me your hand,' Sig hissed, leaning over the wall and reaching down to Drem. He jumped and caught her wrist, and then Sig was hauling him up and over the palisaded wall of the mine, both of them ducking low.

It was as good as full dark; Sig's preparations had taken a little longer than she'd expected. The wall was poorly manned and only sporadically lit, so it took just a few heartbeats to check they hadn't been seen, and then Drem was padding down a stairwell, Sig jumping from the walkway into snow. They crossed an open space and hugged a wall, Drem slipping ahead, Sig confident to follow his lead. A hundred heartbeats and they were deep in the camp, an acid stench burning its way into the back of Sig's throat. Drem turned and signalled, pointing up at the roof of a building, single-storey with a sod roof. Sig was on it in moments, then giving Drem a helping hand. They crawled across the sod, Sig careful to spread her weight. Grass tickled her face. And then they were peering down upon a scene that set even Sig's skin to gooseflesh.

It was an open space, illuminated by many torches, their flames whipped and swirled by the wind. A boulder as big as a keep sat at one end of the clearing, the dull gleam of iron bars highlighted by the flames showing the countless gaols Drem had told them of. Veiled shapes prowled their shadows. The foul stench was emanating from those recesses in palpable waves. In the centre of the clearing stood a table, various butcher's tools spread across it, as well as a profusion of body parts. In places the timber was stained black.

On the far side of the clearing more buildings sprawled. Sig could hear the occasional snuffling and lowing of a bear coming from their direction, though she could not be sure of the exact building.

And in the clearing a crowd of acolytes stood, forty of them, maybe fifty. Other forms moved amongst them, prowling, their movements unnatural, backs heaped and bowed with too much muscle, arms and legs too long for their bodies, mouths and hands razored with tooth and claw that did not belong upon men. More shapes moved in the shadows beyond the torchlight.

Drem did not exaggerate.

'Can you see your friend, Ulf?' Sig whispered to Drem.

He shook his head.

A hush fell and figures emerged from the darkness, a procession, a Kadoshim at its head. He was tall, dark hair swept back and tied in a knot at the nape, the sharp lines of his face and set of his eyes giving him a reptilian appearance. His nose was a thin line.

A chanting broke out amongst the gathered acolytes as he entered the clearing.

'Gulla, Gulla, Gulla.'

Sig slid a hand to Drem and gripped his wrist.

'Gulla, High Captain of the Kadoshim,' she hissed. 'Second only to Asroth.'

The Captain of the Kadoshim walked through the crowd and it parted for him, his procession following behind: twelve, fourteen figures, Sig counted, all cloaked and hooded. They stopped in the space between the table and boulder, forming a half-circle behind Gulla. Two of them came to stand at his shoulder, casting their hoods back. Like Gulla they were pale-skinned and dark-veined, wings furled, clothed in rusted, iron-grey ringmail and tattered cloaks. But they were different, their heads shaved like the acolytes, and they were shorter and stockier.

What are they? Kadoshim? But they look like no Kadoshim that I have ever seen.

'The tide of the great war turns this night,' Gulla cried out, voice sinuous and alien. Cheers and growls and hissing approval rang out.

'My children,' Gulla called, and the two at his shoulder stepped forwards, striding towards the great boulder.

Gulla's children! What foul deed have these Kadoshim committed?

The darkness they have brought upon mankind. A fresh anger bubbled in Sig's gut, a desire to rid the world of the Kadoshim's corruption.

The two half-breeds reached a gate in the rock, the clank of chains and creak of iron hinges, then an animal screech. They reappeared with a giant bat held between them, the huge creature writhing and bucking in their grip, its head twisting and snapping at them, but it could not reach them.

Gulla's children slammed the bat down onto the table, held it pinned and stretched out by its great wings.

Gulla walked to the table, as he did so chanting rose up from the crowd in a tongue few would understand, but Sig knew it all too well.

A hush fell over the crowd.

'*Fuil agus cnámh, uirlisí an cruthaitheoir,*' Gulla cried out.

'Blood and bone, tools of the creator,' Sig whispered. Drem was as tense as a drawn bow beside her.

With a long black nail, Gulla slit the bat's throat, its terrified screeching descending into a frothed rattle, the creature's life-blood pouring onto the table, pooling and bubbling as the creature convulsed.

'Step forward,' Gulla said to one of the hooded figures that had followed him through the crowd, tall and slim. The figure threw back its hood, head shaved to fair stubble that glistened in the firelight.

A woman? Sig thought, though she was not wholly sure; there was something androgynous about this person. Male or female, it drew a sword from its cloak. A black sword.

The Starstone Sword!

Beside her Drem hissed, his body jerking and he almost leaped from the roof, only Sig's hand darting out holding him down. He took a deep breath, one hand reaching for his neck, fingers probing.

Is he taking his pulse?

Drem looked at Sig then, and tears were in his eyes.

CHAPTER FORTY-THREE

RIV

Riv staggered from her bed, the effort almost defeating her, feeling weak as a newborn kitten, but the sight of Garidas dead upon the flagstoned floor, his blood pooling dark and her mam standing over the corpse with her sword in her hand gave Riv the jolt of energy she had been lacking.

She tugged on breeches and boots, a linen shirt, which caught on her back, grating rough as sandpaper, but she managed to get it on.

Aphra ran to Garidas, knelt beside him. She closed his dead, staring eyes. Accusing. Aphra took his hand, smeared with blood, and stared up at her mam.

'I am sorry,' Dalmae whispered. Then, louder. 'Forgive me. I had no choice. I would murder the world to protect you and Riv.'

Aphra was silent, her shoulders shaking, and Riv realized her sister was weeping.

'Mam, why? What is happening?' Riv slurred. 'I don't understand.' She was washed with emotions, shock, horror, confusion. Garidas had said so many things, of Kol and Israfil and improper relations.

Aphra and Kol, involved, Garidas said. This is Kol's doing. He has broken the Way of Elyon, broken the Lore. And Mam has murdered Garidas! A good, kind man; he was offering to help Aphra somehow.

413

Her mam did not look at her, would not look at her, only continued to wipe blood from her hands on her cloak.

'Aphra?' Riv said, but her sister just stared back at her. The stink of blood filled the room, cloying. The weight of it all, murder, Aphra, Kol, right and wrong; her entire life she had been raised to obey the Lore, wanting to do nothing more than obey it.

Purity is removing the ego, Israfil said. What is purity here? What is the right thing to do? She felt breathless, her stomach lurching.

I feel sick. Have to get out of here. And suddenly she knew, she had to see Israfil, to speak to him, to explain Aphra's innocence before this got any worse.

'Get Mam out of here,' she blurted to Aphra as she stumbled past them, out of the door and onto a spiral staircase. Her mam and Aphra called out behind her but she did not stop, staggering down the twisting stairs, bumping and banging into the wall on her way down.

Shouts echoed up to her, the scrape of swords being drawn. She ran on, behind and above her the slap of boots on stone. Riv almost fell through the door that led into her barracks' feast-hall, saw a sight that made her feel physically sick.

White-Wings, close to blows.

Garidas' men, a score or two. They had heard his cry, tried to get to him, and been barred by Aphra's hundred. Some were shouting, pushing, others with drawn blades, ready, threatening, but holding back from that dread step of slaying their own.

Riv staggered a dozen paces, fell against a high-backed chair, her balance feeling all wrong, as if she were trying to navigate the deck of a storm-racked ship. Faces loomed in and out of focus, thought she saw Jost and Vald but was not sure, blinking, shaking her head.

Aphra and Dalmae appeared from the door of the stairwell. They paused, taking in the scene before them.

'Traitors,' Dalmae yelled at the top of her voice, 'Garidas is in league with the Kadoshim.' There was a moment's silence, even the few shouting at one another paused, and then chaos exploded. The sound of steel clashing, screams, blood on the barrack's stone floor.

Riv pushed herself away from the chair and ran through the hall, weaving through a chaotic melee of battle, tripping over fallen bodies, on towards the doorway to the street.

The doors burst open before she reached them, more of Garidas' men were rushing on, drawing blades. A gust of cold air hit Riv like a slap in the face, rain hitting her as if flung by an angry hand, stinging and refreshing. It helped her to focus for a moment and she ran out into the storm-drenched night, gasping in deep lungfuls of air, feeling as if she were suffocating.

A harnessed wain and half a dozen horses were tethered in the street.

The ones Garidas brought here to help Aphra escape. He was a good man, well intentioned, and Mam just murdered him!

She turned and ran through the empty street, rain sheeting down, the stone dark and slippery. Her back itched and burned, like a scab ready to peel, the sensation of new muscle rippling and bunching disturbing her, and the fog in her mind ebbed and flowed, like the tide rising and falling.

What is wrong with me?

Time enough for that later. First, I must do what is right.

As she turned a corner she heard the sounds of battle spill out from her barrack into the open behind her. Turning down another street, she saw figures, more White-Wings. They were setting oak bars across another barrack's door. Riv recognized Lorina, captain of the other hundred that had marched to Oriens. More of her White-Wings were standing in the shadows, waiting. As Riv ran past, muffled voices cried out, thuds hammering on the far side of the barrack doors.

This is all Kol. Charming, handsome, fascinating Kol. A storm is coming, he said to Aphra. What side will you choose?

415

Kol has been arrested, accused of improper relations, Garidas said. She suddenly remembered Kol's hand upon her cheek, fingers brushing her lips, and she shivered.

He has made the storm, has planned for this. Sent the giants away, has Lorina with him, and my sister. But Garidas said he had Kol in custody, that he is being taken to Israfil.

It was all there, in her mind, what was happening, but like a jigsaw the pieces were separate, were not connecting to make the whole picture clear.

On she ran, towards Israfil's chambers.

CHAPTER FORTY-FOUR

DREM

It's Fritha! Tears burned his eyes, the sense of betrayal hot as bile in his throat.

Not abducted by them, or experimented upon and mutilated by them. She is one *of them! Has been one of them all along.*

I am the world's greatest fool.

'It is Fritha,' he whispered, more in control, now, at least enough to not hurl himself from the roof in an attempt to kill the deceitful, lying witch.

What part did she play in my da's death? Was it her that hit me? Took the sword? She certainly has it now.

He felt his body tense again, but controlled himself. He was not about to commit suicide when the chance of justice or vengeance was so slim.

Wait, bide my time. Be the hunter Da taught me to be. But know this, Fritha – for what you've done, I will kill you.

She raised the black sword.

'*Fuil agus cnámh, rud éigin nua a dhéanamh,*' Gulla cried, voice filling the clearing.

'Blood and bone, to make something new,' Sig whispered beside him.

A silence in the clearing.

'Do it,' Gulla snarled.

And Fritha cut Gulla's throat, his two half-breed children stepping forwards and helping her catch the slumping body,

417

heaving it limp onto the table, on top of the still-twitching bat. Fritha sheathed her black sword and reached into some kind of bag at her feet.

'This cannot be?' Sig muttered besides Drem. 'What are they doing?'

Fritha held something aloft, what looked like a severed hand, fingers bunched into a fist, although it was dark and gleaming, and clearly heavy. She brandished it for all to see, a ripple of muttered awe escaping those gathered before her.

'*Fola agus cnámh an Asroth,*' Fritha cried out, and cast whatever it was onto the entwined corpses of Gulla and the bat.

'Dear Elyon above, no,' Sig whispered.

'What?' Drem hissed.

'Blood and bone of Asroth,' she breathed. 'It's Asroth's hand.'

'*Bheith ar cheann, a bheith rud éigin nua,*' Fritha cried out, the crowd before her joining their voices to hers, ringing out in the winter's night. The two corpses on the table convulsed and heaved, limbs and wings entangling, spasming, merging, flesh softening as if they were melting together, their mixed blood bubbling and seething.

'Become one, become something new,' Sig intoned.

Steam spread out from the entwined bodies on the table, a great cloud boiling out and settling upon the clearing. There was a squelching sound, a series of violent cracks ringing out, and then, slowly, the mist evaporated and a silence fell.

We should get out of here, now, Drem thought. *While all are focused on this dread act.*

But he couldn't tear his eyes from the scene before him, his body just as unresponsive.

Upon the blackened timber a body lay, curled like an unborn bairn still in the womb.

'Behold,' Fritha cried out in a voice that did not sound like her own. 'The first Revenant!'

Slowly, as all watched in hushed silence, the body moved, a

twitching that became a ripple of limbs and wings, and it stood. Gulla, but different. He seemed bigger, for one, more muscular, a strength barely contained within his frame. And his veins pulsed with a dark light. His head twitched, raptor-like, as he looked about, long fangs curling from desiccated lips.

'Who shall be my first-born, the first disciple?' Gulla said, even his voice changed, deeper, more resonant, though more bestial, too.

'You?' He pointed at Fritha.

She stared back at him.

'I am promised to another,' she said and, bowing her head, stepped back.

A man leaped forwards from amongst the acolytes that had followed him into the clearing, shrugging off his cloak. Drem recognized him immediately: scar-faced Burg, Wispy's leader.

'Choose me, Lord, I beg you for the honour,' he cried out, voice laced with hysteria and wonder.

Gulla's wings unfurled with a powerful snap, spreading wide and then curling inwards, wrapping around Burg, pulling him closer to Gulla, whose head dipped down, and then Gulla opened his mouth wide, long canines glinting red in the firelight, and he was biting into Burg's neck.

Burg screamed, a terror-filled shriek that gradually subsided into a weak mewling, slowly overcome by a new sound, a hideous, child-like suckling that echoed around the clearing, making Drem's skin crawl as if a thousand spiders were scuttling over him.

Burg's legs buckled and he slumped, Gulla taking his weight as easily as a corn doll, though Burg was still conscious, his eyes bulging and rapturous.

With a shudder Gulla disengaged from Burg's neck and lifted his head. He raised Burg up and placed him upon the table, the shaven-haired acolyte twitching and shivering as if he were caught in the grips of a fever. A single drop of blood ran from the puncture wounds in his neck.

'Drem,' Sig whispered. 'We must get back to Dun Seren. Byrne must hear of this, the Order must be warned,' she said. 'We cannot search for your friend Ulf, this is too important, too dangerous. The fate of the Banished Lands rests upon others knowing of this.'

Drem nodded, but a new hush had fallen over the clearing as Gulla beckoned another acolyte forwards.

We need some noise to cover our departure.

'Is he here?' Gulla called out to this new acolyte.

The figure pulled his hood back, another shaven-haired zealot, though this one was older.

It was Ulf the tanner.

'Yes, my Lord,' Ulf said.

'He's here, somewhere,' another voice called out from the crowd, stepping forwards. A woman this time, shaven-haired as well. It took a moment for Drem to recognize her.

Tyna, Ulf's wife, whom Drem had seen that morning, terrified for her husband's safety.

'Show him,' Gulla said to the acolytes spread about the clearing, bloodied lips spread in a sanguine smile.

More and more acolytes started to push their hoods back, more shaven heads, but they were faces that Drem recognized. Fear seized him, then, a paralysis that threatened to incapacitate him, for they were mostly faces he'd known for the last five years, neighbours, townsfolk, some he'd even considered friends.

Is everything and everyone a lie?

'It seems that half the town of Kergard is here,' Drem wheezed, finding it hard to breathe.

CHAPTER FORTY-FIVE

BLEDA

Bleda sat before the window in his chamber, the shutters rattling with the wind and beating rain. Behind him a few embers glowed on his hearth, all but burned out. He was restless, had been for some days now, and couldn't sleep. He knew the root of it, though it had taken him a while to admit it to himself.

I am worried about Riv.

For as long as he could remember, all he had thought about was the Sirak. About his kin, his dead brother and sister, his pride-battered mother. Arcona, the Grass Sea, nursing his grudges, he and Jin feeding each other's flames of hatred, their spite-filled mocking of all things Drassil, their disgust at any who were weak enough to show emotion, their bitter dreams of justice or vengeance, whatever name you gave it.

*But now I am worried about something – some*one *– else. Riv. My friend.*

It was a new feeling, having a friend. Caring about some-one who had not come from the Clans. Especially when that someone was as wild and emotionally unfettered as an unbroken colt.

But she *was* his friend, he could as much deny it as deny that water was wet, or the sky was blue. She had done some-thing unprecedented that day when she'd given him his bow. She'd forged a bond with him somehow, across the abyss of his pain and scorn.

So, she is my friend. I care about her welfare.

And that was why he'd rushed after her when he'd seen her carried from the weapons-field, almost a ten-night gone, why he'd hammered on her barrack doors, only to be told to go away, that she was unwell and could not have visitors.

Every day he had returned, everyday been told the same thing, whether by her mam or sister. Sometimes a different White-Wing. Even by the bull-muscled Vald once. He'd called Bleda back as he had turned to leave.

'*Don't take it personal,*' Vald had said. '*I've not seen her, either. None of us have. Only Aphra and Dalmae. Riv's got some kind of fever, so they're saying.*'

Somehow that had made Bleda feel slightly better.

Until Jin had spoken to him.

And she's not happy, either.

Jin had told him in no uncertain terms that he was humiliating her, and himself, with his pathetic fascination for Riv. Jin had called her a *bad-tempered barbarian*, which had almost made Bleda smile, a twitch of facial muscle that hadn't gone unnoticed by Jin, and had not helped to soothe her mood.

Perhaps Jin's right. I should be more concerned with my training, earning the right to lead my hundred, and their respect. Certainly Old Ellac had looked at him strangely every time that Bleda marched to Riv's barrack, for Ellac would accompany him, saying he was sworn to protect him, and Bleda had no reason to order him not to do so.

But as Bleda sat here in the dark, thinking these things through, he had come to a conclusion.

I don't care. Not about how I should feel, about how I should behave. Riv is my friend.

He sighed with that thought, a release of tension, and sat a little straighter in his chair.

A sound drew his attention, standing out from the wind and rain. He opened his shutters a crack and peered outside. A movement in the street below drew his eyes, a flicker through the swirling eddies of rain.

A person, weaving through the street as if they had drunk too much wine. A woman, fair hair plastered to their face.

Is that . . . ?

He leaned forwards, pulling the shutters wide.

Riv?

Other forms appeared behind her, following, gaining.

Before he'd realized what he was doing he'd pulled on his boots and was buckling his weapons-belt on, the familiar weight of his bow and quiver feeling like a missing limb returning. He wrapped a cloak about his shoulders and slipped out of his door.

CHAPTER FORTY-SIX

SIG

'Come out, Drem, trapper's son, forger of the Starstone Sword,' Gulla called out. 'And you, too, Sig of the Bright Star. I know you are here, somewhere. You cannot think to ride past a town of four hundred people upon your great bear and go unnoticed.'

Laughter hissed and rippled around the clearing.

'Long have you been a bane to us, a thorn in our flesh, and now you shall be plucked and thrown upon the fire, and we shall feast upon your bones, upon the flesh of your bear and upon the hearts and organs of your sword-brothers.'

As terrified and foolish as Sig felt right now, that made her mad.

There's a time for stealth, and there's a time to kill.

'Come out, come out,' Gulla chanted, laughing, the acolytes taking up the cry, ringing out as they spread through the clearing, turning, searching. A whisper of wings, and Gulla's children took to the air. With a victorious cry they spotted Sig and Drem and sped towards them. One was faster, the female. She thrust a spear down at them. Sig pushed Drem out of its way and grabbed the spear, pulling the half-breed Kadoshim down to her, grabbing a fist-full of leathery wing and then she was dragging herself upright, gripping the wing with both hands, setting her feet and twisting, turning, swinging the half-breed, smashing it with all of her prodigious strength into the roof, an explosion of turf, the creature loose-limbed for a few

424

heartbeats and then Drem kicked it in the stomach, sending it rolling off the roof.

An ear-splitting shriek and its brother was swooping towards them, wings tight as it dived, a sword in its hand. A whistle of air past Sig's ear and a spear was suddenly sprouting from the half-breed's chest. He swerved away, wings beating weakly, and then the wings folded and he crashed to earth.

Below them Gulla screamed.

'Ulfang!'

A roar of rage from the acolytes below as they surged towards the building Sig and Drem were standing upon.

Sig looked at Drem.

'Sometimes the only answer is blood and steel,' he said.

'Ach, but you're Olin's boy, and no denying.' Sig grinned.

'I loved my da,' Drem said.

Sig glanced quickly around, eyes lingering on the dark alleys that led to the wall, only a fast sprint away.

We could make a break for it. Would just need to get over the wall and to the trees beyond. To Hammer.

The beating of wings, and Gulla's daughter reappeared, her hand snaking out and grabbing Drem's ankle, heaving.

For a moment he teetered on the edge of the roof, and then he fell.

Sig's longsword hissed into her hand.

'TRUTH AND COURAGE,' she bellowed as she leaped into the crowd of acolytes surging around Drem, baying for their blood.

She swung her sword with both hands as she fell, carving a bloody path through leather, flesh and bone, the momentum turning her so that she crashed into a new mass of shaven-haired zealots, flattening some, breaking bones, scattering more. Drem was on the ground, pushing himself to his knees.

Sig was on her feet in a heartbeat and began swinging her sword in great two-handed loops. Limbs and heads sprang from bodies, blood jetting in fountains, men and women screaming.

Then something else was running at her, something twisted and misshapen, all jutting teeth and hooked talons. She swung at its head but it ducked beneath, raked her with too-long claws as its momentum carried it skidding past her, links in her chainmail shirt shattering, blood welling beneath, then it was twisting on its heels and coming at her again. Sig lunged for-wards, sword-tip the focal point of her entire body, like an extension of her, legs, torso, arms all flowing into the lunge. The Feral was coming at her so fast it could not adjust its momentum or trajectory, and so ran onto her sword, skewering itself through its broad chest, Sig's blade bursting out of its back in an explosion of gore.

She ripped her blade free, heard steel clash and glimpsed Drem blocking an overhead strike with a spear he must have wrestled from one of his attackers, twisting away from another acolyte stabbing at him, another circling to his flank. In two long strides Sig was there, kicking one in the knee, cartilage and bone snapping, and chopping into another's neck, a spray of blood as she wrenched her sword free.

Drem ducked a wild swing from the last one and buried his spear in the man's chest, left it there when it snagged on bone and drew his father's sword with one hand, a short axe in the other.

'Leave,' Sig barked at him, 'that way.' She jerked her head towards shadows and the wall, in the next heartbeat was run-ning, screaming her fury at a new wave of enemy, a looping swing of her sword scattering them, one ducking low beneath her sword and rising within her guard, too close for her sword. The momentum of her blow opened her right side, left her vulnerable, and she knew there was nothing she could do. The acolyte grinned as he stabbed with a long knife.

There was a wet thud and the acolyte dropped to his knees. Drem ran to it, hacked into its head with his sword, shards of bone erupting. He reached down and pulled his short axe from its chest.

426

He's supposed to be leaving, not hacking Kadoshim's followers into tiny pieces!

Sig ploughed on, knowing to slow down against numbers like this was to die. She slammed into more acolytes, a concussive impact that sent bodies spinning through the air. She stumbled but kept her feet, continued her relentless assault of stabbing and hacking and lunging, her arms drenched with their blood, and her enemies died about her, falling away screaming or silent, bloody and broken. But more kept coming. Blows rained down upon her, chainmail shirt turning some, a stutter of discordant thuds across her shield, red-fire cuts opening up on arms and legs, a dull thump on her shoulder, something more serious on her hip, a flash of pain and then tingling numbness.

No time for pain. No time for dying. Where's Gulla?

It was a maelstrom of blood and chaos, and she was the centre of that storm, carving limbs from bodies, trailing scarlet arcs of blood, leaving the dead in her wake. But there were just too many of them. She tried to keep moving, to be the storm personified, but bodies heaped around her, tripping, snaring, hands grabbing, clutching at her, blades stabbing, and slowly she felt her strength leaking from her along with her blood.

A blow across the back of her leg sent her stumbling to one knee, faces lunging at her and she smashed a fist into one, sent the acolyte crashing to the ground with a pulped nose and fewer teeth than he'd had a few heartbeats ago. A sharp pain in her back, someone trying to stab her, though it felt like her shirt of mail held. She blocked a sword-swing with her blade, rolled her wrists and slashed its tip across a throat, the acolyte, a woman this time, stumbling away gurgling, dropping to her knees as she tried in vain to stem the blood pumping through her fingers.

A crunch to her head, white lights exploding before her eyes, and she fell forwards into the snow-slush, churned with blood and mud, lost a grip of her sword. She lifted her head, blood sluicing into one eye, hand reaching blindly for her sword hilt.

A calm came upon her then, legs all around her, figures seeming to slow in their rush to kill her, as if they were wading through water.

This is my end, she thought, knowing the numbers were too great, even for her and her crew, and she'd given her orders to Cullen and Keld to remain separate, to get Drem out and back to Dun Seren, unless she gave the order, the signal for them to fight. And she hadn't. The numbers were too great alone, without feral man-beasts and whatever in the Otherworld it was that Gulla had become, and was infecting others with.

I hope they got Drem out, she thought as she tried to push herself back to her knees.

CHAPTER FORTY-SEVEN

RIV

Riv paused before the doors of Israfil's tower, leaning upon a wall for a moment. Lights flickered through shuttered windows, high above. A deep breath and shake of her head and she was running on, shouldering the doors open and stumbling through.

Where is everybody? His guards? Ben-Elim, White-Wings?

She hurried up an empty flight of stairs, dragging herself on, ever higher, until she saw a gleam of light outlining the chamber doors. Israfil's chambers, unguarded. Riv heard voices, dulled by the oak doors.

A hand clamped upon Riv's shoulder, turning her.

'What are you doing?' Aphra and her mam hissed at her.

'It has to end,' Riv said. 'Kol. He is a poison.'

Her sister stared at her, face twitching with so many emotions.

'Israfil must know,' Riv said.

'No!' her mother growled. 'You are sick, your mind clouded. You do not know what you are saying.'

'I know exactly what I'm doing,' Riv said. 'I know right from wrong,' and she made to go on.

Her mam grabbed her.

'You are not going in there,' she said, her eyes blazing.

'I am,' Riv grunted, pulling away, but her mother's grip was strong.

An arrow slammed into the wall between them, thrumming.

Bleda stood a score of paces down the stairway, a handful of
his honour guard about him, including the old one who was
missing a hand.

'Let go of her,' Bleda said.

Dalmae's grip tightened on Riv's arm, her other hand inch-
ing to her short-sword.

'Come away with me,' Dalmae said. 'It is for your own
good.'

'I cannot,' Riv said.

'The next arrow will pierce your thigh. I will not hit the
bone, so you may walk again, if I miss the artery. But you will
always limp.'

'Mam,' Riv said, quietly. 'Please. Kol is a poison.'

'But I am so scared for you and Aphra,' her mam said, a
quiver touching her voice, so strong and determined until now.

'Look what he is making us all do. You killed Garidas.'

Shame filled her mam's eyes then, and with a sigh she
dropped her head and let go of Riv's wrist.

'Thank you,' Riv said and ran on. She reached the doors
to Israfil's chamber, glimpsed a hooded figure standing close
by in the shadows of an alcove, but raised voices within the
chamber drew her on. She rushed through Israfil's doors,
the voices became louder, clearer. She staggered through the
waiting room and burst into his chamber, the doors swinging
wide, crashing into the walls, everyone within turning startled
heads to stare at her.

'It's Kol,' Riv yelled, 'Kol is the one.'

She stumbled to a stop.

Israfil was standing before the dark frame of his open
window, his hands clasped behind his back, face a mixture of
rage and disgust. At his side stood another Ben-Elim, Kushiel,
Riv recognized – one of Israfil's high council. Other Ben-Elim
were spread around the room in a loose circle, and in the centre

of the room stood Kol, a Ben-Elim either side of him, each gripping one of Kol's arms. White-Wings flanked them, a dozen, Garidas' men, Riv presumed.

'It's Kol,' Riv whispered.

Israfil regarded her a long moment, his face full of judgement and grief.

'I know it is Kol,' Israfil said to Riv. His expression softened for a moment as he looked at her.

'Sit, Riv. You look as if you are about to drop.'

'But there's more,' Riv said.

'Yes, there is, far more than I ever would have thought possible. Kol has just confessed all.'

Riv swayed on her feet, wanted to tell Israfil all she knew, anyway, in case Kol had kept anything back. But a wave of vertigo swept over her, the room tilting and spinning. She reached out a hand, found a chair and slumped into it.

'So, Kol of the Ben-Elim,' Israfil said, eyes fixing upon the scar-faced Ben-Elim, any vestige of compassion or kindness swept away by the disgust that filled him now. 'You confess to improper relations with mortals, more than one, over many years.'

'I do,' Kol said.

'You know the punishment for this crime?' Israfil said.

'Crimes,' Kol corrected. 'More than once, with more than one mortal. Many more. And yes, I know the punishment, though I think we should talk about one more chance.'

Israfil barked a shocked laugh.

'You will not be given a second chance. You will be executed at highsun, your head taken from your shoulders before all who dwell within these walls.'

'I wasn't talking about one more chance for me,' Kol said, no hint of a smile on his face now. 'I was talking about you.'

One of the Ben-Elim guards holding Kol released him, a glint of something in his fist, a stride to the other guard, a thrust, and the guard was collapsing, blood spurting from his throat, the first guard standing with a crimson blade in his fist. He threw the knife into the air and drew his sword, Kol grabbing the knife from the air and leaping with a burst of his wings at Kushiel.

For a moment Israfil was frozen with shock, then he was reaching for his own blade, as in the ring all about him Ben-Elim hurled themselves at their brothers, stabbing, killing.

Riv sat in her chair, stunned by what she was seeing, blood everywhere, Ben-Elim snarling, screaming, the White-Wings in the centre of the room forming a loose square, not knowing what to do, who to attack or defend. One of them gathered his wits and shouted a command, and then they were making for Israfil, the Lord Protector.

No, this is wrong, the whole world is going insane.

Shapes surged through the open window, more Ben-Elim, ones that Riv recognized from the circle that had formed around her as she'd sparred with Kol, just before she'd collapsed.

Kol was struggling with Kushiel, the two of them spiralling in the air, wings beating furiously, Kushiel gripping Kol's wrist with the knife, pummelling at Kol's face with his other fist. Ben-Elim that had swept in through the window grabbed Kushiel, one hacking at his wing with a sword. A scream, a burst of feathers and Kushiel was falling, Kol ripping his knife free, stabbing it into Kushiel's torso as they fell together, again and again and again.

A hand on Riv's arm: Aphra, with Dalmae behind her, then Bleda and his men. All of them were staring dumbfounded, their cold-faces forgotten. Other figures swept into the room, Ben-Elim, Lorina's White-Wings, some of Aphra's hundred too, all with weapons drawn, joining the fray. Riv glimpsed someone in cloak and cowl.

'Come, Riv,' Aphra said. 'While we can.'

'No,' Riv snarled, 'we have to help Israfil.' She surged to her feet, too quickly, her head spun; she swayed, stumbled forwards, pulling out of Aphra's grip, threading her way through the bloodshed and chaos.

Israfil was trading blows with two Ben-Elim, stabbed one through the shoulder as he rose higher, the other swinging and catching his ankle.

Riv skirted the White-Wings trying to reach Israfil, who was beset by Ben-Elim from above. She crashed into two Ben-Elim, sent them both tumbling to the ground and she reeled away, saw Kol fly at Israfil, slamming into the Lord Protector from behind, slicing at a wing, Israfil crying out and falling, crashing to the ground. Kol landed behind him, Israfil trying to rise, one wing twisted and limp, a spray of blood splattering his white feathers. Kol stamped on Israfil's sword hand, the crack of a wrist breaking, and grabbed Israfil's hair, yanking his head high, resting his knife blade against the Lord Protector's throat.

Riv yelled and ran at them, snatching up a short-sword from a dead White-Wing as she ran, raising her blade for a swing that would split Kol's head. Kol heard her scream and stared at her, part-screamed, part-laughed a feral challenge back at her.

Something crashed into Riv, sent her sprawling to the ground. She rolled, tried to stand, but only made it to all fours, the world a whirling piece of flotsam in a chaotic sea. She blinked, desperate for the spinning to stop, searching for who or what had slammed into her.

It was the cowled figure she'd glimpsed as she entered the chamber, striding now to Israfil and Kol. It stopped before them both, threw off its cowl and cloak, revealing a man with two huge wounds upon his back, scabbed, weeping blood and pus.

A Ben-Elim with his wings taken.

Adonai.

He just stared at Israfil, spoke no words. And then he was drawing a sword and plunging it into the Lord Protector's chest.

Riv screamed.

This cannot be happening!

Somehow she was on her feet, eyes fixed upon Kol, all else a peripheral blur, anger, no, a white-hot rage at Israfil's murder the only thing keeping her upright and conscious. She swung her blade at Kol. He saw, a flicker of surprise as he twisted, blocked with his knife, sending her blow wide.

'Stop,' he said to her. 'It is over, Israfil is dead, there is no more to fear.'

'Murderer, Lore-breaker,' she yelled, stabbing her short-sword at Kol's throat. He swayed, sidestepping her.

'Don't do this, Riv,' he said. 'You are distraught, fevered, you do not mean this, and I do not wish to kill you. Great things are ahead, and you can be part of them.'

She snarled and chopped at his ribs; this time he was too slow, her blade slicing through feathers, its tip grazing a red line across Kol's shoulder as he leaped away.

He looked at the blood leaking from his wound, glared at her.

'I'm warning you, girl, you can be as dead as Israfil if you wish.'

He has changed everything, changed our world, broken every codex of the Lore, for his own selfish desire and to save his skin.

She lunged at him, a short, powerful stab straight at Kol's heart.

He deflected her blade with his knife, sent it swinging wide, and backhanded her with a fist, lifting her from the ground, sending her spinning, weightless for a few heartbeats, then slamming back down to earth again. She rolled onto her back, felt her consciousness flutter away on black wings, tried desperately to cling to it, saw Kol stride after her, knife in his hand.

'So be it,' Kol snarled at her. 'There are plenty more where you came from.'

Through speckled vision Riv saw someone else step between them, attacking Kol, a White-Wing with a short-sword, a flurry of blows, for a dozen heartbeats Kol struggling to defend himself, a red line opening across his cheek, down his arm, white feathers slashed and falling about Riv. He retreated a few steps, beat his wings, rocking his opponent back towards Riv, ducked an off-balance slash and stepped in closer, punching his knife into his attacker's armpit, twisting deeper. A spray of blood as he ripped his blade free, a sigh, and his attacker collapsed, head rolling to stare at Riv with lifeless eyes.

It was her mam.

CHAPTER FORTY-EIGHT

DREM

Drem stared in horror as he saw Sig fall to the ground, one hand grasping blindly for her sword.

No, she cannot fall. We have only just found each other.

It was strange, little more than a day shared between them, but Drem felt as if he'd known Sig all of his life, felt she was kin to him, and the pain he experienced at seeing her fall was all the greater because of that.

He raised his sword over his head and bellowed.

'TRUTH AND COURAGE,' his da's battle-cry.

Mine, now, he thought, *if what Sig and the others said is true.*

He was standing over the body of some half-man beast whose corpse he'd hacked into bloody ruin, the only way to get it to stop trying to bite, claw and chew him. He'd slipped into a frenzy as he had struck it down, fuelled by horror and fear at what was attacking him, felt as if he was walking through some living, waking nightmare.

He ran towards Sig, or where he thought she was, too many of the enemy swirling around for him to see her in the mad dancing shadows made by the torches and wind and starlight.

And he heard his battle-cry echoed back at him.

'Truth and Courage,' a voice cried, a figure leaping onto the table of horrors, an acolyte pushing back a hood to reveal a freshly shaven head, sword and shield in his hand.

Cullen!

Even as Drem saw him, the young warrior was swinging his sword, dancing along the table, avoiding sword and spear thrusts, grasping hands, snapping jaws and slashing claws, chopping and stabbing as he went, acolytes and Ferals falling, more trying to scramble up with him, Cullen's boot, sword and shield boss slamming into them, denying them. Where Sig slew like a force of nature, a strength and inevitability built into her every move, Cullen fought with a blend of skill and joy, smiling, laughing as he drew blood-soaked lines, a precision and mastery to his every move so that it was almost like watching art. A deadly art.

Drem reached the acolytes swarming around Sig's prone form, arms rising and falling. He swung his sword and short axe, screams and grunts, blood spraying as he cut and carved his way through them. Then the ones in front of him leaped into the air.

No, not leaping, thrown.

And Sig rose from amongst them, blood sheeting her face, a flap of skin hanging from her cheek, one eye swollen closed, the rest of her body a similar miscellany of wounds, shield upon her back dented and splintered, but she grinned to see him, blood on her teeth, her sword in her fist.

'You're not supposed to be here,' she growled.

'Friends are a rare thing,' he said to her.

They fought back to back, then, turning, stabbing, cutting, Drem's limbs growing leaden, his very bones aching as blows shivered up his arm, breath a hot rasp in his throat.

Gulla's daughter descended upon them, swooping, stabbing, wheeling away. Sig snatched a weighted net from her belt, swinging it around her head like a lasso and releasing. It wrapped around the half-breed, wings and all, the lead weights' momentum swinging them in snaring loops, and the creature crashed to the ground.

A space cleared around them, hooded, shaven-haired warriors pausing, panting, bleeding. Sig spat a glob of blood. Drem saw a figure on the edge of the clearing, hooded in acolyte's robes, emerging from the shadows and stabbing another acolyte, then slipping back into the darkness.

What?

A figure stepped into the space around Sig and Drem, slender and tall, fair hair shaved from her head.

Fritha, the Starstone Sword in her hand.

She stopped before Drem, out of reach of his blade, held a hand up to the acolytes behind her, a command. For a long moment she regarded Drem with her sheer blue eyes, which he had once thought bright and beautiful. Now he just thought they were cold. A bandage was wrapped diagonally around her shoulder and back.

'Put your weapons down,' she said to him. 'You cannot win. Put them down, and live.'

'What, to become one of those half-men?' He shuddered. 'Or like that?' He nodded to Burg's form on the table, still lying there, curled up like a bairn, twitching and jerking. Cullen fought nearby; silhouetted figures were climbing onto the table, pushing Cullen away from Burg.

'That would be too great an honour. But no, not a Feral. My shieldman, maybe.' She smiled at him, then, and it did not have the effect upon him that it used to.

'You lied to me,' Drem said, thinking of all the deceptions, the smiles and lies behind those eyes.

'I saved your life,' she said. 'I could have killed you, let them slay you in the forest. I forbade them.'

'Why?'

'I know who you are, Drem. Son of Olin and Neve, nephew to Byrne, High Captain of the Order of the Bright Star. You would be a valued prize, especially if you stood at my side.'

'That'll never happen,' Drem grunted.

'All you have to do is open your eyes and see the truth.'

'The truth?' Drem spat.

'Aye, that all is not as the Ben-Elim tell you. That *they* are the great evil, not the Kadoshim.'

'I know the truth well enough when I see it,' Drem snarled. 'Only lies and murder from you, truth and friendship from my friends.'

'Ha, you see,' Fritha said, 'I told you. There is something about you, Drem ben Olin. Something innocent, and loyal. Like a faithful hound. Once you give yourself, your loyalty, it would be unswerving, I think. I would like that. I am destined for great things, you know.' She smiled again, a hint of the future in it, a promise of glory and greatness.

Drem ben Olin. That is who I am. My father's son.

He thought of how he had stayed to find her, that day in the forest, instead of leaving with his da. His da had been alive, then, and was dead, now. Because of that decision. Because of her.

'You are a murderer, Fritha, and I am going to kill you for it. Now, or another time.' He shrugged. 'Justice, for my da.'

'A pity,' she said.

'And I am going to take that black sword from your dead fingers and use it to carve Asroth's head from his shoulders.'

'Blasphemy,' she hissed at him, a crouched snarl, the first real emotion he'd seen from her, and with a wave of her hand the acolytes surged forwards.

Drem stabbed and swung his sword, used his axe more defensively, or to chop at fingers, wrists or arms that came too close in the crush. He was no mighty warrior like Sig or Cullen, but he had spent many years learning how to wield an axe and knife from his da, and the rage he felt for his da's murderer gave him new strength and speed. And these acolytes, while many of them clearly had some blade-craft, they were no weapons-masters like Sig and Cullen. Now that the frenzied blood-rush of battle's first moments had passed, Drem saw that some of them were hesitating, holding back, a glimmer of fear in their eyes. He lunged, stabbed a man through the throat and kicked the body away. It fell back into those behind, a momentary lull, giving Drem a few moments to fill his lungs. A crash drew his eyes to Cullen, still on the table-top, though a Feral man was upon it too. Cullen had kicked one of the torches into the crowd, flames catching in a cloak, spreading, men screaming, and he'd swept up another torch in his shield-hand as the Feral surged at him, all strength and snarl and saliva. Cullen slipped to the side, and as the creature barrelled past him, shoved his burning torch into its torso, flames catching in the tattered rags that passed for clothing, and he pushed it hard with his shield, sending the creature careening from the table into a knot of acolytes. Flames and snarls exploded, acolytes screaming.

Cullen grinned, pleased with himself.

Something moved on the table behind him. A figure shifting, a shadow rising.

Burg.

But not Burg. He was changed, as Gulla had been, a pulsing, rippling sense of malice and vitality to him, like a black halo.

And there is something wrong with his mouth. As if it had grown, too big for his face, teeth appearing sharper, needle-like, and far too many of them.

Cullen sensed something, maybe heard a movement, and spun on his feet to face this new foe. Burg took a few steps, unsteady jerks and twitches, and Cullen danced forwards and buried his sword in his belly.

Burg curled around the blade, then grinned, standing tall.

Cullen tried to rip his sword free but Burg grabbed his sword hand, a blur of movement, and Burg was grasping Cullen, lifting him high over his head, Cullen smashing his shield into Burg's face, with little effect. And then Cullen was flying through the air, crunching to the ground and rolling, coming to a halt a dozen paces from Drem and Sig.

They fought their way to him, stood either side, and slowly Cullen rose on shaky legs.

'Well, *he's* a lot stronger than he looks.'

Drem gave Cullen his axe and drew his bone-handled seax.

'You've got the ambush you hoped for, or a trap, at least,' Sig growled at Cullen as she shrugged her shield from her back onto her arm. They formed a loose circle, Sig and Cullen with shields raised, acolytes all around them, Ferals prowling at the periphery.

'Aye.' Cullen grinned. 'And it's one that's busy stabbing them in the arse!' He lunged forwards adder-fast, axe singing, crunching into the forehead of an acolyte. 'Or the head,' he amended. 'Though for the life of me I do not know how they can stand this,' Cullen cried, rubbing the bristles of his shaved head. 'It's so cold! And it's sure as eggs not going to help me with the ladies back in Dun Seren!'

Drem felt a laugh bubbling up within him, even with death a heartbeat away.

I like my new family.

He wasn't too hopeful on how long they'd get to spend in each other's company, though. They'd managed to stay alive this long because of Sig's ferocity and perpetual movement, and Cullen's position upon the huge table, where he'd been able to elude and leap and dance over every lunge and stab at him. Now, however, they were encircled by a crowd of their enemies.

I think we're going to die here.

CHAPTER FORTY-NINE

BLEDA

Bleda stared into what had once been Israfil's chamber, now more akin to a battlefield. Ben-Elim fought Ben-Elim, White-Wings fought one against the other, and in the midst of it, weaving through them all, he'd watched in horror as Riv had hurled herself at Kol. He'd nocked an arrow and aimed, but bodies were swirling around the chamber like twigs in a hurricane.

In stupefaction he'd watched as Riv's mam and sister leaped into the fray, her mam reaching Riv first, stepping in front of Riv to protect her from a furious Kol. As she fell dead beside her daughter Bleda moved, as if released from a spell. He strode towards the maelstrom, but then a hand grabbed his arm.

'Stay,' Old Ellac said to him, half a dozen more of Bleda's honour guard were behind the old warrior. Something had alerted Ellac to Bleda's stealthy exit of their chambers as he'd set out after Riv, and Bleda had not minded their company. Something about this stormy night had felt sinister and laced with malice.

'I owe her a debt,' Bleda said, the quickest, no, only way for Ellac to understand what he was doing. He pulled his arm free and padded into the melee, an arrow loosely nocked on his bow. Ellac and the others followed as Bleda weaved through the carnage, the stench of blood and faeces thick in the air. For a few moments he lost sight of Riv and Kol, then saw Aphra reach them, the warrior throw herself to the ground beside her sister and mother, then look up at Kol, who was shouting orders to Ben-Elim, orchestrating the madness, though Bleda could tell it was swinging towards Kol and his rebels.

A coup amongst the Ben-Elim, the puritanical Lore-Givers.

Never before had he thought of rival factions amongst the Ben-Elim; it was something that he filed away for further consideration at a more opportune time.

If I come out of this alive.

He was close now, could hear Aphra's wail of grief as she held her dead mam in her arms, for a terror-filled moment thought that Riv was dead, too, but then he saw her chest rising and falling, though her eyes were closed tight.

Unconscious, then.

And he heard Kol shout orders to Adonai, the wingless Ben-Elim who had killed Israfil.

'Take that little bitch prisoner,' he cried, 'throw her in a cell until I have time to deal with her.'

'No!' Aphra yelled.

'She tried to kill me,' Kol snarled at her, 'I cannot ignore that. I am the Lord Protector, now.'

The dark-haired warrior strode to Riv, bent down and grabbed a fistful of her short hair.

And Bleda loosed, his arrow thumping into Adonai's chest. As the Ben-Elim reached to pluck at the feathers, another arrow punched into his throat. Four more arrows slammed into his torso in rapid succession from Bleda's men. Adonai toppled backwards, crashing to the ground.

'You dare!' Kol roared.

'There's another one here for you,' Bleda snarled, nocking a new arrow.

Kol stepped away, into the madness of the battle.

'Take her,' Aphra yelled. 'Get Riv out of here.'

Bleda looked from Kol to Aphra to Riv.

'Please,' Aphra cried.

'Where?' he said.

Two White-Wings converged on them, Bleda shifting his aim, but he recognized them as Riv's friends, the bull-man, Vald, and the stick, Jost.

Aphra yelled directions to Bleda, and orders to Vald and Jost. Then she stood and drew her sword, stalking into the mayhem. Vald swept Riv up in his arms and turned to Bleda.

'Lead the way, Dead-Eye.'

And Bleda did, his honour guard driving a wedge through the chamber, and soon they were spilling out into the corridor beyond Israfil's chamber.

The sounds of battle echoed from all directions, the chamber behind them, the street below.

Ellac stepped close, whispered in his ear.

'We could use this. Strike now . . .'

Bleda remembered the words of his mother, whispered into his ear on Drassil's weapons-field. He looked at Ellac and his men, at Jost and Vald, finally at Riv.

He smiled at Riv, an act of will, intentional, knew Ellac and his men would be shocked.

'I'm taking Riv to safety,' he said, then turned and led them through the chamber, down a stairwell and out into the din of battle.

CHAPTER FIFTY

SIG

Fire was blazing through the clearing, great gusts of wind sending flames flaring. They caught in a timber building, roaring into hungry life, blazing red and orange light onto the clearing, clouds of black smoke rolling across them. Between smoke and flame Sig saw Gulla. He was hunched over another acolyte, drinking blood from her throat, as he had done with Burg. Other acolytes were curled upon the floor, spasming and twitching in some convulsion of rebirth while still others were spread about them in a defensive half-circle.

Guarding them while they are vulnerable.

She glimpsed a shadowed figure on the far side of the table, sprinting towards the boulder that had been turned into gaols for those experimented upon but obviously untrusted. The figure's hood blew back as he ran, another shaved head, but Sig recognized Keld, his beard still wild. He ran to the first gaol, struck at the lock and chain with his axe, a burst of sparks as it shattered, Keld ripping the chain away and hurling the barred door wide. He ran to the next gate and hacked at the lock, this one snapping more quickly, ripped the door open, dashed to the next door as things burst from the open gaols behind him. More cells and chains, more Feral beasts leaping, shambling, snarling from their gaols, throwing themselves into the acolytes that encircled Sig, Drem and Cullen.

'NOW,' Sig yelled at the top of her lungs, her voice ringing out, at the same time the three of them surging through a cloud of smoke towards the enemy before them, smashing them to the ground with their shields, trampling over them, carving them to bloody ruin. In the distance Keld's voice was crying out 'Truth and Courage,' taken up by Sig, Cullen and Drem.

The clearing burst into chaos anew, a place of fire and smoke, steel and blood, ringing with the screams and snarls and growlings of half-men and the dying, and through it all Sig and her companions cut a bloody path out of the clearing. Abruptly they found themselves with no enemy before them. Keld erupted from a cloud of black smoke, a wild grin on his face, and then Sig was running, down a flame-lit gap between two buildings, the others close behind.

Within heartbeats they were at the palisaded wall, Cullen racing up a stairwell, but a burst of wind and Sig's warning shout made him pause – a spear hurled from the sky above thrumming into the stairs just before him. She raised her shield and caught another spear aimed straight at Drem's heart. Sig hacked the shaft away, but the blade still embedded in her shield dragged her arm down. She dropped it on the ground. Gulla's half-breed daughter alighted on the palisade walkway.

'Not so easily,' she hissed, voice as twisted as her body.

Feet thudded behind them, Sig turning to see acolytes and Feral men swarming after them. They stopped a dozen paces from Sig and her companions and a figure stepped to their fore, the shaven-haired woman, Fritha, the Starstone Sword in her hand. Wings beat and a Kadoshim landed beside her: Gulla, a spear in his fist, veins in his body dark and bloated, even his wings seeming to be heavy, weighted with the blood he had consumed. Crimson lines trailed down his pale chin.

'You cannot leave us,' Gulla said. 'I have someone to introduce you to.'

Behind the swarming acolytes a dark shadow loomed, wider and taller than Sig. A great bear appeared, muzzle and head emerging from the darkness, a hint of madness in its eyes. And

446

upon its back sat a giant, broad, wrapped in leather and fur, still masked by the shadows. A war-hammer was slung across its back.

'Ah, well,' Sig snarled, 'if it's time for introductions, let me introduce you to Hammer.'

Sig put two fingers to her lips and whistled, and to her right the palisaded wall burst asunder, timber exploding in a spray of splinters, and Hammer's two front paws crashed into the compound. Her dark fur was covered by a coat of chainmail, harnessed and buckled with leather, gleaming and sparkling in the starlight like a coat of diamonds. She roared a challenge, spraying spittle. Acolytes scattered like flotsam before a tidal wave. With a swipe of her paw she eviscerated one that moved too slowly, her head lunging forwards, jaws grabbing another, the sound of bones cracking, a scream cut short.

The half-breed on the palisade took to the air as it collapsed beneath her feet and swooped on Hammer, hurling a spear, but it was stopped by her coat of mail, skittering harmlessly away.

The other bear roared a challenge of its own, the giant upon its back shouting a command, and it lumbered forwards, charging at Hammer, who was in no mind to stand around waiting for it. She leaped into a charge of her own, acolytes diving in all directions to escape being trampled and broken. Sig ran too, a few long steps, but then Gulla was flying at her, acolytes swarming behind him, and she was ducking swords and spears, sweeping blades aside with her own, barrelling her shoulder into one acolyte, throwing him into the side of a building, where he slid to the ground, twitching.

The two bears came together with bone-crunching force, teeth snapping, claws raking, bellowing. Sig saw Hammer draw first blood, her claws gouging red gullies through the flesh of the other bear's shoulder.

All around Sig battle exploded, Cullen, Keld and Drem drawing tight together, defending against Kadoshim from above and acolytes that had managed to find a way around the two bears as they were busy turning the encampment into splintered ruin. A building disintegrated as the two animals crashed into it, a fountain of shattered timber raining down upon them all.

Sig took the head from a Feral as it leaped at her, body and head spinning in different directions, and strode after Hammer, but something slammed into her side, sending her tumbling to the ground, the half-breed, wings flexing. She had a flat, broad face, hair shaved and growing out in dark clumps, her body heavily muscled. She snapped her teeth at Sig, more animal than human.

A hand rested on her shoulder, dragging her back, throwing her into the darkness, and Gulla stepped in front of her.

'She is mine,' the Kadoshim growled.

Sig made to rise and he kicked her in the head, sending her rolling, grabbed her by her mail shirt and dragged her to her feet, stronger than she would ever have imagined, even for a Kadoshim.

'I have the blood and bone of Asroth flowing through my body now,' he snarled, his jaws opening wide, teeth gleaming.

Fear hit Sig then, a jolt like jumping into ice-cold water as she knew what Gulla was about to do to her. She struggled but his grip held her, those teeth moving inexorably towards her throat.

And then a squawking streak of feathers, beak and talon was hurtling into Gulla's face, Rab scratching, pecking, gouging with beak and claw.

Gulla dropped Sig and reeled away, Rab furiously battering at the Kadoshim, raining insults upon him as well as pain. Gulla's hands grabbed at the white crow, but Rab flapped away, something slimy hanging from its beak, Gulla screaming, a hand over one eye, blood leaking through his fingers and he stumbled into the shadows. An acolyte moved on Sig as she swept her sword from the ground, a spear stabbing at her heart, but a mass of fur and muscle slammed into the acolyte – Fen, taking advantage of the hole Hammer had smashed through the wall. The hound's jaws clamped around the acolyte's throat as they both tumbled to the ground in a tangle of limbs. As they rolled to a stop, Fen stood upon the corpse of her victim, raised his head and howled.

Sig heard Hammer cry out in pain. She stumbled after the sound, through a tableau of destruction, buildings flattened, half-torn down, beams and detritus everywhere.

The two bears were tearing at each other with tooth and claw, Hammer looking much better on that account because of her chainmail coat, though it was torn to strips in places. The other bear was dragging one front leg, its head hanging, spittle and blood dripping, though its spirit was strong and it lifted its head to bite at Hammer's neck. What had caused Hammer's cry of pain was the giant upon the other bear's back as it leaned in its saddle and swung its war-hammer at Hammer's head. She shifted her weight, seeing the blow coming, so that it skimmed her shoulder instead, but there was still power in the blow, and Hammer was battered and bruised, weakening. Slow.

The giant raised its war-hammer high, over its head.

Sig swept up a splintered shard of wood, long as a spear and drew her arm back to throw. Aimed, her arm snapping forwards.

The giant's bear moved, shifting him from the shadows into red-flame light.

It was Gunil.

It cannot be!

But it was, unmistakably. His dark hair, opposite to Varan, his brother, his flat nose from the pugil ring.

The splintered wood left her hand, flying unerringly towards the giant. Towards Gunil, her friend and lover, whom she had thought dead for sixteen years. The makeshift spear hit him high, in the chest or shoulder, Sig could not tell, only knew that he was hurled from his saddle in a spray of blood, disappearing behind the bear into billowing clouds of smoke.

Sig took a step towards him.

'SIG!' Keld, screaming for her to come. He was gesturing wildly at her, standing outside the encampment, just beyond the hole in the wall Hammer had made. Cullen and Drem were with him, darkness and freedom beyond, waiting for her. For a few moments they had a chance to escape, acolytes scattered by Hammer, Fen and the others, Gulla and his spawn nowhere to be seen.

Sig looked back to where Gunil had disappeared, no sign of him amongst the smoke and flame, saw his bear stumble and fall before Hammer's clawed blows.

'HAMMER,' Sig yelled, 'TO ME,' and she began to run, back towards Keld and the others, to freedom. The bear took one last contemptuous look at its cowed foe, then turned and ran after Sig, outpacing her, converging on the hole in the wall.

A figure stepped out in front of Sig, wreathed in smoke and flame, a black sword in her hand.

Fritha, Drem called you.

Sig ran at her, raised her sword, not breaking her stride. Swung.

Fritha moved faster than Sig would have thought possible, twisting away, ducking down, beneath Sig's sword-swing, pivoting around Sig as she hurtled past.

Ah, well, it's time to go. We'll be back with Byrne and a thousand Bright Stars for that sword.

Something slammed into the back of her leg, high, felt like a punch.

She ran on.

In front of her Keld's mouth opened, his face twisting. Cullen shouted something. Sig couldn't quite tell what, as her ears were ringing. She felt weak, suddenly, so very tired. Stumbled, used her sword to stay upright, ran on, or tried, her right leg feeling heavy, not doing what she was telling it. She looked down as she stumbled on, saw her leg was drenched with dark blood.

My blood.

She could feel the strength leaking from her, stumbled on a dozen paces and fell into Keld and Drem's arms as they ran to her, meeting her in the gap in the shattered wall, only a timber post remaining. The two of them could barely hold Sig up, lowered her gently to the ground. Cullen tore strips from his cloak, tied them high about her thigh, took a sheathed dagger to twist within the knot, a field tourniquet. Keld crouched to look at the wound, his face telling Sig everything.

She knew, anyway. To bleed like that, the shock she could feel tremoring through her body already, it was one of the kill-points, the artery in the groin.

I'm bleeding out. Nothing will stop it. Haven't got long.

Hammer's scarred head appeared, muzzle sniffing Sig's face, nudging her to get up.

'Not this time, my old friend,' Sig said, tugging on the fur of Hammer's cheeks.

'Go,' she said to Keld, Cullen and Drem. 'You must get back to Dun Seren, tell Byrne.'

'There's no way in all the seven hells of the Otherworld that we're leaving you here,' Cullen said.

'I'm dead, boy,' Sig snarled, a wave of dizziness rocking her. 'You'll not give your life for someone that's already dead.'

'No.' Cullen shook his head, tears welling in his eyes. 'No.' A denial, not a refusal. Keld just stood, head bowed. Drem looked as if his world had just ended.

'Dun Seren. It's an order. Hammer can take you all. She's your only chance.'

Shouts and yells from acolytes and Ferals as they gathered, the beat of wings, a spear hissing down at them, Cullen chopping it from the sky.

Sig dragged herself to the timber post, began pulling herself up.

She did not look at her friends, but felt hands helping her regain her feet. It was Drem. 'Unbuckle my sword-belt,' she said to him, and he did without question. She threaded it around the post and wrapped it around her waist, cinched it tight.

'Buckle me up,' she asked, and Cullen did.

'Sword.'

Keld put it in her hand.

'Now get out of here,' she said to them, patted Cullen's cheek and brushed fingertips across Keld's face. He looked as if he planned on disobeying her last order.

'They need you,' she said, a whisper. 'I'm trusting in you, my friend.'

Tears filled Keld's eyes and he swatted them away. A twist of his lips as he nodded. Sig squeezed Drem's hand, then she turned to face the oncoming enemy, her body all but filling the remaining gap.

The rustle of wings, and Rab alighted upon Sig's shoulder.

'*Poor Sig,*' Rab said. The crow ran a bloodstained beak through Sig's hair.

'Brave Rab,' Sig said. 'Guide them home. Make sure Byrne hears of this.'

Rab croaked mournfully.

The scuff of boots climbing Hammer.

'Sig,' Keld called down to her from the bear's back, and she looked back at them, her vision swimming.

'We shall never forget,' he said, clenching a fist over his heart.

'We shall never forget,' Cullen and Drem repeated.

'My brothers,' Sig said, a smile twitching her lips.

'Hammer,' she called, loud as she could, even her jaw feeling heavy. 'Take my friends home.'

The great bear lifted her head and roared at the night sky, and then she was turning and shambling into the darkness, breaking into a run. Rab launched into the air, quickly disappearing.

'The trees, where Kadoshim can't follow,' Sig whispered, then turned to face her enemy.

A shape loomed out of the smoke and flame, a shaven-haired acolyte, sword stabbing for her heart. Somehow Sig managed to swing her blade, up, smashing the sword away and opening the acolyte's face from jaw to ear. He fell away gurgling.

Two more, one Sig let the weight of her blade smash into his skull, dropping him without a sound. The second one stabbed Sig in the stomach, Sig headbutting her, nose exploding.

Her fingers were tingling, sword so heavy, and Sig slumped against the belt strapping her to the post. Her head lolled.

Figures gathered before her: acolytes, Fritha, a Feral, growling as it stalked the shadows. Gulla was there, a bandage wrapped around one eye, stained red.

Sig smiled to see his wound, felt saliva drool from her mouth.

Something loomed behind them, taller, broader, a giant stepping close, a bloody wound between shoulder and chest.

'Gunil,' Sig whispered.

He stood and stared at her. There was a glimmer in his eyes that spoke of memory, but it was quickly replaced by something else, a sick half-madness, like his bear's.

'What have you done to him?'

'I found him floating face-down at the bottom of a waterfall, closer to death than I thought possible,' Gulla said. 'He betrayed you at Varan's Fall. Hated his brother and so gave you up to us. The ambush was his design.'

'You . . . lie,' Sig groaned.

Gulla smiled, too many teeth glistening. 'He has been a useful tool since then, and no doubt will be again.'

'You could turn her,' Fritha said to Gulla, her head cocked at an angle, studying Sig. 'Two giants in your service.'

'There's no blood left in her to drink,' Gulla said.

Sig's sword slipped from her fingers.

'Very well, then.' Fritha stepped forwards and rested the point of her black blade against Sig's sternum. 'Gunil, help me,' Fritha said. The giant stepped closer and wrapped his huge fist around Fritha's, who looked Sig in the eye and smiled.

'Gunil,' Sig whispered, could barely believe that he was standing before her. It gave her more pain than the thousand wounds her body had taken.

Fritha laughed, and then she and Gunil pushed on the sword, slowly.

Sig hardly felt the blade enter her body. She couldn't feel her hands, arms, legs, everything going numb, drawing in to some central point, deep inside. Her vision speckled, darkened at the edges. She felt some pain, then, grunted with it, saw that at least half the blade's length was sheathed inside her flesh.

'Hold,' Fritha said, still staring into Sig's eyes, savouring her pain, her death. Gunil stopped.

'We shall hunt down your friends. Kill them slowly, like this. Or turn them,' Fritha said, cold as the starlit night.

No you won't, Sig thought.

She shouted at Fritha, then, as the world narrowed to a single point of light, though it came from her lips as little more than a whisper.

'Truth and Courage.'

CHAPTER FIFTY-ONE

RIV

Riv opened her eyes. She was lying on her back, looking up. Above, she could see the thick timber beams of a roof. A beam of sunlight, motes of dust. She heard birdsong. The familiar creak of branches, scraping, soughing in a breeze.

Where am I? Not home. Not my barrack. Not even Drassil, I think. Though she was not sure how she knew that.

And then the weight of memory fell upon her.

Kol, Israfil.

Mam.

Tears leaked from her eyes, rolled down into her hair. She didn't know how long she stayed like that, crying silent tears, but it must have been a while, because the beam of sunlight had shifted when next she looked. Then a new sound, a baby crying. She rolled over, onto her side; her back felt odd. Heavy. Numb. A big feather floated close to her face, speckled grey.

A feather-stuffed mattress! No wonder I feel like I've slept for a moon.

She stretched, muscles shifting, and ran a hand through her hair. It felt longer. The longest it had ever been.

A fair-haired woman was sitting close by, half in shadow, a baby wrapped in swaddling held in the crook of one arm, feeding at her breast.

'Hello, Riv,' the woman said.

It was Fia.

Riv tried to sit up, but her back felt strange, as if it were heavier than it should be, dragging her back onto the bed, and then there was the thud of boots, and hands were taking hers, helping her up, faces dipping into her vision. Vald, grinning, Jost, eyes wider, odd. Staring at her. She looked at herself, saw she was wearing breeches and a linen shirt, baggy and shapeless.

'Where am I?' Riv asked, closing her eyes for a moment, feeling light-headed. She blinked them open, realized she felt better, physically, than she had for such a long time.

The fever is gone. And I feel stronger, full of energy.

'A woodsman's hut, deep in Forn,' Fia said.

'Safe,' Vald said.

Jost was still staring at her, all white-eyed wonder.

'What's wrong?' she said. He was starting to annoy her.

'Wrong? Nothing,' Jost said. He looked away, eyes almost instantly drifting back to her. No, behind her.

'What is it, then?' Riv snapped.

'Well . . . you've got wings,' Jost said in wonder.

'Don't be an idi—' Riv started. Then she stopped. Another feather drifted idly down to the ground. She looked over her shoulder.

The arch of a wing reared there, big. She took a staggering step forwards and the wing followed her. Her head snapped around to the other shoulder, another wing there, too.

'I've got wings,' she said, fear and wonder mixed.

Without knowing how, a subconscious movement, she unfurled them, a shifting of muscle, a ripple of feathers, and her wings snapped wide, almost filling the room.

'Not in here!' Fia laughed as pots and plates went tumbling and smashing, and somehow Riv furled them back in with a snap. Vald and Jost led her outside, Fia following behind her, and Riv stepped out onto a timber porch, a woodland glade around them. The wings felt heavy upon her back, a shifting of weight and balance that she wasn't used to. Horses whickered somewhere nearby and she saw a figure sitting on a tree stump, tending to a bow on his lap.

It was Bleda.

He looked up at her and smiled, and to Riv it looked like the most natural thing in the world. She smiled back at him.

Hesitantly, she stepped bare-footed onto cool, soft grass and moss.

Then she unfurled her wings – *My wings!* – a smooth ripple of muscles expanding, and looked at herself. Her wings were spread wide, almost as wide as the woodsman's hut. They were not gleaming white, like the Ben-Elim, but a soft, dappled grey.

Riv felt a thousand emotions surge through her – amazement, fear, wonder, worry, confusion, a moment of blind terror – all wrapped around the grief of losing her mam, which ran through her like a seam of silver through rock, and then back to wonder again. Because her wings were magnificent. She felt a grin split her face.

And then she saw a strange thing in the glade before her. Rows of stone cairns, but miniature, as if it was a burial ground for small animals, like cats, or hares.

Or . . .

A weight shifted in her stomach, like a snake uncoiling, rippling through her.

'What is that?' she said.

'Those are the cairns of your kind, Riv,' Fia said behind her. 'A graveyard of bairns, offspring of the Ben-Elim and mortals. You are the first of your kind to live longer than one day.'

Riv looked from the rows of cairns, so many of them, to the baby in Fia's arms.

'And this is the second?' Riv asked.

'Aye, he is,' Fia said, a fierce love in her eyes.

Riv just stood there, all of it washing over her, through her, and her friends gathered close about her.

'Well, what now?' a voice said, Vald.

'Now?' said Riv. She blinked, thinking of her mam and

Aphra, of Israfil and of Kol's betrayal. How her world had changed immeasurably. She looked at her friends, at Fia and the baby in her arms, felt a fierce protection for him.

'We make the world right,' she snarled, an echo of her old anger. 'But first, I'm going to learn how to use these,' and with that her wings were beating, swirling forest litter about their feet and she was rising, unsteadily at first, then faster, more confidently. With a shout of joy she burst through the forest canopy, wind ripping tears from her eyes, and she yelled for the sheer joy if it.